The German Woman

The German Woman

Janet Ashton

BELGARUN
THE NEW FACE OF PUBLISHING

Published 2008 by Belgarun
Typesetting by Gatecutter
Belgarun is an imprint of BGU Limited
Belgarun, Huddersfield, England
www.belgarun.com
ISBN-13: 978-1-84846-003-4

for Christophe

ACKNOWLEDGEMENTS

This is a work a fiction based in tone and viewpoint on the correspondence of the last Russian Empress, so an extensive list of acknowledgements is not needed or appropriate. However, there are a group of historians whose books, one website, and in some cases conversation as well have substantially helped shape the author's understanding of the Empress's perspective, and the factual background of the work. This book would not exist without the contributions knowing or unknowing of Bob Atchison and his assistants Rob Moshein and Lisa Davidson, of Joseph T. Fuhrmann, of Greg King and of Dominic Lieven. Greg and Joe also gave their valuable time to comment on the manuscript.

ABOUT THE AUTHOR

Janet Ashton works at the British Library in the West European Language Collections and has written on Alexandra's life and world and other aspects of modern history for several specialist magazines. She acted as researcher and consultant on a number of significant recent publications in the field.

CHAPTER ONE

Tobolsk, Siberia, March 1918:

Today the new guards destroyed the snow mountain we built at the beginning of the winter.

"When you stood on it people could see you from the street. Someone might try to shoot you."

Now the garden looks small and sad and bare, the fence which the mountain had obscured clearly visible from my window. I can still see beyond it to the church over the road, where people come and go, but in a way it's better not to look. Of course the children feel the confinement most. Today their exercise consisted of chopping some logs for the fire and chasing the dogs out of the house when they dragged some rubbish in. The dogs have been to the town tip again. My children watch them yearningly as they wander freely in and out of the garden.

I do try to cultivate a calm and sanguine spirit, and to keep busy. Before Christmas we spent hours making little gifts for one another and for our people, but now there are more practical tasks to hand - I am darning, because all of our clothes are in holes - socks, stockings, the girls' underwear, even pairs of trousers. The children are in the kitchen making bread, and I feel happy when I hear them laughing. Bless them, they may be bored, but they can still get their pleasure from the simple things in life. We didn't raise helpless young aristocrats, did we, my darling? All that meant most to me is still intact and is here with me. This blessed family that we have raised, the love we have for each other and for them - that's something special. Very few people can claim as much. Beside these things, nothing else matters.

One can't help thinking, though – there's so much time for thinking here. I worry about my children and the lives they will have, and I worry about this country's future, too, though its bitter ingratitude to my darling breaks my heart. He of course has never complained of his own position – not one word of bitterness has ever passed his lips, whatever the papers write about him, however rude some of the guards have been to him, however he might suffer to see his country in the hands of those creatures! It makes my blood boil to think that they dare to slander him – if they could only see him now....

Something terrible seems to have infected the whole world. No country is as it was when I was a child – journalists, politicians, they don't behave the same as they did then. Am I just being nostalgic? I don't think so. I was only born forty-five years ago, but the Europe we lived in then seems centuries away from this world of mud and khaki and big metal trucks. I find I should be ancient by now.

It makes me happy to think about my earliest days, so I try to encourage it – good for the temper. Of course, I always was known for shrieking and yelling, even when I was very small. There were so many of us – somebody was always taking my toys or contemptuously calling me 'Baby', and I wanted to defend myself somehow. How terrified I was nevertheless of Victoria and Ella! I suppose that in my earliest memories of them they must have been around eleven and twelve – I was, say, three – and they were huge and boisterous: – Ella a stout, laughing girl, prone to bear hugs, like my Marie at the same age, I suppose; Victoria a tomboy and a bookworm with a viciously sharp tongue. She has always liked people to know how clever she is.

These first memories of them are connected with seaside holidays on the Belgian coast, when they played rough games of croquet with some French boys, and we little ones were always in danger of being knocked over. We had funny little dolls made of lobster claws which someone had bought us from the shop on the sea front, and I remember the curiously scientific detachment I felt when I leant over my baby sister May and nipped her on the arm with a set of the claws, just to see what her skin looked like when I did it. She set up a wail and I was so startled that I did too.

Mama and the other ladies used to go some distance out to sea in bathing machines drawn by ponies, so they'd be in the water up to their necks as soon as they came down the steps and no-one could see them in their swimming costumes. I don't think they swam, though - they just floated about in the water for a while. No-one ever encouraged us children to swim either, although we waded and went shrimping in rock pools. I regret this bitterly since when I tried to learn as an adult I didn't have much success, and this is why my children were taught almost as soon as they could walk.

Sad to remember so little of Mama. I'm not even sure that I remember her face, although it's so familiar to me from her photographs of course. Rather a long nose and the downwards glance that made her look so sad - strange how that gentle glance has re-emerged in the least gentle or contemplative of my children! I remember her hands very well; I sat on her lap while she taught me to read - in English first, and then in German - and the long white fingers holding the book out in front of me are, strangely, one of my most vivid impressions from my early years. Those hands that I inherited: perhaps her only legacy to me physically; although of course she left me her name.

I used to be so proud of that when I was little! - Having something my elder sisters hadn't beaten me to, because my parents named Victoria after our English grandmother and Ella after our German one, and Irène was born at the end of a war so she got a name which is Greek for 'Peace'. (They were collectively known as the 'Three Graces', sometimes - and to think I had almost forgotten about that!). The English newspapers used to

3

ignore the little variation that Papa and Mama introduced in my name – 'Alix' was so the Germans wouldn't mis-pronounce me as 'Aliiza' – and call me 'Princess Alice' anyway, but I never minded too much.

May and I used to run into Mama's sitting room in the morning and leap on her sofa or slam our fists down on the keyboard when she was playing the piano.

"Good morning, my *weet*heart!" May always said, which made Mama laugh.

She kept a box of her own old clothes in the room for us to dress up in. I would walk around behind her swathed in a crinoline – funny old fashion from Mama's earliest youth! – and copying her mannerisms. It was intended to be cheeky; that was why Papa called me 'Spitzbub' – the imp or the scamp. Mama called me 'Sunny' and eventually the public found out and I was Prinzessin Sonnenschein to the press.

At nine o'clock she used to go to have breakfast with Papa (if he was there) and the big sisters and Ernie. They had German breakfast – lots of cold meat and sausage. May and I always had porridge much earlier on because the nursery was totally under Orchie's sway and she didn't hold with continental eating habits. Even when I was much older I still had the same plain food given me, though; perhaps that's why I've always had the most English habits of us all.

Happy memories of my mother, such as they are.

How upset I was when I talked to others later who knew her better and realised that she wasn't really very happy, herself. What a time she had of it! I know my parents loved each other, but really, they were hardly soulmates. He was brought to England to meet her when she was barely eighteen and she hadn't met many young men at all, unless they were her brothers, and of course it was expected she'd fall in love with him or with his brother. That was her free choice! So she did as required, and in the middle of all the celebrations her beloved father died,

Granny went into mourning for the rest of her life, and my parents got married in a quiet, sad ceremony, tucked away from the public. That was rather like my own marriage service, and it needn't have mattered at all, if she hadn't then had the life that she did. She tried so hard in Darmstadt - she founded all those hospitals and the schools that would give girls some technical training - but people laughed at her efforts and said that women should forget all of that and just concentrate on raising children. And there were two major wars in her first nine years of married life - firstly Hesse-Darmstadt sided with Austria against Prussia, and then with later Prussia against France. How Papa hated the results of those wars! - Germany unified under Prussia; all of the local spirit and democratic tradition slowly squeezed out of the smaller states. That was starting during Mama's life-time and she'd have hated it too, although it hadn't gone as far as it did later. Certainly, though, the wars left Hesse dreadfully impoverished, and there were epidemics of things like typhoid and cholera for Mama's hospitals to contend with. Heaven knows we've had plenty to put up with in our own public lives, but there have been consolations - oh, God, there have been consolations! - And at home in our little nest all was always brightness and sunshine. It wasn't really the same for poor Mama. I think she was rather a melancholy, thoughtful person by nature anyway - it's said she was like her father who died so young of his first serious illness because he just lost the will to live - whereas Papa was cheerful and friendly and liked sport and gardening and never read much or thought too long about anything. Even though they loved each other I suppose that in the end they didn't understand each other at all - they must both have been so lonely! - But she more so, because that was her nature.

In Mama's bedroom in the new palace in Darmstadt there was that window with stained glass and the verse 'Suffer little children to come unto me'. I always knew that this was the window through which my other brother - he came between

5

Ernie and me in age – had fallen to his death one day whilst running around the room. He was three years old and I was one and I don't remember him at all, but I knew that we went to the family Mausoleum in the Rosenhöhe park on October 6th because that was Fritzie's birthday, and May and I chased each other round and round our ancestors' tombs and stood on tiptoe to look at their recumbent statues on the top.

Ah! – something else Mama did for us was to make sure we knew how other people lived. Just before Christmas there were those visits to the hospitals with bunches of flowers and little presents we'd had to make ourselves, so we could see that other people were hungry and sick and had no money for celebrations. Of course in us littlest ones this had no real effect at the time; we just started getting excited because we knew that the visits meant Christmas was on its way. As the big day approached, Ernie, May and I got steadily more wild and over-wrought, until finally on Christmas Eve Papa would fling open the nursery door and we hurled ourselves at him yelling with joy. He seized May and me in his arms and bore us downstairs with Ernie prancing behind, and the door to the dining room would open in front of us and there would be the tree, lit up in the darkness like a picture in some splendid book.

Next day came the goose and plum pudding and mince pies, although we were naturally more interested in our presents, which waited tantalizingly on individual tables, each table labelled with a name.

Christmas 1878 was of course rather different.

I do I'm sure remember Victoria reading aloud to us younger ones from 'Alice in Wonderland'. The book and its illustrations were flavour of the moment in England; I suppose that was why I always wore those white bands round my hair. Ernie was swinging May round and round although he could barely lift her – we were neither of us dainty little girls – and teasing her,

"She thinks the book's about Mama!"

"No I don't, silly!" said May, giggling, and I jumped on Ernie and gave him some friendly smacks. Just an ordinary day, really – probably my memories aren't of the day we got ill at all but of some other one from around that time. At any rate, Victoria gave up with us and put the book down. Shortly afterwards – that day or another – she went to bed with a sore throat, and then I woke up one morning feeling hot and shivery and dreadfully thirsty. That's how the diphtheria started in our family. And of course we all got it except for Ella and Mama, and May, my darling sister and companion, died of it some time in November. She was four years old.

I was six; old enough to get the horrors when they told me, because I didn't want to associate my nearest and dearest with those dead people at the Rosenhöhe. Why did I think like that?! – We weren't brought up as atheists, although many people have suggested that my mother flirted with such beliefs earlier in life. There was plenty of talk about May being in Heaven with the cherubs, but I couldn't help myself thinking about her mortal body, shut away with the ancestors.

Most of all, I was lonely as well. The treatment and aftermath of diphtheria had been almost as nasty as the disease. I remember Mama and Orchie and a hired nurse coming in swathed from head to foot in white, with masks across their faces, and spraying my throat with a scratchy white smoke that I discovered later was potassium chlorate. Now we were recovering, all our bedclothes were burned, and the toys I had shared with my sister were too. Mama had always been mad keen on fresh air and hygiene – she was mocked for this of course, because few German houses however large had a bathroom in those days – but I remember that our rooms now smelled for a while of disinfectant, and Victoria complained about chilblains from the open windows – her circulation has never been too good. I looked at the new toys I'd been given and I felt at a loose end. One afternoon I chanced across the terrible sight of Orchie weeping in a corner, a photograph of my sister in her hands. It was one which had been taken around 1875 for a family portrait Granny was having done, and it showed Ernie in a chair with May and me sort of piled on top of him. Ernie was wearing a kilt and we had white lace dresses with tartan sashes. He and I looked a bit unsure about the whole thing but May who was only a year old was at her most chubby and charming, beaming all over her face with her hand in her mouth. No wonder it was too much for poor Orchie; but I wasn't used to seeing grown-ups cry and I ran away in horror.

Mama fell ill when the rest of us were more or less well again and she died on December 14th, the very anniversary of her own father's death.

Why am I dwelling on all this so much?! – I had wanted to think cheery thoughts and I come back instead to those dreadful days! – But it's hard not to wonder how my life might have developed if I'd had my sister and my mother with me. It's not just a question of the company I so often lacked: – Ernie claims to remember playing on the floor of Mama's sitting room while she played a piano duet with a strange man. Years later, he heard the 'Hungarian dances' and realised that the tunes Mama was trying out were these very ones and that the strange man had been Brahms. She was also great friends with David Strauss, who in a way sort of took her father's place intellectually and who dedicated his *Life of Jesus* to her and terribly upset conventional theology.

Well, after she died, we never had anyone like that visit us at home, because Papa was in no way interested in anything of the sort. Neither, in England, was my Grandmother, so I've always gazed from a distance, and never had the courage to talk to clever people at all.

A few days after Christmas we got on the train and set off for England, which was wonderful. We joined my Grandmother at Osborne, a paradise for a child! – There was the miniature Swiss

Cottage in the grounds, built for Mama and her siblings when they were little so they could learn to keep house. So cousins Thora and Louie, who I daresay were surrogate sisters to me in those days, experimented with me making little cakes and jam tarts in the kitchen. Only Thora was allowed to touch the lighted range. We took our offerings home with us for Granny – Granny never refused a cake when offered! – In those days she was already decidedly round, although she wasn't really very old – she still regularly rode her pony, whatever the weather, with John Brown holding onto its bridle. Brown was with her then, wasn't he? – He died when I was still very small, but I do remember him – how he'd lean over my grandmother's chair at tea time and pour a nip of whisky into her tea. And he used to compliment me on my hair – "Stuart hair, all the way from Mary Queen of Scots – it was nae Sassenach ancestors that gave ye those bonnie red curls!"

Perhaps I'm being vain and it was Ella he was talking to – she was the one with the auburn hair; mine was always lighter reddish-blond. In any case, it comes from the Hesse side, from Papa, although he probably had Stuart ancestors somewhere too.

Well, as everyone knows, all of the aunts and uncles hated John Brown, which of course I didn't know about until later. They complained about his familiarity and his whisky-drinking – in spite of Uncle Bertie and Uncle Alfred being themselves quite often the worse for the wear! Certainly, he was familiar – he quite often addressed Granny as 'wumman' – even I noticed this! – Bless her, though – she was never imposing or frightening to me, and perhaps this was Brown's influence – perhaps by treating her as an equal human being he gave her a new will to live. My elder sisters were quite alarmed by her when they were small and she still lived in the shadow of Grandpapa's death. She was always asking then for less noise, and she used to tap her head and cry 'My reason! My reason!' when faced with romping

9

children. I had to kiss her hand when I entered her sitting room – I had absolutely always known that she was the Queen, you never had a moment's doubt about that – but she laughed her funny tinkling laugh at the things I told her and she made me sit on a footstool while she tried to sketch me. It didn't come out well because I wouldn't stay calm for long enough, but still she didn't mind. My older sisters were annoyed – 'Alix is Granny's favourite'.

Nevertheless I never saw Granny wear any colour other than black, with her little lace widow's cap, and we were expected to be quiet and respectful when later we went on visits to Grandpapa's mausoleum at Frogmore – she would never have tolerated the sort of things May and I had got up to at the Rosenhohe. Granny's generation had very much believed that children were seen and not heard, and if I suppose she had relaxed quite a bit by the time I was born, there were certain situations in which it definitely still applied. She was mad keen on proper behaviour and decorum – nail-biting, gobbling food, and, as we got older, moving fast or inelegantly, were not tolerated for a moment. Still, I was never, ever frightened of her. You never doubted for a second how kind she was, once you'd seen her talking to one of the women from the Balmoral estate, asking after her children and making sure that food and clothes were sent where necessary if the family lacked them. The slightest rudeness to any of her staff was regarded as the apogee of poor breeding – this was her main quarrel with my uncles as critics of John Brown. Perhaps this old-fashioned Tory courtesy blinded her to the human faults of some of her servants, but at least she never abused her position of power, and the same could certainly not be said of all of my uncles.

The best of the uncles was dear Uncle Leopold. No – perhaps not the best in objective terms – Granny always said later that Uncle Arthur was a paragon of duty and good humour, whereas Leopold was often rebellious and frequently short-tempered –

but certainly the best uncle for a child of my age to have around. He came back to Darmstadt with us in the spring of 1879, when Ernie and the sisters went back to the schoolroom and I was alone in the nursery again. I suppose I was still studying there in the nursery with Orchie for only a short while every morning; the others worked away all day.

Uncle Leo had a problem with his leg – I didn't know then what his disease was of course – and he spent much of the time lying on the sofa, in my power. He read to me – lots about the Jacobite Rising and Bonnie Prince Charlie, which was his particular interest – and taught me loads of card tricks for impressing the older ones. One afternoon I slipped on a cold frame while running round the garden and I cut my leg rather badly, so I was given a bandage like Uncle Leo's, which made me dreadfully proud. Papa gave me a box of sweets as a special treat after the accident and how thrilled I was to see Ernie stare at them! It made me feel very magnanimous to offer him one, but naturally he took several, because normally we weren't allowed sweets. I think now that that was a mistake on the part of my parents – it made us so greedy to get them – and I never had the same rule for my own children.

"Greedy little pig!" said Victoria, when she saw our brother with his cheeks full of bonbons.

Poor Ernie; he was rather an unhappy little boy at that time. I have the impression not least from the things told me by Ernie himself that her little son had been Mama's favourite child, especially after the death of her only other boy Fritzie, and he was undoubtedly the most lost without her. There was a legend concocted after her death – in those days of rudimentary understanding of germs and transmission of disease –that she caught diphtheria by kissing him to comfort him for the loss of May – 'the Darmstadt kiss of death' Disraeli called it in Parliament – and poor Ernie lived with this intolerable and unfair burden of guilt all the rest of his childhood. On top of this, my elder sisters told him off constantly, particularly Victoria - Irène was always mild and amiable and didn't often get involved one way or the other; Ella would sometimes intervene to temper what Victoria was saying. If I saw they had upset him I would sometimes now that I was a bit bigger fling myself on them and pull their hair or kick their ankles. Even when he was small Ernie was good and patient with me and May; he was also the only one of the *Geschwister* young enough to want to play with me; naturally I would side with him!

Later in the year sister Victoria decided that the time had come for me to begin my lessons properly, so the routine of seven o'clock starts and two hours of work in the schoolroom before breakfast began for me too. That was with Fraulein Textor, of course, because Madgie was busy with the older girls at that time, but Madgie and Victoria would come in at least once a week to watch what I was learning. I'm sure Victoria even took an interest in my clothes at that time! - This is most unlike her, but I suppose she was at an age when such things are important. Later though it was Ella who took me to the seamstress to be measured, and Ella who chose the patterns, which is far more characteristic. Naturally they made much of how lucky I was - that I didn't have to wear anyone's cast-off clothes as they had worn each other's.

"In those days, Mama used to make our dresses herself - the wars were on and we had no money at all".

Fortunately fashions had changed since they were my age, so I was spared all those wide skirts with looped-up bits at the back - imitation bustles for little girls, which must have impeded play - or if they didn't impede it then they must have got torn a lot. Yes - didn't poor Victoria once have to wear a patched and darned dress at a party with some of our snooty Prussian cousins, as a penalty for climbing through a hedge with it on?

- The bustle was definitely still around for grown-ups when I was seven or so, but I remember I always had sensible straight or pleated skirts on my dresses.

It must have been around the time I started lessons that Toni Becker began coming to see me nearly every day. Hadn't her father been Mama's librarian and private secretary? – That must be how I first met her, although she's always felt like my own special friend – nothing to share with the rest of the family for once! Toni always came in the afternoons, to do dancing and gymnastic lessons. We had wild Scottish dancing and Hessian folk dances when we were small – much later, proper ballroom dances – and Toni was better than I was at the gymnastics. I couldn't stand on my head without collapsing in a heap, and Ernie teased me a lot about this. Never minded Ernie's teasing, because he knew very well that I could reciprocate – he was very nimble and athletic but he always was scared of rough games and horses and getting hurt.

I always wanted Toni to share the rest of my lessons, of course, but probably it's a good thing she didn't. When I was alone in the schoolroom and feeling sorry for myself I had no choice but to concentrate and be interested. And we were so well taught! Madgie was an absolutely inspired tutor, and she chose under-tutors in her own mould. – When I think of the contrast with the way my poor husband had to learn! – Everything taught by rote and repeated mechanically back – verbs, facts, ideas.

Miss Textor and Madgie would tell me something and encourage me to challenge it –

"So – Henry I died, and his nephew Stephen came to the throne. Henry did have a child of his own, but she was only a girl so no-one wanted her on the throne."

"Why, Madgie?"

"Well, girls aren't as clever as boys, are they? – She wouldn't have made a good monarch."

"Isn't my Grandmama any good, then?"

"Well, what do *you* think?"

...and so on and so forth, and of course the ideas she

encouraged us to challenge got more sophisticated and abstract as the years went by.

Victoria keeps notebooks of the things she has read and what she got from them, and she wanted me to do the same. Well, I've never been one for that sort of organisation! but I did love to tell her about books I'd been reading, and read things she recommended, seeing her eyes shine with interest and excitement when I explained what I thought they meant. Generally when I was little of course I agreed with her own interpretation, which smoothed my way a lot, and in my early teens I read Kant and Darwin and Milton under her instruction and had furious arguments with Madgie over politics. Funny that in spite of all her advanced ideas about women's education Madgie was a Tory!

Papa told me when I was a little older that dear Granny worried about Madgie's influence - her cough and her bitter remarks - that she was afraid we would all grow up hard and manly, and she said of Mama, "Alice was very clever, but she was always totally feminine".

So Granny made sure that we were taught embroidery and homely knitting in our spare time, and when she thought she saw a talent for the piano in me she had the Director of the Darmstadt opera come in to give me lessons. Granny herself had a beautiful clear singing voice - a high soprano - and she would sometimes even in her widowhood sing in front of the family at Osborne or Balmoral, which is why I had to accompany her on the piano. I must say that that was torture - all those faces gathered round, waiting for me to make a mistake!

Madgie stayed until I was fifteen, though, because Victoria always stood up to Granny.

Granny's singing takes me back to all those summer holidays we spent in England. Of course we went before Mama died, too, but as I recall we didn't often stay with my grandmother. I remember a borrowed house in Eastbourne in 1878, where

14

I played my first clumsy game of tennis, for one thing. To be honest, I don't think Granny and Mama always got on too well while Mama was alive - I have picked this up from other people, including Papa. Granny found some of my mother's political ideas rather odd, and she was very annoyed that Mama nursed some of us herself because she thought it an animal act and not suitable for a princess at all. Well, I found her views out for myself later, too! - but she was always more forgiving of her grandchildren than she had been of their parents, bless her.

After Mama died Granny remembered only the good about her, as people do - a very human fault. She told us often that we should be as selfless and devoted to family and duty as our mother had been. We went so often to Balmoral or Windsor or Osborne - every summer and part of the winter sometimes too - that in the end there were questions about it in the Hessian parliament and Papa decided it was time to cut the visits down.

"I owe it to Hesse to spend more time there - I am their Grand Duke, and their taxes do pay for your food and clothes!"

In any case, there were times when we simply could not afford to go to go to Britain. Mama had once stayed alone in a small hotel in London on business because Granny said it was too much trouble for her to visit, and she could not afford to pay the hotel bills for any of her staff. For all her kindness, being short of money was something that Granny really never understood. To her, the poor were people who lived in cottages without servants and didn't have enough to eat - not minor German princes whose outgoings in the performance of their public roles exceeded their income.

"If Papa were English," Victoria said, "he would be considered a member of the aristocracy and not royalty at all. Hesse-Darmstadt is no bigger than an English dukedom and it's only because some beastly ancestor sold his soul to Napoleon that we have the right to call ourselves *royal highnesses* at all. It doesn't make us any less a subject of the rotten Emperor than the

Duke of Norfolk is Granny's subject."

"Most English dukes come from families much older than your grandmother's," said Madgie sniffily.

"And our ancestors have been around in Hesse - or central Germany at any rate - far longer than the Hohenzollerns have been in Prussia, but it doesn't alter who the Emperor is. Generally, we have a far more honourable history than the Hohenzollerns, too! - But there are so many German *princes* living in rat-infested, freezing little castles, looking out over lands the size of a postage stamp and huffily telling everyone they are royal or serene of whatever highnesses and looking up their ancestors in the *Almanach de Gotha* to prove it! - it's absolutely ridiculous in this day and age!"

Granny often called Victoria a windbag, but she was very tolerant of her long ranting speeches on the whole.

Which did I like the best of the houses we stayed at in Britain? my children used to ask me when they were small.

Probably Balmoral, for its wild blue mountains and swirling morning mist, even in summer. Wasn't it at Balmoral that I first had pocket money, and used to ride my pony to the village to spend it at the sweet shop? (Papa never knew!) - One of the ladies who kept the shop took Louie and Thora and me into the kitchen and showed us how to make scones and scotch pancakes which we took home to Granny - the beginning of that tradition. There were lots of picnics in the mountains, we children on our ponies and Granny sometimes riding a pony led by her ghillie, sometimes - later - in a little carriage which jolted and shook precariously over the rough tracks. It often rained when we were out there, and we took shelter in one of the little empty stone farm houses that dotted the estate, building a fire to make tea and spreading our jackets over it afterwards so they would dry. Uncle Leopold, who hated Scotland notwithstanding his passion for the Stuart dynasty, one day enlightened us about the little stone huts and why they were empty - the whole sorry history of the highland clearances – but although it sharpened our social consciences it didn't stop us enjoying those picnics, which often ended with a torchlight procession back down the mountain to the castle where Papa and the uncles would have arrived home from shooting.

Sometimes in the evenings Granny used to sing, but mostly the family were called upon to entertain her instead, and that was when we had our tableaux. Hours went into the preparation of the scenery, the whole Royal household joining in – there were always so many people about at Granny's homes! – and then the curtain would rise and we would pose for a few minutes while the family clapped and exclaimed before the curtain fell again and we immediately set about preparing the next scene! Sometimes the scenes were more animated, of course – Ernie striding up and down the stage proclaiming, "England, your beauties are tame and pretentious, compared with glories of brave Lochnagar!"

I am so thankful that all of my children have inherited this passion for amateur dramatics – their sanity could not have survived this winter, otherwise. Two of them are in the room with me now – Olga is reading; Marie is banging on the piano with one finger.

"Let's sing something," she says and sticks her head out of the door to call the others.

There is a long series of deafening thumps from outside, as if something is rolling down the stairs, and Marie shrieks, "What on earth are you doing?"

So I jump up and run to look too, although her excited tone tells me there is nothing to be anxious about. Alexei is standing at the foot of the stairs with his sledge next to him.

"The snow mountain's gone," he says, "What else do they expect me to do?"

Then he comes back to the top, places the sledge on the stairs, sits on it and slides to the bottom again with a wild whoop. I do not want to see this so I go back into the sitting room where Marie and Anastasia start to sing some vulgar song, banging on the floor and the door with their hands, feet, and anything else they can think of, just trying to use up some of their boisterous adolescent energy, poor little things. Every thump from the stairs makes me tense up inside and in the end I hear Nicky order the boy to stop it and to come and sit with his family.

Alexei kicks the wall beneath the window with his heel.

"It's boring! There's nothing to do!"

"Why don't you write your diary?" Nicky says.

"Well, now - guess what I'll be writing?"

Soon it will be time for bed, then breakfast, lessons for the children when the tutors come in from across the road, exercise in the bare garden, lessons for the children with Nicky and me when the tutors have gone home and another evening banging on the piano, playing cards, trying to write letters to our friends and family though heaven knows if they ever get to read them.

Downstairs the guards are having their own party, and the vulgarity of their songs is well beyond anything my children could dream up. When the last lot were here we went to the guard room and sat with them and talked about their families and sometimes the girls even danced with the younger ones! At Christmas we were one big family, when we made a tree for them, and we had home-made presents to give them. These new men are a very different kettle of fish and it's the consciousness of their presence which is giving an edginess to quiet evenings no different from those we have had all winter. They are disturbing the pleasure we have in each others' company, hang them.

Alexei sits on the floor, doodling on a piece of paper.

"What will I do tomorrow, I wonder? Perhaps I'll stand in the yard and twirl a stick in my hand?"

"At least," Olga says testily, "you have Kolya to play with. When was the last time I saw any of my friends?"

It is true that Kolya Derevenko can still come to the house as freely as he did all winter. They have recently put us on rations – two courses at dinner with no soup – but the doctor's young son can come and go for pleasure as freely as his father does for business. We are not totally cut off from the outside world, so we are not prisoners here yet. Still, when we are lying in bed at night and the wind howls around the house it is hard to forget that we are in Siberia.

Tatiana is organizing a game of hide and seek, and soon most of them will be rushing around and yelling like little children; but Olga carries on sitting by the window, looking out into the frozen darkness. It cuts me to the heart every time I look at her to see how quiet and melancholy she has become here. I have bequeathed my poor darling firstborn the most pernicious heritage of all – my mother's personality.

CHAPTER TWO

27 April, 1918, New Style.

The past two days have been painful beyond belief, and long. Only forty-eight hours since the new Commissar, that Yakovlev, came after lunch to say he was to take Nicky away - he wouldn't say where; and I had to face the most terrible decision of my life - go with your husband or stay with your sick child. My heart still feels raw - I am almost afraid to look inside it and scrutinise my motives. Maybe I truly did decide that "a child in his weakness can do nothing; a man can do much," as Our Friend always used to say, and that my duty lay with Nicky; but I am afraid that it really came down to a choice over who I love the most and to putting that love before all things.

Briefly, when the decision was made, we felt calm. We bade goodbye to all those remaining at four in the morning, and climbed into the rough carts that had been brought for us. Of our people, only Botkin, Valia, Nyuta Demidova, the valets Chemodorov and Sednev have been told to come with us. The rest of them remain in Tobolsk with the children, living together under the one roof as they have been since the guards ordered the tutors and the others out of the house over the road a month or so ago. Botkin's children are lodging somewhere in the town, still; he didn't have a chance to say goodbye.

"Eugene Sergeievich," I said to him when I realised this, "we do not have the right to ask you come with us."

"No," our good doctor answered, and he took my hands and looked gently into my eyes, "you do not have the right."

Our blessed household are going into this of their own free will, but I feel angry for the more junior members of staff -

like Nyuta, who is surely not being brought along to act as my chambermaid? – We could do perfectly well on our own, and one can't help feeling that the guards have insisted she come so she can wait on them instead. I remember how often over the winter I lost my temper with Nyuta for her clumsy moralizing or other little faults, and I feel dreadful about it.

Even the stalwart tutors were in tears when we left the house at last. Alone of the whole party, only Nicky and I remained collected. Marie and Tatiana embraced one another with significant looks, and each said, "Look after them," to the other.

The two middle daughters – the flowers of my family! Marie will be a tremendous support and comfort to us on our journey, as she was to me in those dreadful days last March; Tatiana will care for her brother and her sisters left behind in Tobolsk. Alexei was in bed of course when we left, but naturally he wasn't sleeping and I asked M. Gilliard to go up to him and sit with him as long as he needed.

Olga pressed a folded piece of paper into my hand, saying, "Read that when you are alone." And my little Anastasia! – Urged to be her usual funny self and cheer her siblings up when we are gone, she was standing at the window as our carts drew away, sobbing her eyes out, poor wee Shvibzik. It tears my soul to remember them saying goodbye and to wonder when I will see them again.

Several times during the first day, Nicky asked politely, "Where are you taking us? Are we going to Moscow?", but no reply was forthcoming.

The wheels broke, the roads were horrifically rough, half-frozen and swimming in mud; more than once we encountered floods which came up to the horses' chests. That night – last night – we slept in a house which had once been a village shop. We at least had a bed, where we lay clinging together without words listening to our own synchronised breathing in the immense silent Siberian darkness, but Marie was on a mattress on the floor. She got up this morning full of the cheerful resilience of youth and pointed out what a wonderful day it was at last; bright and sunny and very warm. Nicky stood in the window and stretched, then he turned to me and shivered as if a goose had walked over his grave.

"Oh Sunny," he said smiling "I think I've been surprised by joy."

Then we saw Our dear Friend's home. Passing through the village of Pokrovskoe we saw his widow there at her window, making the sign of the cross over us. How strange, how sad, to see her in these changed circumstances: no more Emperor and Empress and subject; instead, we are the poor now; she, the widow of a respected local man, well-provided for at least. Yet it was a comfort too, to see her and remember that we are in familiar country in a way: the homeland of our dear Friend and protector and religious counselor. At rest with the saints, he is watching over us and looking down on us from his heavenly window as his dear family look down on us from their earthly one, making the sign of the cross and smiling.

So now we have come to Tiumen and we are on the train. It seems from the station signs that we pass that we are heading for Omsk. What then? - A show trial in Moscow? - Will we be forced to sign their loathesome treaty offering half the Ukraine to the rotten German army? - This is what we always most feared. But I am looking at myself in a hand mirror, and I can't help smiling; I look so dirty and wretched. Marie is filthy too. I lick my handkerchief and dab it on her nose as I used to do when she was a child, and she swipes it away and laughs.

"What was it Olga gave you, Mama?"

"I'm not going to read it yet. I want to save it until we are somewhere more settled. Perhaps until Olga and the others are with us again."

It is still half light outside. I watch the endless pine forests and the plain passing by. In the next compartment, our girl is talking cheerfully to Nyuta as they make up their bunks. Our own compartment is lapsing into twilight, and although I am aware that Nicky is sitting a few feet away from me, I can barely see him. I smell tobacco and see the tip of his cigarette glowing in the gloom.

"What are you thinking about?" he asks at length.

"Nothing at all, really. I was taking in the scenery and the nature and wondering if there'll be a proper garden where we're going."

"Funny. So was I."

"There, you see," I am smiling as I reach out to take his hand, "we read each other's thoughts perfectly."

"Still the same people, even after all this time," he says, and he comes to sit in the chair with me, although it's not very comfortable, and puts his arms around me and leans his cheek against my hair.

"Bunks tonight," he says, "separate from each other, I'm afraid."

I know he is thinking, At least we are in the same room, on the same train, they have not succeeded in forcing us apart yet. I put my fingers to his lips, in case he was planning to say this aloud, and the pact is sealed. Neither of us will mention separation again.

"Garden," I say, "what are we going to plant in our new garden?"

Naturally it was Papa who so loved plants himself who encouraged me to become a gardener. After Mama died he more or less abandoned Schloss Kranichstein, and we started spending our summers (if we weren't in England) at Wolfsgarten, which didn't harbour too many painful memories. I had heaps of flower beds there. I also of course had a little patch of ground at the Neues Palais in Darmstadt, where people would watch me from the street and sigh about poor little Prinzessin Sonnenschein, playing all on her own, but Wolfsgarten was our paradise. I was proud because Ella wanted to draw little pictures of my flowers, each with its name underneath - she is the best artist among us, undoubtedly, though Ernie is no slouch either. I kept hutches full of rabbits and guinea pigs in Wolfsgarten, and didn't we have a sheep at one point? We also learned to row on the lake, and if we were there in the winter, it was often cold enough for the water to freeze over, so we tried skating, although I doubt we were much good until later when we started going to Russia. Aunt Helena used to be sent to Wolfsgarten by Granny, so I could be with Thora and Louie all summer and pretend we were all sisters. Course, Louie is only two months younger than me but I was always a lot taller so I used to say that Thora and I were the twins and she was our baby sister, which annoyed her terribly! Louie never liked to read or think about things - when I daydreamed sometimes she said I was "playing at being sorrowful" and that one day God would send me some really crushing sorrows to teach me a lesson. Well, she was certainly right about that bit.

Apart from Toni, Louie was the best friend I had when I was a little girl, naturally, but Minnie Cochrane was a great dear too. There were always a lot of English people in Darmstadt. Probably it went back a certain extent to the days when there were Hessian soldiers in the British army, but they really started coming in earnest when Mama went to live there. We used to meet the English children in the Prinz Emil's Garten in Darmstadt, where there was a folly which one team would defend while the other tried to take it from them. Toni and I were the youngest participants, just about - some of the others were almost grown up, and it used to make us laugh when Irène pointed out how many of the boys always wanted to be in the same team as Ella, and would leap gallantly in front of her to protect her from the missiles thrown by the other team. No German children ever took part, except of course sometimes Toni - Darmstadt girls tended to cry when knocked over, and they took dreadful scoldings from their Mamas if they went home dirty or were spotted raising their voices or behaving indecorously in public, poor things. We were very visible in our games, and all the passers-by knew that the Geschwister and I were Papa's children, but no-one ever stared at us. Dear Darmstadt must have been very free and democratic, but we took it for granted at that time.

I had a passion for America from quite early on. The best children's literature in the 80s tended to be American - perhaps that's why I was always desperate to visit; but I had to content myself with learning to play the banjo instead. Prince Ludwig Battenberg, our constant visitor in those days, had of course been to America, on one of his ships. Being Papa's young cousin he often used to visit even when Mama was alive and Victoria was quite small - it was Mama who suggested that he should join the British Navy if he liked the sea, as Germany didn't have much of one at the time, and in any case it was dominated like everything by beastly Prussia. So Ludwig was already a British citizen of some years standing when he became a constant presence in our house and then got engaged to Victoria. Technically Victoria wasn't English at all, but he always seems less English than her, with his German accent which he's still never quite lost.

I was only eleven but I was definitely conscious of how vastly more grown-up than Victoria he was at the time they announced that they were going to get married. What's the age difference? - nearly a decade, I find. - And in any case he'd been at sea for years, and had visited all kinds of wonderful exotic places. (He had a pretty exotic past romantically too, although of course I didn't know anything about that then!) Victoria has always made vigorous use of the age difference between her and me, but she still seemed like a girl to me nevertheless, and now here was this bearded, tanned, broad-shouldered sailor come to court her! One or the other of us younger ones were sent to be with them at all times, acting as chaperone, although as Ernie said Granny said, they didn't need it:

"Victoria is far too sensible to do anything silly!"

She treated her suitor exactly as she treated the rest of us, and one day rowing on the lake she made him wet splashing water around with her hands. He had to take his shirt off to dry it, and Ernie and I saw the huge dragon tattooed across his chest and were most impressed. He had that done in Japan. Papa told me later how pleased Granny was by the match; what an asset to the family she thought the dark-haired, dark-eyed Battenbergs would be, and how a mature, sensible man like Ludwig would be ideal for Victoria. Of course, she had at first not wanted Victoria to get married at all – Granny's generation was steeped in that horrifically cruel custom of training one daughter of the family to remain at home looking after elderly parents – Granny tried to do it to Aunt Beatrice – and because Victoria was so good at managing Papa and the household it seemed as though in our family it would be her. But Granny had the grace to change her mind when she discovered who Victoria wanted to marry, and gave her their blessing. Victoria would be able to spend loads of time with us still, because her parents-in-law also lived in Hesse, and in any case she promised to come back to Papa's house when Ludwig was at sea, and Granny was pleased about that.

What other people thought about the marriage started to be clear when the Hessian parliament refused to vote an allowance through for them. Over the next few years we all got to hear a lot more of what Europe thought of the Battenbergs, and I at first understood that this was simply because they were the children of a morganatic marriage and didn't appear in the wretched *Almanach de Gotha*. Some people felt his humble status was part of Ludwig's attraction to Victoria. Later of course in Russia I heard the scandalous stories about his father's parentage and that of the late Russian empress, because Vladimir used to like boasting that he and Ludwig Battenberg were the grandsons of a Hessian court official. Who cares?! – All this dirt and silliness makes me so ill sometimes!

Having Ludwig in the family was my introduction to the concept of unequal or morganatic marriages, but of course I got to hear a lot more about them very fast!

Papa had explained to me about marriages where the wife takes a lower rank than her husband – why is it never the other way round?! – because he said people would talk about it in the context of Ludwig's parents and I needed to understand what it meant. At the same time he also kept saying how much he would miss my elder sisters when they were gone, and how he needed to find someone to look after the household when he was away with his regiment. I understood these hints when his own secret wedding to Mme. de Kolemine emerged the day after Victoria got married, and there was an appalling row. The older girls knew the lady quite well of course because they'd been so much with Papa recently, and they said she was nice and they didn't see why he shouldn't have another wife, six full years after Mama died. And I started to wonder how it would be to have a new Mama: someone there in the house who was kinder and gentler with me than my bossy big sisters, and would tuck me in at night and go off to parties laughing with Papa. And I imagined our house would be full of music and friends as Ernie thought it had been when Mama was alive. But Granny was absolutely furious with him and no sooner had I been told about the wedding than I heard it was all off.

"It's because she's divorced from someone else," Ernie said, "not a suitable person to have in the house with Irène and you, it seems."

All in all, 1884 was a very educational time for me – I really started to get some glimpses of the adult world – and I felt an interest in it for the first time too.

In the last few days before her wedding, Victoria suddenly became very nervous – she went to bed with headaches, and wouldn't eat, which is astonishingly unlike her normal self.

"It is natural for a young girl to feel slightly anxious at this time," Madgie told me, and then she enlightened me as to what Victoria could expect on her wedding night. I was also given to understand that I should not repeat this to any of my friends.

"Some girls' parents prefer them not to know about this until they marry themselves, which is I think very unkind and silly, but we have to respect it."

Don't think Granny would have been too happy if she'd known about this conversation, but I find that Madgie was extremely wise. Too many of the cousins had horrible experiences as a result of ignorance - I remember this with Ducky, for one - and it ruined the whole relationship with their husbands for ever.

Actually, Missy and Ducky are a very good example of the perils of innocence. Not only did their Mama want them married before they reached eighteen - "so they don't get ideas of their own," - and send them to their bridal beds totally unprepared for what was going to happen, but she didn't even warn them about the consequences. When Missy started feeling dizzy and sick a few weeks after she got married she thought she was going to die, poor little thing! - I can't comment on the physical side of my sister's marriage - the way she acted just before her wedding doesn't suggest she was especially enthusiastic about it! - but at least she knew what she was in for. Thank God we had such a sensible father and sensible tutors! - And this was our mother's legacy too.

Ella's wedding was more imposing than Victoria's, of course, and very significant to me in one special way!

Quite how upset Granny was about the whole business I didn't realise then, but Papa confided to me when I got a bit older how she had pointedly shoved a suitable German princeling in my sister's direction. Did she even have a vague hope for a while that Ella might one day be Queen of England? - If so, Victoria was the only one of us who evaded that particular plan, because Granny also wanted Irène for cousin Eddy, later. She was a terrible match-maker! Just why did she hate Russia so much? Perhaps it was because of the Crimean War, but Papa felt it was due more to poor Alexander II.

"Granny was a little in love with Tsar Alexander when she and he were young, and his murder so many years later shocked her to the core. Every time she thinks of Russia she imagined assassins lurking round every corner," he told us.

It was not entirely fair of her, of course, to characterise Russia as especially dangerous, because in England at that time there was a lot of trouble from Fenian bombs, and at various points in her reign people even tried to kill Granny. But she had made up her mind about it and there was no shaking her. She must have anticipated though, being honest, that one of the sisters would probably go to Russia. Serge was Papa's cousin like Ludwig was, after all, and he came to Darmstadt from childhood - less after his Hessian mother died, but when that happened Ella was already fifteen and Serge had noticed her, probably. Certainly at that age she was old enough for William to be hanging around her, the idiot! - but Ella never had the slightest inclination to be German empress.

Three years later Serge came back, Ella said yes, and another of my sisters was going to a man about ten years older than she was. - Course, I can hazard a guess why in both cases, and the reasons are totally different, because if Victoria's husband was selected for being a man grown-up and sure of himself and established in his career, who'd respect her independence, Serge used his age and experience to dominate Ella from the start. Not that we didn't like him. Papa said Serge was the best of his family, rivalled only perhaps by my godfather the Tsar. None of their other brothers had any principles at all, he said. That bit we certainly found to be true for ourselves in due course. Serge was especially good to me at first, because I was still quite young and he loved little children. He used to tease me that he'd seen me being bathed when he visited with his mama when I was a baby.

"So, Alix, you needn't play the great schoolgirl, because you have no secrets from me!"

He teased me that I'd be lost when we went to Russia for the wedding, because everyone spoke French and I would have to do the same. Ella had certainly told him that this was my least favourite subject!

I remember the journey so well, not least because it took such an age to get there - almost three days on the train, travelling east through Germany on a normal scheduled service as we always did, but being met at the border by Serge's own special train, which he'd sent for his bride. We were astounded at the opulence of that train - I'd never before seen a bathtub with a lip on it to prevent the water slopping when we went round bends! - Then of course there was his own private little chapel, full of colourful icons and screens. I, who'd never even been inside a Catholic Church, let alone an Orthodox one, was most impressed by this display, but Papa cautioned me, "It's all very pretty, but is prettiness really what faith is about? - What are they worshipping here - God or the icon?"

Russia though looked to us no different to Scotland or Hesse, covered in pine forests and lush grass interspersed with lakes and rivers. We bypassed St Petersburg and went straight to Peterhof, as I recall, and at the railway station there I was introduced to my godfather the Tsar and his Empress - Uncle Sasha and Auntie Minnie to me, then, although they weren't really my aunt and uncle. What an imposing figure he was! - Well, Papa was a big, burly man too, but he was dwarfed by the Emperor, and Aunt Minnie looked like a doll. It wasn't just his size, either: his beard was straggly and his features were coarse and weatherbeaten and altogether not what you expect in a man with a desk-job. I was quite scared of him until the next day.

We went to the big palace which of course was also unlike anything I had ever seen - all that white and gold! - Most overwhelmed by the garden, and the big cascade of fountains running down to the sea, all sparkling in the sunlight. And how big the sky seemed, that far north. It being June - or late May according to the Russian calendar which we'd just been told about - it stayed more or less light all night, so I had trouble sleeping the first day. Didn't matter of course - the ghostly half-light over the park and the sea was so beautiful to look at.

The very first evening we were there we had dinner with the whole of the Imperial family - Serge and Uncle Sasha and several of their other siblings, and also of course the Tsar's three eldest children - and that was my momentous first meeting with my precious love! - I remember so clearly how he looked at first sight: small and slightly-built like his mother, with wide cheekbones, a turned-up nose and rather full lips - his father's mouth, though less crude. - Very pretty boy, but not insipid, he had too much colour for that: reddish lights in his yellow-brown hair and big velvety dark blue eyes! He sat next to me and shyly apologised to me in English for not speaking German very well, and I said I didn't mind because I generally preferred to speak English anyway and I was just relieved that Serge had been teasing me, and I wasn't expected to speak French after all.

"Sometimes I speak French to Mama," Nicky said, "but Papa likes us to be Russian and not so old-fashioned-like."

I remember I was a bit surprised that Nicky and Georgy wore sailor suits at their age - sixteen and thirteen - because Ernie had them when little but never after the age of ten. This is just another Russian custom I got used to when I saw that all the young Grand-Dukes were dressed that way until they left the school-room and no-one thought it was especially childish. I also remember that the food we ate was as plain as the food at home, and that Uncle Sasha and Serge drank an awful lot of vodka with their dinner, tossing the entire contents of a glass down their throats in one go. That was most exotic and strange.

Nicky and I were highly amused at the thought that my

sister was going to be his aunt; he decided to call me "Tetinka" or Auntie as well, although I was four years younger than he was.

It's no wonder really that I couldn't sleep – I went to bed feeling sort of mixed-up and excited with everything I'd seen – and as for Nicky! – Well, it was the first time I'd sat and talked at a grown-up dinner table with a strange boy, so it was bound to have quite an effect. Young as I was, I fell immediately under the spell of those deep expressive eyes!

The next day we left our rooms and crossed the park to the Cottage to have lunch with Uncle Sasha and Aunt Minnie. I was relieved to find that they lived in such a simple little house and not in the palace itself – it made them more human. Eventually Nicky and Georgy appeared. They had been to Petersburg to the Imperial Library, they said, to improve their poor minds. I felt half sorry for them, because my own lessons had been suspended for the duration of my visit to Russia, but I would also quite have liked to have seen the Library. When we'd finished lunch the whole lot of us went into the garden, where the great nets were strung from frames, and we all jumped about on them like a trampoline, Uncle Sasha as enthusiastically as any of us children. Because of his bulk, he created a tremendous ripple when he landed, which made anyone near him fly up into the air with great force, screaming with laughter. I lost my fear of him as a result of these games, and also of a drive around the park at Peterhof which we made the next day. Uncle Sasha drove at first, but the horse started to get a bit fractious, and he turned very white and said, "Would anyone else like to take over?"

Ernie looked at him with sympathy.

"Let Alix do it. She likes the brutes, for some reason." – Well, it's true that I could drive my own pony before I was six, and at twelve I'd already started to learn to drive four-in-hand with Papa, so I took over and got a lot of admiring remarks from everyone for that, which was upsetting in turn. I could feel myself getting horribly warm and I knew that my face was going red and blotchy, because my elder sisters had always been sure to let me know that was what happened when I blushed.

Poor Uncle Sasha - he feared horses as much as Ernie does. When he appeared on one in public, it had to be an especially large and quiet one, and the consequence of this was of course that when the equestrian statue was erected to him in Petersburg it looked almost bovine and was promptly nicknamed, "The hippopotamus" by some wag.

At least Nicky didn't see my embarrassment that day - he and Georgy were left at home doing lessons while we drove, and when we got back they came running out of the Cottage laughing and saying that they felt terribly insulted to have been left behind.

We were in Russia for days and days before and after Ella's actual marriage ceremony, and Ernie and I above all had a wonderful time with our new friends. Xenia had a model wigwam (instead of a play house) on the balcony outside her bedroom, which of course appealed to my American fixation. There was also a maypole on the beach with canvas loops suspended from it on ropes - the first time I'd seen such a thing. We ran round and round it with the loops round our waists and then launched ourselves into the air, flying freely on the ropes for a few minutes before coming to rest in a flurry of wet sand. I remember Xenia tearing around with her skirts hitched inside her knickers and being reminded by Irène in her new role as eldest unmarried sister that, "Xenia is only nine and you should not contemplate such a thing any more, at your age!" - as if I would have done anyway!

Time after time I would find Nicky sitting next to me at dinner - I started to think it couldn't always be coincidence and I used to get the strangest hot feeling in my tummy when I saw him coming! One day he wrote me a letter from his schoolroom, which was delivered to me personally in our rooms. Papa, Ernie,

Irène – all of them saw it arrive, and they all looked at each other with smiles and sparkling eyes and teased me dreadfully. The thing is, they didn't actually know which of the Grand Dukes had written it! – But I can't imagine Georgy doing such a thing, anyway. He was great fun but really a very naughty boy who strutted around the park with a huge green parrot on his shoulder, uttering raucous cat-calls when he saw Ernie and Nicky and me lying on the nets telling each other secrets with rather flushed faces. The parrot then joined in – it had a dreadfully exaggerated English accent and it knew a string of English oaths which it had apparently been taught as a means of annoying their tutor, Mr. Heath. Sometimes it flew aggressively at Mr. Heath's head, but Georgy was never properly punished because he was Auntie Minnie's darling. Just occasionally Uncle Sasha would seize a hosepipe from one of the flowerbeds and direct it at his children if he thought they were getting out of hand, but they just laughed at this and leaped about dodging the jet of water. Really, they were such a happy family, it was wonderful to be around them and so very different to Granny's prejudiced ideas.

Nicky and Georgy and Xenia came over to us to pay a social call, and we spent the afternoon sliding on the highly polished floors of the formal reception rooms until Xenia fell over and got a nose bleed and Nicky carried her piggy-back home to the Cottage. We spent a lot of time exploring all the various buildings around the Peterhof park – starting with the dear Italian house down on the shore at Alexandria, where Nicky and I scratched our names onto a window and admired the look of them side by side without either admitting to the other that we were doing so.

On the day of Ella's wedding we went to St Petersburg, and my sister made a state entrance into the capital in a gold carriage drawn by white horses. It was so desperately different from Victoria's marriage! – And Petersburg was naturally very different to Darmstadt. Suppose it was the first really large city I'd been in for any length of time - London was really only a place we sometimes passed through on our way to somewhere else, dirty, with narrow streets. Here we drove along vastly wide boulevards lined with cheering crowds, and there were shimmering yellow and white palaces and churches reflected in the water of all the canals. From the windows of the Winter Palace we looked out onto the Neva, so blue and broad you could barely see the opposite bank, and merging on the horizon with that great sky. How absolutely, breath-takingly beautiful Petersburg can look to the stranger!

"The Venice of the North!" Ernie kept saying throughout the day, whenever he looked out of a window.

The other thing that was stunningly beautiful that day was of course my sister. When you're small you accept the faces of your family as familiar and beloved, but you don't really have an objective standard for deciding whether they are attractive or not. We younger ones sort of knew Ella was considered pretty as she grew tall and slender - she, who'd been so chubby when a little girl! - not least because she always had plenty of boys around her. That day though for the first time I could see for myself how lovely she was in her wedding dress, with her clear complexion, auburn hair, her straight nose and large, serene eyes. Ella's features are like Papa - we all look like Papa apart from Victoria! - but there is something in her expression that reminds me poignantly of photographs of my mother. Victoria, who has Mama's features, always had that un-gentle and direct gaze so unlike her.

The wedding ceremony was very, very long, because they had to have two, of course - firstly Orthodox for Serge, and then Ella's Lutheran service. (Papa said often at that time how glad he was that she didn't have to become Orthodox to marry Serge.). Irène and I wore a junior and senior version of the same white muslin dress - hers long, mine short, she with her hair up and

35

me with mine down – the first time we'd been dressed as a pair. I felt that I'd been somehow promoted by my two eldest sisters' marriages.

Ernie and Nicky were both best men – that was another strange thing, that the Orthodox Church or court ceremony or something required several best men, including a number for the bride, and they all had to be unmarried. They, who the day before had been wrestling on the beach at Peterhof, now acted the perfect young gentlemen, both looking serious and nervous and both wearing military uniform with knee high boots. I liked the soft Russian boots better than the ones Ernie had on, which were shiny and brutal-looking. (A few years later I'd have said they made me think of Prussia). Ernie was growing tall and slender whereas Nicky still looked like a sweet little boy, but when they had wrestled on the beach, it was Nicky who won.

Ella had a lot of jewelry on – most of it was Romanov family jewelry that she was required by tradition to wear – and so did all the other ladies present. Then there were the priests in their highly-embroidered robes, the strong smell of the incense, and the deep boom of the choir intoning the liturgy.

"Decadent, isn't it?" Irène whispered, "I feel a bit sick."

I liked it, though – aesthetically and musically – and Ernie of course got wildly over-excited by all this beauty.

During the wedding breakfast there was a bad atmosphere which spoiled things a bit, because of Ludwig being seated not with his family but with the crew of the *Victoria and Albert*, which he was serving on and which had brought the Waleses to the wedding. Seems Uncle Sasha told Papa bluntly that as Ludwig was of unequal rank he could not be permitted to sit at a table full of Royal and Imperial Highnesses. This was a new, different side of the Tsar and suddenly I too felt a bit sick. A couple of days before Nicky had given me a brooch; now I felt that I didn't want to be taking gifts from members of this family – perhaps I too had breached some unknown piece of etiquette by accepting it! – so when we got back to Peterhof I returned it to him, pushing it into his hand from behind him, so I didn't have to see his expression when I did so.

CHAPTER THREE

It is true that my status changed a bit when Victoria and Ella got married. Certainly our home was quieter and emptier, but it's from this time that I started getting close to darling Papa.

We had rather a quiet Christmas, partly because Victoria was in England with her feet up, awaiting the baby, and Ella of course was in Russia, but also because my dear Hessian Grandmama died around that time. Don't remember her nearly so well as I do Granny – she was shy and led such a quiet life and I was still only 12 when she died – but she was kind and tolerant and we missed her a lot. One always said Irène was very like her.

In spring Ludwig and Victoria came with Alice, who was christened on the same day that Ernie was confirmed – beautiful little baby that she was, with dark brows and brown eyes, like her father. The sensation I felt holding my niece in my arms for the first time is not to be described; I knew immediately that if I didn't have one of my own someday I'd feel I'd wasted my life.

Papa started taking me along to military manoeuvres with him, and that was when I really got to know my native land well – saw the Main, Rhine, ruined castles, forests and little wooden houses, also meadows where edelweiss grew – what nature and history – how civilised, how poetic, even. – Learned that early nineteenth century Darmstadt was at the centre of a scientific and literary renaissance – Stefan Georg and Goethe and Liebig all worked there; in this century my brother has tried to recreate that with his artists' colony and all the support he gave to the Jugendstil. If it wasn't for Ernie, Olbrich and Behrens would probably never have become known. – The Brothers Grimm collected all their stories in Hesse; they worked as philologists in the University at Giessen. – Also the strong connection with the Reformation and the birth of Protestantism – Philip the Magnanimous of Hesse being a great patron and protector of Luther. I was raised to have such a pride in the liberal and intellectual heritage of my state, and to think how it has all ended!! Prussia has meant Germany's ruin!!

The Prussians used to be at the manoeuvres; I saw my cousins Sophie and Mossy there or in England. When Mama was alive of course she had wanted to see her sister so there lots of trips to Berlin (before I was born) and reciprocal visits to Darmstadt by Aunt Vicky's family, but when Mama died no-one showed much inclination to carry this on. Cousin William alone used to come when he was a student at Bonn and try to get Ella's attention, but I was far too young to notice he was there and mercifully I never really knew him until Irène and his brother Harry got married. (Harry never came to manoeuvres because he was already committed to the Imperial Navy – he and Irène must have reached their understanding in England, perhaps.)

In 1870 Papa had supported the unification of Germany, but when he saw the Prussians strutting about the field in their pointed helmets he would sigh and say that things would have been so different if the unification had happened in 1848 and Frankfurt had become capital, as was so nearly the case. Then there would have been democracy and equality between the states and Germany would have been a great civilising influence on the world.

By and large I enjoyed manoeuvres, though, because I would see new parts of Hesse and I would get further instruction on driving four-in-hand from Papa's military friends. Ernie hated going. At fifteen he was put *a la suite* of Papa's regiment, but he only really liked the uniform. Poor thing – how embarrassed he was when he once tried to mount a horse at manoeuvres and in his anxiety took it too fast and went straight over the top in full view of everyone. 'I should have been the man in this family,'

Victoria said, but I don't think dear Papa ever felt ashamed of his son's lack of military prowess; he was just proud to see how like our mother Ernie is in heaps of ways – when he went off to Marburg and Giessen he really thrived amongst the academics. I missed him terribly, needless to say, especially when Papa wasn't there.

We had to go to Berlin when Irène got married, there was no avoiding it. Papa said Granny was deeply unhappy about that marriage as she had been about Ella's, partly because she had intended Irène to marry one of the Wales cousins instead, but also because she considered Harry to be a pale shadow of his not very pleasant elder brother William. Heard that they were both of them unbelievably cold and beastly to Aunt Vicky, and it is certainly the case that later Harry became known for making stupid inflammatory speeches about the might of the German Navy, which William wrote for him. On the whole, though, national pride apart (beastly politics spoils everything in this family!), he seemed a decent sort who could be good fun, and Irène is good for him – made him more English and less Prussian, really, so he behaved better towards his mother thereafter.

The wedding though was not an especially happy event. I was confirmed by this time, that's why I went to the adult parties and saw quite a lot of my much older cousins, who behaved like they always do – William was loud and full of boorish jokes (when he shook hands with Ernie he turned all his rings inwards); his fat stupid narrow-minded Dona was fussing about who took precedence over whom and making her usual remarks about the Battenbergs not being pure-blooded, saying Ludwig shouldn't have been invited to his own sister-in-law's wedding. Charlotte was being witty at everyone else's expense and stirring up arguments. And of course Aunt Vicky was almost mad with grief over Uncle Fritz, who was clearly in agony from his throat cancer (Seems Chancellor Bismarck said loudly during the ceremonies that an Emperor with no voice shouldn't be allowed to reign).

How I feel for Irène, married into that atrociously unhappy family! - But you have to make the best of these things; build up your own little nest and shut out the rest, and she has not been unhappy in her marriage. But how appalling the sanitation is in the Prussian palaces! - and there were predictably soldiers everywhere. Ernie kept repeating the old joke about "Prussia isn't a state with an Army, it's an Army with a state," and we were really glad to go home again. By the end of the year William had of course got his wish and he was Emperor and that was the beginning of the end of everything.

Just after Irène got married, Papa gave me a coming-out party in Darmstadt, which was informal and fun and very different to the pomposity in Berlin. I wore white muslin and had lilies-of-the valley in my hair, which was up at last of course, and people kept saying, "Aren't you like your sister Ella!" which was very flattering. It's true that I'm more like her than the other two - there's the height for one thing (I got to be taller than Irène when I was about thirteen, and Victoria not long after that) and a similarity in the features; but she is darker than I am, and of course she had great poise whereas I've always been sneered at for blushing unflatteringly by some people. No-one in Darmstadt, though.

To celebrate my being "out" Granny had Gretchen Fabrice appointed lady-in-waiting to me, and she finally succeeded in getting rid of poor Madgie. Actually, Madgie was not in very good health, so her retirement was for the best, and Gretchen was really more like a new tutor to me than anything else, albeit tutoring in rather different subjects to Madgie! A big part of her role was to do with poise: chiding me for my language and telling me to take smaller steps when walking - she who was always so soft-spoken and lady-like herself.

The beastly side of being out is that of course everyone feels free to start speculating about who you might marry, which I think is too much when a girl is only sixteen. My first grown-up "season", the winter of 1888-9, was the one I spent in Russia and things started getting seriously complicated. I really think it's too unkind that the whole of Petersburg society was watching and gossiping at the same time.

We hadn't been back to Russia since Ella's wedding - she came to Darmstadt instead - and of course it was the first time I'd seen it in winter and known the intensity of the cold and the silence after a fall of fresh snow. It far surpassed anything we got in Germany, naturally. Ernie and I were enchanted from the moment we arrived and saw the sleighs jangling, muffled by the winter air, along the Nevsky Prospekt; and the frozen Neva being treated as just another road, no fear that it would crack.

We were met at the station by Uncle Sasha, looking as ever rather dishevelled - his clothes never seemed to be cut properly for his great frame, and they hung around him like sacks. He had majesty, though, for all his ungainly size: one glance from this Tsar's slatey blue eyes and people around seemed to know instinctively what he wanted them to do, and would rush to execute his orders. He was a very different person in public from the Uncle Sasha who had jumped around on nets at Peterhof with his children and turned the hose-pipe on them to calm them down. People always used to say they found it hard to recognise that he and Nicky were father and son, because of the difference in build and demeanour. - Nicky of course was with him at the station, changed and grown up since 1884 as Ernie and I were too, so neat and graceful in the uniform of a junior Guards officer and with big, soft shy eyes that right away did something funny to my insides!

These were the years when he was newly-commissioned and was taking lectures in political economy and looking forward to the end of this formal education, about which Ernie and I grilled him constantly.

"I had rather be a soldier than a statesman - because at least soldiers support each other and tell each other the truth," he admitted.

But *Au fond,* what he would truly rather have been given completely free choice in life is a historian, which always amused me because along with French history was my least favourite topic in the schoolroom. I only ever liked the political and philosophical aspects of it; the past per se is not fascinating at all.

It was fantastically interesting talking to him, his mind was at that time like a reverse blue-print of my own. He was not only a historian but he was clearly a linguist - another thing I most certainly am not - and his whole philosophical approach to life was based on instinct and the spirit.

From his historical studies he derived a deeply mystic notion of Russia's destiny; from the tutors -especially Pobedonostsev - this pessimistic conviction that all politicians were liars.

"Maybe it's different in Western Europe - I suppose people are more individualistic and can look after themselves, so you get the advanced democratic systems you've got, and they really work. But Russian society is built around the Church and these small inward-looking communities which are her history and strength and need preserving - I'm lecturing; haven't you had enough of this yet?! - and all politicians and parties serve for here is to pursue self-interest and to exploit everyone else."

Nevertheless, he disliked Pobedonostsev intensely, finding him a cold fish.

"Why doesn't your father just send you to university?" Ernie and I asked. "Then you could have different lecturers."

"Because apparently I can't get too involved in all that - I have to be separate from all sections of society and not get identified with intellectuals, especially. And truly, it would unfit me for leading for the rest of the country - the real Russia."

He really didn't like to talk too long about politics and his position in life - we kept coming back instead to Russia's spiritual tradition and profoundly religious history. Nicky always had a deep and instinctive faith entirely consistent with this, whereas mine was - is - intellectualized and often controversial in line with the way I was raised. Ernie of course was powerfully drawn to all this talk of following the heart, and he insisted we went to the Orthodox service one Sunday. I stood listening like in '84 to the deep beautiful chant of the litany, and in between I looked at Nicky and was quite enchanted with the look on his face, sweet and serious and far away.

"I think he's a sort of religious *exalté*," Ernie said later, "funny character for the future Emperor!"

It was very convenient; there were only a few hundred yards between Ella's house and the Anitchkov where of course the Emperor's family were living for the winter. I used to look out of the window in the early afternoon and see Nicky running up our steps two at a time in a long coat and those soft Russian boots that I'd liked on my last visit - full of energy and looking really too adorable for words! - Then we'd cross the bridge to the Anitchkov and skate and play ball games and slide about on the hills, with or without sledges. Ella, Ernie, Xenia, Georgy were all there, and I met for the first time his most constant companions of those youthful days: Russian cousin Sandro, leader of the group, a smooth-tongued sophisticate already weaving his charms on the 13-year-old Xenia; and Greek cousin Georgie, a huge blond ugly young man who seemed personally closer to him than Sandro was. Also: - "When you go to England, give all my love to our mutual cousin Toria Wales," Nicky said to me, "she is such a kind, jolly person, don't you think?" - They were almost exactly the same age and they had spent every summer of their childhoods together in Denmark; it was pretty similar to Louie and me. - These little reminders of mutual connections of ours made me feel strangely happy - he was part of my world really, for all my grandmother was obsessed with the strangeness and the distantness of Russia from all that was familiar.

Sometimes Uncle Sasha passed by, accompanied by his two youngest children with their spades, on their way to dig the paths clear.

"Papa doesn't like the rest of us any more; we're passing beyond his control," Georgy observed cheerfully.

I could hear the Emperor calling out to Misha and Olga; but he called them "Floppy" and "Badger".

"You see," Georgy said, "listen to that! - he doesn't have petnames for us these days, except that occasionally he's been known to call Nicky 'Girlie'!"

Nicky shrugged and grinned, though he was blushing rather, and Sandro said, "He's a rough tough man and he's right to be so in my view, no-one else will ever be blunt with either of you in this life! - so stop maundering on like some weeping willow, you don't care really and you only do it to feed your own rebellion!"

"There, you see," I said to Georgy, "you've got a petname too now, Weeping Willow!" - he threw snow at me and I kicked a great shower of it back at the three of them, and made a run for the hill. Georgy and Sandro chucked some more snow after me but only Nicky actually followed. It was hard going; as the slope got steeper I found that I was running on the spot and my breath was coming in gasps; eventually I collapsed in a heap, and he flung himself down beside me.

"That wasn't a fair exchange," he said, "we didn't get to hear your petnames. - And don't say you haven't got any; the baby of the family always has loads."

"That's private," I teased him, and he protested,

"You're rotten! - You've heard what my father calls me, it can't be worse than that!" and he drew his collar up and across his face and laughed rather nervously under it.

"What are you doing?" I said, and my voice came out unintentionally soft and amused.

"Embarrassed," he answered, and he looked at me over the

top of his collar with just one eye - unmistakeably flirtatious gesture that made me blush terribly, so that I started talking fast to cover my confusion.

"If you really need to know, my grandmother calls me 'Alicky', my father calls me in German 'Spitsbub' - you know what that means? - and my mother always used to call me 'Sunny', but no-one really uses that any more."

"Sunny," he said, "because of your hair I suppose?"

"Actually, it was darker when I was small. No - I think it's because I was a fat jolly sort of baby."

But he was still gazing at my hair, and I suddenly realised that it was escaping from its pins and falling loose down my back.

"Beastly nuisance!" I moaned, and started trying to put it back up again, "you see, I haven't really got used to wearing it like this yet; I forget I have to be careful."

"Can you sit on it when it's down?" he asked casually, so I answered him jauntily, cousin-style, as well.

"Just about, yes. I know other girls envy that but it gets tangled and then it tugs vilely when it's brushed. Look - I'm going to have to go indoors and do something about it." - I jumped up and started to run off down the hill, and he followed me, catching my elbows from behind and then sliding, pushing me before him until I lost my balance and fell over laughing. And yes - it did feel rather different to horseplay with Ernie!

Every evening almost there was a party at someone's house, and I danced with loads of Russian aristocrats and with my brother-in-law and sometimes also with Nicky. And that was magic. It was partly the music, and feeling incongruously grown-up in my ball-gowns and pearls; but then I could feel the warmth of his fingers through his gloves when he held my hand and my arm, and the cloth of his sleeve through my own glove, and I burned all over. Our eyes are exactly on a level, and consequently they met involuntarily all the time and I saw a sort

46

of sparkle kindle in his as though they were smiling. I held his gaze though I could feel my face going red and all the time I was conscious that our bodies were so close as to be almost touching and I was dreaming of how it would feel to kiss him properly.

We also went to the theatre a lot - Mariinsky or smaller ones - and saw plays old and new. I remember seeing Zola - *L 'Assomoir* I think it was - and hearing Ernie hold forth about the stiltedness of Naturalism and Zola's characters' lack of an internal life, and Uncle Sasha and Aunt Minnie and Papa all looking at him as if they didn't have a clue what he was talking about. At his behest I read the Symbolist manifesto that winter; between them he and Nicky were I suppose already shaking my faith in cold rationalism, in the eighteenth-century *philosophes* to whom Victoria had always steered me. But when I asked Ernie,

"And how does this apply to the conduct of life?" he laughed at me and said, "It's about creating art, not leading your life; you should learn to take everything a little less intensely, you know!"

Then there were concerts in people's drawing rooms, including at the Anitchkov, where Ella sang and the Tsar himself played his big trombone. Nicky, Georgy and I couldn't stop laughing because he looked so large and earnest and out of place with the rest of the orchestra.

"Papa's playing is an offence against the ear," Nicky groaned, and Georgy said,

"What d'you mean? - It's an offence against the soul!"

"Alright!" Serge was angry with them; I saw his cold, hard side more and more as I grew up "you are terribly witty and clever but you should show a bit more respect!" and I found I was giggling, stupidly, uncontrollably, because for some unknown reason this exchange seemed to me hilariously funny. What memories! - God, I could relive these forever!

Bad moments: - there was a little ball at the Alexander Palace given by the Emperor for people his children knew - the first time I had visited Tsarskoe Selo. Nicky and I had been dancing something wild and exciting like the mazurka and when a footman brought us champagne we both simultaneously choked on the bubbles and started giggling idiotically. I had a sudden feeling of unease, and glancing towards the door I saw Aunt Minnie watching us very closely and coolly.

Later I passed her talking to Ella: – "Darling, you must understand that that would never do! And people are talking already."

Ambiguous remark – tried to tell myself she was talking about something very different, but I got the impression I was suddenly being discussed and dismissed as a marriage prospect for the Heir to the Russian Throne just because we'd been flirting! – We who were very nearly cousins anyway! – And, really, not much more than children still.

At least, that is how I tried to tell myself things were.

The reality is that I day-dreamed about him and longed to see him and talk to him when we were apart, and I couldn't but be conscious of the electric physical charge between us.

Back in Darmstadt, I started writing regularly to Xenia, and her letters would often come with a note from her brother enclosed. Then he wrote me letters of his own about plays or operas he'd seen, and about his garden, and funny gossip about his cousins. In June, I got a message from Ella saying she'd had a long conversation with him about me, and how much fun he had had when we visited, and she knew he'd be thrilled if I wrote to her asking her to pass on my good wishes. Really, what was the bloomin' idiot playing at?! – She was clearly hinting that he'd said he had strong feelings for me; and yet I couldn't forget how I'd seen Aunt Minnie warning her off. It confused me horribly, coming on top of me not being sure what I was feeling for him anyway – when do you know that you're in love if you've no experience of it?

I spent the summer at Balmoral riding and fishing with

cousin Louie, and sneaking cigarettes from one of our Uncles. Granny had an amazing nose for tobacco – she absolutely loathed the smell of it and she could tell from the other side of the house if someone was indulging. I once found Victoria smoking with her head in a grate, blowing the fumes up the chimney so she wouldn't be caught – although if anyone was going to get away with breaking Granny's rules, then as usual it would be the blessed Victoria!

And suddenly I found I was drawn more into the orbit of the Waleses than was usual, because I had been in Russia, and they wanted news of their relatives, and I found a new and particular fascination in the company of Toria who was Nicky's soul-mate and from whom I subtly prompted stories about his childhood. Alas, the result of this time chez Wales was that I got my first, unexpected proposal, from my cousin Eddy. He was so much older; never thought of him as anything but a rather indistinct relative – he didn't say much for himself, and sat around a lot gazing out of windows. So of course I said I liked him as a cousin, but no thank you. Granny made it plain that she was very angry about this; I was told what a foolish thing I was doing throwing away the chance to be Queen of England! – But I already had a decided feeling that marrying someone for their grand rank was a bad idea – I knew what I felt when Nicky touched my hand, and contemplating being in the same situation with tall, wan Eddy even made me shudder!

Actually, Granny told Papa privately that I showed great strength of character in refusing Eddy, so secretly she must have been proud. But she said to him too, anxiously, "What idea has she got in her head?" Think, if I'd married poor Eddy, I'd have been a widow by the age of twenty! – My child if I'd had one would be a very young King or Queen now and there'd be no George V. In England's case, this probably wouldn't have made any difference, being a constitutional country.

Next summer, of course, I wasn't invited to Balmoral;

Granny said she couldn't have me and Ernie on account of my behaviour over Eddy, and I was horribly hurt. Suppose I'd come close to an open row with her, like my mother long ago. Instead of Scotland we went to Russia again, although I didn't see Nicky that time. Serge had already by then been appointed Governor-General of Moscow and they were living at Ilinskoe. Nicky'd been expected to pay a visit, but at the last minute he was unable to come. The official reason was that he had to prepare for his and Georgy's long, educational trip abroad to Egypt and the East, but I now know his parents prevented him from coming because I was there. Maybe half suspected it at the time.

Ella's life at Ilinskoe was very informal compared with Petersburg – not so much time spent hanging around waiting for her to finish dressing! (But she still took a look in every mirror she passed!). I remember mostly walks in the birch forests, boating on the river and exploring little wooden villages – my first view of the Russian countryside. Sometimes Ella was recognised by villagers, who would appear at the doors of their houses holding bread and salt as a formal welcome – first time I'd seen that done, though I'd read about it. We went into Moscow as tourists and I marveled at how different a city it was from Petersburg – onion domes and narrow streets.

"This is the real Russia," Serge said, "Petersburg is corrupt, westernised and artificial."

Sometimes there were visitors for cards in the evening, and one day Ella suddenly said, half-nervously, to Papa (but Ernie and I were there too), "You won't listen, will you, if anyone tells you I'm unhappy?"

"Darling, I can see with my own eyes that all is well between you and Serge," he answered.

"Well, good. Because the most fantastic rot does get into the western papers, and there is such gossip sometimes even among friends and family."

Well, it had already occurred to us to wonder why they still had no children – when Serge loved them so – but as a result of this odd little exchange Ernie and I took pains to find out what was being said about their marriage. Undoubtedly, the things people whispered about Serge are the usual filthy-minded bosh our charming aristocracy dream up – that he had raped her and as a result she had excluded him from her bedroom; that he was a sadist; that he visited child prostitutes in Moscow. And then there were those stories about his relationships with other men. Not sure whether Ella knew about these tales when they got married, or even if it had any effect on their marriage when she found out – did she believe some of it?. *Au fond* I do not understand Ella. It clearly suited her to be married to a man like Serge, who guided her taste in everything from literature to clothes, and dare I suggest that the physical side meant nothing at all? – Perhaps it even made her feel good about herself to have sacrificed so much.....

A year after this visit was when she chose to take her husband's faith, which upset Papa and Irène, above all, most dreadfully.

"To think she'll have to confess to a priest! Whatever has happened to her self-respect?"

"Well," said Victoria, "it's a matter of her individual conscience as to whether she feels she needs to do that, and can do it."

As I understood it then, individual conscience was the crux of the whole argument – that the Protestant faith gives a human soul an individual relationship with God, which is denied by the older churches with their powerful priests and their archaic scriptures and services that the simple person cannot understand. At that time, the Russian service still used to be sung in Old Church Slavonic, and I felt that Ella had in some way sacrificed her humanity – arrogant little fool that I was!

Other main family trouble at this time was the next generation. Victoria was so critical of poor little Alice – called her disobedient and slow to speak – seems it took Ludwig's mother to suggest that maybe something was wrong with her hearing which was of course quickly confirmed when they finally took her to a doctor. After that Victoria laid down that no allowances were to be made – Alice would learn to follow the conversation by reading lips, and if she missed what was being said she would have to find some way of compensating. I can well imagine that having Victoria as a mother must be a trial sometimes! (she was demanding enough as a big sister) – Must say that even when I was seventeen it seemed to me a bit strange that she went out to Malta to join Ludwig and left Alice and Louise (poor, skinny little thing that she was then, and only three months old) alone with their nursemaid. Granny fully approved, though – "It's only right that she should put her duty to her husband first."

Well, why couldn't she have taken the children with her as well? – Surely she should have been nursing Louise who needed her own mother's milk if ever a child did?!

Papa and I of course paid our visit to Malta while Ludwig served with the Mediterranean Fleet, and that was when the German Navy came by and there was a great ceremonial meeting with the British ships – how sad now to think how friendly it all was! – Irène came off Harry's ship which was in any case named for her (now she was such a grand Prussian princess and the Kaiser's sister-in-law!) and remained in Malta while her compatriots went on their way. How Ludwig suffered for that later! – when the British press made such a stink about his relationship with Harry and Irène, and how they must have sat together and swapped the secrets of their respective countries' Navies over coffee. – But who on earth could have predicted in the '90s how the friendly rivalry was all due to end?

Irène's main worry then was the health of her little baby Toddy – he would have been about eighteen months old, and they all sat and discussed his terrible bruises and what the future might bring.

"Bleeding in the joints, like Uncle Leopold," poor Irène said. "He could be crippled by the time he reaches his teens, if he isn't taken from us first."

I was horrified and I wanted to know what this disease was, because although I remember dear Uncle Leo being lame a lot of the time, and of course he died so young, I had never realised that he had a chronic disease.

"Haemophilia is the medical name," Irène said. "Means his blood won't clot properly."

Victoria was chain-smoking furiously, presumably - she always is.

"Well, why did you have to go and marry your first cousin?!" she demanded tearfully - I haven't often seen her so upset, "I just knew something bad would come of it."

I don't know why, but at that time we didn't inquire further about where this disease had come from - Victoria was always so knowledgeable about everything scientific that if she thought haemophilia was caused by cousin marriages she must be right. I may have been a bit heartless about it all, too. I was sure that things would change - Toddy would get better or a cure would be found - and I thought Irène's sadness was rather a drag in this lovely sunny country. There were plenty of parties and theatre trips with all the naval officers - I was flirting mildly with Ludwig's protégé Mark Kerr - and also of course the archaeological dig up in the hills above Valetta, which fascinated Victoria and me.

I did worry though that I was leading a slightly aimless life. When Ernie came home to Darmstadt from University for his holidays he would always be wanting parties and fun, so we had fancy dress balls and tennis parties and the like. In between times I started doing the household accounts for Papa, because I didn't want to feel like some idle young lady. It really did shock me to see how little spare money there was to go around, and I think that can only have been good for me - then and in the future. I personally received very little allowance which is why I got into the habit of making all my Christmas presents by hand. They are in any case best that way - shows more thought. Also got involved with all the hospitals and technical schools my mother had founded - sitting on governing committees and the like. Certainly someone had to do it or they'd probably have faded away through lack of interest. Thought this sort of work was going to be my life, and I was quite happy for it to be so - I happen to have been born in a position which while not especially grand or elevated in the scheme of things gave me a certain amount of influence over other people, and this influence must be used.

Mama's precept which informed my education even if she was no longer there to supervise it was, "They must understand that their position in life is nothing other than what good they do with it."

Also, because of this and because of Madgie's ideas, I never expected that I was necessarily going to get married. Girls need to have a role in life beyond sitting around and waiting for a man to arrive.

Well, in due course Max of Baden arrived anyway, and Papa took me aside and warned me that I was going to get another proposal. Almost without a doubt Granny was behind this. I was horrified! - it was worse than with Eddy, because I'd never even met Max before! - Really, I just cried my eyes out - I couldn't even be angry that time. So dearest Papa sent him away.

Mind flies unbidden back to the other one!: - we got alarming news from Ella about both the young Grand Dukes at the end of their tour of India and the Far East. This was when Nicky was been terribly wounded in an attack by a religious fanatic in Japan - sword blow to the head which made a deep cut and left a scar in his brow under his hair. Only the presence of blessed burly Greek Georgie who knocked the sword from the man's hand and chased him away saved Nicky from a second fatal blow. When I heard about that attack it gave me a shock and a deep pain in my stomach, and I thought how unspeakable it would have been if I'd heard I'd never see him again.

Then Georgy was sent home with a terrible cough, spitting blood. Poor "Weeping Willow" (remember that name that we called him in '89?) - the spirit always was a great deal stronger than the flesh. Found out later that he was born with a dreadful respiratory infection and the doctors feared he wouldn't survive. He was even slimmer than Nicky - in whose case the delicate build belies his good health - and in '89 already coughed and wheezed in the winter air. Someone (Aunt Vicky? - with her usual tact) once told me that the brother who came between - the little Alexander who died of meningitis at one year - was a large and lusty baby taking after his father, and it was doubly devastating to the parents to lose him because they were left with such poor specimens in their other sons! Granny said it was something to do with those Danish princesses: - "All of the Waleses were small and born prematurely just because their mother was Aunt Alex, and I always knew that Alex's sister would similarly have puny little children!"

Certainly it's true that Xenia like her elder brothers is rather more Minnie's child than her father's, but both Misha and Olga are big-boned like Uncle Sasha, so I don't think she was being totally fair. Also, of course, Georgy was certainly not the only Romanov who got T.B., so one could actually blame the father's supposedly lusty stock for that legacy. Most of the Romanov men may grow to be seven feet tall, but they never seem to live that long. Poor Georgy was sent to the Caucasus for the air and he never really went home again for any period of time.

Shortly after he went we heard a rumour that Uncle Sasha was trying to arrange a marriage between Nicky and Helene d'Orléans, which seemed an odd choice - dynastically speaking, what use is the daughter of the claimant to a non-existent throne? - That fell through apparently because she was a Catholic and there was then talk about Mossy of Prussia. (Nicky told me later that he'd have become a monk sooner than marry my plain, bony cousin, and over Helene d'Orléans he said he'd renounce his rights if made to do it....).

I had in any case put him out of my head - there really wasn't any hope if his parents opposed it, I certainly didn't fancy the idea of being Empress of Russia anyway, and in any case most crucially to me there was also the religious problem: - wasn't until Ella converted that I really thought about this; but when she did I heard people say why had she done it when she wasn't obliged to? - the only Grand Duke whose wife was legally obliged to become Orthodox was the Heir. Out of the question for me to give up my Church when I'd not long ago been confirmed and had studied the doctrines so closely and believed them so fervently. This had not been the only road open to me - Mama's books could have led me to agnoticism or further if I'd chosen; but perhaps unconsciously under the influence of Nicky's own profound belief I took the other route, I accepted that humanity justifies itself by Faith alone, and it seemed to me that to give up any single tenet of that Faith was tantamount to rejecting the lot. And without faith, what is there in this life? - To what purpose exactly am I living? This point of view was confirmed for me later, when I needed to consult him, by Pastor Sell.

Now I find my mind moving on again into territory I'd rather avoid - can't stop thinking of Papa's chest pains, and how he was reassured by the doctors that it was just a little heart trouble and would get better if he rested (he was after all only 54). So in Papa's case there was no resolution, no question of preparing himself to move into another world - he had a massive stroke at lunch one day and never regained consciousness. Oh God, I can't bear to think about it, even now! - Nine days of unconsciousness with his family sitting beside him and waiting to resume that unfinished conversation.

CHAPTER FOUR

Ekaterinburg, Siberia. 11 May 1918, New Style. So, they tell us that the children will be leaving Tobolsk today. Hope that this is true, that there are no mishaps on the way! - Sig and Zhilik will take the greatest possible care of them, but here, in this place, thoughts start to enter the mind which my soul rebels at putting into words.

Things are better where they are, of that I am sure - they are all safe and bored in Tobolsk, they lead the same old life. Yes - we have had a letter or two - Anastasia has been using the swing in the yard and is whooping to see the sun; Alexei grows fatter and eats well; the dog has a cold. Yet in spite of everything it will be a relief to have them again with us. Their journey should be quicker than ours was, because they will not have the same delay at Omsk while the guards argue with the Regional Soviet over who is to take us. Instead, they come straight to Ekaterinburg. No moments of wondering for them who their commandant really is - has he secretly come to spirit them away to England? We should have known better than to think that for a moment, and even if it had been true, the Soviet was easily able to prevent it in the end.

We have been preparing the other bedroom. The pictures and rugs we brought with us make the big white room look almost homely. But where will our people sleep? Nyuta already has the dining room; Botkin, Chemodurov and Sednev are in the hall. Perhaps the guards will open up some more rooms - we could see when we arrived that it was quite a big house, in spite of the view being obscured by the wooden palisade that they had built in front. Is it to stop others looking in or us looking out? Clearly, we have been allocated only one floor of this house. At first, there were guards on this floor too; had to pass them every time we used the bathroom or the lavatory. Now at least, they have been moved downstairs. Their graffiti remains, though.

'*To all of the peoples Nicholas said If you want a Republic, go fuck yourselves instead,*' it says on the wall of the bathroom. And my Marie has to look at this every time she goes in there. 'Please be so kind,' she has written on the wall next to the lavatory, 'as to leave the seat in the state in which you found it,' and they have replied with an obscene cartoon. Yesterday they confiscated the sixteen roubles she had with her – the others had given it her for the journey. Nicky and I had no money at all, but they still insisted bombastically many times that we should give up our riches. When we arrived they searched the luggage; that was when we realised that things were going to be different here. 'Until now,' Nicky said bitterly, when they demanded to see my things 'we were at least guarded by gentlemen!' 'Citizen Romanov,' bawled the Commandant, 'you speak one more time and we separate you from your family! Two times, you get hard labour!' So I complied with their requests.

And what has happened to Valia? – They separated him from us when we arrived at the house; we don't know where they took him.

Years ago, Victoria came to this town on holiday; but she felt it hostile even then; she remarked it at the time. Strange to think of her in this place. I have no real news of Victoria, not for more than a year. All we know is an announcement we saw in The Times when we were still allowed to receive it that they had changed their name and dropped all German styles when the royal family did. Marchioness of Milford Haven, she is now. Probably she would have preferred to be just Citizen Mountbatten? How are her children? Is Georgie safe? Is he yet a father? Is Dickie out at sea too now? – I thank God I have no sons of service age myself.

And Irène's boys – what has happened to Toddy and Bobby?

- the former especially who is so vulnerable. If he hadn't been needed to set an example they'd never have let him join up at all. One heard such reports and rumours from Germany about revolutions and William killed or deposed - can't have happened just yet, but fear that Irène will have to go through something a little like what we are doing. Or more likely she will be stripped of her possessions and at least allowed to go where she pleases. When it comes to apportioning blame for the war, Harry will not be found wanting, but all my sister ever tried to do was raise her family and live a quiet life. If there is revolution in Prussia, it will take my blameless little old country with it, and Ernie will suffer so terribly to see all his work destroyed. 'Alix, you are going to ruin everything for yourself!' Ella and Victoria kept saying to me these last years; but in the end all of the *Geschwister* are being materially destroyed and without my help at all. Wonder where Ella is now.

The telephone in the room downstairs has been ringing on and off all day. I feel nervous and jumpy - cigarette required. Soon it will be lunch-time and we will be with the guards and their talk and comments again. But it all washes over Nicky now, and even my anger has gone. It is all talk and show; they have not really harmed us, and the talk gets less brusque by the day when they release they won't get a reaction out of us. Some of the boys even blush when they speak to my Marie: they are just young lads like any others. I have not yet given in and eaten meat, although subsisting on macaroni can't be healthy at all. Doesn't matter - the flesh like all earthly things slowly slips away. Not as if we use up much energy here anyway. Daytime spent painting (I still have some watercolours left) or reading; evenings playing cards with Botkin in his room. I haven't been outside since we got here; have pains in the legs too strong for exercise. If we were even to die here we would be ready for it, Nicky and Botkin and me (for the rest, such a thing cannot even be contemplated!!) - perhaps that's why thoughts go back to Papa

59

and his unexpected death all the time. How dreadful it is when you are unprepared and still have a strong hold on life.

Marie and I will need to turn washerwomen if we are to keep up with all the clothes. Nyuta is washing handkerchiefs today but she is not accustomed to it; she was a ladies' maid, and it's slow going. Seems to mean nothing to the guards that her dignity is offended by their requiring her to do this. 'Lackey!' they say, but without much conviction. Her salary has not been paid, because we have no money and the Bolsheviks are not interested in her worker's rights. Yesterday I cut Nicky's hair because it was growing long. Please God, let the children be safely on their way.

I used to have such energy; never felt so dull and beaten down before. Papa's death was the sharpest sorrow I've ever felt, but yet I took myself off to Britain at Granny's invitation ('you and Ernie are orphans now and more like my own children than ever!' she said, bless her) and started to play the dutiful princess there instead. She was going to Wales on a tour of the mining areas, and I went with her, out of interest (even managed to go down a mine and see how the men worked) but also to take care of her. This duty was not without its thorns, of course! One had to share a compartment with her on her train at night, and she was dreadfully restless. Every minute I'd be getting up to open the window or close it again – mostly she preferred it very cold. She was starting to show her age, getting short-sighted and aching with rheumatism, but was filled with enthusiasm for her latest project, which was finding a bride for Ernie.

Ernie'd begun his time as Grand-Duke of Hesse just as he was to go on, introducing his very radical educational bill in parliament. For that the papers called him the 'Red Grand Duke' and I was very proud. Granny though said he didn't worry about answering letters, he was too wild and too young really for the responsibility, and she wanted him tied down. Not sure why she should have thought Ducky would accomplish this. Oh, Ducky was a dear child in those days, but she was hardly mature and steady. Ernie was twenty-three when Granny had her idea, but Ducky only fifteen. Because she was four years younger than me, I never really knew her until they were in Malta with us, when Uncle Alfred was commanding the Mediterranean Fleet. Liked her a lot more than Missy - affected girl that she was, always gazing in mirrors with a silly look on her face and sighing, 'Oh, I cannot live without beauty!'

- Missy used to skip through the meadows holding her arms out to flowers and crying, 'The joy! The joy!'

Ducky I remember was hot-tempered and sulky and thought to be the difficult sister. She and Ernie were very amusing together, but it took him a good eighteen months to propose. In the meantime it was mostly I who played the *Landesmutter* to Hesse, hosting his dinner parties and the like. Also went informally to the University to listen to lectures, because I didn't want to shame him in front of his intellectual friends, and above all I wanted to expand my own knowledge of philosophy and science and the places where they meet. Puzzled me that no-one in the family had ever considered that I might have wanted to go to university properly, but of course in those days it was a real struggle for girls, so they probably thought I would do as my sister Victoria and my mother did, studying in their own time and maybe seeking out clever people to talk to. There were other girls at the University in Darmstadt, though - and of course Ernie wished to encourage this. A good time to be a young woman, the '90s - the first time we had really sensible clothes, for one thing! - I really liked those smart, simple suits and blouses - and the little straw boaters we wore with them. In the '90s the modern bicycle appeared, so the sort of girls who could never have afforded a horse were suddenly rushing all over the place and doing things they liked to do. Used to see them in London, middle-class girls on their way to their jobs as type-writers or lab assistants - they who half a generation earlier would have been expected to stay at home and help with the housekeeping while they waited to get married. If I'd had more time I would have loved to have studied practical science - not easy on your own. In a different life I think I would like to have been a doctor. A doctor of some sort.

People in Hesse put up with me, but naturally they'd rather Ernie's wife than his sister was at his side, and that he was getting on with producing an heir, especially since he had no brothers. When Georgie was born in the Schloss, there were people running round the streets calling excitedly, '*Es ist ein Prinz im Alten Palais angekommen!*' as if he were Ernie's son rather than Victoria's. Shows how proud people were of their state and little grand-ducal family as its representative - never saw them celebrate the birth of the Emperor's children in that way! So much for a united Germany. We had to go to Berlin again when Mossy got married (all the cousins of my age were being paired off, because it was at the same time that poor Louie accepted a proposal from that idiot Aribert who she didn't know at all, and who proceeded to neglect her and eventually accuse her of being barren.)

Nicky was there in Berlin - first time in four years that I'd seen him, and in the meantime the blond beard had appeared - I thought he looked like a Vandyke! - But he was shy and ill at ease; hardly spoke to me at all, and I wondered what was going on. Then Ella and Serge arrived in Darmstadt for the summer, and almost immediately she took me aside. 'Alix, you need to know that if you want dear Nicky he's yours. His parents have consented; he has been told to start making inquiries about your views. He meant to start in Berlin but you were never really alone together.' I got quite angry at first because I always felt she was gossiping, but Serge backed her completely. It was official. And I sat down and wrote him that letter which almost broke the angel's heart, all about my own religion and how I could not be happy with him if I gave it up, feeling I'd committed some sin. Later found out that when he received it he went on a four-day drinking binge with Sandro et al., because he felt so hopeless – sort of thing he sometimes did in those youthful days! I got such a sad letter, it made me howl – 'It's awfully hard when you've cherished a dream for many a year and think now you are near to its being realised – then suddenly the curtain is drawn and – you see only an empty space! 'Oh, do not say no directly, my dearest Alix – do not ruin my life already! Do you think there can exist any happiness in the whole world without you? Oh! Do not get angry with me if I'm starting to say silly things when I promised to be calm....' Can still quote from it, word for word and still have it here with me – and I still feel the anguish I felt, reading it and knowing what he was going through, and looking at it again and thinking that this was a true, passionate love letter from that charming, sensitive, handsome young man who I was now sure I loved in return, and that I was throwing everything away. But I couldn't give in.

Ernie gave in to Granny's hints, however, and his and Ducky's betrothal was announced early in '94. So now in my mind I am in Coburg waiting for the wedding and planning my summer in London with Ludwig, Victoria and the children. I thought it would be diplomatic to stay out of the way of the newly-weds, especially as Ernie was so nervy about it all. Several times he had come into my room saying 'Oh God, I hope I'm up to this! What if it turns out I can't have children?' Well, Victoria fed his fears a bit, saying often that she wished for the sake of the family and of Hesse that it weren't another first cousin marriage, but I said, 'Oh Ernie, why on earth should you not be able to accomplish what practically every other couple in the world can manage?'

On April 4 Nicky and some uncles – Serge and Vladimir, naturally, but also Paul – turned up representing his father; and in the morning Ella summoned me to her rooms and he was there! – That was where he formally proposed, directly she left us alone, and we had a huge horrible theological discussion about the individual conscience in Lutheranism and Orthodoxy, and I kept saying, 'No, I cannot,' and it was torture when he was sitting beside me and all I really wanted to do was throw my arms round him and accept. So he gave up, and the next few days were lawn tennis and walks and plays and huge ceremony when first Granny and then William arrived with their suites. But for me the main thing was hours with Ella, when she repeated to me 'I did it – it didn't damn me. You know, Alix – the Orthodox Church is not so far apart from the Lutheran after all – it's not at all the same as being a Catholic.' And she told me about the lay preachers and *stranniks* and the church's basis in tradition which belongs as much to the simple believer as to the priest. Well, it was the same things as Nicky had said, but coming from her who knew both churches intimately it seemed to have more of an effect.

April 7 Ernie got married, and on April 8 Nicky came to me in the morning and sat next to me for a while without saying a single word. He seemed to be numb with misery, and somehow we'd got past the stage where he felt he had to make small-talk to hide this. I too just sat for ages and gazed at my hands, and in the end I looked up into his beautiful sad eyes and before he could say anything I consented.

Well, the next half day or so is a terrible mess in my memory – we both simply dissolved and cried like anything, as we were to do frequently throughout our engagement – the sweet easy tears of happiness and confusion – and we rushed round telling people officially (there was even a huge crowd of them waiting in the next room for the outcome of our talk!) and sent telegrams and had a thanksgiving service in the Russian church – but in the afternoon we were finally left alone when everyone else was at a party for cousin Bee's birthday, and we walked together in the garden and it was so lovely – being in the warm damp drizzly spring air and holding his hand properly, and being able just to stand still when and where we felt like it and kiss each other again and again - softly at first, but ever more lingering: all those kisses I'd dreamt about for five beastly years, and thought I'd never get. I was wearing a grey dress that day and he a grey suit that smelt of an expensive gentleman's scent, and I have them both still, with me in this place. We talked a lot about those five years, and the days in '89 when we'd been so entranced with each other and too young and too unsure to say a word. 'I used to see you looking at me, so severe!' he said often - and often since, 'and I wondered what you were thinking and why you were looking and I felt all stirred up and - not happy and not sad.'

As long ago as the summer of '89 he'd spoken to his father about me, but got a non-committal reply, and it wasn't until they lighted on Hélène d'Orléans that his parents had even considered permitting him to marry yet. 'Please don't think it was personal, this delay - you are their godchild and they love you, but at first they wanted a very grand political match for me. Trying to be dutiful monarchs and put politics before feelings - but if I did that in such an important area, I'd be too sad to carry out my duties at all, and I have told Papa so again and again.' Decided not to tell Granny that the Tsar hadn't considered her grandchild important enough for his son; but as a matter of fact she agreed with him.

'I never thought the Emperor would permit it!' she said in an unguarded moment, 'the youngest daughter of a minor German prince with the Heir to the Russian Throne! - And Ella! - what has she done? - she always encouraged the boy though she knew so well his parents were against it.' She never hid from me what she thought of my future father-in-law. 'I thank God Nicky is such a gentleman and so different from that Asiatic barbaric father! - But I do wish you weren't going to such a country! - To be exposed to the fast society and the dreadful uncertainty of the politics!' Actually, she could have been a lot more tactful, but she cared for me and was upset, and in any case I was in no mood to be depressed by her words.

Aunt Minnie and Uncle Sasha were a lot more gracious than Granny was, though – I had lovely warm letters from both of them, and I was asked to address her as 'Motherdear'– suppose she thought this was English custom, since Aunt Alex's children had always used the term.

Nicky and I were together for twelve days, doing lovers things. We shopped in Coburg for Easter eggs and sat at the back in the theatre in the evenings whispering to each other and shaking with suppressed laughter because Uncle Alfred kept dozing off in the middle of the performance and dropping his stick with a load clatter. Probably he was tired but he was also the worse for drink as ever. In the afternoons we drove often into the Thuringian hills and picked masses of flowers. It was primrose season, and Nicky had never seen one before because they won't grow in Russia of course. 'Such a beautiful little flower, don't you think?' he said, and he piled handsful of them into my lap. 'It's so golden and fresh and altogether exactly like you are, primrosy-mine!' I said, 'You darling – I could see where that sentence was leading!' and we laughed together, and he asked, 'I'm getting sentimental?' – but really I was overwhelmed by these tender little comments, I couldn't quite believe it was me that inspired them, and I always felt the things I said in return to be inadequate because I know full well that I don't have the same feeling for language. They always came out sounding stilted or derivative. 'Why me?' I asked him sometimes, when my head was spinning, 'why did you spend five years literally fighting for someone like me?' – and he accused me of false modesty and said incredulously 'Is it really possible that you don't know how beautiful you are, and what it meant when you talked to me about all those deep issues, and you really wanted to know what was in my head? You are so serious-minded and clever and so different to most of the people I have ever known, and you

66

dignified me with thinking I might actually be the same.' And he said, 'Can I call you Sunny now?' and I remembered confiding him my babyhood nickname long ago in a frozen garden, and was infinitely touched. Part of the time there it was still Lent, and Nicky couldn't even take milk with coffee, let alone a great many other things, and I was so touched and impressed to see how deep their faith goes in Russia. Made me deeply ashamed of my old bigoted attitude to that church.

Was pleased to see William go back to Berlin quite early on, because he'd been acting as if the whole betrothal was his doing. 'You see, Nicky!' he'd slap him heavily on the shoulder 'I told you to pluck up courage and just go and propose!' - Even then he was patronising my sweetheart as some sort of witless little brother in need of his manly guidance.

We went to Darmstadt for one day, so Nicky could see where I'd come from, for the first time. I showed him Wolfsgarten and the Neues Palais with my mother's bedroom pretty much as it was the day she died - Granny would not have tolerated the possibility that we might change anything any more than she would have changed my grandfather's room at Windsor where she still every day had his shaving things laid out for him.

Nicky looked at the pictures on the walls of Windsor and Balmoral, and said,

'She was very homesick, your mother, wasn't she?'

I agreed that yes probably was; she never in any way let go of her Englishness, but towards the end of her life after various disappointments in Hesse (including of course her marriage) she was more attached to it than ever, and my being born at that time it left a stronger imprint on me than perhaps on my elder sisters, or Ernie even.

'It does seem to me that you are more English than Ella is,' Nicky said. 'Well - it's odd for me, really - because there's a lot of anglophobia in Russia, and although I have English cousins and I love 'em it seems to go against my upbringing in a way to be so totally crazy about an English girl!' I felt obliged then to enlighten about my grandmama's reciprocal feelings regarding Russia, and he said, 'Then I shall be very diplomatic and tactful and try to change her views. The first time I met her, when I was in London for the Yorks' wedding last year, she was so kind and nice to me and not a bit like some people at home had led me to expect. The whole of Europe is terrified of her!'

'I know,' I said, 'and it's strange, because she's not intimidating at all, really; she has a very loving and sort of - well - womanly nature - she likes men to tell her what to do and like my sister Victoria says she trusts the stupidest man's views far more than the cleverest woman's. She was utterly dependent on my grandfather when he was alive; that's why she won't stop mourning him now. I think I'd find that sort of inequality uncomfortable, but he was a huge brain and personality and he really made our family into what it is today. If it hadn't been for his influence on Mama and his ideas I'd have never had any sort of an education and I feel I've missed a lot because he died so long before I was born. He was de facto king of England and some politicians complained that if he'd lived longer he'd have become a dictator.'

'Victoria and Albert,' Nicky said, 'people call it one of the great love affairs of history; I'd like for them to speak of us in the same way some day, wouldn't you?'

'But without one of us having to die young,' I corrected him - 'can we change the subject, please?!'

Back in Coburg I began to study a book of Russian grammar and write out sentences for him to correct. 'Not a single mistake - good little schoolgirl!' he said, and I made him speak to me in Russian so I could hear how the rs *rrrrroll*, and it seems to me his voice even drops an octave when he does so and it makes me all shivery and hot inside. Beautiful, beautiful language, I wish I had the wherewithal to know it like Nicky knows it - all the obscure words and archaic expressions he has made a point of collecting down the years. - And through all this talking the main thing was – getting used to how natural and necessary it felt to hold each other, how warm he was to lean on, how meltingly tender I felt when he laid his head on my shoulder and I could gently kiss his sweet lovely eyes. On April 20 was the first horrible parting – being at the station in front of other people, family and public, and having to be cool and calm and collected. I have never got used to that in all these years.

I was in Windsor after that, and getting heaps of advice off everyone. Georgie York said – the idiot! – that I should consider always wearing low-heeled shoes and Nicky should get his own slightly built up to disguise the fact that we were the same height!! – Well, that's what Georgie has always done himself because his masculine pride is affronted by May's tallness, as if it made any difference! – People always say Nicky and Georgie are alike, which annoys me a little, because all they have in common is the build and the beard, as far as I can see. For one thing, how could one compare Georgie's slightly bulbous pale blue Hanoverian eyes with Nicky's great soulful lakes that were torturing me from his photos the whole time we were apart?!

I got invitations to see Uncle Bertie at Marlborough House and Uncle Alfred at Clarence House, and Granny objected saying it wasn't proper at all. I was also forbidden to go to Ascot for the races. Seems I wasn't to go about in society without Nicky, now – so Nicky and I got a real teasing thing going in our letters about how I'd been planning to attend lots of house parties with the Uncles' fast friends and meet plenty of new gentlemen to put him in the shade. – In the arrogance of youth we did mock Granny quite cruelly for being so old-fashioned! – Nicky said he was writing her very polite and formal letters to charm her and I'd be quite ashamed of his tricks if I could read them.

It was at Windsor that I suddenly started with the pains in the back of the legs, so strong sometimes that I could barely walk. Granny made me see her doctor and he said 'Sciatica' and that it was effectively rheumatic inflammation of the nerve down the leg. I was quite upset – rheumatic pains at 22! – and Victoria said it would cease if I wasn't so obsessed with sitting and sleeping in freezing rooms with the windows open (she always was most un-English in her liking for stuffy hot houses, but it's due to her bad circulation). Granny though said that I hadn't looked strong for about two years – ever since Papa died – and she sent me to Harrogate to take a cure.

Harrogate was lovely, apart from the crowds of people outside the boarding house at all times staring at me as I went in and out. Often felt tempted to put my tongue out at them, it got so tiresome – I'd never had this sort of attention when I was just myself and not Nicky's intended. Trina Schneider was with me in Harrogate teaching Russian all the while, and I was reading about the church – but kept getting distracted by Mrs Allen the landlady's babies for one thing – I'd never yet known any twins, and I remember I was so pleased when she asked me to be godmother and said she was calling them Nicholas and Alix. Then Victoria came with her darling girls, partly so that Louise could breathe the clear air of the moors in the hope that it might strengthen her weak chest. We went on some terribly long drives with this in mind, way into the West Riding, where we would sit on the lovely heather-covered moor and look down at the unlovely black chimneys of Bradford and Leeds deep in the valley – really a dramatic contrast. I never saw England's industrial heartland before – the economic powerhouse of the nation and the Empire.

Of course in Harrogate there were those bath chairs pulled by bicycles – a man sat on the bike and the invalid on a covered seat behind. Victoria and I hired some for fun and had the men race each other – very silly and must have been quite an alarming thing for the badly sick people to have to watch!

After a couple of weeks of doing plenty of lying down and drinking spa water, I was pronounced cured – so then we went to their house at Walton. Nicky was coming on the *Polar Star* to avoid having to pass through Berlin, and mentally I tracked his progress through the Baltic and the North Sea to Gravesend. Then I knew he was on Granny's train to Waterloo, where Ludwig met him with him in a carriage and brought him straight to Me, who was waiting breathlessly for the pet, with a great smile and open arms! – Really, it sounds silly and sentimental, but if heaven resembles anything on earth it'll be those three days we spent at Elm Grove together, Ludwig and Victoria discreetly out of our way in the mornings and no visitors allowed.

We spent those mornings under a tree in the garden, talking and talking, serious things and nonsense. But what an absolutely flaming June! – we were only cool later on when Ludwig came back from his desk work in London and we went out on the river. First afternoon we took an electric launch. Ludwig drove fast – with all our differences of age and outlook and fate, one thing that really unites the whole of this family has been this love of speed! – And we passed punts full of ladies and gentlemen in boaters and blazers and white trousers, sending a ripple that made them rock about and yell with pleasure. From the banks the inhabitants of boat-clubs and water-side pubs cheered to see the launch and we leant over the sides and waved back at them. Nicky was most impressed, having never been in a situation where people didn't know who he was but were pleased to see him anyway. I was touched by this reaction – there was such an innocence about him, and it's never really left him either.

The next afternoon we hired a rowing boat and went out a bit more sedately, although I ended by having blisters on my hands from sometimes getting too energetic, and he took the skin off one finger with the pressure of the ring I had given him. 'It's because I'm so unused to having it there,' he said, 'but it feels wonderful.' – and he showed his injury to Ludwig and Victoria too to emphasise the point. And this I like – that in the Orthodox Church engagement rings and wedding rings apply as much to men as to women so it doesn't look like the contract is only for her. At the time we discussed this I wasn't listening properly because I was mainly preoccupied with watching him row, sleeves rolled up, showing off skinny tanned forearms whose golden hairs stood out in the sun – and I contemplated the delicious possibility that he might take his shirt off.

We all got out of the boat and picnicked on the bank in the long evening. Nicky would keep gently blowing the hair away from my face – it was escaping from its pins and hanging in wisps round my cheeks – and murmuring, 'My precious girlie, you have such a fantastically beautiful complexion – and especially when you're a bit hot.' The feeling of his breath and the memories of him rowing and the stillness and warmth of the evening created such a mood of enchantment in me – I thought I was floating on air all the way home. We walked back from the landing stage a little behind Ludwig and Victoria, cheek to cheek, our arms around each others' waists, not saying a word – and he felt so slender and firm through his clothes where I touched him, and he smelled of fresh clean sweat from all the exercise – and it really stirred my blood. Already that day I was thinking how I longed for the time when we wouldn't have to say goodbye at the end of the evening.

The next day Granny's carriage arrived and bore us off to Windsor and other people. So we paid visits and went to London to the theatre and to Aldershot to see some manoeuvres, and the press got excited because Nicky went into an antique shop and bought some Empire furniture (already Ella was keenly sending advice about how to furnish our future homes). In the garden in the evening we carried on with our talks, exploring one another's souls away from everyone else. Nicky was always glad to be outside and to be able to light up a cigarette where Granny couldn't smell it. 'When did you start smoking?' I asked him, 'you didn't do that in Petersburg in '89.' 'In '89 you see I was still on leading strings,' he said wryly, 'but the next year when I finished my formal education and my father let me go – that's when I instantly acquired a whole raft of vile habits, all of which I want rid of again. I don't suppose Ernie smokes.' I was amused. 'Ernie has smoked like a chimney for years, and so has Victoria and I'm not immune either and we none of us has ever considered it a sin.' I reached out and touched his cheek gently. 'Darling Nicky-love, there is such a quality of purity about you.' 'You wouldn't say that,' he answered gloomily, 'if you'd seen me carried out of the officers' mess at two in the morning, too drunk to walk. I mean it Alix – I don't want to get a self-flagellation thing going here, but your love really uplifts someone whose life has been a complete waste of time for quite a while now.' I said lightly, 'Outrageous, I hope you have a rotten headache afterwards – but don't all young men drink themselves silly from time to time? – I don't want you some colourless plaster saint, you know!' He chuckled softly and said 'I've known many do it far more often! – Honestly, though – I don't want people making allowances for me being a man – I sincerely mean to be good, and I have so often fallen short of the standard I set for myself.'

And while we were in that frame of mind he told me his little story about M.F.K. – And I was just touched that he told me. *Au fond*, though it falls short of the standards I'd ideally want too, so many men have actually done so much worse than this guilt-ridden fling at a time when he despaired of ever winning me and yet believe they have a perfect right to do so. (And he didn't behave badly towards her; she pursued him for years and he resisted for a very long time and always made it absolutely clear that there was no future in it).

'I don't want secrets,' he told me that day 'I want us to belong to each other entirely.' – and he went and got me his diary and put in my hands and said, 'There is nothing in there now that I'd be ashamed for you to see.' 'Silly,' I said, 'I can't read it anyway!' But I started putting messages in there in English because he said it belonged to both of us now, and I began with one assuring him that I thought all the more of him for his honesty and for the pain he showed over his one fall from grace. 'From hereon,' he said, 'no more sins. – It goes without saying that there'll be nothing of that nature ever again – but I mean no drinking myself into a stupor either, it's shameful and disgusting and it's not going to be part of my adult life. Uncle Alfred is one thing, but if you'd seen my father's friends, and the way they go on sometimes over cards – then you'd know why it shocks me so much. I don't want to become like that. I don't think I like men very much, actually!' Of course, another of his youthful faults was a penchant for looking at pretty faces – but that one he is allowed. 'So long as you only look!' I said, and he answered, 'As if I would even do that when I can gaze at your enchanting little face! – Oh, darling – you have got me entirely and forever – soul and spirit, body and heart – I'd like to scream it for the world to hear!' Bless him, he can speak such poetry without even trying; it chokes up the back of my throat. (Uncle Kostia always thought very well of Nicky's writing, and he should know about such things, being the Romanov family poet.)

When we were at Windsor the Yorks' baby was christened with Nicky as one of the godfathers, very amused by that great string of names they gave him (Edward Albert Christian George Andrew Patrick David!): – 'In our church we only have one.' He made me repeat to him the names of my own family, and they seemed to me suddenly rather tasteless and silly: – Victoria Alberta Elisabeth Matilda Marie; Elisabeth Alexandra Louise Alice; Irène Anna Marie Louise; Ernest Louis Charles Albert William and Victoria Alix Helena Louise Beatrice!

I was thinking I would need a new name when I converted – had to be acceptable to the church and Alix or even Alice I didn't think would be, although sometimes one does find 'Alyssa' in Russia – maybe not amongst the Orthodox believers though. 'Alexandra' was always the obvious choice for me, aurally if not etymologically. The patronymic Feodorovna I chose because it was used by Aunt Minnie and also by Ella – refers symbolically back to the father of the first Romanov Tsar; his name was Feodor, and his son prayed before the family icon the Feodorovsky Mother of God when elected Tsar.

Granny was thrilled about the little baby David, because it was the first time the heirs to the throne had extended for three generations. She was photographed with Uncle Bertie and Georgie York and David all around her - four generations of monarchs and future monarchs we thought at the time, although who now knows whether David will ever be king? - Perhaps this war will have brought down the British throne too before then. I badgered Nicky over and over to ask his mother to send me a picture of him when he was a baby, and he pulled faces and described himself as 'a frog-like child' and said he couldn't think why I should be interested; but in the end he got me a photograph of the enchanting little pixie he had been, all eyes and curls, with a little dimple in his chin, and I gazed at it so long he said, 'I'm afraid you've got that soppy look girls get over babies; and I thought you were above that type of thing!' - and I grabbed him and punched him several times in the shoulder.

Father Yanishev came to Windsor to start my instruction. Course, the day of our first meeting was slightly marred by Nicky becoming stuck in the bathroom during the morning and having to stand and shout for half an hour until I finally heard him and managed to release him by dint of a lot of kicking. This put us in a most unreligious state of merriment for the rest of the day.

Most mornings began with breakfast outside in the garden with Granny. As often as not I used to have go and summon Nicky through the window of his rooms, because of that penchant he had then for sleeping in. - Funny how well he's disciplined himself out of that. Sometimes he had the right to be tired; he was invited to regimental dinners by British soldiers and didn't get back until late, and then I would insist on sitting up and talking and kissing all alone until the early hours, because it was the only time we could be really private. There was a certain frisson in that, of course, and it led to dreams that would have shocked poor Granny to the core! – She did tell us off, and she asked Victoria to do the same for reinforcement, about a certain amount of public display. – Well, he was so irresistible, especially when he was talking quietly and seriously to someone with that darling shy expression in his eyes and the little characteristic movement of the head – how could I not be forever flinging my arms around him and covering his face with kisses? 'I thought Alix was more sensible!' Granny said. In her day, couples weren't alone together until the day they married; a lot of people probably didn't even use first names.

She had a lot of advice for Nicky; took him aside on his own and cautioned him about insisting that I didn't do too much. 'She said you had been far too thin ever since you lost your father, but you wouldn't be sensible and the result had been that dreadful pain in your legs,' he explained later. 'She is dreadfully worried about the effect your Papa's death had on you.' He was looking at me so sadly and thoughtfully. 'My dear little bird, you've had so much sorrow in your life already, it makes me quite ashamed. I never felt a truly profound grief.' I wondered about his grandfather, the murdered Tsar Alexander whom Granny had known in youth. 'Yes, that was horrible, the way he died – but the actual fact of his death? – You expect it to happen to grandparents and it isn't nice but it doesn't tear your life apart.' So we talked very frankly then about Papa, and the terrible pain of suddenly not having him there any more when we had become so close, and the anxious feeling that I had at times about everyone else disappearing in the same way. 'My mother died, my nearest sister died, my father died,' is what I said in those terrible moments of self-pity 'it almost makes me afraid to love you.' Nicky was holding me desperately tight, almost too upset to answer. 'Sunny, Sunny, Sunny,' he said in the end, 'nothing is ever going to take me away from you.'

CHAPTER FIVE

Well, after that sad evening, things went mercifully back to normal for the rest of the visit, and we would spend a while talking calmly about heaps of things, only to end up sprawled giggling across the sofa, Nicky underneath, while I tickled him. – And even while we talked, if I leant against him and put my hand on his stomach I could feel him laughing inside, spontaneously, and he squeezed me and said, 'I'm happy,' – and I kissed his dear warm neck and lay close.

He had been most affected by his educational journey to the Far East in '90 to '91, although complaining a bit that all he was allowed to see were officials and uniforms. What interested him most were the philosophies people had out there, and their way of life and how it differed from Europe. In India he'd been annoyed by the behaviour of the British soldiers and administrators and by their disrespect for the culture they were occupying. 'I am sorry – I wouldn't say it in front of Granny, but I will to you because you are young and open-minded and you aren't wholly English – that is an ancient country with various cultures far more elevated and civilised than anything Britain can show – and yet they treat it like its people were savages.'

And: – 'Japan,' he said, 'now that is a wonderful country! I loved it; I really left a bit of my heart in that place. – We'll go there together someday, and visit the temples. – And you will see the frail dainty blossom on the trees – and the paintings and the furniture and the clear bright light – it's all so delicately done and different to Europe and all the dirt and squalor. You know – I have to tell you this, Sunny, forgive me, please – we went to the tea house quarter of Kyoto and we stayed in a geisha house

77

– they are like hotels there – and I watched the whole beautiful ceremony they go through with men, so different to the crude things you see on the streets in the west though in a manner of speaking you could say they are prostitutes, these geishas – forgive me – and it stuck in my mind and ran through my head like water afterwards even while I was asleep. – And I thought – a culture that can prettify that sort of transaction has to be something quite special.' – he bushed deeply and said 'all that follows the tea ceremony is a mystery to me and Sandro can tell more if you really want to know, but – you see – this is a world in touch with its past and its soul and it hasn't been brutalised yet.' I said, 'I wonder if those girls see it like that? – Putting on their little show and everything else so a rich young man like Sandro can feel himself terribly liberated?' and Nicky looked puzzled and argued that their lives were cultured and happy and they simply couldn't feel anywhere near as degraded as those of European street women. 'Degraded?' I asked. 'Well maybe they are – but it some ways it's beyond their control – how else can they support themselves?' – And I held forth about the work of my mother's friend Josephine Butler, and the affair of W.T. Stead and the child he had bought to make a point, and we were onto a wholly different track. 'You're unshockable, aren't you?' Nicky said admiringly at length. 'I simply can't imagine talking to Mama about such things!' 'That,' I said, 'is exactly why such things go on.' – but I'd had enough of moralising, so I steered him back to his spiritual ruminations on the Asiatic soul. After Japan he had traveled back across Siberia and it came home to him that great swathes of Russian territory were purely Asiatic, inhabited by eastern peoples with eastern faiths. 'How many people in Petersburg or Moscow ever go to Siberia?' he said rhetorically. 'It's shameful!'

Now he was possessed by the idea that Russia had a sort of mission to Asia, was the only western power which would treat Asia in any way other than as a conqueror and had a real capacity, because of Siberia, to understand Asian peoples. He was especially interested in the parallels between certain Russian traditions and religious codes of conducts in oriental religions – and one of these traditions was the notion of the *tishaishii tsar*, the saintly leader who ruled by example rather than by terror. 'Alexis, the father of Peter the Great was such a Tsar,' he said, 'and horrible Peter was quite the opposite.' – Believed that Peter had introduced a certain moral corruption into Russia, a rationalising and brutalising element that was at variance with the tradition of the church and community. 'Imagine,' he said 'if one could turn the clock back. Perhaps contact with Asia can do that for us?'

He returned to Russia in mid July, for Xenia's and Sandro's wedding – funny to think of her marrying when she'd been quite a small girl the last time I saw her! – But in fact she was older than Ducky, who was the lady of the house back in Darmstadt. Ducky in fact was in the first days of expecting their little Elisabeth, and slightly confused and unhappy about it all – because of that delightful policy of her mother's of keeping her ignorant. She was such a dear in those days – very open and confiding to me, and maybe I helped her, being older and so much more worldly-wise. Anyway, Ernie was happy, because he knew his silly fears were groundless and his child was on its way.

Nicky was supposed to come to us, and I was sending him violets and planning long, long walks in the woods – then oh such terrible disappointment when he was had to stay in Russia! – because Uncle Sasha was ill with an inflammation of the kidneys. Some sorts of preparations for our wedding had begun then, although of course we didn't have a date set – thought it would be January 1895. I was ordering clothes, specifically underclothes and nightgowns, and there was quite a lot of correspondence about that, and Granny would have killed us if she'd known!

And then came the invitation to go to Russia. I traveled with Victoria on a normal train as far as the border, and there the Emperor's own train and Ella met me and carried me across Poland and the Ukrainian steppe to Simferopol. My first view of the Crimea, that was: a splendid white town with mountains behind, green with cherry trees and vines but with white peaks visible at the top. What a contrast to the dreary flat wheat fields of the Ukraine! – Then we transferred to a carriage (presumably Ella explained then about the laws that banned railways from the Crimean paradise?) and a little further on we met up with Serge and my betrothed and drove for hours through lush valleys full of lilacs, cypresses and ferns – a semi-tropical paradise broken in the distance when we rounded bends by the glint of the deep blue sea. Nicky held my hand in the carriage and squeezed it often, and smiled at me, whispering, 'So wonderful to have you here – your first time in my own country as my bride! Really, when I saw you a great weight sort of lifted off my heart. – And you look even more beautiful than ever!' His eyes were very blue in a face tanned with sunshine; I wanted to smother him with kisses there and then, Ella and Serge or no Ella and Serge; instead I stroked his knuckles with my thumb and whispered back, 'Just wait until I get you alone!'

It was fantastically warm for October and I was astonished and intoxicated by the beauty all around because I was raised by people of my mother's and grandmother's generations to think of the Crimea as a place of horror: Sevastopol, Balaclava, Scutari, the Lady with the Lamp, the Charge of the Light Brigade: these are what English people think of when the Crimea is mentioned, and I said so to Nicky. 'We too.' Nicky said, 'At Sevastopol you can see a cemetery for the hundreds of thousands of Russian soldiers and sailors who were killed by the invading Turks and their British allies. But you can see why they so defended it, I suppose.' 'Here, Alix' said Serge 'you will get a different perspective on that war and maybe you will understand a bit why my brother Sasha, who was only a little boy at the time, has never really forgiven the English.' I was mildly annoyed with him because - actually - I do have enough of a brain to realise that there are two sides to every story. 'Serge doesn't mean to be nasty,' Ella whispered, 'he just means that if Sasha sometimes seems to be anti-British, it's not just a blind prejudice, and you shouldn't think it's personal.'

We came to white-washed settlements, where Tartar peoples would come out to look at us, the women heavily veiled. Each chieftain would take his place on horseback in front of our carriage and gallop ahead of us until we'd left the village behind. There were also Russian people in the Crimea, of course: they greeted Nicky with cries of 'The Heir! The Heir!' - first time I ever heard the Russian word "Naslednik" and it sounded so important and semi-religious. One young man followed the carriage for several miles on his bicycle. I leaned out and gave him an apple I was carrying - never forgot his face - and years later I saw him again, in the war, in a hospital, greatly aged and changed.

Took several hours in those days before the motorcars to get to Yalta and finally Livadia and the Emperor's house. Of course, it was the small wooden house he lay in - rather dark and gloomy in spite of its glorious setting between the mountains and the sea. Went that evening to Uncle Sasha, who was sitting up in a chair dressed in a regimental uniform, but looking whiter and thinner than the previous times I'd seen him. I kissed his hand as my future Emperor, but he embraced me and talked for a while. After that he had to go to bed as he was so tired and it came home to me that he was seriously ill and that I wasn't just here for an extension of our Windsor idyll.

All of the Uncles were there; in the morning Nicky and I scrambled down on the beach where we found Serge and Paul walking. Vladimir hailed them from about halfway up the cliff - you could in any case have heard his voice in Yalta. 'Doctors say he seems better today! I had them report to me as soon as I got up.' This happened a couple of times more, and it began to annoy me. Why was Vladimir getting the reports instead of the patient's own immediate family? – Why was he passing the news onto his brothers first? If Aunt Minnie couldn't bear to hear it, surely they should go to Nicky? Once I was in the room when the report was given, and I saw how Vladimir and Serge would literally butt in if Nicky so much as asked a question – they rephrased it for him as if he didn't express himself clearly enough!

Uncle Sasha was not a good patient and his condition fluctuated a lot. Olga told me – it was the first time I'd really got to know Misha and Olga, they'd been such babies on my earlier visits to Russia – that he would have her smuggle ice-cream into him against the doctors' orders.

Can't remember when it became apparent that the Emperor wasn't going to get better; but it happened fast, although it seemed at the time to take ages. In all, I'd only been in Russia for ten days when he reached the stage of dozing all the time; and then he had to take oxygen and finally Father John of Kronstadt came to him and administered Extreme Unction – all in the space of a few hours. We were standing in his room just unable to believe that this massive awe-inspiring man was dying at 49 from what we'd first been told was a kidney infection. (In fact, nephritis). It was October 20th in the Julian calendar – November 1st , western Europe style. (I was only just getting used to the Russian adherence to the old calendar and trying to think in Julian dates wasn't always easy when I'd just come from the west). He started to have convulsions; then he kissed Aunt Minnie – Motherdear – and muttered something – and she fainted, poor thing, straight into my arms as I stood behind her. There was a kind of rustle of horror through the room and I had to get her out of there and to a sofa and a doctor, and by the time I came back everything was just as horrible as it could possibly be - the body laid out on the bed, priests coming and going, ministers all over the house - it was hardly a family death but it should have been, for this man who was maybe the first Russian Tsar ever to treat his wife and children with respect.

I went to my room because I couldn't bear it - it reminded me of losing Papa - and quite a while later Nicky came to me with a white face and red eyes. I went straight across the room to him and took him in my arms and he cried helplessly, trembling all over, and it moved me immeasurably. 'I'm sorry,' he kept saying, 'I didn't mean you to see me like this.' I felt so terrible for him: 'Oh, Deary, remember that if anyone knows how you're feeling now, it's your Sunny - and the last thing I'd want would be for you to hide your sadness away from me.' I had the sensation of being older than he was; he was so crushed and bewildered by a grief unlike anything he'd been through before, and it was all complicated by the terrible awareness of what he'd inherited. Yet he was going to have to go through everything under the eyes of the world. I could no longer contemplate leaving him as planned to go home until the wedding.

It was that same afternoon that the altar was erected on the lawn in front of the house and everyone present trooped by it, taking the oath of allegiance to their new Emperor. Next day I went to the same place and was quietly received into his church. Thus Victoria Alix Helena Louise Beatrice symbolically disappeared from history and Alexandra Feodorovna was born in Nicky's first Imperial edict! - Servant of God and servant of Russia: I really felt the responsibility of what I was doing, but of course I didn't know where to begin.

Thank Heavens for Uncle Bertie! He and Aunt Alex were there from right after the Tsar's death - she supporting poor Motherdear, he, suddenly, placing himself in charge of the funeral arrangements, holding ministers at bay, mediating between the haggling uncles. Thus we left the house and began our journey north, stopping at each major city so a mass could be sung with local officials. Poor Minnie – Motherdear – looked simply dreadful, and she fainted often. Ella said her heart wasn't strong, although to be honest it's the first and last I've ever heard of that. Can't forget the most horrible thing – that they didn't embalm the body properly, and by the time we reached Moscow his face and hands were already turning black. One took the body from the train there and we went to the Kremlin for an overnight stop, passing ten churches on the way where further litanies were sung. Silent crowds lined the streets and it was sleeting on them in their misery.

Nicky gave a speech to the local nobility. 'I've never done this before,' he confessed to me, 'silly, isn't it?' and he admitted to feeling sick as he stood waiting to go into the room with them. I saw the hesitation as he went through the door; the little backward glance as if he were waiting to be prompted about what to do next, and although his voice came out loud and confident I read the terrible sadness in his eyes at taking his father's place and it was unbearable to me.

Twelve days after the Tsar's death we finally got back to Petersburg and the remaining relatives, who were gathered in the Nicholas station, and the men walked behind the coffin through what seemed like half the city. We ladies were permitted carriages; I saw people look anxiously into mine and cross themselves as I passed, and I found out later what they were saying, 'Our new Empress has come to us behind a coffin.'

Thus we brought poor Uncle Sasha home to the Peter–Paul fortress, and the open coffin lay there in the church for six more days so there could be further services in front of the foreign visitors who were arriving in hordes. By the end of that time there was a terrible obscene smell around it; couldn't bear to think of his family and above all his widow having to notice that – because it was perceptible in spite of all the incense. God, it makes me shudder even now!

I went to stay with Ella and dear Ernie, Harry and Irène

arrived, which was wonderful for me; but Nicky was living in the Anitchkov with his mother and spent his time receiving people. We only saw him for a few minutes around tea-time each day and sometimes not even that.

'Every day,' I remember he said, 'I have that feeling of lightness when I wake up in the morning; you know how it is when you're just becoming conscious and the day stretches ahead. Then the next moment this dreadful memory comes back and I get a feeling as though there's something sitting on my chest. I've been to formal dinners where everyone was laughing and smiling – can you believe it? – and I've had to talk feeling as though I was about to start sobbing. I absolutely dread that before long I'm going to break down in public.' Serge had overheard. 'That you most certainly cannot afford to do, and you will not do!'

Of course I knew before we were engaged how Nicky felt about the possibility of becoming Tsar, but we hadn't talked much about it because we felt it was many years away, and anything could happen before then. One evening he confided that he had no idea of how he was even going to address a minister – his father had never involved him in the process of governing: – 'Poor Papa – he thought he had plenty of time. He wanted me to enjoy being young and carefree as long as I could.' Sandro my future brother-in-law came to me too and he said with some anxiety, 'Don't take this is as a criticism of him on a personal level, but Nicky is such a baby still I simply can't imagine how he's going to cope with doing this job and the people it will bring him across. We grew up together, especially over the last few years, and I have seen the very worst of Nicky – and as I'm sure you know too, this is not a man of the world!' So I was paralysed with anxiety over who we were going to turn to for advice.

The funeral service was three hours long and of course there was such a dreadful crush in the cathedral that three people fainted. Luckily Motherdear wasn't among them. She bore it remarkably well for someone who had lost a good husband and who – let's admit it – has a tendency to make public scenes. Nicky supported her on his arm until the time when he and the uncles had to carry the coffin from the catafalque to the vault. He looked so small and vulnerable and young amidst his uncles' unusual height that my heart ached; some idiot behind me said audibly, 'It's frightening, isn't it? When you think that the whole of Russia is now in the hands of that light-minded youth! – I mean, do you know anyone who's ever had a serious conversation with him?!' One bearer was conspicuously missing: poor sick Georgy, the heir to the throne now, couldn't be allowed to leave his Caucasian sanatorium for long enough even to attend his father's funeral.

And now the one bright memory in all of this: putting aside mourning for a day one week later in order to get married.

There had of course already been an argument about the date: Nicky and I had really wanted it all done quietly in Livadia before the funeral since we didn't think that a big ceremony at a time of national mourning was quite the thing. Ella and the Uncles favoured Petersburg, in the public eye, and they had their way, I don't know how. In retrospect, they were probably right, though: at least we got a few hours when we could forget everything else that had happened.

I drove from Ella's house to the Winter Palace with Motherdear, and the ladies dressed me in the Malachite Room in all those symbolic clothes: the brocade court dress with a golden train, the heavy ear-rings – they are supported by wires as I recall and they cut into the skin above the ear – and the Romanov wedding crown – all the things I'd seen on Ella ten years ago. Then Motherdear and I walked through salons full of visitors to the chapel where my angel was waiting, wearing the Life Guards Hussar uniform – with the blessed Russian boots! – and such a look of love in his shining eyes. That was when it really came home to me that we had finally made it, and were actually going to get married, in spite of the leaden feeling that had lain in our hearts for the past three weeks. I was glad there had been no exciting big build-up - something would have been certain to go wrong if there had been.

We took our lighted candles and faced Father Yanishev, and the service started with his proclamation:'Praise to God's servant the devout and Autocratic Emperor Nikolai Alexandrovich...' I remember who the best men were: for Nicky there was Misha, their cousin Greek Georgie, Sergei Mikhailovich and rotten Kirill; for me, two more Michels (George and horrible gossipy Nikolai), Dmitri Konstantinovich and also silly Boris. Strange to think how time was to make enemies of so many of them! - but on that day the majority were barely even adult: a handsome collection of boys.

And it was all over so fast! - There was a beautiful service with the deep choral singing I'd always so loved, then we went through our vows and exchanged rings, walked round the altar three times with the wedding crowns held over our heads, and knelt down I front of it so I could be proclaimed as Empress Alexandra Feodorovna. Barely a moment to think; and I was so moved anyway that I was only aware of what Nicky and I were doing and didn't think anything of the 100s of people crowded into the chapel around us. My one idea was for us to be committed to each other for ever and as quickly as possible. Afterwards we drove back through Palace Square and down the Nevsky Prospekt to the Anitchkov, and the people standing by the road were cheering for the first time - such a strange feeling! - I'd never really been cheered before for myself though I rode in Granny's Golden Jubilee procession in '87, because the cheers then were for her, and in Darmstadt we weren't exactly given to ceremonial drives.

There were huge crowds outside the house for five hours, cheering and calling for us; several times we went onto the balcony closest to the street. Of course we had no proper rooms because there'd been no time to prepare any; we were in the apartment Nicky and Georgy had shared as boys, and we weren't going away because it wasn't right to do so when in mourning, but this was not important at all. Oh, my Nicky, all that was important then is all that has survived: that 'Me' has full rights to you and 'Me' alone, and there'll be no escaping for you ever again.

CHAPTER SIX

Strange days, the first months of my marriage. Nicky was always tied up with ministers during the day, so if I wasn't studying my French or Russian almost the only companion I had was little Olga. She had lessons, but not that many because she was only a girl so evidently it wasn't too important to her mother that she should get an education. Poor thing, she was really feeling the loss of her Papa. She was his beloved 'Baby Badger'; but as far as Motherdear was concerned she was definitely not one of the favoured ones, even then. Noticed immediately how her behaviour would change when her Mama came into the room – instantly polite and on her guard – very different to the way her elder sister was. What it comes down to I fear is that Xenia is pretty and feminine and pliable whereas poor Olga has Uncle Sasha's big bones and coarse features, and never showed the slightest interest in clothes or gossip. She told me she used to sit under her father's desk when he was working and play with his imperial seal; and when he had finished he would take her and Misha out into the park to light a bonfire or track animals by their spores through the snow.

With Olga I went to Nicky's old schoolroom and looked through his exercise books, all so neat. In this as in other things we are polar opposites: I write fast, I cross out; my desks looked like war zones when I was a child and still do now. It touched me to see how careful his writing even when small, and to look at the desk in his study, neatly laid out with pens and papers so he always knew exactly where he could put his hand on anything. Even at the beginning of his reign he refused a private secretary. I got one in a little while, of course, my Rostovstsev, while Madeleine looked after the clerical tasks, spending much time tidying up and scolding me for leaving such a mess. One day Motherdear found me with Nicky's exercise books, and she sat down with me and talked a lot about his early childhood with a look of such tenderness in her beautiful eyes which are so like his that I felt instantly gloriously close to her. 'Oh, yes – he was desperately proud when he started his lessons; he kept looking so intently through all of the books here and gazing at the pictures. There was one he brought to me repeatedly because of a poem he liked – he couldn't read it himself so I had to go through it again and again and he'd sit beside me staring at my face with a great eager smile. 'Dear Georgy had more fight in him but Nicky was a sweet little child. He had this lovely laugh, very high and unrestrained – his poor father worried that he sounded girlish and had the governess's boy, Volodya, share lessons with him to toughen him up. Of course the result was that when they had done something naughty Volodya would cheerfully take the blame and Nicky could hide behind him, which upset my dear Sasha even more! But I didn't worry – this is how children are.'

I wanted to agree that if my own family was anything to go by, all little boys are sensitive and sweet and it's their sisters who are obstreperous, but I was still too shy of her. Nevertheless she gave me an envelope containing one of his golden curls from his first haircut at three years old. Mercifully, her sister Alex stayed on with her after the funeral, to support and comfort her. Uncle Bertie and Georgie York left quite early; I heard Vladimir say as we saw them off at the station, 'Well, I must say old Wales acquitted himself well over the arrangements! How disappointed the spoilt silly Queen will be to see that her son does have some talents after all.' – Well, all our family knew that Granny had none too high a opinion of Uncle Bertie and wouldn't give him a proper job to do, but to have Uncle Vladimir talk about her in those terms, uncaring whether I could hear or not, was really too much! – It upset me a lot and suddenly I felt rather lonely – with all the goodwill in the world, these people were not my real family and they actively disliked quite a number of my dearest relations.

Ernie, Harry and Irène went even before Uncle Bertie did. I was sad to see my sister and brother go, but to be honest Nicky's succession had introduced a new and unwelcome element into the relationship with Harry. I kept seeing his brother's shadow behind him, just as Papa had told me Granny always did. 'William hopes that you will be making your first state visit a journey to Berlin,' he said. 'Perhaps this coming summer?' 'I can't go anywhere this summer,' Nicky explained, 'We shall still be in mourning.' 'William came to see your father when he was still in mourning for ours.' 'I'm sorry, but I don't want to follow his example,' – a soft, shy voice, because he was afraid of sounding pompous. – – But honestly! – William all but tipped Uncle Fritz out of the throne, and here was Harry suggesting that Nicky – the most loyal of sons and most reluctant of Emperors – behave in the same manner! – Presumably the aim was a renewal of the *Dreikaiserbund* which was still a living memory then – but they were going totally the wrong way about it as usual. – After that I asked Irène to keep Harry from talking politics at family gatherings, and she has done her level best. Nicky's uncles took against Harry, naturally, anyway. The worst that can be said of him is that he takes his job seriously; he tried to talk Naval matters with Uncle Alexei, who promptly looked pained. Later when Harry's name was mentioned at a dinner dear uncle piped up, 'Oh, Henry of Prussia is such a crashing bore!' Sandro who can be very funny when he wishes always said that Uncle Alexei was only interested in his Navy duties insofar as they didn't interfere with his private life, and that his was definitely a case of fast women and slow ships. It didn't take long before I was hearing other stories about Uncle Alexei, usually to do with husbands arriving home to find him emerging from their bedroom, and while these amuse in their own context they become extremely wearisome when they are all people ever talk about. – Actually, he was a great charmer and he caused far fewer problem than some of his brothers – I suppose we remember him with affection.

Poor Motherdear – she quickly started giving dinners again for all these uncles and cousins, although at times she would be in tears at table when she saw someone else in her husband's place. If no-one besides her immediate family were there, she and Aunt Alex often talked in Danish to each other – which in a way is understandable – lapsing back into the familiar at times of great sadness – but it didn't help me feel included. Nicky of course could always manage perfectly well but I can really only pick up words here and there when it overlaps with German. I watched their faces instead – family resemblances are so interesting – and although Minnie had those beautiful eyes Aunt Alex was by far the lovelier of the two sisters. What was it Tennyson called her? – '*Sea-king's daughter as happy as fair, Blissful bride of a blissful heir*' (...*Norman and Saxon and Danish are we, But all of us Danes in our welcome of thee, Alexandra!*)

That was his famous poem to her when she married Uncle Bertie, and it is not just a laureate's flattery. Even when she was fifty she still looked like a young girl, it was astonishing. In time when one saw her and Uncle side by side they had come to look like father and daughter. (Course, he wouldn't have looked as old as he did if he hadn't eaten as he did and become so horribly fat.) (Tennyson knew my mother well too and his poem for her was more poignant; he called her '*England's England-loving daughter, dying so English thou wouldst have her flag borne on thy coffin*'.)

From time to time Nicky and I left them together at the Anitchkov – Xenia and Sandro were never far away, if Motherdear needed them – and went to Tsarskoe Selo for a couple of days, and that was the only thing close to a honeymoon we ever really got.

I always knew that the dear Alexander Palace would be my real home – not least because it is so small. At first Nicky and I were in his parents' old bedroom in the park wing, the room in which he himself was born, which was both amusing and strangely embarrassing at the same time! – But our first weekend there we went racing about the place and exploring, through the state apartments at the middle to the wing near the road. 'Aunt Marie and Uncle Alfred's honeymoon suite,' Nicky said, opening the door to the bedroom, 'I don't think anyone's lived here since.' – He eyed the 1870s furniture with distaste. 'Why did they use such disgusting colours then?! Imagine spending your wedding night here, it would quite put you off...' – I hit him and said, 'How dare you to say such things in my company? You're not with your regiment any more! – In any case, I'm sure the decoration was the last thing on their minds, and the bed looks perfectly comfortable.' – I found I was wincing, 'did you have put the thought of Uncle Alfred and Aunt Marie's wedding night into my head?! – I shall have to punish you for it!' He yelled, 'No tickling!' and he ducked away from me and went across and dived onto his stomach on the bed, and I followed him, catching hold of his foot and pinning him down and wriggling up the bed next to him so I could kiss the back of his neck. He said, '*Spitsbub*! Tomboy!' and I answered, 'I can't help it, it's your own fault for being so adorable.' I let him turn over, and I lay on top of him and held his wrists back against the pillow and put the end of my nose against his, murmuring, 'Every little bit of you, every sweet place – all of you is mine to do what I want with! Oh you darling boy, I could eat you!' 'And I,' he answered wickedly, 'could lock the door here and now....' – but instead he rolled over into my arms and we nestled very close and lay still for a while feeling comfy and listening to the sound of the snow falling lightly against the window. 'I could fall asleep,' Nicky said in a while. 'I love sleeping with you – in the most innocent sense! – having you near and feeling you breathe, and touching your dear soft skin. We won't ever give that up, will we? – Won't ever have separate rooms like other people do, I mean?' I said, 'It's just not to be contemplated!......But we could have this room, you know. I'm getting to quite like the feeling of this bed, and the room would be so much more ours than the one we've got now. Just needs new carpet and curtains, really. Where's the bathroom?' 'Across the corridor, if I remember right,' he said. 'that could be mine, but we'll have to get a new one put in for you just off here; I can't have you wandering the house in your night clothes, someone else might see you!'

'But the existing bathroom is just for this room? – That's very advanced for Europe in the '70s?! – Don't laugh – people in England always told me that in Russia there would be one bathroom for the entire household, and rats running round under the beds chewing up priceless carpets! – And really, that sort of thing does go on in Berlin – I've seen it!' 'Maybe in Berlin,' Nicky said, 'but not here, honestly! – In fact when we were little, Georgy always used to say that could tell what country people came from because of the way they smelt, and the English smelt of fog and damp woollen underwear!' – he started laughing – 'and certainly the Prussians smelt like they didn't wash enough!' 'So what about Russians, then?' 'Oh, leather and tobacco – nothing unpleasant, naturally! – And it doesn't include the ladies, apart from maybe Aunt Marie herself....' 'Is it true, then? – I mean, do I smell like the English do, naughty boy?' 'Lovy-mine, you smell of roses and verbena; it's absolutely intoxicating.' I put my face against his shoulder and breathed him in and said, 'And you do sometimes smell of leather, when you're wearing long boots; but mostly of your soap and scent and also of your own hair and skin, something quite unique and lovely – oh my darling little husband, you are so perfect in every way – how I adore you!'

We got up then; we felt we ought to, things were getting a little overheated for an afternoon; but of course those rooms did become ours, and we threw out the Victorian curtains and carpets and replaced them with flowered chintz and light colours. Where we needed new furniture - as for the mauve room - I ordered it from Maples in London - well-made, inexpensive, modern furniture - because I had no intention of living in a museum. When eventually the house was ready and we showed it to members of the family - notably Uncle Vladimir and Aunt Miechen, needless to say - they made a big show of catching their breath in horror and asking what we hadn't simply imported some eighteenth-century pieces from another of the houses. Well, hang them! - we have a right to a home without the ghosts of Nicky's ancestors breathing forever down our necks. - Wouldn't have wanted to know many of them even when they were alive!

At Tsarskoe we had the chance to have dinner alone without other people, and to go for long drives in the park - first time I'd driven a sleigh, and in the beginning it was a little unsteady, rocking and tipping on the bends - and Nicky's dogs, who always liked to run alongside, would take this as their cue to leap into it on top of us! Splendid fellows, they were, those collies. Iman was the favourite as I recall, not least because Nicky's father had given him to him - occasionally he insinuated his way onto our bed at night although he was supposed to be an outdoor dog. My little Eira who Granny gave me was very much an indoor dog - liked to hang around the table at meal times, and also when he got old and crotchety to fly out from under it and bite at passing ankles.

When we were in town we could occasionally get outside to do some skating, but by and large it was difficult to take exercise at the Anitchkov and I was very relieved to escape to Tsarskoe from time to time - above all for Nicky's sake. He got so pale stuck at his desk all the time when he's always so loved to be active. Anyway I teased him that I couldn't have him getting fat and unfit - with my hand or more probably my lips on his lovely flat tummy. Oh what bliss to cover every inch of that slim, strong body with burning kisses! – And at that time in those long breathless nights we were starting to find things out about each other and to teach each other things that have been perfected down the years, so that almost the chief of the glories of this marriage has been the physical side of it.

In January Aunt Alex returned to England, and after that we found it harder to leave Motherdear for any period of time. I think in retrospect I am less tolerant of her than I was at the time – we were always so conscious of her great grief – but she did start to annoy me. When we came back from Tsarskoe she would rush to meet Nicky with her arms outstretched. 'Oh, darling boy, it's been so sad without you here!'

Well, honestly! – she was saying the same things to Xenia of course – Sandro told me that when they got engaged she screamed at him that he was stealing her daughter and ruining her happiness. At times when Nicky was not for once occupied with ministers and he and I were working together in his study – he on political papers and I on my Russian because I hadn't yet had a chance to even think about the job of Empress – she would come in and begin to make suggestions. One time she asked him to lend one of her friends a lot of money from state funds, which horrified Nicky. His father had left Russia's finances in very good order – whether with the help of or in spite of Mr. Witte I don't know – and she was asking him to set a terrible precedent – one that didn't seem to be part of the modern world at all. So he wouldn't have it and she was most upset. There were also the incidents involving Vladimir and Miechen – how soon I realised that no love was lost between the family of the late Tsar and the family of his nearest brother! – when she'd beg Nicky, 'Darling Nicky, you have got to do something about them. You know your father would have roared at them!'

The major incident that year was Uncle Vladimir using the Imperial box in the Mariinsky theatre as if he were the Emperor

- which of course Motherdear's friends were always telling her he'd secretly love to be. Nicky was upset by this because it was bound to cause such stupid gossip, and he had to write Vladimir that stiff letter: - 'Please don't try to take advantage because I am young and your nephew, and please spare me the necessity of writing to you again in these terms, which make me feel abominable.'

He pulled a wry face when he showed it me. 'I may be head of the family but I don't like writing such messages to an older man.' Motherdear then told us that for many years my father-in-law had had to ban all Grand Dukes from entering Petersburg restaurants. Vladimir was largely the cause of this, having been involved in a very public fight involving Miechen, Uncle Alexei, a French actor, the Chief of Police and a dish of caviar. I can't pretend all of my own family are angels - after all Uncle Bertie got cited in divorce cases and the like and caused Granny a lot of embarrassment, and Uncle Alfred's drinking was legendary - but public fighting is really something else! - I remembered what Papa had said about how of all their generation only Sasha and Serge were worth anything at all, and I sort of understood what he meant. In any case, I got really tired of listening to these catalogues of sins and pleas for something to be done about them - when poor Nicky had so many truly important things to attend to - so one day in a particularly foul mood I drew him as I felt his mother would like him - sitting in a high chair while she stood over him. A pretty stupid thing to have done, and of course she found out about it like people always do. There wasn't a scene - instead she just withdrew from me and was thenceforth coolly polite - and she has never relaxed that since.

I was wretched about Motherdear, and the way I felt physically didn't help either. When I said to Nicky that Madame B. was at least a week late - I who am pretty usually regular as clockwork - he was delighted and we couldn't really quite believe it yet - although like Nicky said with an outrageous touch of pride, 'We haven't exactly left it to chance!' Well, of course we weren't like Ernie, with all his self doubts, but somehow when you know the whole country is waiting to hear such news, you never really imagine it will happen so easily. However, I then fainted a couple of times in church which was a new and unpleasant experience, and after that I was being sick at odd times of the day and my head was swimming. I had had no idea it would make one feel so rotten.

Of course there were no real court duties at all that first year, because of the mourning, but I did have to attend the *baise-main* ceremony in the Winter Palace, where 550 court ladies came to kiss my hand as their new Empress. A most peculiar ceremony – felt dreadfully stiff and shy that all this was for me. Beforehand, I asked Motherdear what to talk to them about, and she said, 'It doesn't matter. It's honour enough for them that you are meeting them.' So clearly Russia was not like England – it wasn't necessary to take steps to gain popularity.

Also there was Easter Monday, all of the Palace staff filing past us to receive porcelain eggs. It was extremely moving, to hear everyone say 'Christ is risen!' with such feeling as we kissed each on the cheek three times – thus ceremony permitted us for once to interact with them as equals before God. We were preparing an apartment in the Winter Palace as our city home, largely because there wasn't anywhere else – all the other Imperial properties were inhabited by one Grand Duke or another. The view of the river from the window of our flat was amazing, but really we didn't want to be in the place – imagine living a house that is half a mile long! – And which has in any case no real garden.

Ella played a big part in the design of our rooms, as she so loved to do – which was kind, but *Au fond*, they felt more like hers than ours. She had N.V. Nabokov who had of course also designed the interior of the Imperial train submit loads of sketches and she picked the ones she liked the most. Thus we got loads of mock Jacobean – which was still fashionable at that point and which Ella always loved – and Louis XV, with a Gothic library. The last gasp of eclecticism, these rooms represented – Ella may be an artist at heart but her tastes always inclined towards the referential – still, I got the modern in too by ordering loads of the vases, etc. from the Gallé factory. Also I made sure that they did my study very simple. In the end, the rooms looked like they straddled the 19th and 20th centuries, which is highly appropriate I suppose. I dread to think what they cost.

The best thing about the apartments in the Winter Palace was that we had an enormous marble and concrete swimming pool sunk in one room, so there would be an opportunity for exercise in spite of the lack of garden.

While our apartments in the Winter and Alexander Palaces were being prepared we went to Peterhof and stayed in the Italian house – where Nicky and I carved our names on the window in '84. Motherdear had gone to Denmark for the summer to visit her parents, and Sandro and Xenia went too and left us their baby Irina. Good practice! – I had by then gone past the stage of migraines and feeling sick all the time, and the baby was moving around. Fighting, actually! We used to sit together in the garden with our hands on my stomach, feeling the movements hour after hour and laughing and gazing at each other with shining eyes, almost unable to believe what was going on. We calculated that it would be due in October, but evidently we got our sums wrong – or she was very late. Everyone from Motherdear down was hoping for a boy, but we were largely indifferent, as I recall – Nicky said, 'A boy belongs immediately to the country – it would be almost better to get one that is completely our own this time.' Also I didn't at that stage know much about the Russian succession law – in my innocence I assumed that any child automatically became his heir.

On balance of statistical probability, we thought we would have a boy – Ernie and Ducky's Elisabeth was born in March; Sandro and Xenia had Irina in July, so we thought ours had to be a boy and we chose the name Paul. This upset Motherdear of course because Tsar Paul was hardly the most august precedent – but we chose it because we liked it, not for him or even for Uncle Paul. I do not like this thing of calling children after oneself or ancestors – very vain and silly and an unfair burden for the child – and strongly resisted suggestions that any of our girls be called either Viktoria or Alexandra. The fact that we repeated Olga is coincidence, really – I liked the name as very ancient and Russian (came with the Vikings – means 'holy', apparently) long before I really knew my sister-in-law who was in any case so young when she became an aunt that it was obvious the name hadn't been selected in sole tribute to her.

Our Olga was born in the Alexander Palace on November 3rd 1895. She was far and away the most difficult birth, as one might expect with the first, although in retrospect I don't really remember the pain – you never do. I just heard later that everyone was in a terrible state because I seemed to be suffering so much: Motherdear prayed openly on her knees, and poor Nicky was weeping. The two of them and Ella were with me the whole time, and Olga finally appeared with the aid of forceps at 9 in the evening when I'd been in labour all day.

The moment I heard her squawk was quite possibly the happiest of my life – chokes me up to think of it now. The others were all astounding too, especially the Boy – but nothing quite compares with the pleasure and amazement and love for the firstborn – holding her in my arms and seeing her move and smelling her unique smell and all while I was so tired that the physical world was all I was conscious of. She weighed ten pounds when she was born – the heaviest at birth of the girls, actually, although she's now so slender, and she's average in height: lots smaller than the next two. She had heaps of hair as well – dark to begin with, but that fell out and grew back blond as we expected. When she was very small she was chubby and even plain and looked like poignantly like the photos of my sister May. Her eyes always were blue but she was at least three before you could see that she'd got the rest of Nicky's features too: the slightly turned-up nose, the high cheekbones and the straight brows that are so much darker than their hair. Funny how Russian she looks, when you consider her ancestry!

My mother-in-law had insisted we get a wet nurse, although I made it clear what my intentions were. 'What if you can't manage it?' she asked. 'You can't feed them on cow's milk.'

Nevertheless, it seemed a strange and medieval idea to me - but as a matter of fact she was right and Olga did resist me at first. She was two days old before experiments concluded successfully in front of not just Motherdear and Xenia but also Sandro - he was such a dear in those days, I didn't mind at all - with me feeding the wet nurse's son and the wet-nurse feeding Olga, after which we were able to swap them.

We had her christened at just 11 days because it was our first wedding anniversary. One took her to the Catherine Palace in an ancient gold coach and she was baptised in the church there, though of course we as the parents were prevented from attending and never saw what happened. The three eldest were christened in the same vest their father wore - before it got stolen - and dressed after the immersion in a frock I made them myself. Oh, and - a piece of her darling soft baby hair was dropped it into the font encased in wax, and it sank well, so everyone told us she would have a happy life. Please God they may still be proven right.

It was quite a while before we could even get used to the idea that she was ours! - But what a joy it was to have our own little child! - As with the others we kept her almost exclusively in our bedroom the first six weeks, so we alone would get the first smiles and could trace the daily changes in her face. We were quickly immersed in the tender undignified chaos she brought with her. We talked rubbish from being so tired with waking in the night because she was crying. I wore loose tea-gowns as much as I could because I was leaking milk down the front of my clothes; Nicky rapidly learnt not to pick her up when he was formally dressed for an audience with a minister because she was unfailingly prone to be sick on him and he'd have to rush off and change again. He was absolutely besotted with her: frequent comparisons were made with his sister's child, who always was smaller relative to her age. They weighed the same when Olga was five months and Irina nine; weeks later Olga was heavier, and chubbier from the start. Their faces are amazingly similar, though!

Olga's coming marked a sort of psychological shift for us: now we had started establishing our own family and didn't have to live in the shadow of the previous generation, and Nicky felt maybe a little less out of place in his Emperor's role. At least, that is what I always felt she has done for him. How can anyone who has been the sort of father he has been to them ever feel inadequate for any position in life, no matter how testing! - And how dare anyone outside the family ever suggest that such a father be called a failure because of things that may have happened to him in other roles! Enough of this - it doesn't help.

A wonderful Christmas we had that year, at the Alexander Palace of course. That was when we established that we would have eight Christmas trees for the household, and I would decorate them personally and choose presents for all of our staff. At first this was so we could get to know them, but I like doing it so I carried on every year after that until 1916. Olga had her own tree in the nursery even then - the revolving one that gave them all so much pleasure over the years. We moved her upstairs to her own rooms just before Christmas, which was dreadfully sad - that moment never got easier, even when we'd been through it five times. It is however completely necessary - you can't have them in your own bed forever, they'd be dreadfully spoiled, and in their position there are always too many people waiting to spoil them anyway. Some of the family used to say that making them take cold baths and giving them only camp beds to sleep on was excessive, but I am glad we did it. You can insist they tidy their own rooms, you can specify that only first names are to be used in the nursery, but every time these little souls go out in public crowds of people gather around their carriage or car and they hear such things said!: - 'I knew that if I only touched her hand, all would go well for me!' 'The Heir! - Oh, the angel! The pretty boy!'

In all five cases to a degree, but mostly with Olga and the last two, we had a certain amount of struggle against the sort of bossiness and arrogance these receptions instill in them, and it would have been much worse if they hadn't been fairly strictly treated at home. They might have grown up like Prussians! When I was a child, no-one called me anything other than Alix; my mother's generation on the other hand even had their toys annotated with their titles: 'Pcss Royal'; 'Pce of Wales'; 'Pcss Alice', etc. and one of my cousins said a funny thing to me once: 'Have you noticed, all the Aunts are very kind and well-meaning, but if they drop so much as a handkerchief on the ground, they never pick it up themselves, they wait for someone else to do it.' (My mother who had a harder life financially than her sisters was undoubtedly an exception to this). I never wanted my children to grow up with that sort of unthinking helplessness; they have to understand like Mama said about us that their position is nothing other than what they make of it; they do not have the right to special treatment and they of all people need to be able to look after themselves a bit and have personal discipline. The behaviour of their Uncle Misha and some of their father's cousins emphasises why this is so.

In those days the nursery was small, but we had established the pattern for light rooms with white furniture and flowery quilts and curtains. The yellow walls and twisty frieze in the day nursery were inspired by the *Jugendstil* and Ernie liked them a lot when he saw them - which he did even before Olga moved up there, because he and Ducky came when she was less than a month old and introduced her to her cousin Elisabeth. (Elisabeth's own nurseries of course were a spectacular blend of Arts & Crafts and the *Jugendstil* well before Ernie became so heavily involved in it.)

The other thing we had already done was have the nurseries centrally heated, so there was no danger she would fall in the fire. I think I have a right to be proud of the way we did our children's rooms, they were so simple but so comfortable and modern and safe - they follow the Fabian Society's dream for all children in this century; may it become so. The English nanny arrived when Olga moved upstairs and almost immediately we had trouble with her. She objected to us going in constantly to see our own child and even to our giving Olga her bath; I was apparently expected to function as a cow and ignore the little one between times. Over the years we have had plenty of problems with nannies, including the Russian under-nurse who drank and was eventually discovered in bed with one of the Cossacks of the guard, but it was especially disconcerting to run into trouble with the first. Finally we had to let her go, and I called Orchie out of retirement - because after all I couldn't wish anything better for my children than being brought up the way I was myself.

So for three years all went well, even though in the end Orchie's age brought her into conflict with some of the younger staff who had different ideas, and she left us in a huff.

After Orchie was dear Miss Eagar, who was wonderful and who stood no nonsense from either the children or the nursemaids. She stayed until 1904 when she left for family reasons and because of the anti-English atmosphere at court during the Japanese war, and I was very sad to lose her. Miss Eagar of course wrote some memoirs and I was happy for her to do so, because they went a certain way towards contradicting the rubbish in the foreign newspapers (above all the British, I am sorry to say) about both Russia and us. Most of the Russian aristocracy had by the '90s taken to British nannies because of their excellent training, so having the same was something even Aunt Miechen couldn't criticise me for. There even used to be in Tsarskoe, later, a little Russian boy called Kirill who was known to Alexei and the other local children as 'the English baby' because of his impeccable accent and his British-type sailor suits (with the tie and short trousers). Everyone went to the English shop on the Nevsky Prospekt for Pears soap and Bovril and children's jerseys, so in this we were for once just like the aristocracy!

CHAPTER SEVEN

For New Year 1896 we went back to Petersburg and took up residence in our new Ella-designed rooms in the Winter Palace. Then followed our first 'season' as Emperor and Empress, which I remember so well and with mixed feelings.

On the one hand, we went together to the theatre (above all the opera) and rode home in a sleigh through the snow with the bells jangling, and it was even more exciting and romantic in the city than in the park at Tsarskoe. We had supper alone in front of the fire and gazed out of our windows at the great frozen river and the falling snow. However, we also went to the parties and we had to give our own. This in my innocence I never dreaded at all; I liked to dance, I'd done a lot of it in '89 and also at the parties Ernie and I gave in Darmstadt - and if I'm not the best at it, so what? - It's supposed to be fun. Nicky needless to say dances wonderfully, he always guided me, and to sweep around the floor holding each other so close and looking into each others' eyes is the most delicious feeling. It doesn't get any better in a public place!

Of course we had to start the season with a big ball at the Palace. When Nicky and I opened the dancing we suddenly got horribly conscious of everyone looking at us - and really it's not the same at all as when you are just two more people at the party! I felt my gloves get damp on the palms and I knew I was blushing dreadfully, and after that we just couldn't wait to go home.

Aunt Miechen and Uncle Vladimir gave a ball which was more fun; the theme was that all the ladies had to wear something on their heads - no tiara-type things allowed - so I went in a red beret as Tatiana from *Eugene Onegin*. (Nicky always did have rather a fixation on this story). Even here, though, we had to lead the dancing.

Ella was of course there to help with her advice - Ella the calm, the graceful, who put out her hand to be kissed with such a sweet smile and everyone in the room fell at her feet. Poor thing, she didn't help at all! - Because imagine walking into a room alongside such a paragon, when you are blushing and don't know anyone and you feel highly unnatural giving your hand to be kissed at all! 'You are so like Victoria,' Ella said to me, mildly amused. 'You know, at one of the first parties we went to she felt sick with nerves and Uncle Bertie had to take her out of the room and feed her - and then she worried that everyone would see her eating supper twice and think she was greedy. But she got over it - imagine Victoria now, worrying about what people think!'

Still, I have seen Victoria get ready for a party - how she rushes down into the hall at the last minute, always a bit dishevelled; and Ludwig is waiting there dark and handsome preening himself in front of the mirror and couldn't be more of a contrast. I don't think she is over her nerves at all!

Ella gave me lots of advice about the people we were going to meet - their ways and peccadilloes and interests. 'Don't be afraid of Vladimir and Miechen; Minnie exaggerates their faults. He is really a highly cultured man, and she is so intelligent. That is the family problem, of course, because Sasha and Minnie never claimed to be great intellects and they always felt Vladimir thought he and Miechen should be in their position.'

Well, Ella is undoubtedly right about the Vladimirs and I might have prized them more for their brains if they hadn't immediately tried to cause trouble over the order of precedence: - I always found it disconcerting that Motherdear was the one to walk with Nicky if we were together in public (after all, he is mine!), while I followed on the arm of a Grand Duke. 'It's

107

because she was crowned Empress first,' Ella said,'that precedence is observed as long as she lives.' 'But if Minnie had any tact,' Aunt Miechen said, 'she would arrive before you and Nicky did and take her place, so you didn't have to go through the humiliation of walking into a room behind her.' - I was inclined to agree, but I had no intention of saying anything nasty about my mother-in-law in public, so I gave her what I thought was a vague smile and moved on. This is probably why Miechen hates me too. By the end of the season she was calling me 'that stiff English ramrod' and saying what a pity it was that Nicky hadn't been made to marry Hélène d'Orléans.

I know this because some of my maids of honour took pains to let me know. They also acquainted me with some of the other stories that were going around: there was that incident where I was supposed to have rebuked a lady for wearing her dress too low, saying that in Darmstadt we didn't do this. Also a tale of me helping a maid black a grate because she didn't know how somehow got to the ears of Petersburg society and caused an unbelievable degree of excitement. And - incredible! - they even heard how Rostovtsev one day at work in my study dropped some papers and I picked them up for him - and even this instinctive act was deemed a terrible breach of etiquette on my part. Some of the maids of honour told me these things because they wanted to help me and show me how to improve my standing; some of them however were just plain spiteful. Also, they talked bosh all day long: really, I don't care whether Aunt Miechen is sleeping with Nikolasha (this was one of the popular stories of the early days), whether Prince X's heir is actually the son of the Prussian ambassador, what priceless gift Uncle Alexei has given his mistress this week ('my dear, she costs the country more than the Navy does!'), whether such and such Admiral is or is not the illegitimate son of Alexander II, or whether Pobedonostsev was or was not Tolstoy's mode for Alexis Karenin. Haven't they got anything better to think about!? -

When I heard the things they were saying about Serge and Ella I began to feel sick, and in due course they started on me. Between 1896 and 1910 I went from being the stuck-up English girl with the ways of a vicarage to being the mistress of poor Orlov - the only true friend Nicky ever had - to preferring women; and then it seems I changed my mind again and decided I would rather sleep with holy men. Let the Bolsheviks do their worst: nothing can compare to the damage the Russian aristocracy can wreak on a person's reputation.

The simple answer as to why they are like this is that they have too much money and not enough to do. Their big aspiration historically was to get involved in the government of the country - many of the ministers were still of aristocratic origins, but this was never enough for them. Quite what they did want is hard to fathom, since representative government could hardly have served their interests unless it were hopelessly skewed in favour of a sort of upper house. *Au fond*, they always felt they knew better than anyone what was for the good of the country, which can hardly be true when you look at the way they live. That winter, I tried to get some of the ladies involved in making clothes to sell at charity bazaars. For one thing, these items sell for a good price, and for another they cost the donor more personally than something simply paid for: perhaps it might make them think. This was predictably not a popular gesture - but good lord, something needed to be done about the conditions of the poor and you'd have thought every little bit helped.

Maybe it's true that much of my family grew up with a political prejudice against aristocracy - Victoria and Ernie are just the same, it comes from our Mother - but I did honestly try to make good relations with them and I persisted with balls and the like for seven years, until the Japanese war was a compelling reason to stop. They simply weren't prepared to tolerate me: they made no allowance at all for me being new to their country and not understanding their etiquette or knowing anyone.

They sneered at my French and they made unkind comparisons between Nicky's modest manner and the determined style of his father (although god knows that when the latter was alive they sneered at him as an uncouth barbarian). One day Vladimir said loudly in my company, 'I pray every night that I may live long enough to hear England's death-rattle.' - and it was petty, spiteful things like that which did for me in the end. Why worry about 'society'? - What, honestly, are the point of court balls which waste heaps of the nation's money on entertaining people who despise us and could never be any use to us politically anyway? This is not the eighteenth century.

Needless to say not all the apples in the barrel are bad. That winter of all the household and the maids of honour I came to know Marie Bariatinsky very well; also there was old Fredericks and Elisabeth Narishkina, both of whom already acted as they did until 1917 almost like parents to Nicky and me. These are people one can cheerfully tease without their marking one down as unsophisticated or provincial, and who do not judge on the impression of 20 seconds. Neither did they condemn me out of hand when I brought Madeleine over from Germany so I would at least have some maids I already knew and who weren't scared to treat me like a human being.

In the family (beyond the immediate) the unmixed blessings were Kostia the poet, Uncle Paul, and in those days most of the Michels (though I never much liked Nikolai of the loose and spiteful tongue) and Nikolasha too.

We remained in Petersburg until April, so I could see for the first time the breaking of the ice on the Neva when the thaw came. One used to say that the sound of it cracking is like a bomb going off; sometimes it can be heard almost at Tsarskoe. It was early May as I recall when we decamped for Moscow and the coronation. The worst of that was weaning our Olga - how we used to love those morning coffee breaks when I'd nurse the little one and we felt so peaceful and united, the three of us. Olga was so forward; she was in short clothes and already blowing bubbles at us and making loads of sounds with her mouth. Ludwig and Victoria, Ernie and Ducky and Harry all came to the coronation – the latter brought masses of people because he was representing William. Of my closest family only Irène stayed away as she was then expecting Bobby and not feeling too famous. As for me, I didn't in fact find the ceremonies at all tiring or stressful – apart from the one obvious incident.

And so we were in the Petrovsky Palace at first because we couldn't enter the city until one had officially proclaimed the date of the coronation to the citizens of 'Our Former Capital'. Nicky had been fasting and we were both praying a great deal – he for guidance; I to take on his absolute faith that his role in life had been ordained by God, because I had still some trouble accepting that idea. The way I was raised, the notion of being selected for such a role seemed a vain and foolish conceit – the Divine Right of Kings – Charles I lost his head for it. Nicky had introduced me to a different way of thinking: the way that says a throne is entrusted by God not so a monarch can abuse power, but so he must take care of the nation and pass the crown on inviolate for so long as it is needed. Even so, I suppose I never have managed to stop rationalising his position, although it has cost me dear in prayers. The evening before we went into the city every choir in Moscow came to stand under our balconies and sing. Many of our guests – family and otherwise – were out there with us, and I could see they were incredibly moved by the swell of the music and by the sea of lanterns all around. At the end of the first song, Nicky stepped forward to the edge of the balcony and started to clap. Undoubtedly this was in no way the 'correct' thing to do – but the rest of us joined in and then the choir went wild with cheering.

In the morning, unforgettably, it was warm and sunny and bells were ringing everywhere. Guns started their salute as the procession left the Petrovsky palace and proceeded towards the gates. Actually, the crowds were so dense that we could barely move, but on that day no-one seemed to mind - bystanders' hats were being thrown into the air, people were kneeling with their arms stretched out or making the sign of the cross and there were no police pushing anyone back. It was so exhilarating!

Motherdear and I had as usual to ride in ancient gold coaches - she in front as ever - and Nicky was ahead of us on horseback. He took his hat off as he rode through the Spassky gate and he tried to call out the blessing to the troops in front of the Kremlin, but they were cheering so loud he couldn't be heard. I only wish I had been one of those soldiers to see their Emperor symbolically emerge into the palace of his ancestors, smiling and golden-headed in the sunshine, like a medieval prince on his white horse - the *tishaishii tsar* that he had ever wanted to be, so protective and gentle, so pure-hearted and brave. Oh, my poor Nicky love....

May 14th was the coronation, that ancient ceremony with modern trimmings. We were up before dawn as our clothes - more precisely, my clothes - took so long to put on. He was wearing the uniform of the Preobrajensky, of course - no other regiment would do for such a ceremony; I had to put on court dress in silver with a train so heavy that if the attendants let it go for a moment I couldn't move and had to signal frantically for them to return.

The rest of the family and the foreign guests were inside the cathedral waiting by 9 in the morning; they had their own procession. At length Nicky and I came out onto the Red Staircase in front of the crowds and the cinematograph cameras that were the first anachronistic touch of the day. We proceeded to the cathedral, and the priests emerged to sprinkle us in Holy Water - really, it was more solemn than our marriage, because that was personal but this was like a ceremony wedding us to Russia - insolubly. And so we went in to the Ouspensky, and bowed to the icon and took our places on the thrones next to Motherdear. She looked pale but composed poor thing - she'd cried constantly for several days beforehand, it reminded her so terribly of her own coronation only 13 years before, with her Sasha at her side. I of course had to sit on the Ivory Throne that Sophie Paleologus brought from Byzantium when she married Ivan the Great; Nicky had the throne of his beloved Alexis, the *tishaishii tsar*, which was totally encrusted in jewels and not really nice to sit in!

Much of the ceremony I don't remember clearly; it was after all five hours long, with a lengthy Mass and much singing. However, one could never ever forget the moment that Nicky went on his knees while everyone else stayed standing, and he prayed for Russia in a firm clear voice that cut through the unearthly silence of the cathedral. Ernie said afterwards he was biting back his sobs the whole time, and what seemed more surprising is that so were half the hard men of the Romanov family - Vladimir, Nikolasha, Serge. After everything's said, they all loved Russia and the dynasty deeply.

Nicky stood up again and I was just gazing at him - I was absolutely transfixed by the humble, serious expression on his face, and his eyes were unfathomable - and the Metropolitan anointed him with Holy Oil and he took the oath to preserve the autocracy and to rule the country. Then he went into the sanctuary to take the sacrament like a priest, with all that implied. And, yes, at that moment the incident occurred that became so celebrated like an omen - the St. Andrew chain round his shoulders broke and fell to the floor. Hardly anyone noticed and he didn't flinch; he came out again, taking the Imperial Crown from the hands of the Metropolitan and placing it on his own head. That was the significant moment - no other European monarch crowns themselves like a priest. I was kneeling in front of him; he took the crown off again and placed it briefly on my head, and I felt its hideous weight and understood why he

113

had wanted to use the Monomakh cap instead. The uncles had vetoed that – rejection of the weight of the Imperial Crown? – you could just hear what people would say about it. Nicky took the Imperial Crown off me again and crowned me with a smaller one, raised me to my feet and kissed me with such a look of tenderness – made my heart glow. It was a special moment for us as a couple, that – when I accepted his burden to share, of my own free will.

We dined apart from the guests, that night – on a raised platform at the front of the hall where everyone else was sitting. Very self-conscious! – But the ambassadors came up one by one to drink our health, and after it was over we were able to walk among people and chat to them, and listen a little to what they were saying.

Uncle Kostia said: – 'He has great majesty, our new Emperor. There is more presence in his quiet dignity than in the most overbearing of people.' 'Perhaps you could tell Uncle Vladimir that?' I whispered behind my hand, and he smiled conspiratorially – he was such a dear man, the only one of his generation who really took the trouble to talk to me for a while and try to know me, and we had some good jokes together. Later I heard him talking about me in a way that flattered me deeply, 'In my view, the young Empress outshines her sister. She has more colour and looks stronger. Ella seems to me white and peaky at times and she looks like she needs to gain weight.' Ernie naturally was thrilled with Kostia. 'Imagine you being related to such a great poet! Perhaps he'd like to give his views on some of mine?' *Au fond*, Kostia is genuinely one of our favourite writers – Nicky, Ernie and me – and his translations of Goethe and Shakespeare and the rest into Russian are astounding too and very helpful to me in learning the language.

What surprised some of the foreign guests was the presence at dinner of the descendants of people who had saved the life of one Tsar or another. I asked Uncle Arthur not to make too much of that when he went home and reported back to Granny – it would only confirm her prejudices about Russia being unsafe when, really, if one assembled the descendants of people who'd saved British monarchs' lives over three hundred years, there wouldn't any fewer. It's just that the British have never thought to honour such people in this way.

The illuminations! – Almost forgot about them – that I had to turn them on by pressing a button that was hidden in a bouquet of roses; and then the whole of the Kremlin was electrically floodlit, and we could barely sleep at night because it came so strongly through our window.

We spent days receiving people, which was bearable if not too interesting, and then, of course, the horrible Khodynka event came along to spoil things. Serge and Ella arrived in early evening to see us, he looking rigid and withdrawn. While he was talking to Nicky on his own, Ella told me that 360 people had been crushed falling into ditches at the Khodynka meadow, where they had assembled to receive coronation gifts. We had been due to go there the next day to greet them. Such a terrible thing to happen – those poor souls – it always hits the poorest the hardest. Nicky emerged from their conversation in tears; he immediately announced that we must cancel the ball at the French Embassy. This Serge did not like, and half an hour later the rest of the uncles arrived, roaring at the staff. 'WHERE THE HELL IS THE EMPEROR?' And thus – a row: – we couldn't afford not to go to the party – the French government had sent tapestries from Versailles – it was so important! 'Why?' I said, 'don't you think the French will understand?– And 'Would you expect us to go if one of the family had been killed?' Vladimir gave me such a sarcastic look. 'That right, Alix. I'm only saying this because the people concerned were just peasants. It wouldn't of course occur to your prim little mind that I might be concerned under any circumstances not to offend Russia's only ally.'

So we went, though his comments on top of the rest of it had ultimately succeeded in making me cry and I know I looked dreadful. I didn't care then and I don't care now - I had rather people knew we weren't made of stone. The Michels were there too but they were glowering; Sandro and Xenia had already let us know that they thought Serge should accept responsibility for the botched arrangements and resign as Governor-General and that we shouldn't have gone to the party. Really, parts of the family used the whole horrible incident as a pretext for airing their hatred of Serge, which was unforgivable and made things even worse.

As the dancing began, we saw the four of them - Sandro, Nikolai, George and Sergei - sweep dramatically from the room and go home. 'There go the imperial followers of Robespierre!' said Uncle Alexei, idiotically. Next day we were able to go to the hospitals to visit the poor survivors, and Nicky announced money for the bereaved families. However it quickly became apparent that there were many more than 360 killed - it was more like 1,500 - and we saw what the foreign press was saying and felt like Nero for going to that beastly rotten ball. I have to say - Serge didn't trouble himself to visit the hospitals. Thus Ella didn't go either. '*Merci Dieu que Serge n'a rien à faire dans tous cela*,' she said to scandalised Xenia at some dinner.

Sandro raged: 'God, how I detest that person! - Flaunting that coldness and arrogance in the face of the entire country!'

Nicky commissioned a full enquiry into the terrible incident, at which point all four of the uncles threatened to resign their posts. So the enquiry was cancelled - it was a dreadful mess, and it ended with Motherdear and Kostia and others sighing that Nicky had been too easily manipulated by the uncles - but what would they have done in his position? - One couldn't so easily lose the uncles' services when we didn't have anyone obvious to replace them. In any case it was important to avoid yet another public scandal. In my view, it was the behaviour of the uncles in all this which was so terrible; they were like a set of spoiled children.

Before the end of the year, Sandro contrived to have a massive row with Uncle Alexei over some question of shipbuilding, and promptly resigned from the Navy. I still feel this was a great loss because Sandro is cocky but he has drive and talent and after that he frittered them both for years when he could have been such a help to Nicky instead.

Terrible Khodynka apart, memories of the year are rather pleasant ones. We went to Ilinskoe after the coronation, where Ella had a big house party. Already Uncle Paul's children were living largely with her and Serge. Paul is a kind, charming man when not in the company of Uncle Vladimir, but he is silly and weak and he couldn't cope with the household or the emotional needs of his motherless babies. Serge on the other hand was so happy to have children around; he was always in the nursery supervising bath-time and the like. With Ella I sensed ambivalence: she was gentle enough when with them but she didn't seek them out - and it was always clear that she liked Dmitri more than poor Marie. Perhaps she felt they were usurping the position of the children she'd have liked to have had herself in a different situation? - I don't know; she doesn't confide. Those days at Ilinskoe were the first since his succession when Nicky had been completely without reports or paperwork or ministerial visits - our first holiday. Until then, I often used to be woken at night by his grinding his teeth involuntarily in his sleep, which made me sad. At Ilinskoe, everyone was lazy. I woke late in a room full of sunshine and air, the curtains stirring a bit in the breeze from the open window, and lay enjoying the warmth of his body lying across mine and watching the sun on his tanned face and shoulders and arms as he slept. Such a delicious tender feeling, one never wants to get up again.

Some people used to sleep after lunch as well; Serge on one chair with his feet on another, a newspaper carefully spread across it so it wouldn't get dirty from his boots. Ella in the meantime

117

took herself off into the garden to do some embroidery or paint while a lady-in-waiting or a houseguest read aloud to her. Nicky and I preferred to go riding, just the two of us. This Ella did not like; she worried that it was too soon after the birth of Olga and I would upset my insides forever. So much fuss all the time! – it reminded me a little of being scolded by Granny when I had sciatica, and told I was too thin and urged to take care and have rests – really, it was excessive, the fuss one used to make over health, it was like they enjoyed it and certainly ill-health still had a romantic image when Granny was young. As I recall someone once decided that Irène – who has never had a day's illness in her life – was delicate in her teens, and for ages she was over-protected and not allowed to do things. It took dear Uncle Leopold to liberate her by promoting rebelliousness. 'I can't help worrying about you,' Ella said to me. 'It's the age difference; you are so much more my child than my sister.' How silly; she may have married Nicky's uncle, but she is less than eight years older me; that is not a generation, and sometimes I felt patronised by her comments. Victoria knows best because she is so clever; and Ella because she is so good. (Such an unkind thing to say, but it's true she sometimes had rather a priggish air.)

Of course in the evenings we often used to visit the Yussoupovs at Archangelskoe, to see plays in their outdoor theatre. Unspeakable Felix I remember very well from those visits – he was about ten years old, a totally brattish boy who used to annoy Serge by putting his hand on his back and announcing he could feel whale-bone. We all knew already that Serge wore a corset – in the style of his father's generation – and it surprised me that a mere child would dare to mock him so openly. Other evenings Ella sang for our company, her rich contralto floating out of the window into the still twilight, while Serge turned pages. Tried to have me sing too, as I sometimes would do in Darmstadt when Ernie played piano for us, but it made Nicky feel uncomfortable, silly thing, so I refused. 'It's just too intimate, singing,' Nicky always says. 'I feel odd hearing you do it for other people.' And he was just the same years later when I used to sing even quite privately with Anya and other friends; he used to put his hands over his ears and leave the room. (Secretly, he was also jealous of my time.)

Ella and I sing more or less the same pitch anyway, so I wasn't really needed. Sometimes she had me play instead; also Nicky and I played duets. This he can do by ear. *Au fond*, although unlike me he wasn't well taught, Nicky has great feeling for music. Alone, I sing for him - the Nightingale song from *Tristan und Isolde* which was always our favourite, and that song from Walton on Thames in '94 -

'*Is this a dream? Then waking would be pain. Oh, do not wake me; let me dream again.*'

Serge was always doing things to Ilinskoe. That summer he had brought a specialist herd of cattle - forget what type - in from Switzerland, and was also having various buildings added on. Nicky and I went around with the camera and photographed the lot. This was the first summer we had our own cameras - principally to take snapshots of our delightful little daughter aside from the formal ones - and nothing was safe. Eventually a couple of years later exasperated Ernie drew me on the margin of one of his albums as a woman with a box Brownie for a head and a huge all-seeing eye in the centre - a bit like the pinhole camera advertisements used to be - and he wrote underneath 'Death by the Kodak person.' I like that. Also I like the science of developing them ourselves; Xenia and Sandro too had to learn this when she snapped him naked in the sea and they dared not send the pictures off! Almost forgot that - how physical they were in the early days of their marriage, before he proved himself true to his Romanov blood and started playing her false. They used to lie entwined on peoples' sofas and he'd have his tongue in her ear, and Ella and Motherdear and the like would be very cold with them!

Well, after our rest in Ilinskoe, we had the state visits we'd been dreading. In the end, they weren't too bad. Austria was first and worst; we knew no-one, and the court of course was totally hide-bound by etiquette. The Emperor was formal and distant; the Empress came to one dinner and I was shocked by her appearance - she, who'd been acclaimed - along with our aunt Alex - as the most beautiful woman of her generation looked thin and pale, a network of wrinkles covering her face, which she kept heavily veiled. Someone told me that she hadn't allowed herself to be photographed since her son's suicide, it had aged her so badly. She ate nothing at dinner and she talked about how she pitied us thrown into our position, and how important it was to find a refuge. Poor thing, she was absolutely right, but I feel she wasn't happy even with the life she'd made for herself away from her husband's court. I've heard she spent it endlessly travelling in search of the mythical place where she could relax.

Austria was upset with me because Nicky and I appeared in public dressed pretty much the same on one occasion - he was wearing a black suit and so was I but with a skirt, and I had a tie on. Exactly the sort of thing one might wear in England to go cycling, but in silly Austria it caused a scandal. Something good came out of the visit, though. We got the agreement that neither Austria nor Russia would create trouble for each other in the Balkans.

We also saw William briefly in Breslau, the visit he'd been hankering after. He was full of obnoxious jokes as usual; Dona was very ugly in the clothes he had chosen for her (she always was even more *unter dem Pantouffel* than Ella was). When they held my baby I flinched involuntarily!

Next we went to Denmark to Nicky's grandparents - a family visit rather than state one - and had fun there; they were such a jolly boisterous family, obsessed at that point with roller-skates. It's true though that if they saw anyone pick up a book they all pointed and made monkey noises. I enjoyed myself but I've never felt I wholly fitted in!

Then - Granny. The two years since I'd seen her dear old face felt like a lifetime; so much had changed. We went to Scotland in the *Standart* - brand new then. Nicky spent an awful lot of money on her, actually, but in a sense it was necessary because she was a floating ambassador for Russia. (How envious William was when he first saw her pass through the Kiel Canal! - He hinted he'd like to receive her as a gift!). Uncle Bertie met us at Leith - it was pouring with rain - and we drove to Balmoral in open carriages. However some distance from the castle we were met by several Highland regiments with flaming torches in their hands and pipes skirling, and they led us to the door, so the final approach was incredibly moving. (Granny of course had made Nicky colonel-in-chief of the Scots Greys as a wedding present, and he was so happy to see them on their home ground.).

Dear Granny was touchingly delighted to have us near her; she kept exclaiming that I had become such a 'stately lady', very different to the skinny girl with painful legs of 1894. Our little love was pronounced beautiful and splendid and mercifully well past the 'frog-like' stage; Granny did say however, 'I do hope she won't become too much like her enormous Russian grandfather! - That would be such a shame for a girl!' I said I thought she took as much after my side - we were all very big babies it seems: - 'I was almost square until I was five'. 'You,' Granny said to my surprise, 'were quite the most beautiful child I ever saw.' She then ruminated. 'Ella was also quite lovely, and even Victoria as a little girl - she has never made the most of herself since. Irène was very plain.' Dear Granny - she never minced words about her family's looks!

I also found that she talked to me now I was married about things she'd never have dreamed of mentioning before. She told me quite frankly that I ought not to nurse my own children; it would interfere with the execution of my duties as Empress and in any case it wasn't at all nice for a well-born lady to make such an animal of herself. How shocked she'd have been if she'd heard me discussing such matters with Kostia over dinner! (Not that one would have done the same with any of the other Romanov men of his generation!). She also said she hoped I would not find myself pregnant too often. 'It will quite spoil your life. This, men cannot understand, even the best of them. They never think of the consequences for we poor weak women.' Naturally, I was dying to giggle. I told her frankly that I had rather liked it – the wonderful intimacy of the feeling when they start to move around. She sighed and said that I was like my aunt Vicky and she had never understood how so clever a person – 'her mind is almost masculine' – could be simultaneously so obsessed with little babies.

The Yorks' little golden-headed two-year-old David was at Balmoral, tugging Granny by her hand to pull her out of the chair; and when he didn't succeed he'd turn to her Indian servant and beg, 'Man pull it!' I saw Granny looking from him to my Olga, and I knew what she was thinking! Really, she was incorrigible!

While Granny and I were driving together and talking, poor Nicky was having a less pleasant time of it. It was only September but it rained constantly, and he was dragged out onto the mountains in it all by Uncle Bertie and Georgie York, who were as ever totally obsessed with slaughtering wildlife. Nicky did not find this fun at all. He sat in our little sitting-room after dinner with his hand clasped over his cheek, which had developed a terrible neuralgia from the cold and damp, and had such a tragi-comic expression on his face that I had to rush to him every few minutes to give him a kiss. 'Oh, poor love!' We were both laughing, but, 'Me don't like being apart from you at all!' he complained all the time. He had also to talk to the prime minister about the vexed matter of free access to the Suez Canal, and the nuisance that Britain's continued occupation of Egypt was causing to Russia and to France as a result. It made my head spin at times, to see him taken aside by these grey-whiskered old men - not just Lord Salisbury but also Emperor Franz Josef and his own grandfather King Christian - by whom he was now in a manner of speaking regarded as an equal. We were two generations out of step with the other leaders of Europe; it was so sad; he should have had more time to learn and to enjoy life, really, before the burden of power descended. (When we were engaged we had planned a long trip to Malta to live near Victoria and Ludwig; that was of course out of the question now). Even William, the only near contemporary on a throne, is ten years older than Nicky and needless to say he emphasised this whenever he could.

It was while we were at Balmoral that one took the first moving picture of Granny. She drove across the terrace in her little tiny carriage, Nicky and I and Uncle Arthur and the cousins walking behind her. I have seen it since, and I note how I put my hand on the back of the carriage, so protectively, because at the back of my mind I feared that I might never see her again. We took the train back through England to Portsmouth where the *Standart* was now waiting, and on the way was when we broke down in Preston station and had to commandeer a room for our suite to have dinner. It caused lots of excitement and attention; that was still a shock for me, who two years ago would have eaten unnoticed in the public restaurant.

Then came the state visit to France - a real contrast to Austria! - As I recall their Navy escorted us halfway across the Channel, and the crowds went absolutely wild to see us; they cheered Olga ('*Vive la bébé!*') and even the nursemaid as they drove by in their own carriage. We heard that blossoms had been tied to the chestnut trees so Paris would look her best!

In Paris Nicky laid the foundation stone for the Pont Alexandre III in memory of his father and in honour of the Alliance that the latter had forged so determinedly. We went to reviews and visited monuments and there was little time for serious talks about anything, because we were only there three days. One night we spent at Versailles, where I slept in a room that had belonged to the unfortunate Marie Antoinette and of course was charmed by her portraits and those of her children. President Faure presented Olga with a trunk bearing a splendid doll and a complete trousseau, all most perfectly made. Far too perfect to play with; they'd have broken everything directly, so the doll and her wardrobe are still in the Pallisander room at Tsarskoe; or perhaps a Bolshevik's little girl is playing with them now?

Went home via Darmstadt and Ernie (avoiding William who made a great drama of it, with sad letters to Ernie about being rejected when he wasn't invited), and by the time we got back to Tsarkoe we were very ready for a rest. Olga was fractious and cutting her first tooth – very late – and we also suspected that her brother or sister was on its way.

CHAPTER EIGHT

I missed the whole of the Petersburg season that year - no hardship!
- because the doctors made me lie down for several weeks; I was
dizzy and sick and generally unwell. We were extremely anxious
for the baby; this was one was so much wanted - as they all were.
I slept for seven weeks on a sofa in the mauve room, Olga's
play-pen near me so I wouldn't miss her development. In the
evenings Nicky brought her bath-tub into the room and bathed
her next to me. When he carried her upstairs to bed she looked
back over his shoulder and laughed and stretched out both arms
to me - it was very touching, except that also did the same for
the soldiers she saw stationed in the park! She went for her first
sledge ride down a hill in the park, perched in her father's lap,
and it seems that apart from one little squeak at the start she was
very calm. When he brought her back indoors her cheeks were
like two little red apples. She was wearing a white furry hat, a
thick cape and mittens, and she looked positively spherical.

Nicky looked forward desperately to Xenia's first visit after
her boy Andriusha's birth: he was imagining our Olga and Irina
pulling each other's hair and squabbling over toys. 'And I can't
wait until she has her own little sibling to fight with. - Loads
of fun, it'll be!' Poor Andriusha was considered by his uncle to
be very ugly. 'But naturally I don't plan to tell Xenia that! Ours
of course will be a paragon of beauty and she probably thinks
hers is too.' From time to time he still had to go town to some
social event; Motherdear had him all to herself then, so she was
happy, anyway.

Thank God, the later months of the pregnancy were much
easier, and our darling Tatiana was born in the Farm at Peterhof

on May 29 1897. Various people sent rather tactless messages; not least Georgy, who telegraphed that he was disappointed not to have a nephew to relieve him of his duties as Heir. By this time I'd got the idea that the law prevented female succession to the throne, but we weren't worried; how dare anyone suggest we might be disappointed in this little beauty! As a baby she was quite different to the others. Her brother and sisters were four-square and blond, with firm pink skin and large heads; Tatiana on the other hand was a long, narrow baby with a delicate little nose, a pointed chin and reddish hair. She weighed nearly nine pounds and everyone said she looked exactly like me. However she is slighter than I am and her complexion was always much darker than mine – that comes from Motherdear. Her hair colour reminds me of Ella. She had such curls when she was little (like her father did) that we kept her hair short until she was four. The name is from the beloved *Eugene Onegin* – a pigeon-pair, Olga and Tatiana, as in the story. They were so funny together. Olga aged nineteen months seemed to change overnight from being my baby into a little girl with a delightful gap-toothed smile and her yellow hair in an alice-band. Compared to her sister, she was enormous, and even her soft infant skin was already much rougher than Tatiana's. You forget how helpless they were when they were born: but put them side by side with a new baby, and instantly you marvel at how much they've learned in such a short time. Olga babbled all the time in a mixture of Russian and English; very soon she learned which was which and kept them apart, she was such a bright little child. She was extraordinarily charming and attractive from very early on; already just after Tatiana was born I could have her in the room with me when I was getting to knew some new maid-of-honour or a lady from a Committee, and she'd sit watching us seriously for a while. Then, suddenly, there'd be a conversational gambit: – 'Look! New shoes!' and she'd be pointing at her toes, showing them off to the potential friend. Seemed to me she'd thought carefully about how to get the lady's attention; she was already well above tugging at my sleeve or playing up. She had a delightful perspective on being the eldest. I remember her sitting frowning sadly at a film show, which showed a little girl whose elder sister was hitting her over the head to make her give up a doll. At the end, righteousness was restored, but Olga piped up:- 'I'm sure the big sister had kindly lent her doll to the little one and the little one wouldn't give it back, so of course she had to be beaten!' She was also outraged by the story of Joseph and the coat of many colours. 'His brothers had every right to try to kill him! – It was wrong for their father to give the nice coat to the youngest!' On the other hand, as they grew up, she very quickly relinquished her authority over the Little Ones to Tatiana. Thus it was power she wanted, without responsibility! Having two children, you feel like a complete family for the first time, and it's so wonderful.

In these the earliest years of our family life, the one and only blot on the landscape was the terrible, sacred task of ruling Russia.

Even the simplest public appearances were a nightmare: I have almost never heard Nicky give a speech in which he sounded anything other than calm and collected, but waiting beforehand he was often physically sick with nerves. Really, there were times would have cursed for my father-in-law for his lack of foresight. Not only did he leave his heir totally unprepared to rule, but he had also when it came to ministers favoured older men – men his own father's generation – who were all very able, but inevitably very soon after Nicky succeeded the poor things started to die in office. And there was no-one to take their place, because his father hadn't got to know anyone new. It was for this reason that we were so painfully dependent on the uncles, the only relatively young, relatively able people we had in positions of power.

Nicky's own friends from his childhood and youth were

decidedly too young to be of use, and in any case most of them showed themselves unable or disinclined to help at all: Sergei Mikhailovich lived for pleasure; Georgie Greece - a strong and capable man in my opinion - belonged to another country; Sandro after resigning from the Navy became addicted to adventure and a life of action and in any case he always had too high an estimation of his own importance as a member of the Family. The only one who was truly loyal was of course Alexander Orlov, who was like an elder brother to Nicky and who consented to become governor of the Baltic provinces, and had he not died so horribly young would have done great things in more elevated roles. As a result of his outmoded and tasteless loyalty he was of course slandered by the aristocracy who accused him of being my lover.

If one looked around for new people one saw only the worst types whose main interest was self-advancement. The reason for this is clear: why should the good and altruistic put themselves forward to help Russia if their only reward is assassination or slander? One has to be a person of exceptional personal strength to put up with that. (Or one has to be in love with the Emperor, like I was, but this is not necessarily a characteristic we would wish to encourage in the ministers!)

Nicky didn't even have a brother to help him, what with poor Georgy being in the Caucasus coughing his lungs out, and Misha a child of sixteen when the reign started. Even as the years passed nothing seemed to advance or change *chez* Misha. Uncle Vladimir sneered, 'Misha has only two interests in life - motor-cars and women.' So what to do? - You can only select the man who looks least worst and hope for the best; and in the end you seek help and advice beyond the political world, because only in other spheres do you find people who are truly thinking of Russia. I worked so hard to get to know the country and her problems; I so needed to be able to help. Used to spend any free morning that I had lying around on the sofa in my mauve room smoking too many cigarettes and reading about the country's history and her political situation. Main problem in those days even more than now was the situation in the countryside which was being systematically pillaged by the Ministry of Finance with its taxes and its refusal to lend money to peasant farmers. Mr. Witte always felt that such loans would be unrecoverable when one had a communal system of land ownership as in Russian villages. Thus it seemed to me his industrial policy was destroying agriculture and simultaneously creating a desperately poor and exploited urban working class with an inclination to riot. Practically and ideologically, Nicky always felt that one way around this was to reduce the amount Russia spent on arming herself. That way, one reduces the tax burden on the poor and slows down the development of heavy industry to a more sustainable pace. Makes it more even, too. Since the days of Peter the Great the whole thrust of Russian industrial policy has been in support of the military and nothing else; such a huge country - dependent on others for the simplest domestic items like knitting needles!

Thus the Hague Disarmament Conference in 1898. What it could have accomplished if other people had been more committed! - Certainly we'd never have had this terrible, terrible war! But those who didn't know him at all said Nicky's motives were cynical, and many of those who did know him called him naïve. These were the politicians. Ordinary people, on the other hand, sent messages of support; we had a wonderful address from the citizens of the United States, acclaiming him as a peace-maker and a great and courageous man. Had he been anyone else I am sure he would at the very least have been nominated for the Nobel Peace Prize, but in '98 it was still in dispute, and in any case it wouldn't have been quite the thing to give such an award to the demon of the liberal western press, the despotic autocrat of all the Russias....Really, some of the rubbish they wrote. Most of the British papers seemed to be under the impression that the knout (outlawed: 1845 – by Nicholas I, hardly the most liberal of Nicky's ancestors) was regularly used on the streets of St Petersburg. One used to see 'artists impressions' of law and order in Russia, featuring a troop of Cossacks riding through a group of unarmed peasant women, whips flailing and hooves pounding. And this from the press of the country that at the same time went to war against the semi-starved Boer farmers, systematically herding their families into concentration camps! – Whereas in Russia we did not even have capital punishment other than for treason.

My first years in Russia really showed me a thing or two about some of the Whiggish assumptions I was raised with, not least that Britain was the trail-blazer of liberalism and her government was the ideal to which everyone else should aspire. Russia has quite a different tradition and quite different needs and it ill-behoves other people to criticise on the basis of their own situation. One can't afford to be narrow-minded about such important issues.

Still, I found plenty in Russia as anywhere that shocked me and shocks me still. My father-in-law's anti-semitic laws were one thing (though it is emphatically not true so far as I am aware that pogroms were ever encouraged by his government or that he allowed the police to stand by and watch them happen). It used to horrify me to hear the things said in the family about Jews. Thus, Serge: 'They are the scum of the earth!' I, aged seventeen, priggishly idealistic, 'How can a soul be scum?' Serge: 'They have no souls!' Even the good Kostia in his play the *King of Judaea* created an atmosphere so frighteningly anti-semitic that Nicky banned the play for fear of what it might provoke. And Nicky himself, my gentle darling who so admired Buddhism and who studied the Indian religions, was known to sigh in horror at the existence of a people and a religion who could have crucified Christ – and he banned *King of Judaea* because he understands the feelings it aroused only too well. This was his father's teaching.

Trouble with laws like the Settlement laws is that they become self-maintaining. If Jews can live only in specified areas, as soon as they emerge they are attacked by a certain section of the population, and then it becomes true that the laws are there for their own protection. Only in the war, when Jews and Christians fought alongside as equals, did the danger of attacks start to diminish and we revisited the laws with a view to repeal. From the reactions of the family you'd have thought we'd proposed a massacre: Sandro, in our bedroom, stamping his feet and raging like the uncles used to: 'Remember this, Alix - for twenty years I've been a friend to you! - For thirty months of war I've kept quiet! But this is the final straw!' Hang him! - I will not run through all that again now.

Sandro in the late '90s was much occupied with Siberia and with Asia. He was part of the various expeditions that made inroads into Korea and China, claiming land for Russia without firing a single shot. In the meantime the bulk of defense spending went on building up the Pacific Fleet, and in 1898 we took Port Arthur without trouble. Nicky was overjoyed: here we had an ice free port for Russia, and as predicted none of the Chinese seemed to mind Russia taking it. Thought it was exactly how he used to say during our discussions in '94: the people in the east accepted that Russians unlike the rest of Europe had certain characteristics in common with them and would act as a force for mutual benefit, and they were accordingly welcoming. Korea specifically asked our protection against the aggressive and westernised Japan. Nicky knew the whole economic and trade future for Russia lay in Asia and that we could not sustain competition with the more active and expensive European states, whose markets were in any case saturated already. The British and the Germans behaved with considerable brutality in Asia: William dispatched some troops to help suppress the Boxer rebellion with a ludicrous blood-curdling speech about how the name of Germany would resound in horror through Chinese history in a thousand years, just as the name of the Huns still resounded across Europe a thousand years after they had passed through. This was why the British press started to call Germans 'Huns', I find. What was it Uncle Bertie said? 'William the Great needs to learn that he is living at the dawn of the twentieth century and not in the Middle Ages.' William as I recall was extremely friendly towards Russia's activities in the Far East, however. One time we met him on the Baltic for a Naval review, and he ran up the signal: 'The Admiral of the Atlantic salutes the Admiral of the Pacific.' Of course it suited him to have Russia turn her attention away from her European borders, but it didn't matter too much. The French Alliance guaranteed that he couldn't try to hurt Russia while her back was turned, just as Russia would give France support in a similar situation. We really thought that no-one could be so stupid as to try to start a war in Europe, and if they did there was always the Court of Arbitration established by the Hague Conference to help.

Really, we were incredibly optimistic for Russia's future, and we had every right to be, in spite of our personal difficulties in finding reliable new ministers. One had to step back from the trees and look at the landscape: - The country Nicky's father left him was stable and peaceful, and all was going wonderfully well in the east. Like he always said, for Russia at least it was possible to establish spheres of influence without destroying the local culture or mistreating people. Of course we weren't without the occasional domestic problem. In 1899 there was the student uprising, but that was diffused by revising the university syllabus and giving them much of what they wanted in terms of the right to free association and so forth. Nicky admires British universities and the way they emphasise the whole person instead developing the mind at the expense of the body. He wanted to see Russian universities become more that way.

Then also - the urban problem of Witte's making. Really,

the workers lived in the most appalling conditions, industry had developed far too fast and their bosses just didn't care. Meant that the trade unions (illegal for one thing) were prey to political influences – people could rightly blame the Minister of Finance and the government for their terrible lives. But Serge knew that wonderful man – Subarov – whose idea was to legalise unions and to establish regular fora for meeting with them so grievances could be aired and addressed, to everyone's benefit. If bosses failed to comply they would be prosecuted. Serge backed this as strongly as I did, though in the end things tended to go wrong with these unions, in Moscow at least, because of the characters of the police spies Serge had infiltrate them. This was not Serge's fault; he couldn't vet the agents all personally; but he was loathed for it in many quarters. The behaviour of the police was one of the things that I dislike most in Russia. Soon got used to seeing agents hovering in the bushes when we were out walking or driving – especially if on a public highway – but what I do object to is police spies compiling reports on my friends and watching them to see what they are up to! *Au fond*, if we choose someone unreliable as a friend, that is our problem; we do not need them followed. But our telephone calls were listened to routinely, and members of the household had their letters opened. No question of sending a private telegram: if Nicky was away at all, I wrote to him with my love, otherwise every word would have been pored over.

Between our marriage and the early autumn of 1898, we were not once separated for more than a few hours. However that September when we were in Livadia – first time since his father's death that we'd visited the Crimea, and things felt a bit sad and strange anyway, but we were trying to have a holiday – his Grandmama died, and he had to go to Denmark for the funeral, such a long way away! – It was absolutely awful, far worse even than being apart in the year of our engagement – because being married, you get so used to being together all the time, and things just go on getting better and better between you as the years pass. Left alone, even though I had our two little cherubs with me, I felt bereft: – couldn't get used to not having him there to tell every little thing to; and the nights with no dear warm body to cuddle close to were awful; I woke up constantly. However there was no question of me accompanying him to Denmark; Irène had come to visit me especially, and I could hardly have abandoned her.

The next year there was another horrible separation, when poor Georgy died. We were at Peterhof, our dear Marie had been born two weeks earlier, and her big sisters were tearing around on the beach, skinny and sun-tanned in sweet white smocks. Then came the telegram that he'd died riding his motorcycle along a bumpy road: a pulmonary haemorrhage had started, and poor Weeping Willow died on the grass verge, choking blood into the lap of a passing nun. Nicky went to Moscow to meet the coffin on its way up from the Caucasus: off to see his closest childhood companion returned to him as a corpse. How he loved and admired his naughty brother! – Kept a box full of transcriptions of Georgy's jokes in his study always, and he used to re-read them from time to time when he needed cheering up.

Inevitably, though, it was Motherdear who was hit the worst – to lose her favourite son only five years after her husband. There was a terrible scene at the funeral – she fell against Xenia just as the coffin was being lowered into the grave and cried out, 'Home! Home! I can't bear it any more!'– then she tried to push past the tomb and get through the door – which was impossible – and poor Nicky and Sandro had to hold her back until a plank could be placed over the tomb and she could cross it and leave. Sandro and Xenia took her home in floods of tears, and Nicky and I just had to stay inside the cathedral and bear the rest of the awful service.

The political consequence of poor dear Georgy's death was

that Misha became Nicky's heir. Uncle Vladimir was second and after that his Kirill. (Motherdear was convinced that Aunt Miechen henceforth spent her days planning Kirill's succession.). Undoubtedly it would have been better dynastically had our Marie been a boy, although impossible to regret her sex on a personal level. At birth she was like her sister Olga; they are still very similar in looks, although in Marie's case everything is more clearly etched: yet bigger blue eyes, a still rosier little face. Her hair is rich golden-brown, darker than Olga's, but when she was tiny it was white-blond. With Marie we gave her a definite family name: there are loads of Maries in both our families, including of course Motherdear and my sister May, but then again there are Marys and Maries and Marias in everyone's families.

She was an angelically good little baby who never cried and had a big healthy appetite: her elder sisters were violently jealous of her. They called her 'Our Stepsister' and when she began to try to walk they deliberately ran into her and pushed her about. Later they excluded her from their games or gave her the menial roles which she was too sweet-natured to resist. She was like a dear little bear-cub, tall and chubby and very strong, inclined to be a bit clumsy or untidy: as a toddler she lost her knicker-elastic a lot and layers of white *broderie-anglais* were forever appearing round her knees below the hem of her frock! Several people said to me that she was very like her Russian grandfather as a child: he too tripped over and broke things and his nick-name was 'Mops' or 'Fatty'. (Thank heavens, Marie has lost her puppy fat in the end, but it was there right up until she was seventeen.) Olga and Tatiana, pointing at her face, would intone together, 'Eyes as big as saucers!' like in the fairy story - which always reminded me of the unpleasant fact that their grandmother never seemed to have as much time for them as for Xenia's children. She - Motherdear - knew the beloved Hans Anderson when she was a child; she sat on his knee and listened to his stories when he visited the

Palace in Copenhagen. To have taken her little grand-daughters in her lap and have passed those stories on first hand would one might have thought have been the most natural thing in the world, but she never did. Very early they learned to be wary in her company; their manners improved astonishingly when she was around, but I felt sad because after all she is the only living grandparent they have.

By the time our Marie came along we had well-established the daily and the annual routine that was designed to make sure Nicky got some time away from his desk (although he never ceased being fearfully over-worked). I remember the calm rhythm of those days with such fondness. No matter where we were – other than on the *Standart* – he was still getting up by seven and going immediately after breakfast and our walk to his study to begin reading reports and receiving ministers. In the meantime I was doing my own reading on Russian politics or I was dealing with some of things I needed to do administratively. Straight away I became involved with the hospitals, because the condition of them was absolutely appalling – imagine a country half a century on from the Crimean War and still with no professional nurses! – Such personal money as I had went into various medical projects, because this needed doing fast; one couldn't wait for the Ministry of the Interior to finish dragging its feet. (In any case, what else is my money for?). I also needed to attend to girls' education – vocational, above all. In Russia, female access to the universities has always been very good – much better than England or Germany – but facilities for those less intellectually able who would need to earn a living were sadly lacking. I also at this time tried to establish in London a depot for the distribution of peasant handicrafts, because I thought the latter would command better prices in England than they could get at home, and help the rural economy a lot.

There were also many, many petitions and letters from individuals to deal with every day – the sort of 'charity work' that is expected of an empress and goes in usefulness beyond merely being able to sort out someone's problems. These type of cases are useful in highlighting a legal or social injustice that is perhaps affecting many more. Nicky also received thousands of these cases a day and he was assiduous in attending to them so that he would know what was going in the nation, beyond what the ministers deigned to reveal. It is so important to this system of government that he should stay in touch, and cases sometimes arrive at the most unexpected of times. Once, at Peterhof, we were disturbed in the night by an official from the big palace, who had ridden over to say that there was a young woman in the formal audience chamber there, weeping and begging to see His Imperial Majesty. Nicky went across to the palace and found out that the girl's intended had been condemned to death for terrorism, but as he had tuberculosis and would die soon anyway, she was begging for his life to be spared. This was duly granted; I can't for a moment imagine him refusing such a request, because there is plenty of research by the Chancellery to ensure that all such cases are genuine.

Where possible, I had the children in the room with me while I was working, although this inevitably became more difficult once they were big enough to climb out of the play-pen as soon as my back was turned and get up to something dangerous. Sometimes I used to get little notes summoning me to see my darling in his office, because he had a spare moment between audiences and needed to ask me something – but sometimes I'd get there and he'd say, 'Nothing to report. I just wanted to kiss your lovely little face!' Lunch was when we mostly saw people – ministers or the extended family, when in Petersburg, Peterhof or Tsarskoe. In Livadia or Poland, it was more often visitors from the countryside around. Always there were people from the household of course, and we wouldn't have the children excluded, although their table manners at times left a lot to be desired and it was difficult to correct them while simultaneously talking to an adult on the far side of the table. (One of the court fogies once said within our hearing that the children all behaved like young savages). Nevertheless, it's important that they get used to being around lots of different people and talking to them. I always dreaded them growing up feeling paralysed with shyness when they walk into a room full of strangers like their father and I do.

When they were very tiny we left them with their nannies when we went for our ride after lunch, although if we drove instead they used to come too, jumping around in the carriage and falling into scrapes. Poor Marie had her finger badly crushed by a carriage door, and Tatiana once got her leg caught between two seats and bruised it terribly. I suppose I was fairly hardened to the sound of their tears, but the agonised wail when the little things have really serious accident goes straight to one's heart like a physical pain that neither Nicky nor I could bear. Later when they began to learn to ride they occasionally came out with us, but to my sadness, only the energetic Tatiana ever really took to her pony in a serious way. The others were all too lazy to want to go out unless they had to.

In winter, in Tsarskoe, we used to spend the rest of the afternoon until the early dusk in the park with them, sledging and skating and fighting with snowballs. All five were incredibly hardy from a very early age; no matter how low the temperature, they go out of doors for several hours a day. I am proud of that.

When we were in town, the opportunities for sport were much more limited – just the little tiny garden on the side of the Winter Palace, a good reason for disliking the place as the children got older and more active. In fact, there were several winters even before 1905 which we spent entirely at Tsarskoe and barely went there at all (thus, there were no beastly balls, either). Twice the reason was that I was pregnant: in '97 I had the difficult time with Tatiana and '99 I was expecting Marie and she was lying at a curious angle that gave me sciatica and made walking difficult and dancing impossible. Then there was '98 when firstly I had measles and then the children were ill repeatedly with coughs and colds and I didn't want to leave them. Motherdear and Granny would have said that childcare was what we had the nannies for and my first duty was to my ceremonial role, but I don't agree. Children in their position will as adults be exposed to all sorts of moral dangers; it's doubly important that they see as much as possible of their parents when they are small in order to absorb all of the values those parents wish. The nannies are there for those times when the parents must unavoidably be away. In any case, I can't bear being parted from them when they are not well.

In 1901 the whole season was cancelled because of court mourning; so in the end apart from the very first one it was only in 1900, 1902 and 1903 when we had to go through the full season from New Year until Lent in town. The children used to get wildly excited before the *baise-main* at New Year, when I went to tuck them up wearing my court dress and kokoshnik; they said I looked like a Christmas tree. I also over the years was commissioned to produce innumerable drawings of myself and their 'Amama', Motherdear, and Aunt Ella and Aunt Xenia in ball gowns and jewelry, and they used to watch me do this with spellbound little faces, as if I was any good at drawing anyway!

Wherever we were, Nicky used to go back to work when our outdoor games with the children were over, and re-emerge at tea-time to see them again. Only closest family came to tea: most often his sisters, especially poor Olga, who was perpetually in flight - first from Motherdear and then after Motherdear forced her to marry the unfortunate Petia, she was running away from him. It was very clear that Olga and Petia would not be having any children - he seemed poor boy to spend his whole life at the gambling table and avoid their home - and she was especially devoted to ours. Later she used to take them to town and give parties at her own house, but when they were small she came to us instead and we sometimes gave children's parties too, with games and a cinema show, that lots of little cousins and above all children from Tsarskoe came along to. Kostia's older boys were very sweet with my little ones, and Paul's two used to love romping with them also, but their chief friends in the family were bound to be Xenia's brood who fitted so closely to them in age: Irina with Olga, Andriusha with Tatiana, and so on. When - as normally - there was no-one else around I liked it best, and we had tea in the mauve room and the children played with each other and scattered their toys round the floor and tried to steal forbidden biscuits from the table. Fat Marie was the most persistent and successful. 'Let her,' Nicky said indulgently, 'it's nice to see she's just a human child - I am always afraid of the wings growing!' Marie repaid him with adoration: she ran straight to him on entering the room, her chubby arms outstretched and a beaming smile all over her face. When he lifted her onto his lap she put her thumb in her mouth and leant against him with her eyes closed and a look of bliss. Little girls and their fathers! - it makes me laugh, because of course I was once just the same.

Between tea and dinner Nicky worked in his study again. It was during these hours when, if I wasn't writing personal letters or reading with my children or seeing the dressmaker or visiting a school or whatever, I sometimes used to feel the lack of female friends. In spite of the ladies about the household, some of whom I was quite close to, for years I never felt I had anyone as near to me as my friend Toni or my cousin Louie had been when we were children. So I used to play the piano on my own in a quiet room and wait until I heard Nicky's footsteps outside the door and the delicious sound of his whistle to me and I could rush out to him feeling as if I'd suddenly come alive again. This was the children's bath-time and bed-time, half an hour of pillow fights with the bigger ones and bathing the little ones, and listening to their prayers before we went down to dinner and to an evening together in the mauve room. Later of course the children were there too, but in the early years there was just Nicky and me, arranging our photograph albums together or reading aloud to one another. Read serious stuff at times, such as works of comparative religion or philosophy, but usually at this time of day it was novels taken from the selection of new books brought us every month.

Perhaps once a week it was that we went to the theatre from Tsarskoe – maybe twice if we were living in town and it was more accessible. But usually we were at home, just Nicky and Sunny, and it was bliss. Of course he had his own sitting room and billiard room and all the places where custom dictated he was supposed to go with the gentlemen in the evening, but he never did. *Au fond* the behaviour of these all-male card gatherings (which he saw in his father's friends when he was quite a child) is part of another world: huge drunken arguments, vulgar jokes – how to imagine him relaxing in such an environment!?

Very often he used to have to go back to his study for an hour or so late at night. So old Sunny would have her bath and go to bed and wait there reading until he was in the bathroom and I could hear him splashing around in the big tub. This is the point where me likes to creep round the door and turn the light off on you in the water, isn't it, my love?! – So as to have you completely at my mercy! Really, the routine was pretty much the same at Livadia in autumn and Peterhof in the summer except that in the afternoons we bathed in the sea with the children instead of playing in the snow.

A few years we went to Poland for the hunting in September, and there we actually took full days off and walked with the guns from dawn until dusk. Lots of visitors came to see us there: it was an easy journey for Ernie and Ducky, and Harry and Irène, and also, alas, for William. We were of course the only people allowed by law to shoot bison in the Polish forest at Belovezh; thus hunting was a social obligation and William came to take gleeful advantage of that, but I must say I loathe it and I will never set hands on a gun. Walk with them I will for the exercise, but certainly not for the vicarious enjoyment of killing driven cattle: there is barely even skill involved. All the uncles and cousins were as mad keen as William: I remember Nicky once lowering his gun when the bison went before him, and Nikolasha roaring some manner of abuse in front of the entire party. (We always had the park at Tsarskoe over-run by rabbits, and although in principle we agree they should be controlled, Nicky who will happily shoot crows or indeed a number of creatures that have a fair chance to get away drew the line very firmly at the bunnies. In any case the children would have been heartbroken.)

From 1898 we took the annual two-week cruise on the *Standart*, which was truly a holiday. No ministers and no governmental papers accompanied us, unless there were an emergency. Thus we cruised along the Finnish coast line, anchoring to go ashore for walks and tennis and picnics. The children we taught to row as soon as they were big enough to hold the oars; later they sailed as well. Nicky showed them how to recognise edible mushrooms, and he cooked what they picked in a tin over a camp-fire with some wine and cream. They learned fast and no-one was ever poisoned! 'When I was a little boy,' Nicky told them, 'my Papa used to promise us he'd eat anything we made for him. So we prepared the most terrible stews with anything we could find, just to see if he'd spit any of it out.' 'Frogs and snails and puppy dog's tails?!' they demanded with delight. 'Oh, undoubtedly. Once we had raw potatoes, but that was a mistake. Aunt Xenia peeled them and left them to your Amama to cook, and she had no idea at all where to begin.' Motherdear unable to cook even the most basic dish? – Somehow this failed to surprise me.....

Such friends we had among the *Standart's* crew! They followed on the hikes ashore, often bearing pieces of equipment such as ladders and ropes, so even sheer rock-faces didn't impede our progress. Sometimes on the beach a maypole would be set up for the giant stride – such as I remembered from the days at Peterhof in '84 – and the children would swing wildly round and round in its canvas loops, shrieking and covered in sand. In the evenings we played quoits on deck or sometimes there was dancing, particularly when the children got a bit older and could join in and gallivant with the young officers. When they were tiny there was always a sailor for each child, following them round so they didn't run overboard or fall from the cabin roofs. This system we borrowed from my sister Victoria who used to use sailors as nannies for her children when they were on board Ludwig's ships – far dirtier and more dangerous places than our dear yacht, though.

Some of the very best of our people are former *Standart* officers: N.P. Sablin, who was Nicky's ADC in the war and such a dear friend to both of us, the very closest we have, to whom one could confide practically anything. Also my friend Lili: her husband was on the *Standart*.

We were also able to go abroad in those days more frequently than later; there were lots of visitors too. In 1897 we went back to Darmstadt for a short visit; the entire family was there and they were introduced to Tatiana and we saw Irène's Bobby for the first time at nearly a year old. What relief when we noted that he was crawling about the floor and bruising himself and there was no sign of the dreadful swellings that afflicted Toddy at the same age. The next year of course Irène's family came to us at Livadia, and in '99 we followed a visit to the Danish family with another trip to my old home. This was the occasion when it was noted that all was not well between Ernie and Ducky. Still, she had a little boy who died at once a few months later; some said it was because she refused to give up riding when pregnant, though when she talked to me of him she wept bitterly and I could not believe she had thoughtlessly endangered his life.

When we were there at Wolfsgarten however - before she was pregnant, I think - she used to slip out of the window at night and ride her horse bareback around the woods and grounds. 'Why does she need to use the window?' people in their household demanded. 'Attention-seeking - that's all it is.' One day one of her horses escaped from its paddock and came into the courtyard in front of the house. Ernie was there and when he saw it coming he ran up the steps. Of course it followed and took a lump out of the seat of his trousers; Ducky stood on the far side of the courtyard and laughed hysterically. Poor Ernie, there were quite a lot of people watching - not only were we there but Ducky's sisters too, and a number of the cousins. Ducky said loudly that it was odd he didn't like horses, he spent such a lot of time hanging around the stables. 'But perhaps the stable boys have superior charms.' I felt sorry for her; she had married far too young and she couldn't cope with the responsibility of being Grand-Duchess of Hesse. Ernie complained that she showed no interest at all in any of his projects. In '99 he already had plans for the Mathildenhohe; he was laying it out with roads and plots for houses. Nicky commissioned the Russische Kapelle, so we'd have a church to go to when we were there; it was the first building in the Artists' Colony. After that came the Ernstludwighaus of Olbrich, the various smaller houses and the hall for the 1901 exhibition. Ernie called two of the streets after Nicky and me: Nikolaiweg and Alexandraweg; none of the other sisters or brothers-in-law shared this honour.

We visited the Exhibition and I was inspired by the plans and by the remodeling of Wolfsgarten that Hugh Baillie Scott did for Ernie. Decided then to make some alterations to our own beloved home. Nicky was a little dubious: 'Are you putting metal window frames in, then?!' - and he joked I wouldn't be happy until the Alexander Palace had been entirely rebuilt in moulded concrete. I always used to tease him that he purposefully took the scruffiest and most old-fashioned furniture we owned for his 'working' study: his ambition was to keep everything like it had been in his parents' day. Nevertheless he liked what I did in the end: the Maple Room and the New Study are in my view highly modern without being out of place inside the house. They are I suppose slightly closer to the French style of Art nouveau than the austerity of Mackintosh or Olbrich – I used sinuous lines rather than the geometric ones which alarmed my poor Nicky so much!

Aunt Miechen and 90% of the court fogies loathed it of course, but I am proud of our work; there are some wonderful touches. I love the tiny row of light-bulbs round the cornice that lights the ceiling up – so beautiful and subtle and much preferable to a central light. Also the way internal balcony connects to the Study, so while I was up there I always knew if Nicky was busy with reports or not and whether I could interrupt. Later, during the war when he needed me to I used it to listen in unseen to the Ministers while they were talking to him down below.

Actually, we had wanted to go to Scotland too in '99, but somehow it didn't happen; thus I never saw dearest Granny again after the coronation visit of 1896.

CHAPTER NINE

It was a horrible winter, the year the century turned: Granny's death was practically the first thing that happened in 1901, and we ourselves had barely got back from the Crimea after the dreadful experience of Nicky being so ill.

At first we thought it was funny; I was in bed because I was two months pregnant and being sick all time, and he had to join me when he started to get a back and headache and the doctors said it was 'flu. Xenia came to tea and laughed and mocked to find us both sick in bed like that. Within days though Nicky was in such pain that he didn't know what to do with himself; the back of his neck ached so. The doctors eventually - belatedly - called in a second opinion, and then they decided he had typhoid and they tried to banish me to another bedroom. I was furious; they had messed up the diagnosis so completely and I refused to listen to them from then on. Orchie and I nursed him; I slept on the sofa near him and had my meals in the same place and I tried to keep the world away.

Nevertheless, the ministers started to assemble when they discovered that he was ill. One day when he was at his worst point and the doctors were cackling about haemorrhages, I was called in to speak to Motherdear. 'Dear Alix,' she said, 'we have to make arrangements for the worst happening.' I asked what did she mean - I wasn't prepared to contemplate the worst. 'The succession,' she said. 'Mr. Witte needs to know the arrangements if Misha finds himself Emperor.' I was so shocked! - I immediately reminded her I was pregnant; as far as I was concerned, insofar as I had even thought about such a terrible thing, I would be declared regent until one learned whether the baby was a boy.

146

There was a precedent for this in Spain. If it proved that the baby was another girl, then and only then did Misha succeed. Witte always had a curiously high opinion of silly Misha. Not long before this Nicky asked him about repealing the Pauline Law to make Olga his heir. His chief Minister and servant said openly, 'I suppose the young Empress is behind this?' and he claimed one couldn't change the law of a hundred years just because the current Emperor had no son. This was odd, because Witte was normally perfectly happy to change the law of centuries, and the grounds for doing so were usually less strong than in this case. But he said Misha was a fine upstanding young man, and changing the succession on behalf of a four-year-old girl was silly. *Au fond*, perhaps he thought Misha as Tsar would be easy to control.

Anyway, I was disgusted that he dared introduce the topic of Nicky's death into our house and to have it raised with me at such a time, and I'm glad to say that several members of the household backed me. Had the worst happened, there were plenty of people who knew what to do; we didn't need to talk about it first. What was Witte doing? - trying to make it happen by sheer wishful thinking?! - I had never liked him much, with his heavy-handed industrial policies and his appalling vanity; from then on I could barely bring myself to be in the room with him. In due course, although he was ill for a month, my sweet Angel got better - as I knew he would when I was looking after him. There is no reason in this day and age to die of an illness like that, unpleasant as it is. He looked dreadfully thin and white though, and for quite a while he couldn't even walk across the room, he was so weak. Then our precious little Olga got it too and was in bed for ages. We had to cut her long blond hair right off, and she too looked so pale and emaciated and pathetic that poor Tatiana when taken to see her in the sickroom couldn't recognise her and cried with bewilderment.

I blame the old house at Livadia for their illness; it was damp

147

and dark and there wasn't even running water above the first floor. It also reminded me of my father-in-law's death. From then on I was thinking about having it pulled down, although admittedly it took us nine years to get round to this. We also moved tactfully to retire the elderly Dr. Girsh; this was when Botkin arrived with his modern training and methods.

Olga was still recovering when we received the news that Granny was sinking. She wasn't sick, she was just old and tired. Victoria wrote that she changed a lot over the winter; from being the round little body she always was in my childhood she suddenly appeared thin and frail, and she could barely see any more. She died surrounded by much of the family on January 22nd (western style). It was so symbolic; she who epitomised the nineteenth century to so many outlived it by just three weeks. That is, if you accept the logical idea that the 20th century began on 1st January 1901. Germany however celebrated its arrival a year early, because William believes he has power even over the calendar and declared that 1900 was the first year.

William also contrived to be the person who supported Granny on his arm for the last hours of her life (Dr Reid on her other side). Just such a shame that he couldn't bring himself to do the same for his own mother later the same year, poor Aunt Vicky.

I was devastated not to be able to go to Granny's funeral – this was the doctors' doing, they are so cautious about pregnancy, although I felt perfectly well – it was by far the easiest one. Nicky sent Misha along to represent Russia instead, and Ludwig and Victoria were at the thick of things of course. Seems the horses pulling the gun carriage with the coffin started playing up, so Ludwig called in a troop of sailors and had them tow it instead. Predictably this caused bad feeling between Army and Navy, but he seems to have started a tradition, because I believe they did the same thing for Uncle Bertie in 1910. England without Queen Victoria seemed impossible; one knew that Uncle Bertie would be a very different kind of monarch and at first we weren't sure whether this would be a good thing. The Russian uncles joked, 'So, Buckingham Palace changes overnight from being a mausoleum to being a mixture of casino and brothel.'(surprised that Uncle Alexei didn't head straight there!) - and they sneered that whichever Jewish plutocrat had lent the most money to the king would be able to control Britain. They simply didn't understand how limited the British monarch's powers are. - But, it has to be said, Uncle's rackety private life worked wonders for England as he gallivanted around Europe with a big cigar and a glass of champagne in his hands. Like it or not (and I don't like it) he who holds the purse strings controls the world these days, and Uncle made friends with all the right kind of people. Practically the first thing he did was to use personal influence to end that hideous, unjust Boer war (which in my view was caused by the activities of his diamond-mining chums) and then because he loved Paris above all things he moved heaven and earth to stop the silly bickering with France over North Africa. Suppose this brought about the *Entente Cordiale*, which upset the Russian uncles. 'England is in alliance with our ally! - One can predict what will happen next!' (I was always thought to be behind whatever it was they feared, of course.) Nevertheless on a personal level we felt that we would not be so welcome in England as when Granny was alive; Uncle Bertie's world is a very different one to ours. I barely knew him as a child (he liked children being entertaining at the dinner table but he was never one for spending much time reading aloud in nurseries like his brother Leopold did) and when we saw him in Denmark in '99 and afterwards he was always bored and restless in the simple, family atmosphere at his parents-in-laws' court.

Motherdear on the other hand found a ready welcome in England now her sister was Queen; she started spending a lot of time at Sandringham and we saw even less of her than before. When she came to us she complained that our open windows gave her backache and colds and she couldn't stand it for more than half an hour. Her own rooms always were horrifically hot, Russian-style, and since she chain smokes I in turn find the atmosphere in her houses practically unbearable.

Ludwig with his worldly past always fitted in fine with Uncle Bertie's set, and the press sniped that his career was bound to advance in leaps and bounds. (There always was a vast amount of jealousy around him even then, because he was foreign-born and he had so much more talent than a lot of his contemporaries who resented it when he was preferred for promotion). That summer he and Victoria came to Russia and we heard all about the sad funeral and this brave new England.

On June 5th (Russian style; 18th in the west) our little Anastasia was born at Peterhof, in our beautiful New, Lower Dacha on the seashore, where all the three youngest were born. She was another fat, fair baby like Olga and Marie, but with the narrower face and straight little nose and chin of her sister Tatiana. Facially, Anastasia looks more like me than any of them, I suppose. From her size at birth one assumed she'd be tall like me too, but even by about three years old she was notably shorter than her sisters at the same age. She used to be slight as well – we thought she'd take after Nicky in stature. At present however just like when she was a baby she tends to be rather plump; I do hope she'll grow more. The country's disappointment when she was born was palpable; I was disappointed too in the moments between the announcement of her sex and actually holding her in my arms, because so many people had said to me that an easy pregnancy probably heralded a boy: 'Girls always cause more trouble.' Nevertheless all that changed when I saw her and held her; I wouldn't swap our naughty little girlie for all the sons in the world.

'Anastasia' means 'Resurrection; prison-opener; one who will rise again', so Nicky freed a whole collection of political prisoners to celebrate the birth. The name is associated with the

Virgin's midwife; in England it was popular in the middle ages, often in the form 'Anstice', but in Russia it is regarded as being a modern name, middle-class, like Tatiana too - the press was happy that we chose it over a more imperial one. Let's not forget however that it was the name of Ivan the Terrible's beloved wife, whose nephew was first Romanov Tsar, so it's a deeply historic name in our family too.

The person who gained most from Anastasia's birth was our sweet Marie, since now she was part of a pair, and had someone to play with even if the big ones persisted in shutting her out. As soon as Anastasia was big enough I used to dress them in pairs - Olga and Tatiana wearing frocks in one design and Marie and Anastasia in another. Later when the age difference narrowed all four used to wear the same matching clothes, and at one point I briefly even had five children in identical sailor blouses and skirts, or in white lace frocks, which was enchanting.

So Victoria and Ludwig were with us at Peterhof when she arrived, and their children too - Dickie, the beloved little 'mistake', just a baby and very much a part of my little ones' generation, but Georgie and Louise were growing up fast (already 8 and 12), and Alice was already a young lady. In fact she is almost as close in age to me as I am to Victoria, and as the years have gone by she's come to seem more and more a young sister than a niece. I suppose she is in character more like me than she is like Victoria, who is not always patient with her. At sixteen she was thoughtful and 'touchy' and already secretly engaged to her Greek prince, Andrea, though her parents thought her far too young. She is tall and blonde and statuesque, with brown eyes and one of the most beautiful faces I've ever seen - even as a child she turned heads. Uncle Bertie it seems said that no throne in Europe was too good for her - this scion of the despised Battenberg line! - but she stuck to her modest minor Greek, and they got married in Darmstadt in 1903 - the first big ceremony for our Russische Kapelle, where the Orthodox service took place. There also had to be a civil wedding and a Protestant service in the Schloss, because Alice hasn't converted. However, she will, she will, of that I am certain – she who thinks so much about her spiritual life and is so in thrall to Ella. As a wedding present Nicky and I gave them their first motorcar, and they drove off on their honeymoon in it through the streets of Darmstadt with half the wedding party chasing them. There were crowds by the side of all the roads; Nicky ended by forcing his way through, head-down, so as to be able to hurl one last bag of rice at the happy couple, and Alice as I recall hit him with a satin slipper and abused him so roundly that he had to give up the chase because he couldn't move for laughing. Verily, his father would turn in his grave! – and some of the Romanovs were predictably extremely sniffy about all of it: 'Those wretched morganatic Battenbergs! – They squeeze their way in everywhere and suddenly they are being treated as equals by half the crowned heads of Europe!?' Perhaps because they have talent and drive? – I remember Nicky once being shown the Battenberg Course Indicator by one of his admirals, who badly wanted the Russian Navy to invest in a few copies. 'My brother-in-law invented that thing,' Nicky said with pride, and the gentleman almost laughed. 'How could your family have invented anything at all?' he was clearly thinking – and that was based on what he knew of the charming, idle Romanov uncles and cousins, for all their snobbish self-esteem.

Alice and Andrea made me a great-aunt when I was 32; but their Margarita and Dolla have been playmates to Alexei and to Ernie's boys, so the generation gap has totally disappeared.

At the wedding, one took a picture which is my favourite of us the *Geschwister* all together as adults, standing arm-in-arm in a row: Ludwig, Victoria, Serge, Ella, Harry, Irène, Nicky, me and Ernie on the end. We all look happy and smartly-dressed: the one thing I don't like about it is that Ernie was then alone. He and Ducky waited until after Granny's death before they parted company, because they knew what a divorce would do to her, who had been so instrumental in arranging the marriage. Nevertheless, they separated before the end of 1901, Ernie went off on a long visit to India and thought and wrote poetry, and thenceforth he only had his child six months a year, which nearly broke his heart.

She was such an enchanting creature, his little Elisabeth, my godchild: tall and dark like Ducky. He called her the sunshine of his life, but she was watchful and sensitive too, as a child raised in such an atmosphere inevitably would be. How terribly she envied her cousins their large family! – In Darmstadt in 1903 she persuaded Marie and the two big ones into her bed, and then she summoned us all upstairs to say goodnight. Of course we found four little girls in Elisabeth's room and only Anastasia in the one my children had been sharing, and we had to fake great surprise and anxiety at all of this. 'See, Aunt Alix!' Elisabeth was laughing, 'Papa has four children now and you've only got one!' Later in the visit Tatiana was discovered playing in bed with a box of matches, which her cousin had given her as a memento. She was to strike one in case she should wake and feel lonely during the night. We relieved her of them very fast, but I couldn't help thinking some displacement was going on – it was poor Elisabeth who was likely to wake feeling lonely in the night.

Ernie and she came back to Poland with us after Alice's wedding, and she had a splendid time riding huge horses in the park (another way in which she took after Ducky). Olga and Tatiana followed her at a distance on their childish ponies! Because she seemed so well and active, we didn't worry when she developed a temperature; we went off to the theatre in someone's house that evening, and when we came home she was dying of heart failure and there was nothing anyone could do for her. It chills me to think about it: of course it was ghastly typhoid, but a rare form that lay dormant for ages and then killed very suddenly.

153

We just could not fathom why everything had to go so wrong for my poor brother: the death at birth of his other child, the divorce, and now finally this! – At that point his whole life lay in absolute ruins around him. He took her poor little body back to Darmstadt and interred her in the grounds of the Rosenhöhe, because he couldn't bear to shut her away inside the mausoleum – who can blame him? – A very pretty simple little grave, with a kneeling *Jugendstil* angel at the head, and just the words: 'ELISABETH. 1895–1903' on the stone. Ernie says that when the time comes he wants to be buried near her, out in the open air, away from all the ancestors: – 'Why did she die alone? Why can't we all die together?' Victoria told me that he used to same the same thing when he was a little child and our brother Fritzie died, and that Mama was touched and encouraged him in it. I find that type of brooding most unnatural in a child, although I can understand why a bereaved parent might do it. There can't be any experience more lonely than outliving a person who should have outlived you.

That was the lowest point of Ernie's existence. The next year thank God he met Onor who has made him happy and given him dear little Don and Lu.

Ducky in the meantime turned up in St Petersburg on the arm of Cousin Kirill: there were stories circulating about them even before the divorce. Of course their union was illegal in Russia – they are first cousins through her mother and his father – and for ages Kirill hesitated. (No doubt he was afraid of damaging his chances of succeeding to the throne; it wouldn't be any other consideration.). In 1905 in the midst of all the trouble abroad they took the plunge. Nicky immediately stripped Kirill of his title and naval rank and ordered them out of the country, which was exactly the way his father used to deal with these illegal marriages (though actually only one happened in his reign). The result: a terrible scene with Uncle Vladimir: shouting and bellowing and issuing threats of resignation until Nicky backed down a little and let them come home. Ducky then used her position to spread stores about my brother and stable boys around the capital, and she entirely lost my sympathy for a time. Whatever Ernie has done, she was hardly blameless herself. All we his sisters wanted to do was forgive both of them for sins committed at a time of terrible unhappiness and let them get on with new lives, but she seemed to actually try to make that impossible. (Incidentally I know for a fact that none of even Ducky's own sisters can stand Kirill: he is cold and cowardly and selfish and probably not even faithful, but she has made her bed and now she lies in it, poor thing.)

Kirill and Ducky were not the first in Nicky's reign to flout the law: Uncle Paul took that honour when he married his mistress without the specified imperial consent. It was at that point that Serge and Ella assumed formal as well as informal responsibility for his first family. However Paul's new marriage was eventually recognised as indeed it should have been, since there were children (one born before the marriage): let the parents bear the consequences of their own actions, but don't visit them on the next generation. I don't want to dwell on all of this, it makes me ill: with all the privileges they have had, the very least one can expect of family members is that they should obey the law, whatever their personal view of it. Either that or they should renounce everything and look after themselves: they cannot expect imperial privileges to come without obligation of any kind.

Ekaterinburg, May 24th 1918, (New Style). The children have come at last! – Yesterday, in the space of an hour, we were told that they were a distance from the town, then that they were in the station, and finally that they were at the house. They came in with the boy, Sednev's nephew Lenka, and Kharitonov; all the others were kept out. Nevertheless the tutors had been with them throughout the journey, guarding and protecting; now they are somewhere in this town, still trying to find their way back to us. Why can't they come in? – So needlessly cruel when the children are so attached to them and they have nowhere else to go, here in the depths of a foreign country.

My poor darling children, they had a terrible time on their journey. Part of it was on a boat and Alexei was locked into his cabin with Sig and Zhilik; the girlies on the other hand were forbidden to lock their door; they barely slept a wink for fear of what might be going to happen. Such utter torture – all over now – we are together again: Sunny and Sunshine and all our five treasures.

And what a surprise – I have had a letter and packets of coffee from Ella! She is not too far away, it appears; she is in Alapaevsk with Paul's boy, some of Kostia's sons, and Sergei Mikhailovich. Seems they are living in an old school house and have the freedom to grow their own vegetables. How I envy that! We in our turn have the windows painted over now.

The kitchen boy Lenka Sednev has been ill; I have been nursing him; I am so used to doing this and it fills the time, besides.

Last night the girls slept on the floor as there were no beds ready. Their luggage was taken to the guard room downstairs. Alexei is in Marie's former bed, and I am sitting beside him. Getting into it he knocked his knee and thus he groaned terribly all night – no-one else had a wink of sleep. Nicky looks grey and exhausted today: 'Sometimes I think he does it on purpose.' Still – poor suffering Baby! He is asleep at the moment, and I sit watching his face as I did when he was really a child, deep in innocent slumber. It's not a child's face any more: it is angular and at the moment too pale, half-frowning even in sleep. 'Mama,' Alexei wept, ill in Tobolsk before we left, 'let me die! I'm not afraid to die! I'm afraid of what they will do to us here!'

His coming was so auspicious for Russia and all: cheered the whole difficult summer of 1904. On a personal level too it was a great joy: it reaffirmed my faith in myself after the miscarriage which was so nasty and alarming. August 1902, that was: I'd been pregnant as far as am I aware for nine months (fact is, M.B. never came back after I stopped nursing Anastasia, and at the same time as that happened I began to feel sick again). I'd not seen a doctor (why should I? - I was an old hand by then, and the majority of women don't see doctors when they are pregnant - it's not an illness!) and although the baby didn't seem as lively as the others had done I had no reason to think anything was wrong. But then instead of a baby, M.B. turned up as if it had never been absent; I went to the doctors and was told that there was no pregnancy, I was simply anaemic. They were wrong, of course (unbelievably!): next day I had a miscarriage, but the baby was so tiny one might have supposed it a two months child - whereas I knew I'd carried it for nine. 'Missed abortion' I think the horrible term is. Either that or I had genuinely been anaemic for the first seven months but somehow it had been conceived anyway - no-one could give a proper explanation. Something went badly wrong, perhaps it simply failed to grow.

We were absolutely miserable: what an end to nine months of waiting! - Though it could have been worse: imagine how awful if the child had been still-born a normal size! Petersburg society of course had its own explanation: seems I'd had a false, 'hysterical' pregnancy as a result of wishful thinking. Xenia came to sympathise with me on this: she believed it too! - But - why would I? - False pregnancies are what barren women have: I never had the slightest problem getting pregnant, myself.

The person widely blamed for all of this was our first friend, M. Philippe, who was nothing but a kind, simple man, who talked to us about God and life and his thoughts on both. Certainly his views were theosophical in the broadest sense of the word: he was interested in all religions and in their expression, and his medical practice led to him being prosecuted by the French government because he stepped beyond the bounds of the conventional rationalist European and as a result he wasn't licensed. This upset the bigots, and Petersburg society talked the most unbelievable rubbish about him: he was supposed to claim that he could change the sex of a child in the womb: hence it seems he convinced us that I was about to produce an heir when I wasn't even pregnant. Ella cross-examined us about all of this: she could not accept him as nothing more than a lay-preacher in the Russian tradition. 'He isn't Russian,' she said, as if that meant anything at all!

In retrospect I suppose this was the beginning of the difficulties between Ella and us, but at the time it wasn't that important: we saw her infrequently and all was usually calm and normal. From 1900 we were going to Moscow for Easter every year, because the atmosphere was better than in ghastly Petersburg: this event and a brief period in winter when they came to the capital for parties was all we really saw of Ella and Serge. The children had fun in Moscow: they ran through the Kremlin museums and climbed in the coaches. 'I want this one!' Olga would order, 'Have it brought back home for me!'

For all my efforts, she was difficult and imperial around six years old; I worried about the effect of their isolated existence. They none of them, for one thing, had the slightest conception of what money was for, or any understanding of commercial transactions. When Olga and Tatiana first visited a toy shop in Darmstadt - they couldn't go in shops in Russia of course - they seemed frightened to choose anything. 'If we take the toys, won't the little girl they belong to notice?' they asked. 'Then we shall get into trouble.' When eventually they were persuaded to buy something, the owner passed them change across the counter, and Olga laughed, 'Why are you giving me money?'

Their father is not much different. For all the spartan simplicity of his upbringing, he has always been astonishingly naïve about financial matters. For one thing he used to boast to the dandies on the *Standart* that he wears cotton socks (theirs were silk!) and they are sometimes darned to save money. On the other hand, he used every Easter to commission two eggs from Fabergé, one for me and one for Motherdear, without even thinking to inquire what they cost! When I teased him about this, he used to tip his head back and screw up his eyes in that smile and say, 'Well, I never was a businessman.' He also used to select jewelry for me from displays that the shop-owners brought him periodically; again he bought on the basis of what he liked without thinking twice. Bless the pet – I used to laugh, 'Oh, bad Boy – how you do spoil me!' – but I wasn't having him do this for the children, who are so impressionable. When each was born, we started making them a necklace by setting aside one pearl. At birthdays and Christmas thereafter, another would be added until the necklace was complete at sixteen, and then they would be given it. Until then if they wore any jewelry at all apart from their watches, it was coral or cheap glass beads. That is plenty for little girls.

Eventually we started to give them pocket money, and they were to understand that was all they got. From such a fund they had to buy their own note-paper and presents for friends, and – later – their own soap and scent. Not until they were twenty did we plan give them any power over the household funds I administered in their names, and which paid the salaries of their nannies and bought their clothes, and so on. This way, perhaps, I succeeded in bringing them down to earth? – But some are more so than others by nature. Marie always had the simplest tastes and the most open, friendly manner; her brother also is so careful with his funds that one might call him stingy! It was Tatiana who always showed the most interest in clothes and pretty things, on the whole. When she was quite tiny she would come down to me in the morning and demand to choose my dress and to brush my hair for me, and help put it up. Personally I had rather do without the fuss! Why can't clothes just be simple and functional and easy to put on?! – I remember my dear friend

159

Lili coming to see me once in one of those ridiculous hobble skirts - looked like she could barely walk, so I made her run in it, and sure enough the silly narrow hem of it tripped her up immediately! The only thing I think I really care about is having fine nightdresses and underthings - and of course that is not exclusively for my own benefit.

My beautiful, graceful Tatiana was popular with the public quite early on. Once I remember we were driving in Tsarskoe from the station to our house, and a little crowd got around the carriage and cheered the children and tried to touch them. Tatiana gave them a long, thoughtful look with those dreamy-looking eyes, and then she put her tongue out. This was greeted with delight; they could see she was just a normal, natural little girl. (Nevertheless I was angry with her.) She took eagerly to people outside the family (Olga, alas, was shy), and we used to find her at parties in a circle of little admirers, happily bossing them all around. When she was five we had a state visit from the Prince of Siam; Tatiana circled around him with a big smile, looking him up and down. 'Shake hands with the gentleman,' I told her. 'That's not a gentleman,' she retorted, 'it's a monkey!' - I was excruciatingly embarrassed. - 'So are you a monkey, Tatiana!' - But the good gentleman was very amused, they became the best of friends at once.

Olga was about five when we started to look for tutors. At first we had Piotr Vasilievich for mathematics and Russian; Miss Eagar and I dealt with English between us, not always very diligently, I have to admit. The big pair were on the whole rather good students: Olga had natural talent, and Tatiana great perseverance. (The little ones on the other hand are all exceedingly lazy). Olga, in fact, seemed to be good at more or less everything she did. She drew well, she had a sweet little singing voice (where did she get a soprano!? - the last soprano on my side was dear Granny! and her paternal grandmother is a contralto too) and she is the only one to have properly mastered the grammatical structure of all the languages she speaks. Klavdia Bitner who taught them in Tobolsk had plenty to say about the standard of the Russian spoken and above all written by the others; I know for myself how imperfect their English spelling can be.

In Moscow in 1903, Olga made her first confession. This was quite a day for us: she had symbolically reached the age of reason.

1903 was also the year of the canonisation of St Serafim, when we made our great journey to his hermitage at Sarov and were greeted on all sides by the real people of Russia. What with one thing and another - pregnancies, children's illnesses, the daily grind of ministers and papers - we had not until then had much of a chance to visit the deep countryside and see something of the real nation. It was a marvelous experience: one feels refreshed by contact with people from outside the horrible city circles; people with serious concerns and genuine lives to lead.

Serafim was a popular saint, a true *starets* or holy man who had lived simply according to monastic rule and was revered by the whole nation. He was a healer too; he had reputedly healed members of our family even - Nicky's great-grandmama, my namesake Alexandra. It was so important to us in every way that he be glorified: it would be a sign to the people that the Church was a living force in Russia still, and responsive to the will of the Believers, the true Russian people. Without this holy unity of people, Church and Tsar, there can be no real Russia, and no real Church either: I understand how this is historically true as well as true in a spiritual sense, and Nicky and I were so eager to show it.

We had discussed before we went that we intended to bathe in the stream outside the hermitage, where Serafim had been wont to cure people. I had been in Russia long enough now that I should be able to do such Orthodox things without feeling strange, and we wanted to be sure that the miscarriage the previous year would leave no lasting physical effect. Certainly the doctors would not be able to help, they had been hopeless in their diagnosis anyway. So we went into the water together the evening after the canonisation, with no-one else around – though God knows the police can't have been that far away – and I emerged with such a sense of calm and elation and such joy that we had been able to share this experience. (Not all the sensations evoked by being out of doors in the water at night with my darling husband were holy ones – so naughty in a place like that!)

By Christmas I knew that I was pregnant, although we didn't tell many people in case something went wrong again. I said I had 'flu as an excuse to stay away from beastly parties when I was feeling sick. That was the last season of parties ever scheduled in the Winter Palace, and pretty soon they were cancelled, because of the war: - - As I remember we had just got back from the theatre on 23rd January when Nicky was given the telegram telling him that the Japanese Navy had sailed unannounced into Port Arthur and torpedoed three of our ships. No-one could believe it; all the world knew that Japan was upset by Russia's protection of Korea, which they regarded as theirs by right – but to deliberately start a war! – In the morning Palace Square was full of students cheering and singing hymns and shouting abuse about the Japanese. Nicky went to the window and saluted them, but I knew what it cost him. In 1898 he'd been called by some 'Nicholas the Pacific' because of the Hague Disarmament Conference. Part of the aim of the Far Eastern policy had been to break the traditional militaristic approach to expanding ones spheres of influence. Yet now he had to send men off to lose their lives.

– Neither of us had any real experience of a country at war. Nicky as a little child had seen his father go off to be involved in one of the endless skirmishes in the Balkans, which had however almost no impact on life in Petersburg; I had never even seen that much. Pretty soon though the capital was full of grey troop trains, of white-clad doctors and of regiments in their drab winter greatcoats: we were not so stupid that we had thought modern war would look like the colourful spectacle presented by paintings a hundred years old, but the devastation was more total than anyone had anticipated. Our Pacific Fleet was besieged in Port Arthur from the beginning: there soon came that day when the *Petropavlovsk* - the flagship, the pride of the fleet - made a valiant attempt to break through the minefields and was blown to pieces. Only around six men survived in all, and one of them was cousin Kirill, whose first action on being taken ashore was to have violent hysterics. He has never been on active service since; such a terrible experience, one would sympathise if he were a nicer more humble man.

I was at least able to turn the ballrooms of the Winter Palace into something useful - they became workrooms, where people could sit to make clothes and bandages for the army and navy. I liked to join in with this, and to my surprise some of Petersburg society agreed to join me. Even the precious children were commissioned into the war effort: they sat frame knitting in the afternoons, turning out scarves - and Anastasia not even three years old.

In July the internal troubles started with the murder of Plehve - that could have happened any time, there had been a spate of terrorist attacks even before the war started - and the consequent elevation of Mirsky to Minister of the Interior. What a mistake that was! - He was Motherdear's friend and nomination; she appeared at Peterhof to argue that he must be given the post if the government wasn't to lose the confidence of 'educated society'. Plehve it seemed had been widely regarded in the upper echelons as a brute; Witte warned him said Motherdear that he was making his own assassination inevitable. Still, no matter what the necessity for reform, we shouldn't have set about it during a war. We so hoped that Motherdear was right about the line to take, but Mirsky proved an absolute disaster, a real effete aristocrat who ran about fussing over trifles when he should have been taking energetic steps to accomplish the big things. His meagre reforms served no purpose except to raise expectation and make the strikes and discontent that inevitably follow from a nasty war worse than ever. My father-in-law would have been shocked if he'd seen his dear Minnie push such a man into such a position; but Motherdear never did have any coherent political strategy – it was all a matter of personalities with her.

Ella and Serge were visiting us at Peterhof, and they were in despair. Very sensibly in retrospect, he said that reforms should be planned, and should come in peacetime when the government was strong and invulnerable. She seemed to me to be a condition of near collapse; she kept talking about the need to shoot and imprison strikers and terrorists '*pour encourager les autres*' and Serge ticked her off unpleasantly several times for being emotional, illogical and feminine. I was very worried about her; there were troubles in Moscow and it seemed to be preying on her nerves – she who had always been so calm.

On July 30th we were at lunch with them when I started getting strong pains; I went upstairs and Baby dear was born less than an hour later, weighing 11 and a half pounds. He was the easiest birth of all, but he was a huge splendid boy, barrel-chested and fair, with a nose and chin like mine, and his father's cheekbones and straight eyebrows. Xenia when she saw him said he looked like a warrior knight!

From Peterhof one can hear the guns firing in Petersburg; I lay there in bed after his birth and counted them and imagined the joy on the streets when people heard the 102nd shot, then the 103rd, all the way up to 300, and realised they'd got a Tsesarevich at last. A ray of sunshine for Russia in the middle of the horrible war.

Because of the war we named the whole Army as his godfathers (Irène, also born in a war, had Papa's regiment as hers, this was our

164

precedent). We also for good international relations asked Uncle Bertie and William, and then Alexei's great-grandfather King Christian. Our Olga aged eight was a godmother to her brother – all of the girlies were at the christening wearing miniature court dress and looking adorable – the elder two slim and dainty, the little ones so chubby you could eat them! – We were as usual in agony about the christening because with each successive birth the people who carried the baby during the ceremony got older and older. By the time it was Alexei's turn there was a real danger that the ancient Metropolitan and Princess Golitsyn would between them manage to drop him into the font! And the name – well, that was for an ancestor this time: Nicky wanted the boy named after Alexis the Mild, the *tishaishii tsar*. And it was good to break the endless cycle of Nicholases and Alexanders and Michaels in the family.

CHAPTER TEN

Ludwig stood proxy godfather for Uncle Bertie, and he and Victoria were also present with us at the blessing of the Baltic Fleet in October, when it set off on its journey round to Asia to relieve the poor Pacific Fleet. The miracle is that Ludwig's presence received no negative comment at all in the British press; in those days it was accepted that he was not going around Europe betraying Naval secrets but that Uncle Bertie had sent him to Petersburg to smooth over problems. England's attitude to the war hurt Nicky deeply: of course as Ludwig said they were allies of the Japanese and as such they could hardly be overtly friendly to us, but the Japanese alliance itself had been an aggressive act aimed at Russia whose influence in the Far East was so resented by London. Thus not only did England refuse to allow Russian ships to refuel in British ports, but she prevailed upon France – our ally but hers too now of course – to say the same thing. Only Germany showed us any friendship at all in this war which we didn't start, and her motives for doing so were purely selfish anyway.

No sooner had Ludwig gone back to London after trying to explain England's position than the terrible Dogger Bank incident occurred and brought us to the brink of war. I know people think it sounds ludicrous – how could the Russian Fleet possibly mistake a squadron of English fishing boats for the Japanese Navy, even in heavy fog? – but there was at the time very good evidence that the Japanese were indeed operating in disguise in peculiar places such as the English Channel – the Port Arthur attack itself is evidence that they were good at slipping unnoticed into places where they shouldn't have been. Of course this does not excuse the Russian Fleet steaming away in a hurry when it realised that it had accidentally fired upon civilian ships and killed some men; but the latter in its turn was a crime in strictly human terms, and no reason for the British Fleet to give chase as they did. Thank God for the Court of Arbitration, and also for Uncle Bertie, who effectively called his Navy off. As a result of the Court session Russia paid reparations to the families of the men killed, as was only appropriate, but also to Britain, which in my view wasn't. Ironic, really, that the Court of Arbitration established as a direct result of Nicky's Hague Disarmament Conference came to rule against Russia; but this is the objectivity one would hope to find in such a body.

Nevertheless the feeling about England remained in Russia very bad indeed; in May the next year when the Baltic Fleet was annihilated by the Japanese at Tsushima, it was recalled bitterly and often that the British had built the Japanese Navy. It goes without saying what this did for my popularity in Motherdear's beloved 'educated society'. I was used to this from Uncle Vladimir; now, though, Sandro was also aggressively anti-England, and he made this known every time we saw him.

Sandro and Xenia were with us at dinner on February 4th. I remember that Nicky was trying to steer the conversation away from political topics, saying peaceably, 'What will happen, will happen. In the end it's God's will and there's only a limited amount you or I can do to change it.' Sandro was laughing. 'What is this, Nicky?! – You call yourself a Christian! – Some of the things you say sound to me like pure Islamic fatalism!' Nicky laughed too, 'And you, Alessandro – for your part, you're a megalomaniac.' Everyone was in a jolly mood; I have to admit we'd broken our usual rules about excessive alcohol consumption and we'd been drinking port for a while; even us ladies had a few glasses. Sandro always tended to have that effect on parties, though – man of the world that he is. 'Well,' he said 'how can we put our respective worldviews to the test?' Nicky moved across to the sofa near the door. 'I am going to sit here, and we shall see whether you can remove me with your active intervention, or whether it's God's will that I remain.' So Sandro seized him by the arm and tried to drag him onto the floor; but Nicky got hold of the back of the sofa with his other hand and stayed in place though he was laughing ridiculously much. Sandro then tried to tip him off but that didn't work either. 'Alix - help me! How can I shake the passivity of this husband of yours?' Nicky pointed at me and threatened 'Don't you dare betray me!' so I did. 'Subtle methods first - tickle him, Sandro!' He took my advice and thus Nicky fell onto the floor in a matter of moments - and it was around this point I believe that we were interrupted by old Fredericks coming to tell us that Serge had been blown to pieces crossing Red Square.

Poor dear Ella: she heard the bomb go off and she ran out of the house knowing at once what had happened, to find the remains of her husband scattered bleeding in the snow. Oh God, I can't imagine anything more horrible!! - And according to what witnesses said she started gathering him up in the folds of her dress and crying out, 'Hurry! Serge hates mess!'

The police and the Ministers absolutely forbade us to go to Moscow for the funeral; they were thinking what was all too close to the surface of my mind too - that it could have been Nicky. Serge's murder was just a month after that awful Blessing of the Waters ceremony and Bloody Sunday - the whole winter just a catalogue of horrors. Was the Blessing of the Waters not even the very same weekend as Bloody Sunday? - Because Mirsky's panic and indecision over the former effectively caused the latter. Of course the city had been on strike, and Mirsky was flapping about the reception Nicky would get when he appeared in public. As matters turned out, he was well-received by the people of Petersburg. I was standing behind the window in the Winter Palace (I wasn't due to appear: it was nearly time for Baby's feed) and I heard how they cheered when he walked onto the Embankment with Motherdear beside him. Then the ice was cut and the priest blessed the river and one started firing the salute. All of a sudden I saw the policeman near Nicky fall to the ground; then there was splintering crash as one of the windows of the Palace broke and I could see people running in all directions down below. Motherdear fainted but Nicky just stood there calmly and the salute went on and the ceremony was over. After that I ran to meet him as he came back inside and I flung my arms round him and held him so close I thought my muscles would seize up forever. My darling Treasure - that was the second attempt on his life, though Mirsky's investigation said different - claimed that a live shell had been loaded purely by accident into the cannon!

We went directly back to Tsarskoe as we'd planned anyway, and two days later were told by Mirsky that a march was planned by some petitioners on the Winter Palace and he had ordered troops into the city to deal with any trouble. What he should have done of course was arrange for Nicky to meet a group of the petitioners; but Nicky wasn't told until it was too late to go to town and the situation was hideously volatile. Thus the next morning the people marched on the Palace and the troops fired on them to make them retreat (fearing thousands would be crushed otherwise) and 92 people were killed and there was the most appalling international scandal. Undoubtedly that 'liberal' Mirsky behaved like a complete idiot and the direct result was a huge rash of strikes and marches; however the foreign politicians and press in their turn were vilely hypocritical about the whole thing: it was used above all in England to demonstrate the moral bankruptcy of the tsarist regime. This in spite of the fact that I remember the first Bloody Sunday: the Trafalgar Square dem-onstrations of '87, when English troops shot at and rode over hundreds of unarmed demonstrators. I don't know why it is that when a similar atrocity occurs in Russia it is always deemed four times worse, and why they had to imagine that Nicky was in the Palace and had personally ordered the shootings and watched it all. Thus Serge's murder was just one more hideous thing, although the most personally painful because of the effect on Ella as much as anything. Poor Serge - he had his faults (he was it is true cold and arrogant as Sandro always said), but he was cultured and consistent and she was nothing without him: he guided her intellectually, politically and spiritually and he showered her with jewelry and her one function while Serge lived was to appear beautiful beside him. She didn't even have a say over how her own house was decorated - maybe that's why she took an interest in ours!

Practically her first act after the arrest of the murderer was to visit him in jail to try to convince him how wrong he'd been, and she offered to pray for his soul, because Serge was so concerned with the afterlife and redemption. A rumour went round later of course that she'd offered to intercede with Nicky to spare the man the death penalty if he'd only confess that he'd been wrong; this is part of Ella's personal hagiography and completely untrue - it would have been so out of character for one of her (i.e. Serge's) political views. 'I have nothing to do with earthly justice,' she always says. For a long long time after the murder she was a pathetic lost figure: one feared she'd never get through it. Eventually though she filled the house with nurses and with soldiers wounded in the war. She participated herself and used her own and Serge's carriages to take the men for drives when they were convalescing. Thus she was terribly criticised by the likes of Aunt Miechen and her sons for 'spoiling' them, but we her family were glad that she found something useful to do at last.

Meanwhile 1905 carried on getting worse. In May came the battle at Tsushima, from which the splendid Baltic Fleet emerged with just three ships left. This is what happens when two modern Navies face each other: no-one sails away in defeat. The world should have learned something from this, but it didn't.

At this point the Army's reinforcements reached the Far East and prepared to engage Japan in land war. In spite of their spectacular success so far, the Japanese could not go on indefinitely; this was our great hope. Victory would have stopped the internal situation from getting any worse. However, Roosevelt intervened at this point with his suggestions for a Peace Conference. Witte was sent along because whatever his other faults he was not a man to give in easily; he laid down terms so stringent that no-one expected Japan to accept them. Sounds terrible to say it, but – it's a shame they did. A few more weeks of ghastly war would have been Russia's salvation. However Witte came back as the broker of an honourable peace, full of scathing comments about the United States and the uncivilised ways of its citizens (he hated the food and didn't like the fact that they drank water at dinner; I heard later from Uncle Bertie who was great friends with Teddy Roosevelt that the latter had in turn found Witte arrogant and vain – as good an analysis as any I have heard!).

One truly good thing came out of it all: Roosevelt suggested that the Hague Conference be reconvened, so in 1907 Nicky formally called it and we went through the second round of unsuccessful disarmament talks. There was scheduled to be a third in 1915 – how ironic! – But the principle is there and established now, and maybe one day – one day! – it will bear some fruit. As will the Court of Arbitration.

In the meantime the main threat was England, alas. Our *Standart* cruise that summer was not its usual calm self- Nicky wouldn't be permitted any rest at all in that dreadful year. We knew before we left that William would be coming aboard at Björkö for discussions of the international position and as I feared he sprang up the ladder from his electric launch with a great big smile, seizing hold of Alexei and bouncing him in his arms: – 'So – my little godson! Such a fine strapping lad! And have you used your gold mug yet that Uncle Willy gave you as a christening gift?'

I said he hadn't; it didn't seem quite appropriate for the nursery. William laughed loudly and answered to Alexei, 'Never mind, my boy – In a few years, eh? – you'll come to Berlin and Uncle Willy will give you your own Prussian regiment and you can drink wine from your cup. Mark my words Alexei – he who does not enjoy wine, women and song remains a fool all his life! As you will learn to say one fine day, *Wer nicht liebt Wein, Weib und Gesang, der bleibt ein Narr sein Lebenslang!*' I wanted to turn away in disgust, listening to his silly boasting, so at variance with the way he truly lives his life!

– As soon as William had released our Sunbeam, I took the children ashore out of his way and the big girls fished from a jetty all afternoon while the little ones made mud pies at the edge of the water. Alexei tried to help, but at that time his idea of using a spade was to stick the tip of it into the wet sand and then thoughtfully flick the whole thing upwards so that everyone was showered with mud. Marie, Anastasia and he finished up filthy, soaking and shrieking with laughter. When we got back to the yacht, Nicky and William were still talking in one of the cabins. I had tea with some of the dear officers, and eventually Nicky came and sat on the back of the cane chair next to me with his feet in the seat. I remember I smiled up at him and said, 'You wouldn't do that if it was you that had to wash the cushions.' – but he didn't seem to be listening. He lit a cigarette and said slowly, 'Sunny, I've got us a treaty with the Germans.'

– Several months earlier there had been talks about a possible treaty, a draft had been made, but nothing had been concluded. It now emerged that William had brought the text with him now, and that Nicky had signed to make sure it wasn't suddenly withdrawn, although he wanted it kept secret until he'd talked to the ministers and above all to the French ambassador. – 'I don't know – he tries to be friendly, but he has this amazing instinct for putting my back up every time he opens his mouth! – You know, he said to me when I hesitated to sign without consulting first, "Nicky, if only you knew what a battle I have had to bring my ministers to heel! You simply can't go inviting them to share your power - you'll have no end of trouble later! - Just be thankful that you are thus far still a true autocrat - make your own decisions!" Sometimes with him around, it's as bad as listening to the uncles!'

William went back to Berlin and was faced by the threatened resignation of Chancellor Bulow. So much for the autocrat he actually believes himself to be.

My poor Nicky also was terribly harangued by the ministers; no-one believed that such a treaty could be activated without upsetting France and possibly breaking the alliance. Perhaps they were right, but they had in no way tested the waters yet for France's reaction as Nicky had intended. Thus Russia withdrew with some embarrassed little coughs from that treaty, as if poor Nicky had done something stupid by trying to form a protective bloc against the aggressive power of England and Japan so they would be wary of starting anything new. And if all had been ratified beastly Germany which in the end has turned out to be the biggest threat of all would have been neutralised at the same time.

Instead, the next year, we ended up in the Triple Entente of France, England and Russia, which felt more natural to me perhaps - but which has allowed William to spout screeds of bosh about being 'encircled'. (Encirclement nevertheless might as everyone believed have deterred him from starting a war if he'd been any less mad and Prussian.)

The whole of 1905, all this ghastly war and politics stuff hung over our sweet family life like a dark cloud; Nicky and I could never put it entirely from our minds even when we were alone with our five little chicks. From time to time we had to leave them (only the second time I had ever done this) and attend military reviews in different parts of the country - which of course was frightfully interesting and gave us a rare chance to see the real Russia, just like when we went to Sarov. - This was the year wasn't it that Zhilik joined the household as French tutor to Olga and Tatiana - though at first of course they called him respectfully, 'M. Gilliard'! - I sat in the classroom with them for the first few weeks, partly to make sure that they had books out ready to begin when the poor man arrived, because otherwise they'd have certainly tried to delay. Our Olga of course took to French straight away; when he explained the purpose of the auxiliaries, she listened carefully, and then observed, 'I see, Monsieur - the auxiliaries are the servants of the verbs. It's only poor avoir which has to shift for itself!' He liked her brains and her cheek and I saw that he could handle her sulky moods and Tatiana's occasional tendency to tell fibs, so I withdrew from the lessons and sent one of the ladies instead. I felt for one thing that my presence made Zhilik nervous. Marie was at this time taking her first lessons in the other classroom - always a little alone, poor middle child, because the result of this was the bond of sympathy which developed between the two babies left in the nursery and shut her out a bit. When eventually we sent Anastasia to the classroom as well, Alexei's great joy was to break in on one or another pair of sisters and disrupt the lessons, racing round desks and laughing until he was captured and carried off. It hurts me to realise it - but for all her calm, even personality, Marie always bore little scars from her middle child's position. If needled or scolded by the older girls, Anastasia would put out her tongue and run off and climb a tree; Marie however used sometimes to burst into tears and wail, 'Nobody loves me!' - and she was pathetically eager to please them: - 'Mama, Mama - don't you think Olga and Tania are old enough to have their own rooms now?' - and - later - 'Mama, don't you think Olga would like to let down her skirts?' Olga and Tatiana exploited this mercilessly; when she followed them around with the look of adoration in her huge blue eyes, they said, 'Oh, look, it's that puppy again - that fat little *toutou*.' My Mashka, my steadfast support and comfort – I hope you realise at last that you are every bit as precious as the other four.

By some miracle, I almost forgot!: – before peace was concluded came the ghastly mutiny of the sailors on the Potemkin; all the officers were murdered, the whole world was shocked and most of Crimean ports had to placed under marshal law as a result. Concluding peace with the Japanese as the victors did not help the situation in any way at all. There were riots and murders all over the Caucasus and in Moscow, and to our eternal shame several members of the family started preparing to flee Russia. Sandro and Xenia were among them. (Wonder where Sandro and Xenia are now? – Quite likely that they really have left this time.). Other members of the family starting acting as it were the end of the world and behaved in a way that just caused Nicky further anxiety at that terrible time: – this was the summer of Kirill and Ducky's sudden marriage, and also of Misha's little scandal with the girl Dina, which kept Motherdear much exercised throughout the year in case he took it upon himself to marry her.

One day on the way to Gatchina to see Motherdear, Misha fell asleep at the wheel of his motor and overturned it in a ditch – could have killed his sister Olga too as she was beside him, but astonishingly neither was hurt at all. Just everything about Misha confirmed to me how important it was to have Baby, to keep the throne out of such unsuitable, feckless hands. But he was a charmer, though! – The children adored him. He used to tear packs of cards in half just to amuse them. (He has his father's great strength: Nicky remembers the latter bending pokers for them, and knotting a silver fork at the dinner table to throw it at the Austrian ambassador who had no doubt annoyed him with some comment about the Balkans.) Most people we talked to insisted that the common theme of all the riots and troubles that year was a demand for representative government. Allegedly this had to do with the failure of the autocratic government to deliver victory in war. Mirsky's half-hearted reforms raised expectations without actually delivering much change and thus didn't help at all: people felt they needed more radical change and probably with the government weak and discredited they could get this by violence. Only a wavering government would have appointed Mirsky in the first place.

My poor darling Nicky. He spent hours and hours alone with the ministers discussing the options. Very strongly he felt and I felt – knowing what we knew about small towns and the countryside from personal experience and from letters we receive and even more so from reading – that those who made such demands were a decided minority, city-based and usually well-educated. It annoyed me to think that the legitimate aspiration of the striking workmen to better conditions were being exploited for political reasons by various constitutional activists.

Nevertheless the options were limited; this vocal minority made life difficult for everyone. One could do two things: suppress it roughly for the sake of the peace of the rest of the country, or give in to its demands. Motherdear along with her high society friends was in the latter camp – although had my late father-in-law been alive in 1905 he'd have very decidedly done the former – no doubt about that at all. How her views had changed without him there! She urged Witte upon us, saying he was the one man who could act as Prime Minister through a period of great change. Nikolasha, hard man of the Army, who might have been considered for the post of military dictator if the other path was to be followed, told half the family that he would shoot himself in Nicky's study unless Witte were appointed and a parliament convened. 'It is all very well for Nikolasha,' Nicky said sadly. 'He can make these gestures and try experiments and never mind the consequences. I, on the other hand, have a responsibility before God for the future of this country and I can't take precipitate steps.' Nevertheless he was persuaded by their arguments in the end: this was the only way to lead Russia out of chaos. Thus he signed the 17th October manifesto and we got the Duma which was a thorn in his flesh ever after and the cause of so many of this country's present problems. Neither did Witte deliver the peace that he promised.

Nicky never really liked this man, so arrogant and vain, who caused so many problems for the cities in the rushed way he industrialised when he was Minister of Finance, and who had also shown himself so uninterested in the problems of the rural population. Briefly at the turn of the century, Nicky started to meet with all the ministers together in the hope that this would make them act in unity and we wouldn't have this endless problem of one department trying to cancel the orders of another directly a decision had been taken. On one occasion Witte and a colleague started a huge row right there front of him - screaming and bellowing at each other as if the person they served was not even present. Thus Nicky left the room and the result was that people said he had no stomach for a fight. So unfair! - Surely the biggest fight of all is the battle to keep oneself in hand and behave well and courteously and come to agreements? - and it's just such a shame the ministers couldn't manage to do likewise. They so often forget that they serve the country and not their own careers. (In the end, it seems you actually have to treat them like my father-in-law did: when one threatened to resign in a fit of pique, he took him by the lapels and bellowed, 'You will resign only when I tell you your work is done!')

Witte in 1905 began his job as Russia's first proper Prime Minister in a mood of pacification; but when the manifesto failed to produce instant peace he changed his colours and tried to hang and shoot everyone. In the end he lost the confidence of the entire country and above all of the person who had been persuaded to trust him to bring in sensible, planned reform. Such different personalities - but Witte acted like Mirsky all over again.

The first Duma opened in April 1906 in the Winter Palace, and at first it seemed that all might go well. The electorate was deeply unrepresentative, of course: such a lot of deputies from Petersburg and Moscow, and so few from the peasant majority. However I had planned a ceremony to welcome them to government, which involved a church service in the St George Hall with the deputies and ministers. Motherdear, Xenia, the other Grand-Duchesses, the ladies and I were in court dress; Nicky and the ministers and the men of the family wore uniform. When this was over he went to a platform and the throne and read a speech asking them to come to aid in bringing new peace and prosperity to Russia. Motherdear and I stood on the platform in front of him; naturally, she sobbed loudly throughout his speech.

Nicky's voice was loud and firm. (I have only once seen him give an address that showed any anxiety or nervousness, and that was very early in his reign – the 'senseless dreams' speech to the Tver town council when he told them that he would preserve the autocracy as his father had done. Serge was behind that speech but I got the blame as usual amongst those who disagreed with its sentiments.) At the end of the speech a cheer broke out in the Hall, then this spread to adjacent halls where loads of spectators were standing, and echoed huge and magnificent around the Palace. I couldn't help it: I was sobbing like Motherdear does, and poor Nicky was too, we were all so moved by such a display after the terrible times the country had passed through. So we left the Hall, and the Duma went to its permanent home in the Tauride Palace, and immediately the mood changed and the fighting and speechifying and histrionic gestures began, and the disorders in the country continued. Hence Witte commenced his embittered retirement, resulting eventually in a set of self-justifying memoirs which did Nicky who had no means of replying a lot of harm in the eyes of public opinion. One day, my love, you will write your own story for the world to see - and if you don't then Sunny will do it for you!

Oh, I hate to think of all this - but in a way it helps - aids understanding of what has happened and why.

- Things started to quieten down when dear old Goremykin was returned as Prime Minister and Stolypin became Minister of the Interior. Stolypin faltered at the end, but for five years he gave sterling service - the man who finally addressed the peasant poverty problem and started selling them state land very cheaply like horrible Witte refused to do in case he couldn't get the money back. Also dealt very firmly indeed with arson and political murder - ended with the press calling the hangman's noose 'Stolypin's necktie'! - Beastly painful job, but he was the man to do it. And time after time he confronted and defeated the Duma who repaid the trust Nicky had placed in them with such stupid bickering and arguing that one time they quite literally brought the roof down.

At Peterhof in the summer of 1906 one could still hear disorders going on: the Naval base at Kronstadt mutinied, and we got the sounds of gun shots right across the bay.

We had Paul's children with us a lot that summer. Ella's increasing devotion to nursing meant it was no longer so practical for them to live in Moscow with her. On the other hand, she had fought tooth and nail to keep them away from their father and his new wife, so her growing indifference to them left them in rather a hole. I felt terrible for the poor things; Nicky relaxed the rules relating to Paul's access, and we had them around us too whenever we could. Marie was already at this time sixteen years old and Dmitri fifteen and a cadet, so the problem didn't endure long: the next year Ella announced that Marie was engaged to William of Sweden, and could Nicky as emperor sanction the marriage? - So he agreed, a little surprised as the girl was so young - but after all, Alice Battenberg got married at 18, and that is a success. However poor Little Marie P. appeared at her wedding with red eyes from crying and she told any who'd listen that Ella was forcing her into a loveless relationship with a man she barely knew. All I can say in Ella's defence is that she didn't know Serge too well when she married him, but it worked in its own peculiar way, so maybe she expected the same thing to happen here. However she chose Serge of her own free will, and against quite a lot of opposition in fact.

Dmitri was sad to see his sister go; these two in their sad childhood clung together like Ernie and I did (though ours was not nearly so unhappy - at least we had Papa). Olga and Tatiana were too young to see the pathos of him: they looked up to Dmitri as a glamorous older cousin who took them on exciting bicycle rides around the park. He was most charming and golden-haired and athletic: one could see that he'd be big trouble before long! (And he has been: he has completely spoiled and wasted himself on loose Petersburg women.)

Our children were reaching their most enchanting age as a group. The eldest was ten that summer and the little one two. We have a film taken (their first as a complete group) as we boarded *Standart* for our little holiday: they are wearing sailor skirts with caps and reefer jackets and they come cascading in a row along the decks. Marie and Tatiana are holding Alexei's hands and all five are laughing delightedly. Suddenly they stop and jump round in a circle, and then Babykins hurls himself onto his back and sticks his solid little legs into the air. Really, such naturals before the camera! - Just like later when they did their plays for the family.

Still, Anastasia spent the summer getting into scrapes. Poor little *Shvibzik*, first she had diphtheria - can't imagine where she caught that. I took her across to the Farm and shut myself up with her and her injections of serum, and Nicky and the others remained at the Lower Dacha until she was well again. This is still a nasty disease, still has the potential to kill if not treated properly, and I couldn't help thinking while I nursed her of her

English grandmother and her Aunt May, whom she of course greatly resembled at that age.

Sometimes, curiously, when Anastasia looks at me sideways with a sly little smile, I see my mother in her face as well, although I can't picture a personality more different to poor Mama's gentle soul! She is, however, dreadfully temperamental, and that does come from Mama, however manifested. My poor mother was a sensitive, tortured soul; Anastasia like me and Victoria and like Olga takes offence and loses her temper far too easily. She terrorised all her little cousins from a very early age: they hated to play with her because she pulled hair and bit and scratched and she cheated if she felt she was losing a game. Adults on the other hand were inclined to spoil her because she is so amusing: already in '06 she had her little ritual when we boarded the yacht of crouching in the corner with her hands over her ears and such a hilarious expression of horror at the sound of the salute. Irène once said to me, 'Well, sister Sunny - you've got your own little *Prinzessin Sonnenschein* in this one.'

No sooner was she recovered from diphtheria than she almost drowned, swimming too far out to sea on quite a rough day. She always was fearless to the point of being foolhardy. A wave swept her under; closer to the shore everyone else resurfaced, but she didn't appear, and Nicky immediately flew off in the direction of where she last been, and dived down and pulled her back to the surface and the shore. Well, she was alright again pretty quickly, but it gave us a fright, and Sister Olga who is her godmother and loves her dearly said mawkishly, 'I do worry that that child isn't meant to be with us for long. Only five years old and already she's nearly died twice.' (The other time was of course when I was driving with her as a baby and the horses bolted - I had to jump out and seize them from in front, and thank god the precious little one lay unhurt on the seat all the while.)

Victoria was with us at Peterhof that summer, after an extended visit to Ella in Moscow. Victoria it was who looked long and hard at the bruises on my son's legs when he ran around in little white shorts, and she said quietly, 'Alix, does he always get such terrible big patches when he hurts himself?' – I said no – because he doesn't; most of the time his bruises look no different to any other child's. 'I spoke to Ostrogorsky our paediatrician about it when it happened before,' I reassured her. 'He thought it might be a touch of anaemia and he dosed him with iron.' 'It has happened before?' Victoria persisted. 'From time to time, yes. It worried me at first but it always goes away.' 'Alix, I have seen the exact same thing in other boys in our family. Don't you remember Toddy's bruises when he was this age? – I think you need a specialist blood doctor very fast – I don't want to alarm you, but it seems to me there's a strong likelihood that Alexei's got haemophilia.'

– In my heart, really, I had feared something like this. When Baby was three weeks old he bled for three days from the navel, but he was so healthy and cheerful throughout that episode that we told ourselves it was just a little vein the doctors had forgotten to tie off – and in any case the blood is quite prone to clot poorly for a few weeks after birth, isn't it? – Then there was the fact that his funny bruises were so intermittent. Irène's Toddy and poor little Henry whose haemophilia is much more severe than Alexei's used always to be black and blue when they were learning to walk – they looked as though someone had been mistreating them. So I took comfort from the ignorant diagnoses of the doctors and accepted Alexei might just need iron from time to time. – And something else: – no-one ever told me that a disease like this was a possibility. I remember Victoria sighing over Irène's boy and saying, – 'I told you not to marry your first cousin!' – we all thought that haemophilia was a sort of mutation that came from near relatives marrying each other; for that reason I never thought it would touch Nicky and me.

But yet somehow, even before Victoria spoke to me, I was half wondering whether we needed a specialist. Baby was growing extremely active and adventurous and he bruised more and more badly so no amount of iron could help him. We appointed the haematologist Derevenko to the household, and I had a long talk with him about it all and he told me about the hereditary pattern. 'It runs in families, and is passed through the women, though only the boys get it. I remember reading an article in the *Lancet* many years ago about Prince Leopold - Your Majesty's uncle, I believe? - which used the word haemophilia in connection with his poor health, though I haven't heard any reports that any of his brothers are also sufferers. Certainly King Edward seems to be in rude health! This is unusual - statistically half the sons of any woman who is carrying it - and Her Majesty Queen Victoria must have been carrying it - will have it and the other half not. Equally, half the daughters will carry it. Hence in Prince Leopold's generation your mother must have been one of those sisters affected, and passed it on to you and you tell me to Your Majesty's sister Princess Irène.' 'So Ernie was lucky not to get it,' I said.

    - Then I found out from Victoria something I had never known before - that Frittie our other brother had been a haemophiliac, although this tended to be forgotten because falling from an upper window would have killed any child. Victoria being the eldest knows most of our family's little secrets and most feared haemophilia of any of us, although even she did not understand how it was inherited. This is ironic, given that Victoria is the only one of us sisters to have produced two perfectly healthy boys.

    One thing is evident in all this: it is my fault that my child has this terrible problem. My fault too that statistically two of his sisters will go on to have haemophilic sons of their own. My fault that the Heir to Russia's throne was born with a high probability of not living to succeed. 'You should have married someone else who could have given you a healthy son,' I said to Nicky after this conversation. He sat next to me looking fiercely at his hands, and answered in a low voice. 'Just as you should have married someone who didn't stand a fair chance of being assassinated. – You could have lived in a quiet and peaceful country and not had to worry whenever your husband went to town whether you'd see him alive again. You could have had real friends instead court ladies who place etiquette before all else. You could have raised your children to do what they want to do in life instead what God has decreed they must do, like it or not. You needn't have even had a son. Sunny, I had no right to expect that any normal human being would ever marry me - you'd have to be mad or horrible to take on such a job willingly. But instead I got the most perfect being in all the world, who gave up her country and her religion and her peace of mind for my sake, who has given me five wonderful children - of course I am biased but I think I never saw such beautiful children anywhere - and who is my companion and my support in all that I do. I loathe being Emperor - I hate it and I always knew I would hate it, and if I didn't have you beside me I don't know that I'd have had the strength to carry on. So never never let me hear you say again that have failed me in any way, because it just kills me.'

The other thing Derevenko said was that the disease is incurable; it persists all their lives, although many haemophilic boys if they live thus long find they have fewer attacks when they stop growing. I have clung to this knowledge: the main thing has been to steer him through childhood without anything terrible happening, or any lasting damage. Irène's boys were a terrible warning of what could happen. When Alexei was two, Toddy was already seventeen, and even then had permanent problems with his joints because of repeated bleeding when he was a child: he feels stiff and arthritic on cold mornings and sometimes can barely walk even when he's not in the middle of a bleed. But still worse: little Henry died aged four from a cerebral haemorrhage, not long before Alexei was born.

However, even poor Irène has Bobby as well. Try as I might,

I can't help raging against fate that my only boy had to have haemophilia. Why was it Alexei, when there was a one in two chance that he might have been completely healthy!?

We decided very early that Alexei's illness would not be discussed within the Romanov family. The only person who knew was Nicky's sister Olga, who was so often with us. As far as the rest were concerned – and that included Motherdear and Xenia and Misha until it became unavoidable when he was about eight – he was just rather accident prone. There are several reasons for this. For one thing, if he is expected to grow up with a healthy mind, he needs not to be treated as an invalid by everyone he meets. At home it is different, at home he is just a son and a brother 90% of the time, so we can make allowances when we have to for his physical difficulties. To people outside the immediate family it is different: if they know about him, he comes to them as 'a haemophiliac' and not as a normal little boy who happens to have certain difficulties. This is very bad. When I think about it, I almost understand why Victoria was so brutal with Alice over her deafness, why no allowance was ever made – except that I still think Victoria went a little too far in behaving like that even at home.

Secondly, there were political, dynastic reasons for keeping the illness a secret. In 1906, the worst thing that could have happened would have been a revelation that the heir to the shaking throne had a potentially fatal disease. Thus keeping it from the wider family prevented it becoming known in the country at large.

And there was also pride. I could just imagine what Uncle Vladimir and Aunt Miechen and their dear sons would have to say about it all: 'So – Queen Victoria's granddaughter has brought this illness to the family. One almost wonders if it was British plot to destroy the dynasty.' Makes me angry – because the Romanov clan is hardly one that has been historically famed for its good health. Only Uncle Vladimir of the six sons of

185

Alexander II even made it to his sixtieth birthday. They have no room at all to be sneering at anyone else. My cousin Ena I know has taken haemophilia to the Spanish family, and her eldest son has the disease. Her husband - half a Habsburg, with all the insanity and physical frailties that implies! - has it seems had the gall to proclaim loudly that he doesn't feel he need be faithful to her any more, since, 'Through no fault of mine my heir has been born with a disease that came from my wife's family and not my own.' (There used to be rather a funny vulgar poem about Ena going around Uncle Bertie's set in the days when Alfonso was still interested and she had a baby every year: -

'*One month's pleasure; Eight months' pain. Three months' leisure; At it again! O, what a life, For the Queen of Spain*'.

There - that's cheered my thoughts up!)

CHAPTER ELEVEN

On the subject of having court ladies instead of friends, like Nicky said: - 1906 was the year I made the acquaintance of my dear Lili Dehn, who came to be introduced to me at Peterhof as a young lady about to marry one of our *Standart's* officers. She and Karl took a house in Tsarskoe when they returned from honeymoon and I saw as much of her as I could because she is a funny, sensible person who leads a simple life and is not part of the beastly court. In due course we were godparents to her little Alexander, as Titi is really named - in my honour.

Also Ania at this time was growing closer. She did a stint as a maid of honour in 1901, but I only really knew her a little later when I heard she was in difficulties with men. Ania it seems was in love with Nicky's dear true friend Alexander Orlov. At the same time she was being courted by that Vyrubov character, who I knew to be a Naval officer and a veteran of beastly Tsushima. He was also younger than Orlov, and as Anna was only twenty-two it seemed far more appropriate that she should marry him than a widower with children - who in any case did not really show much of an interest in her. Thus I recommended she accept Vyrubov's proposal, they got married, and one day when I was having tea at their place in Tsarskoe Vyrubov came home, the idiotic police didn't recognise him and refused him entry to his own house. Next day poor Alexander Taneyev came to see me in a terrible state and told me that his daughter had come home to him. Her husband had last night given her a dreadful beating as punishment for causing his exclusion.

I felt abominable. It was I who persuaded her to marry this man; turned out he was a drug addict and his nerves were completely shattered by Tsushima; he hadn't even managed to consummate the marriage, Ania said. She got an annulment and that summer I took her on the *Standart* with us – not as a lady-in-waiting or some such thing, but as a sad young woman who needed to recover from a terrible experience which was largely my fault. She joined our family walks ashore and our picnics with the ship's staff, and she sat with Nicky and me on deck in the evening while he read aloud or the band played balalaika music. The whole time she poured her heart out, and I eventually reciprocated. Ania is not the cleverest person in the world, and not even the nicest at times, but she is a simple soul, entirely guileless, whose prime motivation is her desire for affection. All of her virtues and all of her faults stem from this one need, which is such a refreshing change from the majority of people we know.

That was the summer we all but lost our beloved *Standart* – a great adventure, especially in retrospect! – If I remember right, we were moored a little way out to sea all afternoon because it was very hot and Nicky and the officers wanted to swim in deep water. The children, Ania and I went ashore and waded around amid the rocks for a while and took photographs (Olga had just been given her own camera, and I was instructing her).

When we got back on board the gentlemen were still in the sea a little way off, and I leant against the railing with a pair of field glasses, all alone, and watched my darling's naked athletic body as he glided through the shimmering water. Afterwards I hid the glasses because I didn't want Ania looking too! A little while later we were playing quoits with the girls on deck when I heard him whistle to me from the big saloon, and I felt my face get pink like always – so silly, an old married woman like me! – and I ran off to see him. He was now in white Naval officer's uniform, with white tennis shoes, which I adore. 'A little bird tells me you were out on deck with the binoculars earlier on,' he said, his lovely eyes twinkling. 'And if I was?' 'Well, how do I know that you weren't peeping at one of the gentlemen, eh?'

'You don't, my child. You'll just have to trust me.' 'With all these dangerous gentlemen about? Never!' 'In that case, how do I know that I can trust you with Ania? - Oh dear - am I going to regret bringing a pretty young lady on board?!' I put my hand over his eyes and added something like what I often say, 'I shall put you in dark glasses, I think, to keep all those gay butterflies from seeing your irresistible eyes. Maybe then I can keep you.' Nicky linked his arms round my waist and put his head on one side and said, 'You can keep me forever if you give me a kiss - but WITHOUT DELAY!' As if I ever need a second invitation! - We spent quite a long time then being totally blissful like we do when alone on a sunny afternoon.

I remember it all so well because we'd hardly emerged from the saloon when the entire yacht shuddered violently. Tables fell over, Ania's tea-cup flew out of her hand, the girls hurled themselves dramatically against the walls of the cabins. We had hardly steadied ourselves before the Little Admiral appeared and said we had hit a massive rock. He had radioed for help and fortunately it wasn't far away because we were followed at all times by a Naval destroyer.

The life-boats went down and we herded the girls and the non-Naval staff into them - the former with many protests - they didn't want to go; they were eager to be on board until the last. For a few moments it wasn't clear where Alexei was; last seen, he'd been playing on deck with a basket of kittens belonging to the 'ship's cat'. Tatiana was now holding the basket on her knees in the life-boat, and several of the others were pinning the struggling kittens down, but their brother was nowhere to be found. A look of panic spread across poor Ania's round pink face; she should have been watching him. However in a moment the sailor Derevenko, who in those days was his on-board *diadka*, appeared holding him by the hand; Alexei had just been to have his hands and face washed for tea. Nicky leant over the side watching the water creeping rapidly up, a stop-watch in his hand. He calculated that we had only twenty minutes. He and I wanted to be the last civilians to leave her, our poor wrecked beauty; in the meantime I pulled sheets off the beds and starting filling them with pictures and other irreplaceables from the cabins and salons.

We spent the night on board the destroyer, from where we could see the sad black hull of our beloved *Standart* slowly settle and sit still; she hadn't sunk completely after all. We were all filthy dirty and we slept in sailors' bunks. In the morning we had sad work keeping the children out of the engine room; they went wherever they pleased on the yacht, and they refused to understand that on a serving ship their presence might not be so welcome. Fortunately Motherdear turned up in the *Polar Star* and we transferred to that for the journey back to Russia. Even here the accommodation was inadequate for us all; I shared a single bed with Alexei, the girls were crammed two to a bed as well, Nicky was on a sofa, and Ania in the bathroom!

All of the children were naturally absolutely thrilled to have been involved in a ship-wreck! Nicky and I were downcast though of course because we thought we'd seen the last of our beloved holiday home, the only place we were entirely free from the cares of state. Miraculously, she was salvaged and refitted, and we were able to put to sea again the next summer as usual. That was the summer that Uncle Bertie paid his visit. It had to be on the yacht; our police felt that getting the King of England and the Emperor of Russia side by side on dry land would be simply too tempting for the terrorists. Such were things since 1905. The days when dear uncle had walked through the streets of Petersburg behind my father-in-law's coffin along with not just Nicky but also half the kings and heirs in Europe were well and truly over for us. The British press made much of this; they wrote some utter bosh, especially about the children, who were a real hit with the visitors.

Alexei knew that Uncle Bertie was his godfather, and he stood alongside throughout the formal piping aboard and welcome, flapping his hands at his side and bouncing up and down until he was noticed and swung in the air. I was quite alarmed; Uncle was puffing terribly and Alexei was by no means a light child. He was nearly four and he looked quite grown up - I'd had his hair cut short and put the frocks away for ever (he wore them only intermittently even as a baby; this custom had started going out of fashion already then). His colouring also started changing around this time; he used to be a blond curly baby but he became auburn-headed, like Tatiana, and his hair grew very straight. For the visit he wore an English sailor blouse (with the tie) and blue shorts. Such a solid, handsome little boy!

All five tinies quickly got the idea that Uncle likes naughty children; he encouraged them to race slices of toast down his trousers, butter-side down. I remember this little trick from my own childhood.

Uncle brought a very large entourage with him; besides the family and household there were a number of politicians and Naval personnel. One day, Nicky tells me, he was talking in the dining room with several of them when he noticed looks of discomfort on their faces - even winces. They were all standing with their backs to the table, whose legs were obscured by a long cloth. He carried on talking and watching for a minute or two until he saw what was causing the discomfort: a small hand repeatedly shot out from beneath the cloth and pinched the backs of the gentlemen's calves. Nicky lunged forward and pulled Anastasia out from under the table by her hair - not hard, but she understood the message. Little children find the undersides of tables irresistible, though - Alexei when brought to chat with guests at dinner would often disappear beneath the cloth and emerge with a trophy such as a shoe. When ordered to give it back to its owner he once inserted a strawberry into the toe, so that the poor lady got a terrible shock when he put it back on her.

191

Jackie Fisher – once Ludwig's friend, then already his mortal enemy – was First Sea Lord in those days, as I recall. He was certainly there with Uncle, and he danced on deck every night with Sister Olga, whom he'd met somewhere else and appeared to adore. He was old enough to be her father, easily.

Our children sometimes joined in the dancing, when it was of the communal type. I remember my little Anastasia leaning backwards and swinging on hands as she gallivanted around in a ring – and poor Marie losing her shoes if she went too fast. Olga and Tatiana were obsessed by roller-skates at that time; they careened about the deck and Aunt Alex joined them, in spite of her stiff knee and her advancing years. This was poignant; how unlike her sister she was – imagine Motherdear joining their games! – but she should have done; it was she who was their Amama after all.

The downmarket British press when we saw it on our return was full rubbish about the 'four little Grand-Duchesses' and how the carefree laughter they knew on that voyage was unlike anything they ever experienced at home, besieged on all sides by terrorists and revolution. Most of the papers had also decided that Nicky and I weren't happy together – partly on the basis of the way his uncles and cousins and ancestors behaved, they couldn't imagine that a Romanov could ever be a good husband. I remember that when Elinor Glyn published *Three weeks* it was all over the papers that this silly story of a spurned, adulterous queen and her English lover who begets her heir was based on our marriage!!! (In truth I think it was more likely Cousin Missy). All this makes me laugh: picture the Gothic horror of our family life, shut up behind high gates outside which the mob is howling. From time to time a troop of Cossacks sallies forth to mow down peasants with their knouts. Inside the Palace (grand and Byzantine, of course – courtiers in long robes like the sixteenth century) the evil Tsar is consorting with his strings of mistresses and dreaming up ways to further oppress his people.

His pale-faced little children ask each other in whispers why they can't go into the garden like other children do. The empress meanwhile has fled to Ruritania with her upright English lover. It would make an excellent film: in fact it undoubtedly is one by now, except that the Empress is no longer the outraged innocent.

Uncle Bertie made Nicky Admiral of the Fleet of the British Navy; this was what most upset the better quality British press. He - England's ally - was abused in Parliament as 'a bloodstained creature' not fit to wear the uniforms of the Mother of the Free. This makes my blood boil.

The next summer we went to England, though, returning Uncle's visit. It was the first time since 1896, and we landed at Cowes for Naval reviews and the like. Of course things felt very strange: dear old Osborne House was given to the government by Uncle Bertie who'd never liked it, and it became a convalescence home for soldiers, with the Naval College where my Battenberg nephews were educated in its grounds. It was sad: I would have liked my children to have seen the Swiss Cottage and the toy fort where I used to play as a child, and to have handled the little gardening tools that belonged to their grandmother and had her name on them: it would have made that part of their ancestry real for them. Instead it seemed like history.

David Wales took us around the Naval College and told us horror stories about his treatment there: he was nick-named 'Sardine' (being too small for a whale!) and the other boys took pains to remind him of his unimportance - they poured ink over his head and on one occasion left him for hours with his neck trapped in a sash window. Well, they all have to put up with this kind of treatment at school: Georgie Battenberg did too, although because of his easy personality and humble rank he suffered less than this little prince. What the more obstreperous Dickie went through later was appalling, though: he fought and argued and ended up with only one friend, and because of the date (it was 1914) he suffered his German name quite especially. I don't know how Victoria can have borne leaving him there, knowing what he was going through, but she did. I suppose it strengthens their characters, but I am not convinced that the English public school is the right place for all children and I'm glad I never had to take any decisions about whether to send mine.

Nicky and Cousin George had their photograph taken in front of the College with their respective heirs: a nice picture, Nicky is wearing a double-breasted blazer and white trousers with turn-ups and he looks a bit casual and dashing in the way he stands! - Georgie on the other hand always stands rigidly upright, and he mocked the turn-ups: 'Is it raining?!' - he is obsessed with clothes and 'correct' dress like Uncle Bertie always was. When Alexei was about eight and he went through a phase of telling the court fogies if he thought they had their decorations awry or something wrong with their uniforms, Nicky used to tease him, 'You've got a big streak of your godfather in you!' However this sort of obsession is normal in a little boy. In cousin George it simply mirrors his interest in stamps: he is a dear old fogy and a pedant at heart. I never at all disliked him, though. Nicky and I have more in common with him and May than we did with Uncle Bertie's entourage: they like a quiet life with their family. When George succeeded to the throne eleven moths after our visit to England, Nicky was quite happy: loads of his cousins on the Danish side stood to inherit thrones (one used to call old King Christian 'the grandfather of Europe') but apart from Karl in Norway, who was elected, George was the first of them to share this burden with poor Nicky. It was funny to see the English papers call him the 'young king' (after Uncle Bertie and Granny, they found it strange to get a monarch who had little children and wasn't grey!) when he is three years older than Nicky who had already been on a throne for fifteen years! I have to say, it seems to me that Georgie is rather harsh with his children, though: he roared and bellowed at David every time the boy put a foot wrong. David was rather a fragile-looking child at that time, and none of the pictures I have seen since have corrected that impression. He was fifteen but he certainly looked younger: on the photograph with his father and Nicky and Alexei, our little Alexei was almost as tall as he was (alright, I exaggerate, but not that much) at not quite five! However, the officers on our yacht were very interested in David: for a couple of years afterwards when they wanted to tease Olga they used to hand her an envelope which when opened would reveal a picture of the little prince. And I know Motherdear and Aunt Alex would move heaven and earth to get Olga or Tatiana for Princess of Wales. Not that it matters any more.

The events of 1905 undeniably had a big impact on our public lives: not only did the police want those state visits have to be to quiet places where there was no terrorist threat, but also we found that we were simply too busy to get the court balls going again, even had we wanted to. So after 1904 we never really lived in town, and the flat in the Winter Palace was shut up permanently. It seems so distant now: those halcyon nineteenth-century days at the beginning of our marriage when Nicky and I used to set off for a drive around town without police escort, and were acclaimed for our 'democratic' style!

On the other hand, we were hardly hermits at Tsarskoe. Motherdear used to complain that we were cutting ourselves off from the world (by which she meant from society) but the fact is that there were always people for lunch, and ministers and administrators to be received morning and evening, and military reviews to attend and places to visit. The only place apart from *Standart* where we were truly informal was in the Crimea, where no-one bothered us for days at a time, and where we were able to go shopping on foot in Yalta just like anybody else. (I remember being told off for thoughtlessly trailing a wet umbrella across the floor of one shop: its owner didn't recognise me and quite rightly ordered me to use the rack by the door. I'd have got away with it if silly Ania hadn't been offended on my behalf and loudly addressed me as 'Alexandra Feodorovna', thereby embarrassing the poor man terribly!). After our 1909 visit – the first for several years – we pulled down the old unhealthy wooden house and commissioned a new one in Italian style. Partly, the Italian style reminds me of Osborne: after seeing that house again, I think I wanted to recreate it for myself, although I planned that the interiors should be prettier than the ones my grandparents designed! (I remember quite particularly: they had modeled the hands and feet of their children as babies in marble, and arranged them on desks as ornaments: it made a most macabre effect! – We of course have a statue at Tsarskoe of the whole of our beautiful Tatiana as an infant, but the effect of the full child is less peculiar!). Also of course both Nicky and I went to Italy when very young: in 1891 I was in Florence and Venice with Ernie and Victoria, looking at scenery and paintings, and the crumbling glory of all those beautiful buildings. Nicky went to the south of Italy on a cultural tour as part of his own education: mostly he was besotted with the little white towns and the blueness of the sea, which are so like the Crimea. Thus we built a white Italianate villa of our own, nestling against the stunning green of the mountains, and it was ready for a visit in 1911.

It was good for the children to have the Crimea: I mean not just for the easy life they could lead there, but also for the things they saw, which broadened their education in a human sense. From when they were small I had them visit the sanitariums: they should understand that this paradise has its sad side too. Of course there were heavy criticisms of this: some idiots thought the children would contract tuberculosis from a visit, and I was castigated for irresponsibility! (Normally one accuses me of over-protecting them). They also used to assist at the charity balls, manning a stall at which they sold drawings and paintings they had done themselves. I also taught them embroidery like I too was encouraged to do as a child: I am much better at this than I ever was at drawing, and it is an outlet for the artistic side of my personality. Only Tatiana showed much desire to emulate this, though Anastasia and Alexei both like her have an enthusiasm for more practical handiwork: they knit very well, and for him in particular this has been a blessing at times. Marie we discovered to be the one with the most talent for painting (Olga is good but not as good): curiously, she uses her left hand by instinct; makes me wonder whether she might have been left-handed if not trained to use the other one by the tutors. Poor wee Toutou, that may explain why she was always so clumsy.

In 1908 after the visit from Uncle Bertie, we had Sig join the household. Uncle complained about the children's 'Hibernian' accent that they picked up from Miss Eager when they were tiny and from a Scottish tutor who taught them English before Sig came. I was powerless to do much about the accent: I don't want to force them to be doing elocution lessons in the evenings! A real English tutor we thought could take care of such things in the normal course of lessons, so Mr. Gibbs came. I wanted them to be respectful but they quickly found out that his first name was Sidney and his father was a John, so he was called Sidney Ivanovich for a few days, and after that 'Sig', for his initials. When I attended classes I was horrified to see that he would test them with his own book lying open on his desk: I thought they could probably see the answers from where they sat, but he assured me they were far too honest for such cheating. It seemed to me for a while that he might lack firmness: however when the time came Alexei brought out the iron in his soul, and all my misgivings went out of the window.

Alexei by nature is not necessarily any more difficult than any of his sisters (none of whom are angels): however, his unique circumstances have at times made his character impossibly tough to manage. When he was tiny he was terribly spoiled in the nursery by Mary Vishnyakova: because of her anxiety about his illness, she couldn't bring herself to say no to him. And then of course he was aware very early of who he was: at one year old he went to military reviews with us and the soldiers cheered him, and he clapped his hands and shouted 'Hurrah!' back at them, which delighted everyone present. When Botkin's wife came to meet us for the first time, he was about four. She spoke to him and he turned his face away with an indignant look – at that age he was quite shy of adults. Silly Botkin laughed and said loudly, 'Of course the Heir is angry! – You have no right to speak to him before he has addressed you!' – And clever little child that he was, I've no doubt Alexei heard and duly noted this. Thus by the time he was five or six he used to make his little pronouncements if interrupted in his games: 'Run away, girls – someone has called to see me on business.' On one occasion he walked into the room next to Nicky's study, where a minister was awaiting an audience. The man didn't move. 'When the Heir to the Russian throne comes into the room, people have to stand up!' Alexei trilled. Fortunately Nicky came in at that moment and heard him and made him apologise. In some ways, of course, it was easier to cure his arrogance than it had been in Olga's case, because he was the youngest. Whatever he might be to the public, at home he was Alexei Romanov, 'number five', and his sisters sat on him very firmly when he was obnoxious. At times it was embarrassing: I remember him spotting his little friend Kirill (the 'English baby' of Tsarskoe) when out driving, and asking for the automobile to stop so the child could get in. Marie and Anastasia were asked to move over to make room, and they brusquely refused. Alexei repeated the demand, the three of them had a loud argument, and he leapt out of the car and raced away into his friend's garden, shouting and yelling, in full view of several passers-by.

Nature of course had other ways of reminding our poor Little One that he was not a demi-god. When he was small, he was well most of the time: his worst problem was the big blue bruises which could make him look frightful, particularly when they affected the face. The strain in these years was on Nicky and me: living in a constant state of alertness and mild anxiety in case something serious happened to him. The two things we most feared were nosebleeds and internal (especially brain) haemorrhage like the one which killed my nephew Henry. Thus we took steps to make sure that his risks were minimised: Derevenko and Nagorny his sailor *diadkas* from *Standart* were engaged as permanent nannies to follow him around, restraining him from taking too many risks and catching him if he fell.

We also explained to him when he was five or six about the need to avoid risks, but inevitably he ignored this when he could. His toys were very extravagant: it was necessary to give him things that would distract him from wild games. Thus the model railway in the nursery had moving figures on it; he just had to flip a switch to set them off. The signals and scenery were terribly elaborate. In quiet moments on wet afternoons, Nicky and he would play with this for hours. – There were also battleships and aeroplanes, a tepee like his Aunt Xenia had long ago in '84, and regiments and regiments of toy soldiers. He liked to line them up and drill them and dream about being a medieval tsar leading his troops into battle: then Anastasia would race into the room and kick over several rows and there'd be screams and tantrums and fights again.

Anastasia, much like me (in this as in many things!), never cared greatly for toys. When she was very little she had one beloved, hideous doll, half-bald; later she spent most of her time climbing trees and playing out of doors. When it rained they all five used to run up and down the slide in the Mountain room at Tsarskoe, polishing the surface so that it became ever more slippery and dangerous. The girls rode their bicycles in the corridors of the state rooms, and naturally Alexei wanted one too but it was too risky. We got him a pedal car, which of course didn't go as fast as their bicycles would, and he wailed, heart-rendingly, though it wasn't exactly true, 'Why should other children have everything and I nothing at all?!'

I suppose in some ways, 1905 did affect our private life as well as the public one.

Of course, the affect was partly positive: with no ball 'season' and no winter in Petersburg we could spend even more afternoons and evenings than before just being a family. On the other hand, for several years, we were too busy to go abroad apart from the state visit. Thus I didn't see Darmstadt between 1904 and 1910, and we weren't able to attend dear Ernie and Onor's wedding or the christenings of their boys, even though Don is Nicky's godchild and Lu is mine. But my family came to see us instead. In 1908 we had Victoria with Louise and Dickie at Peterhof. Next year as we sailed through the Kiel Canal on the way to England we stopped off at Hemmelmark and Irène, Harry, Toddy and Bobby, Victoria, Louise, Dickie and Ernie who were all staying there came aboard for a couple of days, which was great fun. Alice and Andrea came from Greece and saw us, and when they continued on to Denmark they left my two little great-nieces Margarita and Dolla with us for safe-keeping. Alexei was thrilled to have them: for once he was not the youngest most powerless child in the house!

- We all felt a certain amount of anxiety at this time over Ella. In 1908 she had started getting rid of her worldly possessions and preparing to found a nursing order. This was the natural extension in a way of her activities with the wounded soldiers immediately after Serge died, although we weren't sure why she wanted her nurses to be religious ones. She fell into terrible conflict with the Church for one thing: the Synod argued that there was no such tradition in Orthodoxy as a nursing order: this she borrowed from the Catholics. Ella doesn't think of doctrinal issues, she just does what she feels she needs to do, which in my view is far more Orthodox than the Synod's approach anyway. Then of course the family were upset: Aunt Miechen said Ella was planning to retire from the world. Victoria and I were annoyed by this criticism: so far Ella had given no sign that she herself planned to be one of the nuns: we thought her role would be limited to supporting and administrating. This is entirely consistent with the way she was brought up; our mother was so interested in medicine too, and Ella would be leading a far more useful life than she ever did when she was married to Serge and thought of nothing but clothes and parties. Then, however, in 1910 she took the veil, and we were all a little bit shocked. She had led until that point a life which was anything but religious, and now here she was walking around in a grey habit and drawing everyone's attention to herself. I remember we were afraid she thought herself a saint - putting aside the worldly life and giving herself to God and the suffering and all that. It is a big moral role to arrogate to oneself in full view of the world. I have been mean-spirited about this at times, but it's hard to see one's very human and imperfect sister take on such a guise.

Victoria of course ended by supporting her: she said that Ella was simply doing her best to be good and useful, and that her very cool calm nature would guide her and help her preserve balance in this new role. However there should be more to such a vocation than simply a desire to be useful. She could have done that in the secular world.

Victoria's daughter was uninhibitedly admiring: from the beginning of the endless cycle of wars in which Greece has been embroiled since then Alice's one aim in life has been to become like her Aunt Ella. She goes to the front and sets up hospitals and assists with refugees in the most harrowing circumstances. I admire her very much, although Ella it seems has not bothered replying to Alice's letters about her work because she is so wrapped up in her own. *Au fond*, there is no real chasm between Ella and me. I have never really understood her, but on the social level all is the same between us as it ever was. She is my sister and I love her: I just cannot understand why it is that religion which should bring people together so often causes such problems in our family.

The main topic on which Ella and I have disagreed has been, of course, Grigory. Ella was hostile even to our first Man of God, Philippe, though she knew nothing about him. She listened to the rumours which accused him of table-tapping and séances and the rest of the mumbo-jumbo that certainly Nikolasha his patron was involved in. One story even held that he believed he could make himself invisible when he wore a certain hat! – In the end we had to part with him because the police discovered that he was a Freemason and had other connections illegal in Russia, but this had after all nothing whatsoever to do with his ability to speak to the soul.

Grigory came to us first in 1905 through the agency of Nikolasha and Peter and Stana and Militsa to whom we were so close then and who had introduced us to Philippe. As a matter of fact they always have someone they are enthusiastic about, but this was less apparent in those days than was the fact that they were intelligent people with a very broad philosophic approach to religion. Like us they sought the divine spirit behind the narrow expression, although without the more scientific background that I have they tended always to go further: certainly they dabbled in spiritualism and other such rot; they seemed to swallow everything the theosopohists swallowed, hook, line and sinker, even if they were only experimenting. In the early days this was unimportant. Militsa learned Farsi in order to be able to read Zoroastrian texts in the original (and this is the woman who Petersburg society claimed thought herself invisible when she drove with Philippe!). Naturally these sorts of interests were likely to be a real bond between them and Nicky and me, especially when so much of the Family was so unfriendly, and they were with us a lot in those days.

Grigory had come to the attention of the church because of his healing skills: he arrived in Petersburg from Siberia in 1902 I believe but it was a while before Nikolasha heard of him. Of course then neither they nor we realised how significant a healer would be in our lives; we simply received Grigory as a wandering Holy Man, a *starets*, whose wise words could shed light on spiritual problems. Just another lay preacher, really, although he was quite a lot younger than most of the startsi, and we knew that he was married and had three children back at home, which is rather different from most of them. Clearly, he had a vocation to have left all that behind, although he did tell us frankly that his own father believed he was trying to escape his peasant's life, and said of him, 'Grisha has turned preacher out of laziness!'

We only saw him a couple of times in the next two years, but Nicky did mention his healing skills to Stolypin when the poor man's daughter was hurt in that hideous bomb attack on his house. In due course though but I can't remember when exactly we realised that Grigory could help Alexei.

Before anything really dangerous happened, the main problem was the pain involved in more serious injuries: turned ankles or pulled muscles which slowly leaked blood into the tissue around. Listening to his yells was just agony: we who'd never been able to bear hearing his sisters scream when they were genuinely hurt now had to sit through far worse - this endless, agonised sobbing when his little voice started to sound hoarse and weak like an old person's. He sat up in bed and he wailed to us with one hand outstretched and the other in his mouth, his little face crimson and seamed. And that was just the muscle bleeds of his infancy. We had no idea then about the pain of bleeding into the joints.

The doctors could do absolutely nothing apart from pack on ice and hope the bleeding would stop. But Grigory had the power to heal him instantly: just a touch on the forehead and Tiny would start to calm down. His tears would stop and eventually he went to sleep; then in the morning he'd wake looking rosy and healthy again and in a day or two he'd be up. Sometimes just a phone call from our Friend was all it took.

People have said to me it's faith healing: if one believes strongly enough, one gets well. So I read Mary Baker Eddy and delved into these ideas, and they did not explain how Grigory could help when Alexei was so young he didn't know what faith was. Late 1907 was when the muscle bleeds started; when I felt for the first time the true spiritual impact of what I'd done to my son, and I'd sit and comfort him and hold him while he cried: my perfect baby, my beautiful chubby little boy, tall and strong and rosy – wailing in misery and incomprehension against the disease I'd transmitted. And Nicky stood next to me and touched my cheek, and walked with the girls and came back to me with sweet little stories of their games in the park while their brother suffered, and knelt down before me while I looked into those eyes that are like a window into heaven, full of purity and love and gentleness; eyes that have never for a second blamed me for what his child was going through, for bringing a torment like the outside world into this little home that was his refuge, that was so perfect. I remember for the first time reading Fet who comforts me now, and oh my Nicky, in those days in the first hell of his sufferings I wanted to quote to you melodramatically (but I meant it, this is the effect your love has):

> *'As a bright angel from heaven*
> *In the radiance of the quiet fire*
> *Pray from your tender soul*
> *Both for yourself and me*
> *With words of love*
> *Banish the doubts of my spirit*
> *And shield my heart*
> *With the wings of your prayer'*

Darling Angel, you don't know what you are to me, how much and how often I pray to be worthy of your love. Forgive me if ever I have grieved you, and believe me deary it was not willingly done.

CHAPTER TWELVE

In due course people realised that Grigory knew us, and this did him no good at all.

One started coming to tell us stories about his past life: drinking and womanising and what have you. The police handed Nicky a report suggesting that he had been carousing somewhere in Petersburg; Nicky double-checked the dates and pointed out that on the evening in question our Friend had been visiting us twenty miles away at Tsarskoe. It was the old, old story: we only have to like a person for the gossip and the jealousy to begin.

Grigory never made any secret of the fact that he'd had a sinful youth. Part of his personal philosophy was that an individual was better qualified to know God's forgiveness if they'd also tasted sin. Petersburg society of course drew various crude and unsubtle conclusions about his doctrines from this idea. They used his surname against him, too: though there had been Rasputins in his village since 1700 Petersburg claimed the name meant "dissolute" and had been invented for Grigory alone. So after that, he tried to change it.

Just to be sure about him, I sent Ania and also Father Feofan who was then our own confessor to Pokrovskoe with him when he was visiting his family there, and they observed the simple life he led and the esteem in which he was held by his neighbours.

Ania was a devotee of Grigory very early: he warned her that her marriage with Vyrubov would not be happy, and when this turned out to be true she was most painfully impressed. In time of course her understanding became a little deeper and more mature than this. Needless to say, she saw nothing to worry her on the journey; but Feofan admitted to us that Grigory slept with a lady on the train on the way there. Father Feofan had no real difficulties reconciling this fact with the picture he had formed of a genuine Holy Man, and he helped Nicky and me come to terms with this contradiction as well. *Au fond*, Grigory was a poor man who suddenly found the world at his feet as a result of his great gifts and it is hardly surprising he was sometimes tempted to go back to his old ways when so many offered. I have that book about the saints, *Iurodovye sviatye russkoi tserkvi*, which Feofan gave me then and which makes it quite clear that the Orthodox Church can tolerate lapses in its holy men, especially when they are from simple backgrounds.

Ella got involved because of Sophie Ivanovna.

I had not really wanted my children to have a governess: I need to bring them up to be what I want them to be, without other people's ideas coming in. However for parts of 1908 I was none too well: I started getting palpitations and shortness of breath on exertion, and Botkin made me rest and do nothing for several weeks, especially since he was aware that my Papa had had heart problems. I got better but the symptoms recurred a few months later, and then again after that, worse and longer-lasting than ever. I have no doubt whatsoever what has caused it: it is due to anxiety over Alexei. The constant background feeling of worry has acted on the muscles of my heart. It's having the fighting instinct constantly aroused but very rarely needed which does it: the blood rush has to find an outlet somewhere.

As far as the children are concerned this meant that I was not always at that time able to see them as much as I wanted to. Certainly if ill I couldn't be in the schoolroom with them in the morning, nor could I participate in the winter sports because Botkin refused to allow me out in the cold, or the games that went on in summer during the walks, even assuming I was up to going out. Because of work Nicky was not always able to join them for the walks, and he certainly couldn't spare the time

207

to oversee lessons, so they had to have a governess, and Sophie Ivanovna was appointed because she was an intelligent woman from a long line of poets and historians.

Pretty soon we started to have disagreements with her: she had her own ideas about how little Grand-Duchesses should be raised, and these involved a lot more pride and grandeur than I ever wanted. They were still so young; in 1909 when matters came to a head Olga was barely thirteen. Nevertheless Sophie Ivanovna objected violently to the fact that during one or two of his visits to us Grigory came up to the nursery when the children were in pajamas and dressing gowns. He told traditional stories from Siberia, and then he would help Alexei say his prayers. He was so good with children; the three little ones spontaneously acted out the parts of the animals in his stories, and they listened fascinated when he rebuked them gently for picking flowers: 'Doesn't the flower too have a right to a life?'

Sophie's problem was not, thank god, anything dirty-minded. Even she drew the line at suggesting that Grigory had obscene designs on these small girls. However she didn't like a peasant speaking to her charges as though he was their uncle. So we asked her to leave, and she went straight off to Moscow screaming rubbish to Ella about this charlatan who had gained terrible influence over us. She also before she left managed to whip Mary Vishnyakova into such a state that the poor thing claimed she'd been seduced by Grigory - whom incidentally she idolised, her attitude was very different to Sophie's. Well, he didn't even visit us often enough to get to know her, and it is most unlikely that he was ever even alone with her anyway. Botkin thought that she was on the point of having a nervous breakdown: poor thing, she had cared for Alexei for five years, so one can quite see how she came to be in such a condition. Therefore she went to a rest home in the Crimea for a while, Alexei was left to his sailor nannies, and the girls never had another governess. If I wasn't in a fit condition to look after them, they could be with one of the ladies-in-waiting instead. This state of affairs has worked ideally.

In autumn 1910 after my latest and worst attack with the heart, Botkin ordered me off to Bad Nauheim in an attempt to get it properly sorted out. - I had had enough, it just seemed too much that this thing kept recurring, and I couldn't take long walks or ride or even rush up and down the stairs to my chicks when I needed to. My poor Nicky came into me in the mauve room at intervals throughout the day and sometimes I felt so sorry for myself lying on the sofa like the heroine of some early Victorian novel that I really cried, which upset him dreadfully. 'Oh darling, I can't bear it when you're sad - you that are my sunshine and support and are so strong and brave! - I'd do anything, anything, for you to be well again!' And I felt so guilty for the worry he was going through, especially when his mother came on one of her rare visits and reminded me pointedly of what a hard life he led, 'The last thing he needs is to see the person he loves most suffer like this.' - But she said it accusingly, as if she thought I was malingering to get out of my social duties as Empress. We still hadn't told her about Alexei.

Anyway, we went off to Hesse for the first time in seven years, and stayed at Schloss Friedberg, a short train ride north of Darmstadt. I took my cure and saw various doctors, and Nicky went to Frankfurt with Ernie to buy antiques, and took a trip with the two eldest to Bad Homburg vor der Höhe, where they were all so happy because no-one recognised them most of the day and they just walked anywhere they felt fit. At the end of the afternoon, some journalist spotted them and then a crowd gathered which spoiled things a bit, but they enjoyed themselves on the whole.

I loved to watch the growing companionship of the three of them at this time - it was of course changing from what it had been when they were small and he was their jolly playmate; now they shared much more. Olga at thirteen got her own regiment, the Elizabethgrad Hussars, and then Tatiana at the same age the

Voznezensky Lancers, so they rode beside him at reviews like real Grand-Duchesses with a public role when I couldn't go. They started in Darmstadt that autumn going to the theatre as well.

Olga had changed a lot over the preceding fifteen months. She went very fast from being a skinny little tanned girl with wispy blond hair to looking suddenly much taller than her sisters. Her hair was thick and shiny and always well-brushed, and beneath it her face appeared small, rosy, with a dear little turned-up nose and pointed chin and a charming natural smile. So fresh and pretty and so like her father, whom I think she loves more than anyone. Nicky talks to our clever Olga about topics he has never mentioned in front of the others, but I see the look in his eyes when he turns to Tatiana, and I know who the other woman in his life really is! The others noticed too, and if they wanted a favour there was a hint of jealousy, especially from Marie, when they decided together, 'Oh, *Tatiana* must ask Papa to grant it!'

Olga and Tatiana at Friedberg and afterwards at Wolfsgarten were enjoying a wonderful new, grown-up friendship with their cousin, Ludwig and Victoria's Louise. She is nearly seven years older than even Olga, but suddenly they had interests in common with her for the first time. I permitted them after they got M.B. the first time, to stop taking their cold morning baths and switch to warm ones instead, and they became very fascinated by scenting the water and then scenting themselves. In Darmstadt with Louise and me they were shopping for their own future favourites: *Rose Thé* for Olga, which is close to what I always wear, and Jasmine for her sister.

Louise is a darling girl, a carbon copy of Victoria in some ways, if rather less intellectually-inclined. Her health was never very good - she had so many coughs and colds as a child, and by 1910 she was already plain and thin through illness. Like her mother, she hides a great heart under a brusque manner, and she devotes herself to her parents in the way that Victoria was devoted to Papa and us littler ones after Mama died. As a result, Louise is the clear favourite of both Ludwig and Victoria. I do hope that one day she will have a life of her own, though. Her sister Alice was at Wolfsgarten too with the wee girls, and we saw Ernie's precious Don and Lu for the first time. Alexei was enchanted with his little cousins, especially the smaller one, whom he kept picking up and towing around. One day he sat on the front of a carriage, bouncing up and down and clicking imaginary reins, playing coachman to Margarita and Dolla who were in the back. Suddenly his sisters and Dickie appeared and harnessed themselves to the shafts; they actually managed to pull it some way before they fell in a heap.

Ernie had a new artistic interest that autumn: he founded a school at which Isadora Duncan was to teach her funny Greek dancing. Now Don and Lu have started going there, to their great disgust! Isadora Duncan came to do a season in Petersburg as well and was the cause of many sad conversations between Sandro and poor Xenia. He always did like American women.

Also we got to know Onor really well at last. She has been such a blessing for Ernie, so calm and cheerful, and unlike Ducky she took a real interest in Darmstadt and in the projects my mother had set up, so that unlike Ducky she has been loved by the people there. At Wolfsgarten everyone said to me that I looked wonderfully well from the cure, and one of the Nauheim doctors presented a report suggesting that Botkin had misdiagnosed me, and there was no biological heart problem at all.

Well, I know that the origin is psychic not organic, but that does not mean that the symptoms aren't real! – What he was implying was no less than 'silly, hysterical woman, she's imagining it all!' Isn't it always the way? How do you deal with women and shut them up and belittle them? – you tell them that they are 'hysterical', 'nervous', 'neurasthenic'. In the last century they even used to lock them up! Well, I am none of those things. I am energetic and determined and I've never had hysterics in my life, but it didn't stop some of my family saying some odd things to me. Hence, Ernie, 'What are you doing to yourself, Alix? Why can't you accept that nothing's wrong? – You can't take Alexei's illness onto yourself, you know – It won't help him for you to be ill.' I see what he thought: I was punishing myself for the boy's haemophilia. I denied it quite angrily, and Ernie said, 'So why hasn't your miraculous Holy Man/healer healed you, then? – It's as if you don't want to get well.' I pondered this one for a while, and I've asked myself if he was right, and I've thought myself well, but in the end the symptoms have always come back. Three to four times a year I find myself totally knocked up for two weeks or more, and Botkin makes me stay in my room and work there until noon, and use a wheelchair moving around the house if finally I get up at all. It isn't ideal, but at least life can go on in a manner of speaking. And yes, it does always happen as when the boy has been through a trying bout of bleeding, but this is not surprising if I stay awake at his bedside for days.

Olga 'came of age' officially in November 1911 – her sixteenth birthday. We were in the Crimea staying in our new Italian house for the first time, and the priests had been through blessing the rooms with incense. Ania was our guest, and we were singing a lot at that time – her soprano and my contralto – and Emma Fredericks and Sonia Orbeliani who were part of the household at that time joined in too. I went round hanging pictures and re-hanging them by the hour, and planning gardens, and spent loads of time as usual in the Crimea organising the bazaar on behalf of the sanatoria. All the children came to it that year, carrying black collecting boxes round their necks for further donations, and Alexei was with me behind my stall a lot of the time, wearing his Russian sailor uniform with a *Standart* cap and attracting great interest. I lifted him onto the table and he sat cross-legged and bowed at the customers with great charm and decorum for once. Another day we motored up to the top of

Ai Petri and climbed around on the rocks and looked out over the stupendous cloudless view of the mountains and the sea and wanted to stay permanently.

It was so perfect there now we had our new house; only one thing truly remained to be done - a house-warming party, in honour of the birthday of our darling first-born. I was so glad for her sake that we were there and not in rotten Petersburg, which would have been such shy work. In the Crimea things can be simple and informal, and true friends and nice people can come along.

The morning of her birthday Nicky and I gave her her diamond and pearl necklace and ring, made of the stones we'd collected for her since she was born, her first jewelry of any value. That night she came to the party wearing a filmy pink dress with her golden hair up for the first time, and she looked so young and shy and touching that her father's eyes were suspiciously damp. He danced with her and with me, and we gave her a glass of champagne with her supper which made her giggly. Then Nicky danced some more and finally left her alone with a gaggle of young officers, cousin Dmitri keeping a watchful eye over all. We went out onto the terrace and looked up at the stars. It was a warm night as usual down there and one could smell flowers on the air. The mountains were black against a dark blue sky.

'Now we're the older generation,' Nicky said, and laughed delightedly. I was less impressed: 'Tomorrow she'll back in the schoolroom squabbling with her sisters.' But it was different, having a 'grown-up' daughter; I knew that foreign princes would be casting their eyes towards Russia now, and I didn't like it. 'Sixteen is so young to be considered of age.' I said resentfully, and Nicky agreed. 'Remember me when I was sixteen? - In theory I'd have been allowed to rule Russia, but I was a child, wasn't I?' I said, 'Old enough for me to love you, though, and I was even younger. Imagine - I was Marie's age!' 'Marie falls in love daily,' Nicky smiled. 'It doesn't mean anything, though – except I'd never say that to her!' 'And it meant something for you, at twelve, did it? Something permanent?' 'Silly boy, how can you ask that?!' He looked at me with ironic coyness through his eye lashes, and said, 'Just – since we came here, I haven't seen too much of you. You spent so much time organising the bazaar, and you've been beastly singing all your evenings lately. And I wondered – will it be my turn sometime?' I was touched and amused. 'Are you jealous of my friends?' 'I'm jealous of anything that takes your time away from me. Darling, I does love you so eternally!' 'Sweetest of sweet pets!' – I took his head between my hands and tilted it forward a little to kiss his eyes – 'No matter how big old Sunny's heart is, no matter how thoughtless she can be, you know, don't you, who comes first? Who stands nearest and dearest, and holiest and best? – 'Cause no-one has a husband like mine – so gentle and good, so pure-hearted and trusting of everyone!'

The dancing was winding down now; we went to say goodnight to our darling girl, and I stayed with her a while as she got ready for bed, listening to her nonsense about who she'd danced with and how that made her feel, and I was touched that she told me, because I at her age couldn't have faced confiding in anyone like that. Nicky I found back on the terrace, smoking with Dmitri. I knocked the cigarette out of the latter's hand and said, 'You're too young for that; I shall tell your Aunt Ella! And go to bed – it's late!' The silly boy gave me a salute and sloped off, and I took both Nicky's hands and smiled teasingly into his eyes, 'And now you too, my poor jilted angel; we go by-by.'

We did spend a lot of time at Livadia for the next three years; since we'd designed the house ourselves, it felt like our real home. Also, of course, the climate is wonderfully good for Alexei. At six, I think, he started having joint bleeds, and days when he'd wake in the morning unable to bend an elbow or a knee, or when the knee would flex and fill with fluid and grow as hot

214

and red as fire. Also of course the pain increased; he had sleepless nights of crying and groaning, when I read story after story to him, trying to take his mind off it, and for a while it would work, but a new wave of pain would set in and the wails began again. In the day the pain is generally less, but after those nights he was good for nothing; he dozed or played listlessly with his toy boats. Then there'd be the days or weeks of recuperation, lying in bed or being carried around by Derevenko, getting bored and complaining and refusing to concentrate on his lessons. He was miles behind where he should have been academically; his writing was appalling and he refused to speak a word of English to any of us, although he always understood perfectly well; I even read to him in it most of the time. His stubborn will broke me in the end; thus Alexei is the only one of them with whom I've usually talked in Russian, and his own must have suffered as a result!

At Livadia he was always a different child. It is the cold northern climate that affects his joints; in the Crimea there is no pain or stiffness at all; it's just the anxiety and uncertainty we have to contend with, and that is my problem but thank god not his, poor wee Sunbeam. The endurance he builds up there lasts several months of winter too. Thus we were there in spring and autumn 1912, and twice similarly in 1913, and in early 1914 too. Ernie and Onor were with us on the first of these visits; they were in Russia for ages that year, arriving at Tsarskoe and travelling down with us on the train.

In retrospect, it seems this journey was the first inkling we had of difficulties with Ania.

She was jealous of Ernie since he took our attention away from her, and I suppose that after several years of living in each others' pockets we were bound to start to find annoying little traits in one another anyway. The whole of the last winter Nicky and I had been going to her little house in Tsarskoe several evenings a week, even more than in the past, to tease about her the coldness

215

of her floors, and compliment her on the toffee she made for us, and all the things that kept her dear unaffected soul happy. If we didn't go to her she came to us and sat in the evenings in the family circle, reading aloud while Nicky and I played chess, or playing bezique with me when Nicky read, and so forth. If we couldn't see her when she wanted she sulked, especially if she discovered that we had been visiting someone else instead. At some point this stopped being touching and began to annoy me. It was no longer possible to confide in her; she was acting more like a spoilt child than a woman. At the same time, I felt terrible for her, because so many people had it in for her due to her being my friend; how could I just drop her?

This was also the period of the terrible rift with Grigory. In 1911 he went to Palestine on a sort of pilgrimage; of course, he had always wanted to visit such a place, but we too thought it might be a propitious time for him to go. There had been one too many reports of bad behaviour – women and drinking and the like – for which he had no alibi. He freely admitted to this; he said that he was led astray, but we started to feel that a little more self-discipline was called for – it was too much, to have the Minister of the Interior and heaps of bishops come to us and complain about him all the time. One day at Tsarskoe he was even over-familiar with Nicky's sister right in front of us – stroking her arm and asking was she happy.

Not only Ella but Victoria and Ernie as well had given me lots of conversation about him at Wolfsgarten, 1910. The main idea was that he was damaging our reputation through his association with us, and it all accumulated to a need to see him less, for his sake too, since his association with us left him open to attack. Simply not fair on a man who is not used to it, and who has done so much good, whatever his faults. So he went off to the Holy Land and wrote a book of his thoughts on it; powerful and moving stuff, Grigory back to his best, as when we met him. I had them printed later so people would have a chance to get a balanced view.

Then, however, he did something absolutely unforgivable; he gave some letters the children and I had written him to that idiot Iliodor, whom for some reason he believed to be his friend, and before we knew what had happened they were all over Petersburg. A hideous betrayal of our privacy, especially given the way Petersburg society thinks! – Thus the slightest expression of spiritual need in any of these letters became to them a personal need; they not only started to say that Grigory was my lover, but he was the lover of my little girlies, my innocent babies, too!!! No doubt the real letters were embellished and downright fakes added to the collection in the circulation – and that vile Guchkov of the Duma used it all to make political capital in the newspapers!!! – Well, clearly, the filthy minds of the city don't help, but Grigory had betrayed our trust anyway: – One doesn't give away letters from friends, even if there aren't idiots waiting with open hands to receive them. I stand by that even now; we weren't unfair to ask him to stay away at that time; it maybe taught him circumspection. We made it very clear to him that he wasn't to come to see us again, although this left us with a feeling of anxiety: what about Baby? – What if something should happen to him?

Ania was distraught; she would hear no wrong of Grigory. On the train to the Crimea – she was coming too, because she'd nothing else to do, and I felt sorry for her in spite of my growing irritation with her – Ania seemed strangely bubbly and cheerful. One time we stopped in the middle of the Ukrainian plain, and the children slid down the embankment on tea trays, getting covered in dust, with even the court fogies watching from the windows and cheering them on. 'Oh, wouldn't Father Grigory love to see them like this! – Bless their simple souls!' Ania said, and then she burst out, 'And he shall see them! – Oh, I've got such a wonderful surprise for you!' – At which point she revealed that he was on the train! Well, we put him off it, and continued our journey; but it was clear to me; Ania's first allegiance was to Grigory now and not to us.

Ernie raised the topic again too, in the vineyards at Novy Sviet during an expedition there. We had had lunch outdoors with Prince Golitsyn, and he had brought out his best wines for us (which I drank a little of for politeness, though only really like port), and gallivanted about in his Tartar dress being exotic and amusing. It was quite a chilly day for a Crimean spring, and down on the beach after lunch everyone was playing 'ducks and drakes' because it was too cold for paddling. The children were wearing riding boots and long cardigans; my Tatiana looked slender and grown-up and elegant, and I think it was around then that she got to be taller than Olga is. I was watching Nicky too, racing across the shingle and throwing rocks overarm, and looking still so slim and youthful next to Ernie – although they are exactly the same age my brother had started getting a bit paunchy and middle-aged; it was quite a shock.

Everyone was feeling peaceful and cheerful, and Ernie did rather spoil it for me. 'You know, Alix, people think that Rasputin man has political influence now.' I shouldn't have been startled; two years later I wouldn't have been; spreading such an idea was Guchkov's dream. 'That minister Vladimir Kokovtsev spoke to me about it the other day. He is convinced that Stolypin was falling from grace before he died because he spoke out against that person to Nicky. He also thinks you were glad about Stolypin's death for just the same reason. Did you say something to him about history moving on and Stolypin's role being over? Because Kokovtsev claims you did.'

I was horrified; I remember Stolypin's death all too well, not least because he was assassinated in the theatre under the eyes of Olga and Tatiana. 'I meant that history moved on politically!' I said angrily. 'His role was over – he was losing his ability to handle the Duma. It doesn't mean I was glad he died!' 'Kokovtsev thinks you were. He also told me that he knows he too will fall soon because you are against him and so is this Rasputin.' 'If he falls, he falls because he can't work with Krivoshein,' I said. 'And Krivoshein is the best Minister we have.' Ernie looked at me sadly. 'You don't understand what I'm saying, do you? - The truth is not important; all that matters is perception. This person is damaging you, Alix. These ministers think he has some sort of a hold over you and you will move heaven and earth to protect him. And if Nicky is thought meekly to give in to you, it will damage him too.'

I was furious and humiliated; how dare Kokovtsev discuss me with my brother - the closest person in the world to me, outside my immediate family! - as if he would sympathise? We men - we understand each other; we shake our heads together over these silly women! And Ernie himself - to come back to me spouting this bosh: All that matters is perception; people can say what they please about us with impunity, and we have to bow down to their prejudices. So strong were these prejudices that they hadn't even noticed that the object of their contempt was himself in disgrace - so what, truly, were we to do? Nicky made a big mistake in 1905. When the press was given its freedom, one important constraint should have been added: a libel law. Without it, a free press is a license for anarchy to men like Guchkov.

Ernie looked into my collection of religious and philosophical works, and he put his head in his hands. 'There is nothing we can say to you, Alix; we simply do not have the erudition to fight against whatever it is that is going on in your mind and soul.' He sat looking at me with tears in his eyes. 'I am so sad for the way life has turned out for you. It just seems to me that you've had one long catalogue of misfortune since you went to Russia. I mean - the wedding almost literally over your father-in-law's coffin, the health problems, Alexei's illness, the way some people have acted towards you. I don't like your mother-in-law, she is a spoilt, ambitious woman, and I think her conduct when you were newly-wed was unforgivable. She never even lifted a finger to help you find your feet with all those people who go out of their way to harm you now, and who will use this Grigory to harm you more.' 'Oh Ernie, don't be maudlin,' I said, although I appreciated and was touched by his concern. 'No-one gets by without their difficulties, and the only one I would wish away if I could has been Alexei's illness. The rest means nothing when I balance them against the joy I've had. You know how perfect our family life is.' 'Yes,' he said, 'but I wish Nicky were a tougher character, or he had more time for study, because then he could perhaps lead you away from whatever theory it is that's got hold of you - whatever philosophy it is you are using to prop up your belief in this healer. Instead, he just follows, intellectually. Nicky is a saint and an angel, but he doesn't know how to deal with you!'

Poor dear Ernie was more than usually upset when this long visit came to an end, as if he had a premonition of what was going to happen. He held me close to him for a long long time, and he kissed Nicky very gently and said to him in German - the language of his poetry not his daily life - '*Ich habe das grosse Gluck, dass mein Schwager mein Bruder ist.*'

1912 was the year of the centenary of Borodino, and we visited the battlefield and met a man of 112 years who had fought against Napoleon. On the train on the way back, Alexei got hold of an unfinished glass of champagne belonging to one of the suite, and drank the dregs of it. After that he was very gay and wild, and he went around the train burping and saying in a hollow voice, 'I can hear my tummy rumbling!' 'You see,' I said, 'he may look like me, but he's a true Romanov by nature!' Nicky understood. 'If he turns out to be a boozer,' he smiled, 'I will disinherit him.'

We thought it was time to start his French lessons; he was nearly eight, just a little younger than the girls had been when they began. I have to admit, Zhilik was disappointed in our daughters. Olga especially, because he'd had such high hopes of her to begin with. So did I. When she was twelve or so she used to take books from my table where the librarian laid them out even before I had seen them. I was happy for her to have anything academic, it is good for her, but she liked novels as well, some of which I wouldn't necessarily want a girl of that age to see. I warned her off, but she said cheekily, 'I am just making sure that this book is a proper one for you to read!' Yet the fact is she found studying so easy that she just gave up trying, and her work started slipping backwards. Later in the war I managed to find her things to do and read that stimulated her mind, but she always did spend so much time sitting on a window sill just gazing out and dreaming. Her half of the bedroom was always in a mess, and this of course infuriated Tatiana, who ultimately would give in and start to tidy up around her. Tatiana was less naturally academic, but she was at least interested in her studies, and she has kept her serious reading up more than Olga has. She has the best piano technique, too, without ever practicing much.

Marie did alright; she is lazy but not strikingly so like Anastasia is, and she has the least academic ability of all of them I suppose. I don't care too much about this so long as she makes the best of what she has got; brains aren't everything in life. Anastasia when she was a tiny little child was the most sharp and analytical of them all: I remember how she would climb on the nursery table and jump down, until Miss Eager threatened her with a smack. "It's better to jump and be smacked than not to jump at all," replied our naughty girlie after weighing the options – so poor Miss Eager tied her to a chair, which A finally concluded was a punishment severe enough to stop her jumping again! She has an ear for languages like her father does; she could do very well. Her French accent is flawless according to Zhilik. However she was bent from her earliest days on avoiding hard work of any kind; she even tried to bribe the tutors by bringing them bunches of flowers so that they wouldn't give her bad marks. She sat there under their noses writing little notes which she smuggled out to Nicky and me, 'P.V.P. has set me a problem which doesn't want to solve – such pig and filth!' We punished her too, but she just didn't care. In Tobolsk Sig told me frankly that her school books look as if her intellectual development has suddenly been arrested. I agree: in writing she is incapable of analysis of any kind, and this is so ridiculous in so sharp a child.

Zhilik was worried about Alexei from the start. He hated the way the sailors followed him and ran to catch him if he fell over. One day he came to me and spoke openly:

'Alexis Nikolaievich is a capricious child with a very strong will. If he is not allowed to make his own mistakes in life, he will grow up totally without self-control.' He was absolutely right. From a moral point of view I never liked the sailors being there; but it was always a question of having the courage to take chances with Alexei's physical well-being. I dread him growing up like my poor Uncle Leopold did, hating his mother for keeping him on a short rein, always trying to escape and make his own life, but I kept putting off the moment when we'd cast him loose from his nursery bonds. Certainly by summer 1912 he no longer looked a baby. He was tall for his age and skinny, running around on the Finnish coast in a pair of striped bathing drawers and hurling himself in and out of a hammock with his little friends. His best chum outside the family was always Dr Derevenko's Kolia, but he played too with the sailor Derevenko's boys, and Xenia's youngest three, and the little Greek princesses, and Kostia's little afterthoughts, Georgy and Vera. So we pulled the *diadka*s away and let him make his own mistakes. Almost immediately he slipped and fell off a desk while putting a picture up, and he banged his knee and had a painful bleed. But that passed.

Irène was with us in Poland that autumn, for the shooting. We were at the lodge in Spala, which I already didn't like; so dark and poky, one needed the lights on all day. There were

222

so few bedrooms that Irène's boys had to sleep in the dressing rooms.

Baby was unwell from the start. He had had an accident at Belovezh just a couple of weeks before, getting into a bath tub – he had a nasty bruise at the top of one thigh for a while. It gave him trouble, spreading a bit into the groin, so that he had to go to bed for a few days and lie as still as possible to help the clotting. I lay near him, my heart playing up, while the rest of our party was out from dawn to dusk in the forest. I hated that: we looked pale and felt bored and needed air.

As soon as the doctors said it was alright we moved onto Spala. I took him out into the woods for a drive. We'd not gone far when he went quiet; then a little further on he clutched at his stomach and a terrible line appeared between his eyes, like an old man. He screamed and gripped my sleeve, so I turned around at once and began to head back to the lodge – but no matter how we drove it made things worse – slow drew out the agony, fast sent spasms of pain shooting though him with every jolt of the little carriage. That was the beginning of our anguish, the most nightmarish appalling experience we have ever been through: as long as I live I won't forget how my child looked and sounded after twelve days of bleeding, when he no longer even had the strength to cry, and he was lying on one side with his left leg drawn up against his chest.

We knew what was happening: the haemorrhage flexed the leg, making the thigh joint as big as possible so as to reduce the anguish as it filled with blood, but after a point it couldn't bend any more and still the bleeding continued. It had spread up into his stomach and his temperature was dreadfully high. My baby, my naughty, noisy sunny little boy was groaning with his eyes rolled back in his head, 'Oh, God, have mercy on me! Oh, God, have mercy on me!' The room was full of doctors: horrible, depressing sight – and they wouldn't leave him alone: every hour they were poking and examining and taking his temperature, and every time they touched him he would somehow find a last reserve of strength and a terrible wail would come from deep inside him. It was all I could do not to fly at them and shake them by throat; I wanted to scream, 'Leave him alone! Leave him alone!' – and every sound was like a hot knife in my heart. But of course I didn't say a word; I acted like I always act, for his sake – reading to him, and stroking his forehead and his poor, wet hair, and when I couldn't bear it any longer I was lying on the bed next to him with my arms around him and his little yellow face pressed to my neck, hour after hour. Sometimes he fainted, but he never got a wink of sleep. When I had to sleep Nicky would take my place, or Irène – she who knew so well what we were going through, and quiet and calm and gentle as ever – but with deep suffering lines scored in her own brow when she was near him. One day Tatiana came in, although I tried to stop her; she has seen plenty of suffering, this child, in the T.B. clinics, but I was less happy to let her know exactly what her brother was living through. 'I can cope with it, Mama,' she said simply, and she sat with him a long time, chatting away to him without flinching, although he looked dreadful and his groans never left off. She was just starting to show us what a character she has, Tatiana, little lionheart.

Outside his bedroom life was going on as normal, because it had to. I would hear his sisters playing tennis; or neighbours would arrive to go shooting. Anastasia ran shrieking past the window in pursuit of her cousin: 'Bobby! Bobby! When I catch up with you I'm going to beat you! My hands are itching!' One day she and Marie put on a play: scenes from the *Bourgeois gentilhomme*, as rehearsed with Zhilik in French class. It was quite a big event for them: people were coming from the surrounding estates, and full costume was arranged. I had to go; cruel to let my little girlies down on this day they'd so looked forward to in a different life.

I was sure that people would be able to hear his screams from the little improvised theatre: amazingly, they couldn't. I chatted away and tried to enjoy the show, but my mind was not on it, and halfway through I had to slip out of the room and listen: and his groans were audible from there, deep and heart-rending and worse than ever. He sounded as if he was about to die. I started to run towards his bedroom, and I was wearing court dress, so I had the stupid bloody train of it to contend with, and in the corridor I passed Zhilik, standing in a doorway: our eyes met briefly and he shrank back, as if he hoped I hadn't seen him and didn't know that he knew what my official life as Empress really means. But I saw the expression on the dear man's face, and I knew more than ever that we had a friend here - someone we could really trust with our secret and our child. Anyway, we've had no option.

Alexei was no better when I went back to dinner with our guests. Nicky threw me an anxious glance as I walked into the dining room, but although he wanted reassurance I could only shake my head. When half the guests had gone I went back upstairs leaving Nicky to get rid of the rest, and I found our son silent now. 'He is very weak,' poor Feodorov said quietly. I sent him and all of his colleagues out of the room, and sat down on the edge of the bed, holding Alexei's cold waxy little hands and kissing them over and over again. Irène came and put her own hands on my shoulders and said gently, 'My darling, believe me, never a day goes by that I don't think about my little Henry and wonder how he'd be now, twelve years old. I'd have given up everything to have him live, and for Toddy and he to be perfectly healthy. But when I think that he wasn't, and that if he'd lived, he'd just have to go through what Toddy goes through year after year, never letting up, one session of agony after another until all the fight is gone out of him, I can't regret his death - not really - for his own sake. So, think, if you have to let the Baby go - perhaps in the end it's the best thing.' Nicky had come into the room and was standing listening, and suddenly Alexei

225

opened his eyes and said loudly like a child in some dreadful old-fashioned book, 'When I am dead, please build me a little cairn of stones in the wood.' Poor Nicky rushed out of the room with his hands over his face, and Irène propelled me after him, taking my place next to the bed. Nicky and I sat in his study for a while and held each other, and although he wept bitterly my eyes felt hot and dry. I had no right to cry for my own grief when I caused all this in the first place.

During that night we released a bulletin announcing to Russia that the Heir was ill. Of course we didn't say exactly why: there was mention of a gastric haemorrhage but not its ultimate cause. We felt we needed to get this out, because everyone seemed to think that the next one would announce his death. I was simply not prepared to contemplate this: I am not the same gentle person as dear Irène, and I can't let something so precious to me – to all of us – go like that. So I did then what I had tried to avoid doing: I telegraphed to Grigory in Siberia. And some hours later the reply came back: 'God has seen your tears and heard your prayers. Do not weep, the little one will not die. Do not allow the doctors to bother him.'

Irène had in fact already sent the doctors to bed, because she thought the situation was hopeless. Alexei was given Holy Communion, and although there was no immediate change, within a day he got some real sleep and his groans grew calmer.

CHAPTER THIRTEEN

Alexei could not walk for a year after Spala. I am told he was lucky; that such bleeds can cripple a child for life, so severely has the bone and tissue in the joint been damaged. That knowledge didn't help, looking at him. I don't know – when they are born they are so perfect, their skin is so soft and has its own particular beautiful smell; and then they grow – or at least mine did – into rosy toddlers with firm, rounded limbs and they are still so pure and unblemished. But now here he was looking like a little old man – white and waxy, with that poor twisted leg and bones that stuck out, and a little face all seamed with suffering. It was torture to look at him.

He had mud baths, and treatment with an electrical apparatus called the Föhn system, that warms and relaxes the tight muscles. As soon as possible, a metal brace went onto his shoe, holding his leg firm. Bit by bit as the leg slowly straightened, the brace was let out.

And in the meantime we spoiled him rotten in the material sense; I simply couldn't help it, after all he'd been through poor little man he needed some paltry recompense. So he got his dog as a pet that Christmas; and for his ninth birthday we gave him a miniature motor of his own. This was a Mercedes bought in Germany, though our own have mostly been Bellevilles and Ernie will always sing the praises of the Opel – Hessian car – when asked for his view. Alexei drives the wee motor himself, but really he was most interested in the dog. The basket was waiting under the children's tree on Christmas Day, and the dear child shrieked with pleasure when he looked inside. 'A puppy! A puppy!' The puppy tore about the room leaving a trail of devastation, and Alexei announced that he would call it 'Joy', which made his sisters laugh. 'It's a boy dog, silly! Joy is a girl's name.' Anastasia, big lump that she was getting to be, was sitting precariously on her father's knee. He tugged her hair lightly. 'It also happens to be an adjective. Do you know what an adjective is yet, eh, Shvibzik?' We went through the usual ritual that it's me who blows out the candles on all the trees, because I am the only one who knows the breathing technique to get the top ones – but I must say that that year it was a struggle; once it was all over the strain of Alexei's illness caught up with me and messed my heart up nicely for quite some while.

It didn't help that the coming year was the Tercentenary of the dynasty, and we were scheduled lots of very public appearances. Some of these were an absolute joy, of course: we went on a river cruise to Kostroma to trace the origins of the dynasty, and as ever it was wonderful to get into the real Russia, and to meet real people. We journeyed of course to the Ipatiev monastery where young Mikhail Romanov was in sanctuary when the boyars arrived to tell him he'd been chosen as Tsar. (How funny that the house we are in today is the Ipatiev house – we the last of the dynasty).

Of course we also had the church services in Petersburg, with poor Baby carried in the procession by a Cossack, carefully positioned so his leg wouldn't appear to be bent. We announced that he had a sprained ankle, but he looked so white and pinched and anxious that a little sigh of pity went up from the crowd. Then the worst thing was the balls: we had to give one in the Winter Palace for the first time since 1903, and seeing our old flat again was unbearably poignant, the way I was feeling that year. I remembered the theatre trips by sleigh, and eating dinner a deux in front of the fire, back in the early days of our marriage. – And the two of us sitting by the window drinking coffee, while I was nursing our Olga – how we just gazed at her the whole time, and marvelled over her. And Kostia told me I outshone

Ella....: – yet now I looked at myself in the mirror and I saw an anxious face and a too-florid complexion, and I was fatter than I am normally – than I like to be – because I was so short of breath so often that I could barely take a bit of exercise. (and Ella of course was thin and wan and ethereal as always in her nun's robes). I could find the odd grey hair if I tried, as well. I mean, really – I don't like vanity or obsessive interest in clothes and the like – but I don't like to see myself looking such a wreck either.

I had to leave the party pretty early on, because Baby had had some pain in his leg – it was the blood reabsorbing – before we went down there, and I couldn't get him out of my mind. I needed to go check that he wasn't suffering, that he was being taken proper care of – so to have to stand there smiling at these idiots going by, and having my hands kissed, and murmuring small talk to them – is this really what life is for!? In ten years nothing had changed; it was still the same old gossip and malice – and as usual our family was providing plenty of ammunition. The major scandal was of course Misha's marriage, and somehow the whole world knew that he had sent us a telegram in the middle of the boy's dreadful illness letting us know that he had married his mistress – mother of his son, conceived while she was still married to someone else ('you have to arrange a quick divorce,' Misha coolly said to Nicky at the time, 'because I can't contemplate my child being raised as another man's') – in case he soon found himself Heir to the Throne again, in which case it would be impossible! – It was the heartlessness of this act which hurt Nicky more than the illegality of his brother marrying without the necessary consent.

And little Marie P. was back from Sweden after her marriage to William – the marriage Ella was so eager to arrange – fell apart, and there was of course plenty of chatter about all of that. At our ball, Marie did seven dances on the trot with Dmitri, and Nicky laughed at them, and teased Dmitri, 'Give another lady a chance!' but I had one of the equerries order them apart, because I could just see what Petersburg society would be saying in the morning about this particular sibling relationship.

The names on everyone's lips were Stravinsky and Diaghilev (but not often for their art) and Poiret, and the ballgowns were narrow and bright-coloured and cut off above the ankle, and after a while I couldn't bear this trivia and rot any longer. I started feeling rather light-headed, and I could hear my own breathing. I signalled wildly to Nicky, we left the room amidst a rumble of resentment and as soon as we got back to our apartments I fainted - horrible feeling - and before that I'd only ever truly fainted when I was pregnant.

Naturally 'society' was resentful that I'd left the ball so early, but within a few days they had something else to talk about, because this was the summer that Nijinsky went on stage wearing an unusually revealing costume of his own design. As he leapt across the boards, Motherdear peered hard through her opera glasses from the Imperial box, and then she swept to her feet and out of the theatre - and the poor man was dismissed from the Imperial ballet!

The other nuisance I remember from that year was the nonsense with Ania. Well, in retrospect, after all she's been through for us, it seems unkind that I made such a fuss about it, but at the time it caused me masses of angst. We were in the Crimea as I recall recuperating from the celebrations, when she started her silliness. I was spending my afternoons lying on a whicker sofa on the balcony, reading or going through papers while Nicky walked alone. In spite of the tercentenary, he was busier than ever that year with sheer desk work, and he barely had a moment to take any exercise. 'Oh look at the poor Emperor,' Ania gushed when she saw him. 'All alone. Shall I go and join him?' 'He likes being alone,' I said, 'it clears his head when he has so much to do.' 'But maybe he'd like to discuss his work with someone?' she said, and she went bounding off in his direction, and walked with him a while, although since she was so fat it cost her loads of effort to keep up. Then she always wanted to be his tennis partner, which mildly annoyed him because he is so good and she of course with her bulk is anything but. One day he was ragging our dear friend N.P. – who was one of the ADCs at that time – about red socks, and wanting to know how on earth did anyone find time to go shopping for coloured socks. Well, wouldn't you know it but Ania went into Yalta and got him some – and when he was on the tennis court she'd call out to him to show her that he was wearing them. He laughed and pulled his trouser leg up a little way. Well, I tried to tell myself that she looked on him as a sort of benevolent elder brother and that was all.

One afternoon we all went up to Kozmenets, and I was in a wheeled chair part of the way because of the state of my heart. Nicky and N.P. hooked their walking sticks onto it and pulled me up the slopes, and we were all laughing madly by the time we got to the lodge. Marie – my great galumphing girl – for some reason stuck a chair in the middle of the pond, and climbed precariously across to it while her father lashed at its legs and hers with his stick, and we knew that any moment she'd go in the water. Which she duly did. Nicky sat down at a table on the terrace, sprawling forward over it and still laughing, and Ania of course flopped down beside him. Marie's eyes were on her instantly – even now she looks daggers at anyone who tries to take a second of her beloved papa's time when she wants him for herself – and she said with malice, 'Mama – look what Ania's doing!' I did look, and I could see that she was kicking at Nicky's ankles under the table. He grinned, and then he got off his chair and sat on the table instead, and held his hands out to me with his sweet smile and his eyes crinkled up. My heart lurched with such adoration for him – really, more than ever – and I was unspeakably furious with Ania. How dare she take advantage of my friendship to try to steal my husband?!

I didn't say anything then, but in bed that night I found I

was crying when he was kissing my face, and he was shocked. 'Sunny – what's wrong?' So I told him then 'Ania – flirting – and hanging around you – and buying you little presents and dropping hints about how you confide in her.' 'My darling, why should it bother you? – She is in love with our family life, don't imagine it's me personally interests her, and in any case you know how she's always infatuated with some man or other – last week it was N.P. – and you used to joke about how you'd brought her as a temptation for me just to test me!'

I was silent for a bit, and then finally I told him, 'That was different then. Then, I was healthy and beautiful, and now I am a wreck. But look at her there – all pink cheeks and big soulful eyes.' 'No, that's you.' Nicky said softly. 'My darling love, poor fat Ania looks like a cow! – Do you really think I'd be interested in her in any way whatsoever when I have you? Look at your sweet darling face in the mirror – and then at me, too. You may not be too well at the moment, but I'm not without my own signs of wear and tear: I have lines round the eyes and my hair is getting thin at the temples. Suffering and experience does these things to us, and I don't think we are necessarily any the worse for it. We grow together and our love just gets better and better..... Well, that's my little lecture for the day over with! Look – me show you.' – and he started kissing my shoulder, and murmuring, 'Darling Girlie – skin smells like oil of roses. – And every time you put your arms around me I just want to melt into your softness and warmth – and so does Boysy – forgive me! – but you make me constantly aware of his existence when I'm near you. I doubt Ania would know what to do with –' I put my hand over his mouth and we both giggled unkindly. He started kissing the palm of my hand, and I completely let myself forget about everything besides the warmth of his lips and his hands, and the feeling of his skin against mine and all the while he was whispering, 'Sunny, my life, my soul, I love you and adore you and I am faithful to you to the end, and you know that now for

232

nineteen years and don't you ever think otherwise.'

I was happy then, and calm, but eventually several months later even I did have to speak to Ania about her constant silly attempts to flirt with my husband - embarrassing for him and so demeaning for her. She made scenes and accused me of mis-understanding her, but during the war she used to send him the most inappropriate letters (via me, so I had ample opportunity to study them) and say the stupidest things to me: 'You have your children to console you; I miss him more.' I wanted to shake her, 'Listen to yourself! Do you have any idea how stupid you sound saying such things about someone who at best looks on you as his wife's friend, and at worst barely knows you exist!' - but I never said it, because it was just a bit too cruel. I went on putting up with her even at her most unbearable and rude, for two reasons: one was the never-ending guilt I feel about the marriage I pushed her into, and the other was Grigory.

Knowing how nasty people are and how much rot they talked if he came to see us at home, Nicky and I after 1912 used to go to Ania's house to meet up with Grigory, because of course she carried on seeing him far more often than we did. Before our rift in 1911-12, he used to come to us maybe four times a year. After Alexei's illness we saw him at Ania's as often, at least until 1916, when it got to be a bit more frequent. Grigory used to get angry about people criticising Ania, actually: he said she was a 'heavenly adolescent' and one should be tolerant of her little foibles because of all her good points. Well, that's what I used to think generally anyway before she provoked me: she is honest and loyal, bless her, and eventually I calmed her down and persuaded her how unfair she was being to Nicky with her behaviour. This I know for a fact: no matter what Grigory might have been tempted to try with other women in his darker moments, he never for a second looked upon Ania in that manner. She was like a spiritual daughter to him, and he treated her as tenderly as he did his own children.

This didn't stop idiots talking: God, the things they said about her! – Already in 1913 they were claiming she was Grigory's mistress and she lived with him in Petersburg. They also as a variation said she slept with both Nicky and me: that story started even earlier. Poor simple soul, to be so maligned just because she was a friend to the most hated people in Petersburg. In 1917 I did what I could for her: I advised her to ask for a physical examination to prove herself a virgin (since I knew the marriage with Vyrubov was never consummated). Poor thing, she'd have found it terribly distressing and I doubt she'd had such a thing before, but it exonerated her: not just of the slanderous gossip, but also of the related political accusations: she is out of prison now, and that thought consoles me here. She has suffered so disproportionately to any harm she ever did.

Once more I had to read letters from the sisters and Ernie (who'd heard from Irène all about Grigory's role in Alexei's recovery) telling me that for our own good we should send our friend away. As if that was likely after what had happened the last time we did! 'See him less then,' Irène – peacemaker as ever – suggested (when we barely saw him anyway) 'send for him if you think Alexei needs him; but don't see him otherwise.' How could I explain about the spiritual balm that Grigory's conversation brought – it wasn't just a question of Alexei's health, it was every possible spiritual concern connected with the child. Never mind the learned priests – Grigory was the man who reconciled me to my own role in my boy's illness by saying simply that Alexei could bear it, it would strengthen him, 'God sends a cross according to the back.' 'But that's just a religious platitude,' Victoria always said, which annoyed me immeasurably, 'Surely that's the point, isn't it? Doesn't a reading of all the eschatological theory in the world bring us in the end back to the simplest explanation?' 'There's too much of me in you – you should never have married such a gentle man,' Victoria said to me the last time I saw her. 'You know how it is with Ludwig and me – I am not his "little woman" and I certainly don't blindly follow his lead, but he knows how to tell me to shut up!' I started laughing at this, and I couldn't be annoyed with her however much I resented the tone of what she was saying, and I'm so glad of that now.

In the winter of 1913-14 there were again several parties – little dances at home in Livadia, then later a couple of larger ones in Petersburg that other people gave and Olga and Tatiana were allowed to go to. Tatiana was sixteen and 'of age' in June, just recovering from horrible typhoid. All her hair was cut off during the illness, and in the official tercentenary pictures of our family she is wearing a wig. By winter though it was growing back sleek and straight and dark auburn, and she parted it on one side at that time and tied a ribbon round it – she looked very modern and quite beautiful. Tatiana's eyes slant up at the corners like my mother's and Uncle Leopold's did, but her complexion is paler and darker than the British family's – she takes after Motherdear in that respect. Exotic-looking, I should call her. Any old clothes look wonderful on her tall, slim figure.

She was a great hit at parties, and she was eager to go to them as well, whereas Olga was perhaps indifferent at the planning stage although of course she enjoyed herself when she actually got there. Their first big Petersburg ball was given by their grandmother at the Anitchkov. I stayed until midnight, until I was sure that they were having a good time, and then I went on the train back to my Baby at Tsarskoe.

Nicky remained with the girls, and in the morning I woke feeling cold with a sad empty place next to me. I put my kimono on over my night things and went looking for him and I found him sleeping on the sofa in his study, like he used to do occasionally when he'd been working half the night. I knelt down next to him and whispered, 'And how long did those wild girlies keep you up?' He groaned, 'What time is it?' 'Half past seven,' I said, 'when did you go to bed?' 'Five o'clock! But

235

I've got an audience at nine, I can't sleep in.' and he jumped up directly. Such was our experience of the gay youth of our big girls. We did intend for them to have fun: we were fully reconciled to holding a big ball at the Winter Palace in the new year of 1915, at which they would make their official 'debuts', and we expected to have many many more sleepless nights waiting for them to stop dancing. It was fate that disposed otherwise.

We went to Romania, didn't we? Sailing across from Yalta on the dear *Standart*. - That was the first official trip abroad since 1909, and the ostensible reason was to discuss various diplomatic issues between our countries; long-nosed Sazonov was hoping to detach Romania from her alliance with the central powers. I also however suspected that the old King wanted his great nephew to take a long look at our Olga; so did she when we got there and Prince Carol came forward to greet us on the jetty. She and I did not enjoy the day as a result: I didn't really like the look of the boy, with his fat pink lips and round pink face - looked like a sensualist, and as if he might run to fat quite early. Certainly his mother had. Missy in her youth was considered a great beauty, not least by herself, and I hadn't seen her for years. Thus it was a shock to find her with a round moon face wearing a dress like a tent and gushing over my daughter. Olga looked sulky, as she certainly can do when things aren't going her way. She took her hat off and trailed it along besides her like a little girl - like Anastasia was doing. Pretty soon the bright sun brought up a rash of freckles on her nose, and her bare forearms were turning brown. Carol paid her the most peremptory attention.

We went to lunch. The old Queen turned up amidst all the display without any decorations on. I was embarrassed for her and I took off my own St. Catherine Order, but Missy gave us a deliberate look and kept her jewels on: clearly there was no love lost between her and the Queen. There was nothing between Missy and her husband either - he so stiff and Hohenzollern; she so full of drama. Various rumours attend the paternity of their younger children. Altogether this was not the kind of family atmosphere I wanted my cherished, innocent eighteen-year-old child going into, so I took Missy aside after lunch, and I said frankly, 'If any attraction is born between Olga and your boy, I will be happy for them, but I don't want her making a marriage of state to a man she doesn't love.' 'No indeed!' said my cousin with feeling, 'I absolutely agree – no compulsion.' I felt warm towards her then, though her assured 'royal' manner scares me stiff – *Au fond*, she knows what I mean about arranged marriages, because of what their mother's narrow mind and ambition did to her and to Ducky (and indirectly to Ernie too).

Horrid Carol kept on staring at my Marie. She and Anastasia always looked relatively older for their ages than the big ones had: at fourteen she was physically very mature, and tall, strong and healthy, but mentally she was absolutely a child, as indeed she should have been at that age. Of course, he did make a bid for her a couple of years later, when Nicky rebutted him quite strongly: in retrospect one could see this coming in 1914.

On the yacht on the way back, Nicky sat down to some work, opening up letters and chucking their envelopes into the sea. I was near him, sewing I suppose. Olga appeared. 'Papa,' she said, 'don't make me marry that idiot!' Nicky was very moved. 'Darling, there is no question of anything happening without your consent.' 'Good!' she said. 'I am Russian and I mean to remain Russian!' – and she stalked off. He and I looked at each other with distress: we had never talked about marriages to any of our girls; they knew nothing about the family laws that would make it well-nigh impossible for her to marry a Russian because he would be either a commoner or too nearly related. That evening for the first time we talked about it together, and Nicky said tentatively then that maybe these laws should be relaxed: why should they not marry 'commoners' if they so wished, and if it meant that they could stay near us. 'One could change the law in the abstract before it happens – I am not adapting it to suit a particular case otherwise I will be inundated by the cousins, and I'm not changing anything to suit their whims!' But it was so depressing having to think about it: it chills me to contemplate children getting married in their teens.

Nevertheless Irina did, as Xenia had done before her. That summer Olga watched her closest cousin, the companion of her nursery bath-times, become a bride, and a year after that she was a mother. So ridiculous: Xenia a grandmother at forty: to see them at the christening one would have thought she was the mother and Irina the baby's elder sister. She acted the mother too when Irina and Felix went off so often and left the little child with her.

I would never ever have allowed a daughter of mine to marry Felix Youssoupov.

- Knew him since he was a cocky little boy who used to touch Serge's stays through his uniform: Zina Youssoupova was a very good friend of Ella, and Felix in his teens gained a sway over Dmitri that alarmed my sister. She ordered them apart, and thenceforth for a time Felix was very scathing about her, sometimes in my hearing – although he knows full well that she has effectively been a mother to Dmitri and has every right to be concerned. Ella it was who told me about Felix's theatre trips dressed in Zina's gowns and jewelry, his appointments with Dr. Badmaiev to be 'cured' of some personality trait the nature of which was all too obvious. Even Dmitri admitted to being surprised that Felix should think about marriage. There is something altogether unhealthy and hysterical about the whole atmosphere around Felix: he used to live in a flat decorated entirely in black, and he affected to see the world through a haze of opium smoke. At all times he carries, ostentatiously, a volume of Wilde. Naturally this is not Wilde the author of the *Soul of man under socialism* or the satires: Felix is exclusively interested in Dorian Gray. He likes the occult and he often wears his hair long, old-fashioned 'aesthete' style.

Sandro and Xenia didn't believe a word of what Ella said; they let their child go blindly to the altar. Alas, one has seen so much of these types of marriages, and the unhappiness they bring - above all there was Ella and the odd home life she had with Serge and terrible stories that made her so miserable. Also poor Mavra, haunted by the blackmail threats against Kostia after his periodic trips to the bath-house. But all this pales into insignificance besides the fact that Felix made himself a murderer. How can Irina live with him now?

Of course, the first attempt on Grigory was in that summer, but it had more to do with his private entanglements than with his friendship to us: that woman Gusseva was an agent of the madman Iliodor, was she not? - And as Grigory did not want the matter investigated, people said she was a prostitute and he had a history with her himself, though it wasn't true: he didn't know her, and she was no prostitute; more a kind of fanatical *exaltée*, of the type Iliodor had around him. - But it was a terrible shock to hear that he was in hospital in Pokrovskoe with a dreadful wound to the stomach, and for several days it was touch and go as to whether he'd live. Poor Baby was not too well: he pulled his ankle on the ladder of the *Standart* jumping into a dinghy and it gave him loads of pain for a few days - we needed Grigory then, and he was in no position to help at all. Naturally at the time this all had more significance for us than the assassination in Sarajevo - who could have believed that Austria would use it as a pretext for going to war with Serbia?

So symbolic - we had visits from both our allies that summer. Firstly it was Admiral Beatty's fleet which sailed into Kronstadt for a Naval review, and Georgie Battenberg was one of the officers and had a marvelous time showing his cousins over the flagship. I am as proud as ever I was of my ties to this great Navy, and at that time Ludwig was First Sea Lord and working like a slave. We barely saw him, the last years before the war, but he was due to come in 1914, bringing Dickie with him when term at

Osborne ended. Marie looked forward to it very much – Dickie was her infatuation as a little girl, although naturally it didn't last with her beyond meeting another new boy. He has been more constant – when last I heard from Victoria she said he keeps her picture by his bed even now, silly boy!

Ludwig and Dickie didn't come, because of events, but Victoria and Louise were in Russia for a while – that was when they took their cruise up the Tura and visited Ekaterinburg and other places in the Siberian borderland. They came back to Petersburg with tonsillitis, and our doctors insisted on their isolation from the children – usual panic – so I alone went to the door of their room to wave at them and tell them that I'd arranged for thick coats for their journey in case the weather changed or it took longer than expected. That was the last I have seen of Victoria. She left a great many things with me – clothes and jewelry that she didn't want to carry across Europe at that time – and the Bolsheviks have them now. Ludwig too – he will have lost money in Russia because he had so much invested in mines and the like. I wonder how they will live after the war?

Monsieur Poincaré came in July, and there was a full range of ceremonies for him. How distant it seems now, that great military review, when all the officers were in their coloured ceremonial uniforms for the last time – mile upon mile of them stretching across the dusty plain of Krasnoe Selo, their voices like the roar of the sea when they prayed aloud for Nicky and our ally. The children were all in uniform, as I recall, because by this time Marie and Anastasia had their own regiments – Kazan and Caspian – like the bigger ones at their age, and Alexei is Hetman of all the Cossacks from birth. And I – my Crimean Uhlans. But we rode in a carriage together (once only – at their Jubilee – I led my regiment on horseback; this the girls never did though they have faced the troops from the saddle, and Alexei was not permitted to ride). Nicky alone was on a horse, facing the soldiers and calling out to them, 'God bless you, my children!' always such a moving moment, and his voice is clearly heard across the field. 'God bless your Imperial Majesty!' they cried back as always. I could weep to think of it now. Then there were fireworks and a Naval review, and big ceremonial dinners, and finally the President's fleet steamed away across the Baltic and we could relax. Briefly.

In the morning we heard about Austria's ultimatum to Serbia. How stupid it all was - they'd traced the assassination to a group with Serbian links, or so they claimed. But no-one thought it meant war, still - twice in the past ten years we'd come to the brink over the Balkans, and it had been averted; *Au fond*, they are not worth fighting over and I never really believed....

But it all escalated so fast. Russia was playing for time, urging both sides to arbitration, and Austria ignored us - they just lined up at the Bosnia-Serb border and refused to back down. Serbia called upon the ancient alliance. Somewhere along the line they claimed they had accepted the terms of the ultimatum, but Austria had ignored this and just started shelling.

Well, our mobilization was not universally popular. Grigory for one sent Nicky a telegram, the gist of which was why should a single Russian die for the sake of the ungrateful Serbs. Then also Witte with his broader more cynical perspective was rushing around Petersburg saying that the idea that the idea of the Serbs being Slavs and 'blood brothers' to whom we owed a duty of care was just romantic rubbish, and we should leave them to get what was coming to them, we couldn't afford a war. It's easy to criticise when you don't have to make the decisions, but there was a lot in this. For the first and last time in my life I found myself of a mind with Witte.

The counter to it was the military and the ministers - Nikolasha and long-nosed Sazonov above all - with their hardened arguments about Russia's status as great power depending in standing up to Austria. I feel so sad for sweet Nicky's sense of chivalry and duty to Serbia, and how wrong it all went. But

Russia and Austria were evenly matched: the struggle could have been contained if Germany hadn't got involved.

Strange, dreamlike days. I remember Nicky being with Sazonov and the ambassadors for hour after hour, but I remember him escaping too and coming down to the garden where the three younger children were playing with a huge wooden swan on wheels, and the big ones and I were gardening. Nicky wanted a walk, and he brought the swan along, and at one time I remember that I was sitting on the back of it, and the rest of them were pushing or pulling it and we were laughing, and everything was so normal. We were as usual at dear Peterhof, in the Dacha down by the water. On July 18th (Russian style; in Western Europe it was 31st) Nicky was very late for dinner. The girls and I sat waiting, and they bickered gently amongst themselves as normal. 'Mama,' (this was Olga), 'can you ask Anastasia to stop making smells!' 'I can't help it!' the little one protested, 'I've had a worm – I'm trying to get rid of it!' Olga tried to slap her, not entirely light-heartedly. 'Spoilt little scatological brat!'

I sent Tatiana to look for their father but as she was getting up he appeared anyway and said from the doorway, 'Germany has declared war on us.' I was horrified, 'Why? What has happened? – Why didn't I know about this?' – I was shocked because our general mobilization had been accompanied by assurances to William that only Austria was targeted; Nicky wanted rotten William to act as arbitrator; until the eleventh hour he was pleading for the whole matter to be sent to the court at The Hague. Now he said to me, 'I don't know, I can't imagine; it seems that none of the assurances I have given have had the slightest affect on William or anyone in Berlin. Now I have to go back to Sazonov.' 'France will be next, then,' I said – the terms of the Alliance made it unavoidable; Germany was attacking us on Austria's behalf, our ally would come in too. 'Yes.' Nicky said. Several of the children started crying, and he held out his arms to them with such a look of anguish in his eyes. How in Heaven could we afford the human and financial impact of a European war? – And on a desperately selfish level, how could we sleep easy with so many dear ones on the wrong side?

Two days later we went to Petersburg by boat for a formal declaration of hostilities. The Neva embankment was crowded with people; they hung off the bridges and cheered and shouted and waved their flags. There was a popular song I remember from those days; it was printed in the papers, and if they weren't singing it then, they were within days: –

'Uncle Fritz has gone quite barmy; Wants to have a boxing match! But who leads the German Army? Willy Whiskers, stupid cat!'

(Funny how all the hatred immediately crystallised upon Germany and on William personally; it was as though the ancient national enmity for crumbling Austria didn't count any more).

Many more people were out on the river, bobbing about in their sailing dinghies and steamers. We walked through the crowds on the quay and into the Palace – Nicky and me and the four Girlies. Baby was at home with his poor sprained ankle, alas.

In the Nicholas Hall he took the oath not to make peace while a single enemy remained on Russian soil. We went onto the balcony, and we were deafened and swamped by the singing and noise from the crowd below. It was like the coronation all over again, except in a different city, the city where usually there was protest and complaint: at last, in Petersburg, one really felt the holy unity of Tsar and people – if only it didn't take a national crisis to pull everyone together like this. But even the Duma behaved well in those early days.

And of course Germany was stupid enough to violate Belgian neutrality on its way to attack France, so on August 4th (Western style) Britain came in. We went to Moscow for another ceremony in the second capital, and the crowds there were waving the three red, white and blue flags – Britain, Russia, France – curious coincidence that they were all the same colour.

For me, my family was split down the middle. Victoria, Ella, Alix - Allied countries. Irène, Ernie - Central Powers. Husband leading Russia; a brother-in-law at the head of the British Navy and a nephew serving in it. But also a brother in the German Army, a brother-in-law high up in the German Fleet and two nephews serving in that. Such agony, especially for my Ernie and our little old country, dragged willy nilly into this war which will ruin it, thanks to the idiotic ambition and pride of rotten Prussia. It even went through my mind that William would send Ernie to the Russian front to revenge himself on Nicky and me, but thank God he went to France instead. Letters crept through via the family in neutral countries like Sweden and Greece: Ernie described how he walked amongst his colleagues and how alone he felt, and what all the pain and suffering was doing to his sensitive soul. 'Oh God if I survive this war I will spend the rest of my days searching the universe for some means to ensure that it never happens again.'

CHAPTER FOURTEEN

Most people in those early days were full of wild optimism. They were in fact mad. A huge crowd ransacked the German Embassy in Petersburg (a lovely modern building: Peter Behrens - Ernie's friend - designed it) and pulled the bronze horses off the roof. In all the allied countries there were attacks on poor little dogs because they happened to be Germanic breeds, and that December I had to have a row with the Synod when it tried to ban Christmas trees because they were German in origin! Nicky received a great rush of petitions from people with German-sounding names who had been in Russia for generations but who suddenly wanted a Russian name too (just like Petersburg at once became Petrograd). There are multitudes of such people: Stürmer, Mekk, Fredericks (or is that Swedish?), Benckendorff, Hohenfelsen, to name just a few of those known to us. Heaps of people from the Baltic too. Once upon a time I had a terrific argument with our Mossolov because he insisted that the name of the Imperial Family was not Romanov at all but Holstein-Gottorp, like the father of Peter III. (He: 'This must be right, the Almanach de Gotha says so'). Well, it's a moot point as to whether any of the current family descend from Peter at all (Catherine the Great was his wife after all, and she even implied in her memoirs that the son wasn't his), but it just goes to show how old and strong are the racial and cultural links which tie us to our enemy.

Nevertheless, the utter rot some people did come out with! 'This isn't a political war,' Aunt Miechen said, 'it's a dual to the death between Slavism and Germanism.' She who had been Princess Marie of Mecklenburg! But then, those Mecklenburgs did always claim Slavic descent, I suppose... For us, the worst thing happened in England. It took just weeks for the furore whipped up in some of the newspapers about the Navy being led by a man with a German name to force Ludwig to step down as First Sea Lord. And after he had done so much to ensure that the Navy was actually ready for the war when it came: the narrow-mindedness is too colossal! Poor Ludwig, it broke him entirely, and on the only picture I have seen of him since, he looks an old man.(Well, he isn't young, he is actually more or less a generation older than I am in terms of years, but he was in good health and fit until his resignation).Victoria too - what has happened to her? - she was only fifty-one when the war broke out, but she never tried to nurse or anything like that as Louise has done - it's as though they are in retirement now. It was the press's doing, but Aunt Miechen let people know in no uncertain terms who she thought was to blame for his misfortune: 'If his wife could have kept her mouth shut for more than ten minutes at a time, he wouldn't be in this mess. Naturally people thought he was a spy when she went round Europe proclaiming that Henry of Prussia passed German secrets to him - they were all wondering what English secrets he'd passed to Henry of Prussia.' Poor Victoria - like me, she has fallen foul of Aunt Miechen in some way or another - and in any case Miechen was using her alleged faults as a none-too-subtle means of attacking me.

The war changed nothing as far as the Family was concerned, I simply couldn't believe it. The young Grand Dukes and Princes went on with their parties; Miechen held her salons for intrigue and gossip; Nikolai Mikhailovich spread rumours in the Yacht Club; the theatres were open, the dance-halls were open. One time I discovered that one of these halls was using my name, advertising an evening's entertainment with proceeds to one of my Committees - well meant no doubt, but hideously frivolous to be thinking of the tango, etc. at such a time, and I went wild and got it stopped. Nicky banned the sale of alcohol for the duration of the war, but this had no impact on the Grand Dukes, who simply dipped into their own cellars. Just three of them were noticeably involved in the war effort: Nikolasha of course and Sandro with developing the air force, and Sergei his brother with munitions – the result being severe failures in the supply, and a number of financial scandals around him and his mistress. However the War Minister lost his job for that instead because the Duma was down on him – so all was well and as normal....

Dmitri went sporadically to the Front, but he and most of the other young ones contrived to develop a series of health problems which prevented them doing much at all. Only Kostia's fourth boy Oleg went seriously, and was almost immediately killed.

Misha who had been living at Knebworth House in England until 1914 returned to Russia and made many demands relating to his wife's status, though he was a decent commander who became popular with the troops. Uncle Paul was ill the whole time. Kirill, Boris and Andrei V. took turns to be ADC to Nicky and didn't even bother thinking up an excuse for not being at the front.

On the whole, the women did better. Marie P. and Sister Olga and Kostia's Tatiana were all nursing from the start – but even here one heard wild stories – for instance that Tatiana K. got the St George medal just because she'd visited an area where shelling had once taken place – really cheapens it, and I was angry. How I hate the spectacle of these kings and princes who parade around the world covered in decorations they have done nothing to earn – William was always the worst, but they were none of them exempt, apart from my sweet love. His father appointed him Colonel, and he has steadfastly refused to promote himself further, which is as it should be. Nevertheless our Benckendorff came to me to and asked that one send Cousin George a Russian field-marshal's baton, and when I said no, he doesn't command and one doesn't play with such nominations, he looked at me as if I'd gone mad. Quite a shock - it brought straight home to me how far the court fogies lie from me in political terms - and they are indicative of the whole of Petersburg society. Still living in the (early) nineteenth century; and the same alas was true of so many people running the war: old men sending young men to their deaths. I did what I could about this - any time I heard of a regiment or division commanded by an elderly time-server I took steps to get him removed. Several of them we 'kicked upstairs', which is to say they were given ceremonial roles on the Headquarters staff, where they could do no harm. England however had many of them in positions of great influence, and the result was the hideous massacres on the Somme and at Ypres. They tried to fight a modern war as if it were still a question of cavalry and foot soldiers slugging away, and the casualties were just appalling.

So many familiar names. From England my cousin Maurice, almost at once during the retreat from Mons. Here, Oleg K., and then poor Botkin's eldest boy, and our priest's son too. Benckendorff got the telegram and asked me to break the news to Father Alexander - one of the hardest things I've ever done, seeing the tears running silently down his poor brave face and into his beard as he thanked me for letting him know. As far as Germany was concerned, there was my godchild, my friend Toni's boy, nineteen years old. Mossy my cousin lost two young sons; Moritz Riedesel zu Eisenach who taught me to drive four-in-hand lost three.

'I so want to help you, dears!' Tatiana said. 'I wish I was a boy and could go off to fight.' Nicky and I had to say, 'Sweety, thank God you're not!' I found plenty for her and Olga to do on the Home Front. Each chaired a Committee to help refugees, POWs families, etc., and I was so pleased that they were truly involved in the administrative work. Teaches them to think on their feet, alone and without me telling them what to do always. They worked in the store at Tsarskoe on collecting clothes and the like for the troops and making sure they found their way to the right people. I also had the two little girls involved in this when they weren't at lessons, and all five children knitting scarves, jerseys, etc. to contribute. Each child funded in his or her name a hospital train to carry the wounded back from the front, and the two eldest were actively involved in the administrative aspects of this. One had to move fast with regard to the hospitals and the sanitary trains, otherwise many would have died unnecessarily – casualties were so high from the start. Thank God I quickly managed to get 85 hospitals set up under my direct control in Petrograd alone; for the first time almost I didn't find anyone obstructing me or objecting to the principles of what I was doing. They all recognised the national emergency. Ella's old house on the Nevsky Prospekt where only Dmitri now lived in his little flat became the home of the English Hospital, and the Big Palace at Tsarskoe was ready very quickly to receive the wounded in spite of some people saying of course that this wasn't appropriate. (What else was it being used for, exactly?!) – Thus we could walk or motor across to it very fast each morning and begin work.

I needed to be nursing personally – partly because all hands are required at such a time, but also so I could feel in myself that I was offering some help that cost me more than just my time and money. So many were giving so much, it's the least I could do. Also, it was a consolation in some ways when my darling was away from me, as he was so often after November 1914. He went first in September on a week-long visit to the Front, to see the wounded and cheer up those going out again. In October he was away at Headquarters for slightly longer, and then much of November and December, coming back for Christmas on 18th (see how I remember the exact dates still!) and staying with us then for a whole blessed month. Really, his first instinct was to place himself at the head of the Army, and of course he couldn't forgive himself not doing so in 1904 and he felt this was part of the reason Russia lost that war – it looked like the leadership was not properly committed. In 1914 all the ministers were very much against his taking supreme command and so incidentally was our own personal spiritual adviser and Friend – although one was not at that time paying too much attention to his views, because he'd been so against the war anyway and he persisted in sending letters warning Nicky about it all, 'Dear friend, I say again, a menacing cloud is over Russia....they kept wanting war, evidently not knowing that this is the end. Don't allow the madmen to triumph and destroy themselves and the People.' In retrospect – how right, but at the time it was very unhelpful to be reminded that war was a bad thing when we had all our attention now on trying to win it. I remember that Ania was saying he wanted to see us, and I said, 'Let him wait a few days, I'm busy.' She let me know that Grigory was angry about that; he put the phone down on her.

Nevertheless for various reasons Nicky didn't take command; he put Nikolasha there instead, a disastrous move if ever there was one, but popular with the ministers and Duma and part of the Army. *Au fond*, maybe my darling has a lingering belief anyway that such jobs are best given to members of the Family, who have a vested interest in the doing their best, as Sandro always used to say, and are trained for the Army from birth. Well, maybe they do have an interest, but it doesn't make them any good. Nikolasha was always part of the war party – he and his Balkan wife, hang her – and violent, hysterical and unbalanced to boot. His fault and Witte's that the Duma existed, though he was no sort of liberal by any means. Whatever his personal loyalties, he was without doubt the tool of a right-wing militarist faction who wanted Nicky off the throne and a sort of wild demagogue figure in his place. Also, he was an incompetent commander, and we reaped the consequences of that. Nicky at Headquarters in 1914-5 was in his shadow in the worst sort of way, and all the Ministers were even going straight to Nikolasha for their orders

– but at least the troops got to see their Tsar often and to know that he was with them in spirit.

I in the meantime was going to the Catherine Hospital in the big palace after church in the morning (suddenly with the war we became like Ella and there were services daily!). Olga, Tatiana and also at first Ania came with me, and together we went through the two-month course of clinical and anatomical lectures, and learning to work under supervision. Firstly we were only permitted to stand by, holding ether cones or handing instruments across to the qualified staff, but there was so much that needed doing, I couldn't wait to get started. Every day more men arriving on trains from the trenches, all of them dirty and feverish and some with maggots crawling through their wounds. This latter was shocking at first but of course it is a good thing – they keep the wound clean until the nursing staff can get to it. It is less good if you meet that sickly-sweet smell of rotting flesh, because then you know that gangrene has set in and an amputation will probably be necessary. Such a painful feeling to assist at operations of this type and to have a whole leg passed across to you, and to know that it will go to be burnt like a piece of refuse. And they have to learn to live again without it.

But this I had expected: this is the conspicuous side of the physical wounds. What I had not appreciated so well are the hidden ones: that men can get gangrene anywhere, and perhaps in a sense the consequences of a wound in the groin can be harder to live with for a normal man. The younger girl nurses I sent out of the room when we came to dress wounds such as these, it was simply too distressing. My two young girl nurses were simply marvelous. So cool-headed and so gentle from the beginning, even on the day they saw their first death (poor man haemorrhaged during his operation). Ania on the other hand got bored by it all – not enough attention being paid her personally – and she was shockingly rough at some of the wound-dressing. She preferred it if she could escort parties of injured when they were taken off to convalesce or wherever, because then she flirted madly with whoever had particularly caught her attention this week, and she enjoyed the appreciative things they said about her. On the other hand, she put lots of own money into the war effort (and she didn't have much of it) and she was not at all a bad administrator, so without a doubt she was doing her best according to her talents.

She and I and maybe Isa or Nastinka of my ladies often used in the afternoons to go off to other towns and visit the hospitals I had there. Best not to warn the staff that I was coming, since otherwise they panicked and put on a show, so I used to turn up in my Red Cross uniform and enjoy their reaction when they realised who I was. Also of course went on longer trips which took two days or more – off to Vilno in November, stopping that time at 2 in the morning to pay a surprise visit to a hospital train we came across, apologising all the while for waking them all up. Before Christmas I was in Moscow for more than a week with Nicky and of course Ella as well, checking the hospitals there and enjoying doing war work with my husband beside me for once.

In the evenings at home in those days we would go to our own hospital again, and the three little ones with us, to chat with the wounded and play cards and board games and try to cheer them up (I know I am a bad loser, but the children didn't have to tell the soldiers so!). There were film shows and concerts in there too for their benefit, but I think they enjoyed the children's nonsense the most – they who were missing children of their own, or little brothers and sisters. Sometimes the dogs would come along with us and add more entertainment. At this stage I think Alexei had Joy, Anastasia had Shvibzik, named after herself, silly child, and Tatiana had just acquired Ortino from her flirt Dmitri Malama. Poor little Shvibzik, he died of a cerebral inflammation in 1915; that was when our Jimmy came to replace him.

I couldn't always be there with them, though, because there was as ever admin work to be done and things to read and people to see, and if I didn't do this in the evenings I had to sacrifice a day's hospital work instead. Fortunately I slept horribly badly without my angel there (also probably drinking too much coffee), so I got loads of reading done in the night, particularly of newspapers because Nicky never got the time. Important to keep up with events and public opinion – in the allied countries as much as Russia. Used to hurt me to see differences between us and our Allies underlined – above all between my old (half) country and my new – since these were almost always to the detriment of the latter. For instance there was an English nurse called Edith Cavell who was doing wonders at the front line in Belgium, escorting wounded men under fire and the like, and you would never find a middle-class Russian lady up to that kind of coolness. (On the other hand our chief surgeon in the hospital was Princess Gedroitz and this you don't find in England I have to say – the education system is better for women in England on a general level, but here there is better access to university studies for those who can get there). Also England at once produced a great crop of war poets – and literature is supposed to be a Russian specialty – so where were ours!? (Answer is, at home, because the best-educated and literary-minded were all busy avoiding service). The notable thing was – how many immediately felt the war to be a good thing, and cathartic. (Rupert Brooke saying how God had 'caught his youth and wakened him from sleeping' in a world 'grown old and cold and weary'). Well, this is crazy, to welcome it like that, but so terrible a war simply has to end by purifying people – one can't witness such utter horror and continue to be dry and hard and materialistic as before, it's simply not possible.

Seeing the wounded, knowing what they went through and what their families went through worrying about them, I felt bad to be suffering so selfishly not to have my Nicky there, but

I couldn't help it. We had so rarely been apart until then – never more than a few days perhaps once every couple of years, if that. So quiet at home in the evenings (better for this reason too to go to the hospital) and so sad and cold in bed at night, and such a horrible feeling waking up in the morning and always turning automatically to give him a kiss, and not finding anybody there. I was the only person sleeping on the ground floor in our wing; it felt strange. But overhead were the sounds of Marie and Anastasia lumbering about and playing their gramophone records sometimes quite late in the evening (so would phone then to tell them to go to sleep). The children always wanted to sleep in my room when their father was away; when she was quite tiny Olga would say, 'I am the eldest, I ought to stay with you when Papa's not here!' and thus now there used to be great battles between the little ones, with Alexei proclaiming his rights as 'man of the house,' and Marie and Anastasia vigorously disputing that he had any. One evening Marie phoned me to ask was Anastasia still with me as she hadn't come upstairs yet, and I went into the dressing room and called her name. 'I'm here,' came a mournful voice from the mezzanine floor, 'I'm sitting on the lavatory seat picking my toenail because I'm afraid to go upstairs in the dark.' Cunning little madam! – I let her stay with me that time, but they didn't get to make a habit of it because I keep the light on half the night and they'd end by being tired out and no good for anything.

Sometimes though one or two of the dogs stayed with me: Ortino above all because Olga complained that he snored and she couldn't bear him being in the room with Tatiana and her. In the early hours I wrote my long letters to Nicky and in the summer I got up at this time and watched the sun rise behind the trees, and how the soft pink mist shimmered on the grass, and one could hardly believe half the world was at war.

By the spring of 1915 things were starting to go badly. The first months of the war the politicians (idiots) were saying it would be over by Christmas – such rot, anyone with half a brain could see that it would be a long one. Once again, they were living the nineteenth century. We made good inroads into Austrian and East Prussian territory at first, but they were the defenders and their army was better supplied than ours and they started to drive us back. Nicky in those earliest months made loads of visits to parts of the country he'd never seen before, raising morale. He was in the Caucasus and he wrote me beautiful poetic letters about the mountains and sea and the wonderful fruit gardens, and wondered why I was not with him too. I knew what he meant – somehow one works so hard normally that one never gets to see new places and has so few new experiences. We would have exchanged all the homes in different places across Russia for the simple right to be like other people and to have the romance of being able to take a journey somewhere completely new every year if we felt like it.

He went also to towns in Galicia newly taken from the Austrians – and this worried me. Too triumphal, too early. Sure enough, we then had the humiliation of the slow Russian retreat, and we heard that old Franz Josef was passing through towns where Nicky had been just weeks before. In no way does this look good to the world, and the Duma started making capital out of it. That, I simply could not believe. In France and England the whole of parliament rallied behind the government; ours tried to undermine it. Well, of course, it was built on a vastly different premise and unlike theirs it didn't participate in government itself, but it did surely have a vested interest in making sure that the war was prosecuted successfully, and unfair criticism isn't the way to do this. One could see exactly what was going to happen. This huge country, too dependent on foreign industry, insufficient rolling stock to deal with the supplying of both food and munitions in a prolonged war, was racing against time to victory. The government was trying to shore up the home front for long enough to attain that, and the Duma was pulling in entirely the opposite direction. So from then on there were three clear questions to be addressed: how to improve the military situation; how to deal with the supply problem; how to shut the Duma members' mouths. Everything we did from then on in aimed to solve these problems; and clearly in the end we failed.

The first step was to get rid of the rotten C.-in-C. Germany's advance into Poland had completely unbalanced Nikolasha; I always knew he'd be knocked for six at the slightest setback. He and his staff starting apportioning blame right, left and centre, beginning with poor old Sukhomlinov, whose ultimate ministerial control over munitions they blamed for the defeats. And naturally the press and the Duma took up the refrain until the poor old man had to go; he even ended in jail for a while of course when they decided he was treacherous as well as incompetent. Yes, Nikolasha got a real spy mania going. The most surprising sources warned us about this. Even Nikolai Mikhailovich, my worst enemy in the Family apart from Miechen, wrote Nicky a letter telling him that Nikolasha was dropping wide hints about how my 'German' birth (personally the term I'd use would be 'Hessian', not the same thing at all) made me suspect! I was not the only one: they got several people arrested. In Moscow riots were stirred up and a rock was flung at Ella's carriage. A crowd outside her Convent screamed at her, 'Away with the German woman!' and even accused her that she was hiding Ernie in there. She who had always been so loved.

Finally they started on the most abominably brutal and stupid thing of all, namely herding the Jews out of the western borderlands on the grounds that they were likely to collaborate with the German invader and speed our defeat. Nicky wrote to me naively that these people were fleeing their homes and making terrible difficulties for themselves, and I was furious. I had been to the depots in Petersburg and seen them arriving; every day I went with Tatiana through the piles of papers her Refugee Committee received. I read and heard the stories – and

Nikolasha was trying to persuade his sovereign and master that these people were voluntarily leaving their homes!

In midst of this chaos the Duma started demanding that all the Ministers it didn't like be removed, and against his personal instincts Nicky pretty well gave in to them that time to shut them up. He kept dear old Goremykin in as Prime Minister to keep the new ones in line, though.

Well, it was like 1905 all over again: concessions in time of war, concessions from a position of weakness rather than strength. Opening the floodgates so they all think the time has come to start making demands. And to what end this concession? So the Duma can claim credit for victory without actually having contributed anything of value beyond its nominal approval of the ministers? So they can panic at every set-back as they did at this first one and saddle us with one incompetent after another and end by losing us the war? – Either way it's not a good policy and whatever they may have thought in Petersburg and Moscow it would not be a popular policy in the country.

I was so worried about my poor Nicky at that point. He had been at Headquarters throughout the terrible defeats, and his mood was totally changed from the beginning of the war. He got pains in his chest which worried me hugely, and when he came home on a visit his eyes had such fathomless sadness, it haunted me for days after he left. I couldn't bear to think of what he was going through on his own; even the ADCs at HQ with him were people who he knew less and wasn't close to. (at the beginning of the war he had N.P., who was now off himself with his own regiment). No-one to confide in, no Sunny to caress him tenderly when he was low, and give him courage and back him up.

All my married life I have been chafing quietly against the bullying by one person or another of my gentle husband; suddenly at a time of national emergency I wasn't having it any more. You don't give in to people like Nikolasha and their tools

257

in the Duma: you remove them. And he did. He was home with me for the whole blessed month of July, and he ended by going with his own first instinct and placing himself nominally at the head of the army.

In practice of course it was Alexeiev who commanded, but that is not the point - Nicky was there as a symbol of the government's commitment, of the unity of the civil and the military which Nikolasha had so undermined but which was so needed at that hard time. He told me his decision when we were sitting on the balcony together in the evening, smoking and watching the moths flitting about in the dusk. It must have been pretty late if the dusk was gathering, when you think what time of year it was. We had been visited by Grigory in the week who simply said to him to go with his instincts (though G. personally had always opposed the idea, he was speaking as a spiritual adviser here and not as a man with his own opinions). We had also been to Communion together that day, and Nicky said simply now, 'Yes, I will do what conscience tells me to do. This is how I have always tried to conduct affairs - usually it works better than cold reasoning.' I was overjoyed. I said, 'Oh darling, you won't regret this - I know it. This is the beginning of the glorious times!' - but I was a wee bit anxious as well - as a wife - because although it was a moral weight off his shoulders I couldn't help thinking of how much more work still he would have to do. 'We need to get that strong man to look after the civil side of things and keep the Duma in control,' I added. 'I mean - quickly, before it wears you down.' He was looking at me with a smile, and he said, 'You have been so fierce and determined all this time - really, I admire you more than I can say.'

This was the bad period of Ania's convalescence after her hideous train accident: she was well out of danger but she realised she wouldn't walk again and she was being hopelessly demanding of everyone's time. The children who used to love her when little now pulled a face if I asked them to pay her a visit. She was alright usually with them (although she liked to have them crawling around her arranging cushions for her legs, etc.) but she affected to faint if I so much as jogged her bed too hard. All this coming on top of worrying so much about Nicky and about the war meant I found it increasingly difficult to keep my temper in check with her. Not just her either; the minor stupidities of people in the household set me off as well and I spent heaps of time apologising. So: – 'Fierce and determined?' I said, 'you mean, The Cow gets it every time she opens her mouth the wrong way?!' 'You should arrange your time to suit yourself,' Nicky said. 'I truly wish her well, but she has her parents and her sister and loads of friends, and she doesn't need to be with us so constantly.' 'It's nice she can't come here in the evenings,' I admitted, 'I want you to myself these days, we see so little of each other now.' I was lounging on the sofa, and Nicky came across then and knelt next to me and looked into hard into my eyes. 'Be calm,' he said firmly, and I laughed at him and rubbed noses with him and put my arms round his neck. 'Oh, come here, wee one – me spends much too much time waiting with yearning arms these days.' He obediently lay down on the sofa next to me and I whispered, 'Ah, sweetheart – precious, sunny, big-eyed darling – you are so brave and have such a hard life and me so wants to make it easier for you. Me feels so much a mother to you sometimes.' He smiled wryly and put his hand over my mouth, 'Enough! – Very *ne nado*!' but a few moments later he said, 'Won't you help me, then? – I mean here and in town, while I'm at the *Stavka*.' I was startled. 'How do you mean?' He opened his eyes again and looked up at me. 'I mean – be my eyes and ears in the rear. You can see the ministers for me and keep them in line.' I was actually quite shocked. 'Me – talking to ministers about government matters?' 'Yes – why not? – You need to have more confidence in yourself, Lovebird – it seems to me that you were born to do a job like that.' 'Bossy and meddlesome, you mean? – Really, though – I have tried before, but I felt very strongly the ministers didn't like me. Remember Kokovtsev?' 'Kokovtsev wasn't the same as dear old Goremykin.' 'No – but others will be. There's a certain type of man – doesn't like a woman with too much to say for herself. I mean – even in our household there are plenty though they try to hide it – Mossolov can't bear me, and Fat Orlov stinks of valerian every time he comes into my presence it's such an ordeal for him, poor man!' Nicky was quite indignant. 'How could you possibly think anyone didn't like you?!' – But I am less sweet and trusting than he is, and I knew their feelings well.

It was hell seeing him go back to the *Stavka*: worse than ever although Nikolasha and his set weren't there any more. By this stage they had settled on Mogilev as permanent HQ of course: quite a distance back from the original station at Baranovichi, because of the enemy advance. Still further away from me. So we went through the usual beastly business of saying goodbye at the station with half the world looking on, and when I got home and went to dinner with the children in the playroom I immediately started writing a letter to him. I was eating and trying to listen to them chatting too, and they were all firing at each other with their water pistols, which was their little fad just then. In the middle of it all Olga first and then Tatiana broke off and came round to whisper in my ear, 'Papa says to tell you he loves you frantically, more than ever – a real *puits d'amour*.' Then, afterwards, when I went to the mauve room to finish the letter, the three little ones appeared one at a time and also gave me sweet messages from their father. I was so touched the way he'd done this that I absolutely howled like a baby! – darling, not many men would think to set up such a scheme to make their wife happy!

Alexei was worrying me about a cinema that had been taken of him and Joy in the garden. He was whirling round and round with a stick in his hand while the dog jumped about him. I thought it was charming and cheerful and should be shown publicly, but he was distressed by this. '*En faisant des pirouettes?* - The dog looks more intelligent than I do!' I decided I think then that the time had come to send him with his father. He was not by any means a baby any more, he was all but eleven and sharp and funny and bright, but he remained very behind in his lessons because of all the interruptions. He had had to study that year even during the Christmas and Easter breaks when the others were free, partly to keep up while he was well and partly because he was so naughty when he had too little to occupy his mind. His French was getting to be very good because he so liked Zhilik's company, but Sig complained he ate sweets with great concentration during English lessons and looked for excuses to leave his seat. Everyone worried about the fact that he hadn't started on fractions yet and he couldn't decline the cases properly for Russian numerals.

So I resolved that he was going to go to the *Stavka* after Nicky's next visit home. - Felt that living with the soldiers and seeing so much of the war at first hand would mature him and occupy his active mind; it would compensate in some ways for the academic gaps by broadening him out. We always strove also for ways of making sure he didn't grow up as shy as his father: that always was Nicky's foremost problem (attractive as it is from my perspective), and the *Stavka* experiment was part of that. On top of all this, he was the Heir to the throne of a country that was going through a terrible and momentous experience - a once-in-a-century experience, I did hope - and he needed to understand fully what that was about. The troops too needed to see him - an inspiration and morale-booster. - And I wanted Nicky to have his company - someone to cheer him up as all our treasures cheered me up when he was away.

But it was so hard, letting my littlest one go! Nicky was home a few days in September and while he was with us we got the boy measured up for khaki private soldier's uniforms and greatcoats. His sailor suits went into the drawer never to

261

re-emerge: such a sad day – no babies any more! – Besides, sentimentality apart, I could hardly bring myself to relax when he was out of my sight. He had never been away from me for more than a few hours and it brought back the time after Spala when being apart from him used to bring on a panic attack almost with wondering how he was.

Briefly after they went off, I kept waking in the night suddenly with my heart pounding and the feeling that something dreadful was about to happen. I remember saying his prayers for him up in his bedroom, and then I would go to his smaller pair of sisters who were bathing and chucking scent around – always violet with Anastasia, usually lilac for Marie, isn't it? but she did experiment – and try to be cheery with them. Sometimes for a treat they used Nicky's big sunken bath, and water went everywhere. As autumn came on, they drew their beds together at the centre of the room for warmth. Anastasia had bronchitis and I moved Marie in with the big ones, but as soon as recovery began she was back again, and she would hide under the bed clothes when Ostrogorsky came to listen to Anastasia's chest, and be very embarrassed if he pulled the covers back too far and found her there in just her nightgown. My merry little girlies – they were the sunshine in my quiet home, lost without its centre.

Olga on the other hand was a worry. She broke down from time to time after a day at the hospital, and when I reminded her about Committee work that needed doing she would snap at me, 'I'm tired! There are plenty of other people who can do it instead – why should it always be us?' 'Because there is a war on,' I said to her, 'and in any case I want you to be useful – I didn't bring you up to be a doll.' 'I am not some little princess from a petty German court!' she raged at me, 'I am the daughter of the Tsar, and maybe I would like for once to do something which demands dignity!' 'All the dignity you've earned,' I always used to say sarcastically – and by this stage I had sometimes lost my temper with her. But she was anaemic and run-down, and the war was heavy on her soul, my poor sensitive girl – so I took her out of nursing for a while and let her spend her time reading and larking around in the garden with the little ones. Therefore, if I didn't go in to work for whatever reason, it all fell upon Tatiana. Tatiana coped with it.

CHAPTER FIFTEEN

All through the autumn with Nicky at Mogilev old Goremykin brought his reports to me. There was another stupid Duma revolt involving the demands of the so-called Progressive bloc but he faced it down with far more dignity than his younger, stronger colleagues, and the Bloc fell apart. We thought we'd found our 'strong man' to look after the wartime government.

Needless to say, the rest of the ministers had it in for him and made his job hard; Grigory came to me with complaints about him, presumably on the basis of things one was saying in rotten Petrograd, whose views he passed to us all the time – he was so keen to help. We ignored all of this, but before the end of winter the Old Man asked to be relieved of his posts. He said he was simply too old. Nicky well before this had to be rid of Shcherbatov from the Interior post. That one made a good impression on me at first but he was useless in controlling the excesses of the press, and we had a load of bosh again about spies and about how Grigory was controlling the government. I ask you?! – Did any of our allies put up with this sort of demoralising stuff from the press in wartime? – Britain is even censoring the soldiers' letters. Then S. managed to provoke a strike in Petrograd by locking up a load of innocent people, and generally he was a rotten lot all round. One bitterly regretted Maklakov who had been pushed out in June by the Duma and Nikolasha's people.

As for our 'strong man' that we so needed: it should have been Krivoshein. Before the war, back in his days of sparring with pompous Kokovtsev, Krivoshein was 'heir apparent', the man most likely to be Chairman of the Council of Ministers someday although he was so invaluable in Agriculture. But by

1915 he wouldn't serve. He was one of those who protested Nicky's decision to assume supreme command, and just after that he resigned. Alas for our last truly brilliant man – and alas for my poor darling who found himself left with so few real choices at such a hard time. It's treachery, truly.

In place of Shcherbatov we got Khvostov – my first attempt to select a man for minister and oh, God, how I regret that mistake! – No doubt about it, it was entirely and completely my fault. In 1911 he had been considered briefly for another post but old Khvostov, the uncle, warned Nicky that his nephew was unstable and too young. Dear old Goremykin too said to me that Khvostov was not to be trusted; he made inflammatory speeches in the Duma about Jews and Germans – at a pinch, he was one of Nikolasha's lot. But we were desperate; he came to see me and actually he impressed me. He had given plenty of thought to the problem of supplying the cities and the troops, and he had good ideas about managing demobilization at the end of it all. Fat man, but with plenty of energy, and I felt maybe they had taken against him because of his age and spontaneity. He was youngish but he was no boy – my age, and I'd been doing this job for twenty years! Being of the Duma helped of course; he would keep them calm. I even used to make affectionate puns on the meaning of his name – he was 'the tail' to Nicky and me, as if he was a friend, hang him!

My next choice was a good one though: in place of Krivoshein I suggested Naumov, who did his job well and for quite a long time, for all that he was one of the idiots who had persistently moaned about Grigory's supposed influence. This was the sort of man we needed: one who would put aside his personal prejudices (probably he despised Nicky and me for 'tolerating' Grigory) and use his great talents for his poor country's good when she so needed him.

The 'tail' Khvostov however just went completely mad. Wasn't long in office before a terrible story emerged via the newspapers and via Ania: Khvostov had tried to get the police to have Grigory murdered. Our Friend's poor cats had been poisoned first as an experiment – such a ridiculous touch it would have been funny if not so cruel! – And Beletsky of the police who was once the tail's friend turned upon him and initiated a terrible correspondence in the press which shamed them and everyone else before the eyes of the world. 'Russians are not accustomed to see their ministers behave like the Mafia!' thundered Beletsky, just in case anyone had failed to get the point. Well, on its own, this disgusting little story wouldn't have harmed anyone except Khvostov himself, but coming on top of all the things some people were starting to believe about us, it must have done absolutely loads of damage to Nicky's standing: fancy having a Minister of the Interior who turns out to be a criminal! – I will never never forgive myself for that.

And Grigory of course – I felt so bad on his behalf. This man helped us, on several occasions saved the life of our son, and he had no more involvement with the Ministers than any holy man in the church had ever done. Of course he would approve and bless our choice or otherwise just like John of Kronstadt or others did for Nicky's father, but this is a traditional role, and one never subjected Father John to such treatment. Fancy trying to kill him just because he was our friend! – I could never get to the bottom of the motivation, because the fat Tail was a monarchist – probably that was the problem. It was this old old story like Ernie and Victoria and Ella always said – that his perceived interference was damaging us. As I see it, that was the fault of the Duma and the press who spread such stories, and it was up to the Minister of the Interior to shut their libels up – not to try kill Grigory! To be leaving poison around his flat – where his little girls also lived! It says much about a man – this inability to keep a sense of perspective on matters such as who the Emperor will have as his friends – and that too was the problem with having Samarin for church affairs.

He again was the Duma's choice, and he spent his whole term of office carrying on about Grigory instead of thinking about the churches and congregations. After that he fell into a huge conflict with some of the Bishops over the question of canonising John Maximovich - some narrow doctrinal point, usual Moscow bigotry - and sent off some wild telegrams calling me names ('foolish woman', etc.) and accusing Nicky of undermining him by siding with the Bishops. Absolutely wonderful. Getting rid of him at the same time as Shcherbatov (and Krivoshein resigning too) cannot have looked too good in terms of consistency, but this reflected more on the Duma for having insisted on him in the first place than it did on Nicky - or at least it should have done. The press started going on about 'ministerial leapfrog' - and certainly if Nicky hadn't given in to the Duma in the first place it would have looked better - but as in 1905 with Mirsky hindsight is a wonderful thing.

The Khvostov business was just a nightmare, though; my fault, and made things simply worse than ever. It really dented my confidence in my judgement - and until then I had been feeling quite happy about it. Of course I never really wanted to be involved; I was scared stiff of having to talk to these people on political matters - whether using Russian or French, I was afraid it would desert me, and in any case I would show my ignorance of so many things and make Nicky look bad. Old Goremykin helped me a lot; he said I was '*l'energie*' and kept him up to his job, which made me laugh. Then also there were the doom-merchants - mostly members of the Family - who would come to say that Nicky should not have taken supreme command, it would damage him a lot when there were defeats. This annoyed me, and I would show them the foreign newspapers and how they praised him for his commitment to his allies and to successful prosecution of the rotten war - and I reminded them of the terrible things that Nikolasha's command had brought about because in the autumn of 1915 we were still reaping the results of his persecutions in the Baltic states as well as of Jews in Byelorussia and the Ukraine. And when I'd finished holding forth they were convinced – or if they weren't they didn't dare say so! – and I felt more confident in my political abilities. I even won Miechen for a while, paying her a visit one afternoon in town, and talking long about the need for strong united government in time of war – she absolutely agreed. And Ducky too – sitting there looking old and ugly with her long equine face poor thing – she was a marvel in the war, she nursed in areas under fire and she won the St George Cross and alone of the family she really deserved it.

Sometimes coming out of an audience with the Old Man or Naumov or whoever I would catch sight of myself in a mirror and it made me laugh with astonishment – 'Look at me with all the Ministers suddenly!' The Khvostov business dented all that for a while, but in time Nicky found Stürmer to take both Interior and also the Council of Ministers so the Old Man could retire. Stürmer had been a good provincial governor; he was no Krivoshein but he would do as our 'strong man' to keep the ministers in check and the supply system working, and even the Duma were happy when Nicky visited them (my advice) to introduce him and say he hoped they would work well together and sort out the supply questions. I felt better about things then: far more effective to placate the Duma than to close it down and have another huge storm in Petersburg – Petrograd – and Moscow. – And mostly when I wavered I just had to think back to Nicky's tired eyes and thin face – suddenly he looked much older than before the war – and that spurred me on.

Beginning of 1916 the whole family went on a journey to the south, and although we were working – I inspecting hospitals, Nicky seeing troops – it felt like a real holiday. Of course what with I at Tsarskoe, he chiefly at the *Stavka* since war started we hadn't been near any of the places that normally gave us a change of scenery (even if the ministers had always followed). – In 1915 I was just one day at Peterhof, seeing hospitals. I looked at our house there – our dear Lower Dacha – where so many of the dear children were born (all but Olga and Tatiana – T. was born nearby in the Farm) and at the sea and the little yacht the *Alexandria* which once used to carry us out to our beautiful *Standart* and it felt like a million years since those peaceful days. So sad – and thus in the south we didn't go near Livadia although we were tempted – simply not the right time to be taking a break in such a lovely place. The journey itself was enough. In the Crimea though we passed through Evpatoria and the children went onto the sand while we were working – that was sufficient, they get pleasure out of the simplest things as we brought them up to do. At public appearances the girls ran down the steps behind us jostling into one another and laughing like high-spirited babies, and I had to turn around and joke with them, 'If you don't stop at once I'll tie you all together in a row on a string, and that'll look very grown-up, won't it?'

Down there we saw more of Tartar life than ever before and went to a service in a mosque – the girls and I too, they relaxed their rules for us – and also visited the Jews of the Karaite sect. My heart was bursting with love for this great diverse empire and all its traditions and all it could one day be, and I launched forth to Nicky about the behaviour of our troops in Turkish territory, and how they should leave everything as they found it and not mess up places sacred to other peoples' culture or religion like the English do. We had so many plans for peace when finally it would come.

But oh God what a hideous war! – By and large things went much better for us with Alexeiev in command, but the ghastly inhumanity of it all! Back at home I had a steady stream of Red Cross informants coming to me with news of our front and the western front and the impact on life back in the villages. Ian Malcolm (remembered this man from the coronation in '96, when he was an attache at the British Embassy) brought me expanding dum-dum bullets that were banned by Nicky's first Hague Conference and were suddenly being used anyway. Also the British and the Germans threw gas at each other's troops though that had been banned too. There were zeppelin raids on London; I heard our own air force buzzing constantly overhead, preparing themselves to defend if anything should happen. Irène wrote to me officially as from the German Red Cross to ask about the treatment of their prisoners of war, and I investigated and was not happy with what I found but when I tried to do something about it - apart from the humanitarian angle, it makes sense to treat them well, since then the Germans will do the same to ours - Petrograd society said this was because I was with them in spirit. (Ania was good at letting me know what people were saying about me, sometimes well beyond the point that I could tolerate.)

Inflation of course started climbing well beyond the hike in wages; lots of new notes were printed and these proved so flimsy that people were able to copy them and use them to cheat shop-keepers or cab drivers. This was the sort of useful detail that Grigory passed on and which would have escaped us completely otherwise because hanged if the ministers bothered! - but thus Nicky was able to arrange a pay rise for those in government employ, and to order an investigation into minting methods.

The generals kept him at Headquarters the whole spring and summer of 1916 - right through the agonising, glorious days of the Brusilov offensive. As he couldn't come home the girls and I started going often to see him, and I was so glad finally to see the *Stavka*, and to experience how he lived there. When first HQ settled at Mogilev Nicky had lived in a wood nearby in his train, but it started getting damp so he moved into the former Governor's house with his suite and the Allied representatives. The house was really not nice - dark and old-fashioned - but especially after Alexei was there it was obviously better to live somewhere that was at least dry. It touched me to see how they slept on campbeds side by side, and I heard how the boy woke his father up early in the morning and chatted away until Nicky chucked a pillow at him to quieten him down. Then Tiny was having lessons while Nicky saw the generals and the ministers (they came periodically from Petrograd to give him no peace) and when I was there I worked on the train and let our girls run wild in the neighbourhood with the ladies of the suite (usually took two with me) chatting to people they met and seeing provincial life. They came back in time for lunch, and Olga was often in a state of distress about some evidence of poverty that she'd come across, 'There was a little child on crutches, and I asked and he said it was perfectly curable only his parents couldn't afford treatment! – I am going to put money aside to help him myself.' – because we had just given her control of her private income that used to be looked after by me. Later on I discovered from Isa Buxhoeveden that so rattled had Olga been she'd forgotten to ask the child's name or address; it was Tatiana walking calmly behind who'd picked up the details – such were the differences between our two good-hearted big girls. Tatiana's Refugee Committee had by this time grown to be almost the size of a government department, and she, eighteen years old, now handled much of the administration without my help. I said to Nicky, 'Do you see what we have here?' and he answered, 'She's just like her mother' – but she isn't. True, her bossy managerial side is like mine, but it's not me that bequeathed her so patient and hardworking a nature, my love!

We used to have lunch in the house (or – better – when it was warm – in a marquee in the garden) with the suite and the foreign generals, and I must say I was horrified by the way Alexei used to behave. He'd wait until Nicky was talking to someone and then he'd start shoving salt cellars, mustard pots and anything else he could lay his hands on down the table towards one of the Allied contingent, demanding that they count in three seconds how many pieces they had. Other times he'd get up and improvise a game of football with a screwed up napkin or whatever lay to hand, and he'd be nagging the generals to join in – which they often did, because of course his spirits were irresistible to anyone not required to teach him discipline. Since he was a little tiny child we've had trouble with his table manners: he was never much interested in food and he would lick his plate or tease other people at lunch just to pass the time away. Now at *Stavka* Zhilik came to me in despair and wanted the boy brought home to me, but I refused to budge. Certainly he was out of hand, but the benefits of being in that environment outweighed everything else. He had just come on so much in terms of the way he looked at other people: his manners were so much gentler and more humble and like his father's. 'It really is nice of you, you know,' he said holding out a hand when a favour was done – not the same child as the spoilt little autocrat of the nursery at Tsarskoe Selo! – And he went around the hospitals with such calm and sweetness, and held the hands of people who suffered with a look that told them how deeply he understood what they were going through. 'You didn't tell me there were boys like that in the army!' he yelled one time at Nicky, when he'd seen a fifteen year old with horrifying wounds, 'he's the same age as I am!' – He wasn't, but he looked it. Every time I saw Alexei he was taller by what seemed several inches. When barely twelve he was already nearly as tall as Nicky. Slim and straight in his corporal's uniform – he had been promoted – and with the contours of his face starting to appear from beneath its childish roundness. When he was tiny people thought he was like me, and indeed his grey eyes and his nose and chin are very much so, but his cheekbones are wide and Romanov, his eyebrows are straight, and he will be an almost perfect blend of both sides of the family. He complained because I kept forgetting to send his corporal's salary – 'I've had nothing to eat! Soon I shall have to start selling my books so as to be able to live!'

I looked at him and his great solid sisters Marie and Anastasia (both a bit fat then), and the pride was mixed with sadness – no babies any more! – In the afternoons we went on motor rides along by the Dnieper, and we got out and walked and I talked to local peasants' families and held their babies and whistled to them like I used to do with mine – the expression of fascination on their tiny faces! – and I felt such a pain inside and I wanted another one.

We walked in the woods and I saw where Nicky picked the flowers he periodically sent me in his letters. Some days we built bonfires on the banks of the river, and the children baked potatoes like in Finland. We also went onto the river in an electric launch, or we walked through fields and lay down to rest in hayricks, where the girls pleaded for cigarettes and were sometimes given them too. 'When you're not here, we don't often do this,' Nicky said to me. 'I am working and Babykins goes out on his own with Sig or Zhilik. He brings me so much life and sun, but I still long terribly for you when you're not around.' – And he would kiss my hands and cheeks and say, 'I get a little peck of a kiss from him in the morning and the evening but I don't get any real ones – soft and warm and with non-resistant lips!' He made me laugh, rolling around in the grass and trying not to let the girls hear us, and I said, 'How old are we?!' 'In my mind,' he said, 'forever twenty-six and twenty-two, like at Walton in the summer of our engagement. I must say you always looked so demure and I was completely bowled over by how passionate you were! – I am sure I've committed most of the seven deadly sins in my time, but thanks to you the most consistent of these has been lust.'

And he was right – it was like our engagement again, because what with me living on the train and him in the house at HQ and him never being able to come home we didn't sleep together for six months and I started having the most colourful dreams, like in '94 but more so, due to experience. Also we had at that time that lovely book which was so much like our own story – the struggle of 'Boy Blue' to persuade his friend Christabel to marry him against her rational objections (she was ten years older than he) which had nothing to do with her heart – it was like Nicky and me over the religious question. 'I fought for you,' he said, 'and against yourself too! – Like this Boy Blue, only more tenacious.' And she, Christabel, the blue-stocking type trying to be good but prone to the odd cutting remark – she was rather like the young Alix H. The garden that most of their conversations takes place in reminded me of later when all was resolved, and the garden at Elm Grove where we talked for hours and explored each others' souls – that book was oh so special to us the summer of 1916. Of course the critics were hideously snooty about Florence Barclay, and they talked about the 'Jane Austen of the servant's hall' and made scathing remarks about Daily Mail readers, and I wanted to write to the poor woman and tell her that actually her simple, well-written book meant the world to two people from a different milieu who just sometimes feel they'd like a break from heavy literature and bad news. I have always read philosophy and pure science for pleasure or enlightenment and I'm not so intellectually insecure that I can't enjoy something very different once in a while, hang them!

There was a real peace at *Stavka*, far away from Petrograd and all its gossip and panics. 'I have a sense of perspective here,' Nicky said, and could see what he meant. I liked to sleep on the train because the noise and lights of the station around us were a comforting disturbance and very different to the buzz of Sikorski's and Sandro's air force passing overhead like at home.

Usually I didn't take Ania to the *Stavka* with me: it was so much nicer without her. However one time she did come because Grigory rang to rebuke me for being unkind to my nearest friend (which she wasn't! Felt at the time that N.P. was very much closer, we could talk to him about anything). I felt bad and agreed to give her that treat. Of course she went around the house during the day listening to conversations, and then she came back to me and told me that all the Russian generals and most of the foreign ones were in despair at my being there – 'She has come to bring the latest orders from Rasputin.' Made me sad; I never thought the nonsense had spread there too. And of course while I was there Nicky got rid of long-nosed Sazonov and moved Stürmer over to Foreign Affairs instead, and I knew they would all be saying this was my doing. As a matter of fact I wouldn't have done it then: Stürmer was asking to relinquish Internal Affairs but I'd have kept in office anyway – there had already been too many changes that year, what with the various problems at the War Ministry and the matter of rotten Khvostov on top of it. Stürmer feared the Duma although he had always been much more popular with them that the Old Man had, and in any case they were so much less confident of themselves since Brusilov's victories had demonstrated how right Nicky had been to remove Nikolasha and order civil and military to work together. In retrospect I can't help feeling that if we'd kept old Stürmer to his post all would have gone well. The main problem as usual was the question of supplies, and he felt himself at a loss to solve it. I was kept very well informed on this matter by a variety of people: Ian Malcolm for one was travelling all over the country with his Red Cross detachments and he came to me in despair about the inadequate state of the railways for moving food to the cities. One time we stopped all other trains for several days just to get provisions into Petrograd, but of course Internal Affairs and Agriculture were required to collaborate on this and they wouldn't. I could see what was needed: we had to put the matter of supplying into the hands of one person, who would logically be the Minister of Internal Affairs – and Stürmer I am sure could have done it if he'd hadn't turned out to be another beastly coward. If we had to have another change, Protopopov seemed to me like a good choice. He was Vice-President of the Duma (no popularity problems there); he was a successful business man who understood economics, and when he'd been in England and France recently with other Duma deputies had a made a great impression, so that Cousin George and others wrote asking why didn't make more use of this talented man. Well, he was a free-market Whig type so he was bound to go down well in England. I personally favour a more interventionist approach to the economy (look what Witte's free markets did to the workers in our cities), but I am not an expert, we were in an extreme situation, and in any case who else did we have? So Protopopov got Internal Affairs. And good lord didn't he fail us!

In October Nicky relieved Sturmer of the Council of Ministers and Foreign Affairs and I was in despair. This followed the visit to Kiev and I suspected he had been brow-beaten by his mother and Sandro while he was with them there: they always did bow to the fluctuating waves of society opinion, and 'society' hated Stürmer. On Nicky's part this sort of consideration is much less important, but he like I had had enough of the old man's timorousness – the difference is that I wouldn't have indulged it. Poor Nicky was looking again like he had during the crisis of 1915: big hollow eyes and a nervous smile. If anything he was worse.

When he came home to me for a while at last, he was as usual hounded by the ministers, and he came out of meetings with them looking distracted and saying, 'I need to go outside for a while. It's so peaceful in the garden, among the trees. I can almost forget I'm so near ghastly Petrograd.' I asked him to summarize for me what had been said and sometimes he couldn't, he hadn't been concentrating. It drove me to fury: 'What are they doing to you, these cowards!? Why can't they just get on competently with their jobs and not give you this constant worry?' So he got rid of one of the worries, and of Bobrinsky from Agriculture at the same time, because of the same old supply failures. When I heard the name of Stürmer's replacement I was horrified:Trepov, hard conservative, loathed by the Duma. No doubt he meant to close it and make things yet worse in the cities, and certainly he wanted rid of Protopopov who had barely been in office two months. In fact he said that unless the latter went he would not take the job.

I went to see Nicky at Mogilev; I said, 'What is going on? – Why are they trying to damage you by instigating yet another rotten change? You know what people are already saying about "ministerial leapfrog".' Nicky said, 'I can't have Trepov without getting rid of this Protopopov, who has in any case still shown no sign of decisive action to sort out supplies.' 'He hasn't had long,' I pointed out; and then I said because I thought it might sway him, 'Our friend blessed this choice of yours, you know that.' Nicky made an impatient little gesture with his hand, 'Please don't drag him into this, it isn't fair to me or him. When he agrees with your views you take it as a sign from God, but you ignore him when he doesn't, and that is the truth, Alix. Please respect both of us a little more.' I was shocked beyond words, and overwrought as he was of course he was right; I dropped references to Grigory at once, feeling deeply ashamed.

Naturally Nicky kept Protopopov: there was no question of his letting himself be dictated by Trepov, who had no alternative candidate to offer anyway: Trepov would serve with whatever colleagues his leader thought fit to give him. Nicky was tired but full of resolve – 'Darling, forgive me if I've been moody or unrestrained; I'm under terrible pressure and if I hadn't had you here backing me I'd have gone to pieces in front of him. Now I'll be calm and firm with them all again.' I ached with pity and love for him, my poor harassed dear; I covered his face with kisses and repeated again and again, 'Soul of my soul, joy of my life, I'd die for you! These men are all petticoats, but I am your first servant and I have trousers on unseen.' – Little joke between us, always made him laugh, but I didn't feel like an especially nice or cheerful person after the experience of those days.

Back in Tsarskoe I issued an order taking the relevant areas of the supply system away from Agriculture and giving sole responsibility to Internal Affairs, and I ordered Protopopov to get decisively on with his job. Of course he was barely in office before his friends in the Duma turned against him and started saying he had syphilis and was going mad. 'Of course he has only developed this disease since I appointed him,' poor Nicky said, despairing.

Paul Miliukov stood up in the Duma and made a stupid, irresponsible, inflammatory speech about the whole internal situation: 'Gentlemen, if the Germans had decided to use the opportunities they have to influence and suborn in order to disorganize our country, they could not have done a better job than the Russian government has....the nagging suspicion has become a clear realization that an enemy hand is influencing the course of state business....how can anyone refute these suspicions when a handful of dubious persons manage the most important state business in their own interests?' He went on to accuse Stürmer of having been a German spy; he mentioned a lady who had 'launched him on his career' and who had now 'returned to Petrograd' to further the German cause after months with agents in Montreux, and he said her name (which he oh so chivalrously would not mention) was in all the newspapers – and the name in the papers was that of my poor old Mistress of the Robes Zizi Naryshkina. They had confused her with someone who was actually still abroad with German agents – and this public pillorying nearly broke the dear old lady's heart. Then he ended up: 'Gentlemen, without harboring any personal suspicion I cannot say what role in this played a certain antechamber through which Protopopov also advanced to a ministerial chair....this court party which appointed Stürmer is the court party grouped around the young Empress!'

Ella came to see us after this, and she begged us to send

Grigory away. 'A certain antechamber – you know what that means – the whole world thinks that to get a ministerial seat one only has to pay a visit to Rasputin's flat, offer him money and it's guaranteed.' 'Rasputin' – she used the name deliberately. *Au fond*, it's his and has belonged to his family for generations, but the uneducated always thought it a nickname connected with dissolution, and they used it scathingly. This was exactly why Grigory had tried to change it. 'It can't be denied,' Ella said, 'there are always political people hanging around him.' 'Grigory receives all sorts of people for all sorts of reasons and certainly they do not all get ministerial posts,' Nicky said quietly. 'Yes, some may hang around him in the belief that it will help them, but it doesn't, anyone can see that if they pay sufficient attention, and I object to the likes of Miliukov exploiting this true, simple man of God for political ends. He is a good-hearted Russian with a gift for words and a concern for the poor and when I am unsure or depressed I have a conversation with him and I always feel better. I will not be separated from him for the world.' 'The whole world also apparently think that I am a German spy,' I told her 'do you want me sent away as well?' She ignored that; she started getting excited, 'You say people are exploiting him for political reasons, but it's not just that, is it? – Look at the way he behaves – it is damaging you so much! – He takes bribes for sure –'

I cut in on her, 'People are silly enough to give him money to try to get things done, that much is true – but he passes it on to the poor. Remember, Ella, that Ania Vyrubova is constantly visiting his flat; she sees how simply he lives and what people he receives. She is not the most worldly person, but others have been there too and don't find anything remiss. Nikolai Sablin you don't know – but talk to Dmitri, for one – or Felix Youssoupov, they are there a lot these days. Felix apparently needs treatment for something; you might like to ask what it is in case Dmitri is involved.' 'Poor Felix,' Ella said, 'why does he turn like that to that man! – When I've told him so often that his sins of the flesh are as nothing compared to the purity of his soul.'

I was thunderstruck; I said, aggressively, 'So you accept that the two aren't mutually exclusive?' 'We do know what goes on with Grigory,' Nicky put in gently. 'we aren't totally naïve. With any man of God you always find a bad self-interested element in his following.' 'You'll know then about the drinking binges,' she said, and she started to cry. 'He tells me has been drinking more of late,' I said, 'it isn't wonderful but it isn't surprising after Khvostov tried to have him killed.' I was speaking more frankly than I would normally do with her. All my life she's played the wise elder sister and poked her nose in matters of ours she has no business touching, and my usual reaction is to push her away – but I was needled by her implication that we were some sort of innocent fools being taken for a ride by a debauched charlatan, and I meant to defend myself. 'Alix, he was seen drunk at the station here on his way to see that Ania,' Ella said, 'Someone reminded him that the police were certain to note it and you'd be angry if you heard about it, and he stared cursing you wildly and quite obscenely. Then there was the incident in the restaurant when he took his trousers off and boasted about what he could do with you and with Olga and Tatiana – and he goes quite openly to bath-houses with all types of woman, and has them back at his flat. I may be in Moscow but I hear all; the Family are simply in despair –'

I was furious. 'It ill-behoves anyone in the family to start preaching about other's behaviour! When you think of the illegal marriages, and the infidelities! – the *ménage à trois* of Sergei and Andrei and that woman! – and the strings of women Boris has had! Why do they think there's one law for them and quite another for the poor? – Exactly what behaviour has the most power to damage Nicky –the occasional lapses of a Siberian peasant – which one so grossly exaggerates! – or the constant self-indulgence of nearly all his relatives?!'

'Better if I hadn't come!' Ella said. 'Oh God why is Victoria so far away? - at least you pay nominal attention to her!'

Dear Nicky managed to smooth things over and calm us down, and we went then to see the children and laughed over Olga's kitten climbing up house plants; but I have not seen Ella again since that day.

Next thing was that our Mossolov, my prime enemy in the household since Nicky sent Fat Orlov off to join Nikolasha, offered Grigory a bribe to get away from the capital. It was rejected, but our friend was nervous, and the last time Nicky and I saw him at Ania's and asked for his blessing he said, 'It's time now for you to bless me.' Ania rang him one day just after that to ask his advice on my behalf on some matter to do with Alexei, and was very upset that he bellowed at her - she, his little friend and 'daughter'! - saying, 'What else do they want from me? Haven't they already had everything?'

On December 17th she flew across to our house in great agitation saying Maria had phoned to ask whether her father had come straight to Tsarskoe, since he hadn't returned home after his visit to Felix the previous evening. Of course Ania hadn't seen him either and she was in a state. I immediately made inquiries - and in fact the police were already sniffing around Youssoupov's place because of shots that had been heard in the night. The policeman who had been hanging around at the time - they were always watching Grigory, and not always for his own protection - said that man Purishkevich of the Duma came staggering out boasting about how they had 'shot a dog - Grishka Rasputin, the false prophet'. In the morning though Felix said Purishkevich was drunk and talking rubbish, Grigory had never been there, it was a real dog that had been shot, and he even produced a body. But no-one could find Grigory and the whole thing was like some hideous melodrama. The characters and status of the people involved! Purishkevich, for heaven's sake! - Duma deputy of the far right, chiefly known for going into the chamber with a red carnation stuck in his trouser fly. Spent most of his time making up silly little verses about his colleagues. Felix - high nobility and Xenia's son-in-law! - with all his little ways. And Dmitri. Nicky's first cousin; Ella's foster son, once a constant guest in our home and even a flirt of our daughter Olga. The blow he had rendered us was quite terrible. How had they planned it? - Over dinner in a restaurant with the champagne flowing? At some bath-house with the boys and girls of easy virtue looking on? What exactly did they hope to achieve?

Grigory's body turned up next day, beneath the ice of the Malaya Nevka. It was tied and battered: they'd shot at him and clubbed him with hysterical brutality; it's just agony to imagine the scene. They told people they'd poisoned him with cyanide too. I had them under house arrest immediately; Nicky was on his way back from the *Stavka* and not in a position to act. Back came Felix's reply cool as anything,

'The Empress is as much a subject of her husband as anyone else and making such an order is beyond her competence.' But they stayed where the police kept them.

No sooner had Nicky arrived than Uncle Paul turned up and demanded to know by what right I had had his son arrested, and wasn't terrible damage being done by letting the whole world know that members of the Imperial Family were involved in a murder?

Nicky was simply furious. 'Before the whole world I am filled with shame that the hands of my kinsmen are stained with the blood of a simple peasant - and you are telling me I will save face by pretending it hasn't happened!'

We buried Grigory in the corner of the Alexander Park, always intending that in time his body would be taken quietly back to his own village: he wasn't even in consecrated ground. What sheer hell it all was. We were thinking constantly of Alexei and the times Grigory had saved his life, and wondering what would happen the next time he had a bad bleed and doctors couldn't help. We were full of personal grief at the loss of Grigory's prayers and spiritual advice, and for the poor children too there was such a feeling of horror – the first time something so awful had happened to anyone they knew, they suddenly felt utterly vulnerable. They had seen war wounds and sickness, but they understood the purpose of one and perhaps the sad inevitability of the other; never before had their precious souls been touched by an act of pointless brutality. This applied still more so to his own poor little Maria and Varvara, left fatherless at school in Petrograd and with their mother far away. Nicky told them they should look on him as their father now, and they came to see us many times at home between then and March – far more often than Grigory himself ever had. They are just the age of Marie and Anastasia, and all got on well together, no doubt to the horror of the dear Family.

Also I kept remembering what Grigory had said to Ania the last time they spoke 'What else do they want? Haven't they already had everything?' – and again and again it comes back to haunt me: this man died because he helped us; this man gave everything because of our spiritual needs and above all the needs of our son. You can glorify him as a martyr to the hideous behaviour of the rich and powerful, but how on a human level do you live with the guilt?

CHAPTER SIXTEEN

Dmitri was ordered to the Persian Front and Felix to internal exile: more one could not do without the hideous experience of putting them through a trial and letting them wash their dirty linen before the world and drag us through the mud with them too. Almost incredibly, that letter then came asking Nicky to release them, and it was signed by half the Family: Aunt Miechen and all of the Vladimirovichi including Ducky; Sergei and Nikolai Mikhailovich (naturally); some of the Konstantins including even Mavra, my friend; and Uncle Paul and little Marie P. of course, interceding for her adored brother.

Nicky simply returned the letter to the senders, having written on it, 'No-one is allowed to commit murder; I am surprised at your request.' Neither of Nicky's sisters signed it thank God, nor Misha nor Sandro even, but what hurt most of all, well beyond the letter from the family, was hearing that Ella the saintly nun sent Dmitri a telegram which the police picked up, congratulating him on his role. Her great friend Zina Youssoupov wrote to Felix in similar vein and adding that all that remained to get the government back on course was to 'get rid of Her'.

I watched Nicky absorb all this information and my heart ached so much for him. Until much later I withheld from him the letter Grigory had left for him but which little Maria passed to me. I can quote verbatim: 'Tsar of the land of Russia, if you hear the sound of the bell that tells you Grigory has been killed, know this: if it is my brother peasants who have killed me, then all will be well: remain in Russia and rule in Russia for many generations. But if it is your relatives who have wrought my death, then not one of you, that is to say, not one of your children or your family will remain alive for more than two years: they will be killed by the Russian people. Brother will kill brother, and for twenty-five years there will be no nobles in Russia.' And of course I understood the implications already: what sort of a signal does it send to the country when even the Tsar's family are turning against him and killing his friends? But nevertheless I hoped that he was wrong: I refused to believe that an entire system of government could collapse because some members of parliament and some superfluous princes have lost all sense of perspective.

It was a bad winter, though. The boilers on many of the trains froze and then burst, which temporarily disrupted food supplies to the cities. Protopopov, hang him, came to us often and held forth about the Physiocrats and his theories about the self-regulation of price and inflation, and then one day he said simply that he wasn't up to the job we had given him. Nicky turned towards me with an anxious look, and I was furious. 'No-one is starving, the war is going well, we can't afford another change - please get on with the job we have entrusted to you and which you begged for, swore you could do and appear to be doing effectively so far.' - So he carried on and I don't think he messed it up completely, but I was bitterly disappointed by his cowardice: the least setback and for all his bombast this one like all the rest had simply tried to buckle. I didn't receive any of the other ministers alongside Nicky, but he did ask me to be on my balcony between the Maple Room and his study so I could hear what was being said without them being aware of my presence. I was frantic with worry about him and his inability to concentrate for more than a few minutes, and his physical health was also breaking down - he had flu very badly and he coughed for ages. I wouldn't let him go back to the *Stavka* after Grigory died, and in any case he had no inclination to in spite of his feelings about the atmosphere in Petrograd: we really needed to be together. The new story in town was of course that he was an alcoholic: some idiot who'd seen him drunk a few times when he was about twenty-two had written a book suggesting that this was the reason for his distracted air. Never mind twenty years of overwork and a family who won't behave decently! The other theory was that I was feeding him hashish to keep him in a state of mindless euphoria so I could do what I liked.

The Duma was going on about me more openly than ever, realising how little difference Grigory's senseless murder had made to government policy: they were seriously undermining Nicky all the time. (Rotten Shulgin: 'She is very clever, far above all around her. Her domination of her husband is an open revolt against the autocracy. It poisons the very instinct of monarchy. Just because of the weakness of one husband to one wife the sovereign offends his people and the people offend their sovereign. How awful to have an autocracy without an autocrat!')

Both of the allied ambassadors behaved vilely: Paléologue was forever in Miechen's salon exchanging gossip about everything with everyone; Buchanan went about openly telling people he thought I was a spy and that information I had passed to Germany had led to the torpedoing of the Hampshire and to Kitchener's death. This man I knew when I was a child: he was British *chargé d'affaires* in Darmstadt and his daughter is a friend of my niece Alice, and yet still he affected to believe this.

Sandro wrote asking to see me; I didn't want to see him. He wrote to our Olga next, inviting himself to lunch. I was in bed with one of my beastly monthly headaches and for the past few days Nicky had gone no further than the Mauve Room in his dressing gown, too tired and achy to carry on with normal life. All this had been explained to our dear brother-in-law, but he wasn't interested in sparing our health. Thus Nicky went to lunch although he wasn't particularly up to it, and then afterwards he brought Sandro through to see me as Sandro requested. I wasn't wild about him being in our bedroom and with his horrible roué's eyes on me in my nightdress: the old closeness evaporated with his fidelity to Xenia – but there was not much I could do about it since he was so determined.

He took a good look at the icons on the wall and said rudely, 'This place looks like a bloody pagan temple, Nicky!'– and then he sat down and waited, with a quizzical look: – 'Don't you have work to do?' 'I'd rather stay,' Nicky said simply, and Sandro shrugged. 'If you insist; but you may not like what you hear.' Then he said to me, 'I need to speak bluntly as I would to my confessor' – patronising me by taking the religious angle – 'You are leading the government towards destruction. The people you have appointed – and I say you because I am aware of who is behind this terrible ministerial leapfrog – have left us in a situation from which the only exit is revolution unless you very quickly find yourself a set of ministers who are answerable to the Duma. I hate the very idea of constitutional monarchy, you know I do, but at the moment it is the least ghastly option.'

I said, 'In June 1915 a number of ministers were appointed who were acceptable to the Duma, and none of them proved up to the job. Furthermore, their appointment was a result of blind panic and spy mania on the part of the Duma. Do we really want that situation recurring every time we have a military set-back? Do you think that's the way to run a war?' 'In theory I absolutely agree,' he said 'and things would have gone perfectly well if you had chosen competent people to direct things. Instead we have this parade of blunderers and idiots who are ruining us all, and the only option to save our own skins is to accede to the Duma.'

'What exactly is it that this "parade of blunderers and idiots" have done?' I asked. Sandro said something about the scenes they caused in the Duma, and I gave him my usual rejoinder about Petrograd and Moscow and the Duma itself turning on more or less everyone we appointed regardless of their credentials and being deeply unrepresentative of the country as a whole. 'You could well be right,' he said, 'but the fact is that the people who matter are against you. The people with the loud voices: the natural supporters of the crown, and it isn't loud mouths in the Duma who have caused that, it's the policies you have been pursuing.'

Then he elaborated at great length on what he meant, and of course it all turned around what he'd heard about plans for Jewish legal emancipation and for forcibly requisitioning aristocratic land to sell to the peasants. 'You can't conceivably be thinking about giving equal legal rights to the Jews who openly incite trouble wherever they go and who make up ninety per cent of the real left revolutionaries – it would be simply chaos! – And to take away land from the very people who hold the extremists in check – don't you know what that will do? – The Slav peoples have no discipline; give them an inch and they'll take a mile. You may think that if you do this you'll find yourselves in a sort of populist paradise of Tsar and people, but what you'll really get will be anarchy. I know this isn't Nicky's doing – Nicky is a product of the same upbringing I am – all this is you and your family's odd ideas. Remember this, Alix – for thirty months I have kept quiet while you've dragged this country to ruin, and I can't sit silent any more! – You and Nicky may not care what happens to you, but you have no right to drag your relatives with you over the precipice!' He was purple with rage by the time he'd finished, and then Nicky said softly, 'You know Sandro, what annoys me in all this is that you don't even have sufficient respect for my brain and my will-power to credit me with making my own mistakes. Do you wonder that my wife, who is the only person in the family who has ever backed me up, is now the only person in the family whose judgements I really trust? – And you and the rest of them respond to this by turning on her and saying the vilest things about her and laying every one of my perceived errors at her door. Does it surprise you that I wanted to stay in the room with you? Please – can you leave now.'

Such was the quality of the family's argument with us.

Nicky's sisters were disgusted by it all; Olga said, 'Mama and Aunt Ella may be listening to rumour, but they at least have your interests at heart when they criticise. None of the others is thinking of anyone but themselves.'

My spies in town (Ania's father and others) told me of some of the fantastic stories that were going around about family plots: that Motherdear had moved to Kiev after giving Nicky an ultimatum that either I went or she did; that a specially-arranged aeroplane would crash onto Nicky's motorcar and kill him; that Dmitri would be recalled from Persia, forcibly married to our Olga and the pair of them placed on the throne. I didn't believe for a second that even Nikolai Mikhailovich or Miechen would get involved in anything so wild as these plots, but the point is that the whole of Petrograd believed they would, such was the atmosphere they had stirred up.

One of the newspapers openly summarised the ideal programme:

"1. Emperor to be deposed

2. Young Empress to be shut up in a convent

3. Dowager Empress (with Grand Duke Nikolai Nikolaievich) to be appointed regent to Alexei II"

Late February it was that Nicky received a message recalling him to *Stavka*, and for his sanity he was quite glad to go. Nevertheless, it was beastly hard on the heart that he had to go at so difficult a time; I remember being in his compartment on the train before it left, and sitting on his knee and holding his face between my hands and kissing him long, long over and over again, so that when I released him for a more than a moment he whispered with a mischievous little smile, 'Sweet Sunny – you won't be dreaming about catholic priests tonight!' – but he was coughing still and his mood changed quite rapidly, 'I must say I'm dreading the lonely nights; my camp bed is so hard and stiff and my feet get so cold I can't sleep.' I had a big hollow pain in my stomach. I said, 'I wish I had wings so I could fly to you in the evenings and cheer you up – I've got visions of you sitting alone with your book and no-one you know well there to talk to you and make you feel warm and share your jokes. Oh darling – I know it sounds sentimental but I do so want to want to be there at night to tuck you up – and I could bend over you and bless you and gently kiss your sweet face all over, and then you'd feel less sad.' 'Please don't worry and feel miserable,' he said shyly, 'when I'm alone at night, I shall try to feel your arms round me, and I shall imagine I'm nestling tightly up to you, and feel safe and cosy and loved.' I was blinking tears back; I gave him a great speech, 'My precious one, you know what kind of childhood I had, and I was happy and I had fun, but it was oddly short on affection, with my father being away all the time and my mother dead – and the nurses were employed to be strict and fair, and the sisters were fairly stiff-backed too – I think there's something wrong with Ella, actually – but royal training is like that there, you know – in Britain and Germany. So with you it's been like a torrent of suppressed feeling all the time – all the pent-up love I couldn't express when I was little has gone into my feelings for you, and that is because you have so repaid it and have needed so much tenderness in return. I remember seeing your family the first time, and your big boisterous papa and your naughty brother and sweet little pixie Xenia to whom you were always so protective, and it was worlds away from mine, I was the little last one on the far end of that family that had once been happy too before my mother and my sister and my brother died and the bigger ones grew up. You were all so full of life and warmth, and of course your father was a true Romanov and there must have been violent bad temper there too, but you have none of that in you – you have nothing but the sweetest side of your inheritance and you have made my married life perfect bliss – so forgive me if I cry like a great baby when you go away, but though I have our five treasures they not one of them means anything near what their father does and I can't bear the time without your sweet presence near me.' The ADC came then to say that the train was about to move and I was in tears as I went to the door; the last thing I said was, 'Farewell, Lovy-sweet, my Little Boy Blue; come back soon!'

Over the next couple of weeks I was so glad I'd told him all that; with a family history like mine I guess you are inclined to treat each parting as if it were your last and pour out what is on your soul. Either that, or you bottle it up completely like my sisters seem to do most of the time.

Alexei had been playing with two little cadets from Petrograd the week before. One of them had a bad cough, and pretty soon we got a message that he had gone down with the measles. Alexei and Olga were themselves in bed with twenty-four hours of Nicky going, and then Tatiana too not long after, and finally to cap it all Ania caught it. I had moved her out of her house and into ours already because she kept getting such dreadful anonymous dreadful letters – such cowards people are – so much of the hatred against us was directed towards this poor harmless young woman, and she was accused of political conspiracy and all manner of sexual crimes – she whose marriage had never even been consummated – just because she'd known Grigory well and had acted like our go-between. I put her in the park wing where Nicky's parents had once had their rooms, at the far end from us, which was a real nuisance when she got ill, logistically speaking – I spent my whole time trailing back and forth between her and them, changing sheets and preparing drinks. My children were good though the big ones were actually quite ill – Tatiana went deaf for a while – as is the way with measles in adulthood. The Cow however thought she was dying and made terrible scenes all the time and had not just me but several nurses from our hospital and her own doctor running around her constantly. My dear friend Lili Dehn who of course came to see me one day and ended up staying longer than she intended said wryly and with great truth, 'Ania brings out one's maternal side – that is to say, half the time one wants to pet and amuse her, and the other half one wants to murder her!'

Nicky was due back five days after he went away. In the meantime bread and fuel riots started in the capital, as I had feared they would. Protopopov in spite of his protestations about being useless had laid plans for dealing with them, but his own name featured on the banners the rioters waved. 'Down with Protopopov!' 'Down with the war!' 'Down with the German woman!' It was a hooligan movement, really, students brought onto the streets by the mild weather; if the temperature had dropped again they'd have gone back inside. The problem was that a couple of regiments started mutinying and joined them, and that induced whole-sale panic in the Duma and other quarters. Those regiments – they were reserves, badly trained and badly disciplined, and irony of ironies they'd have been at the front if Grigory hadn't advised us of the trouble that calling up the second class would spark off. Nevertheless Nicky sent a stiff message to the ministers telling them to pull themselves together and do what they had to, and then on February 28th he started home.

Same morning Ania's father turned up at our place, saying that his car had been commandeered in Petrograd by a mob. Several mansions in the capital had been looted – such a shame, that included the home of Catherine Radziwill, who wrote a vile anonymous book about me and who had been giving an extravagant party only the night before – all these symbols of aristocratic corruption and more so to none than to me.

Fat Rodzianko of the Duma sent a message asking me to leave Tsarskoe for my own safety, but I pointed out that with children ill I was not even going to consider it. In any case it sounded like he was over-reacting. Derevenko who had been visiting the hospitals around us came home to check up on the invalids and said that as far as he had heard the entire network of railways around Petrograd was now in the hands of rioters. This worried me: how would Nicky get to us? – And then even in the sickrooms one began to hear terrible noises – glass smashing and shouting voices, and somehow we got to know that a huge crowd of mutinous soldiers was on its way to us with god knows what in mind. On the way they were breaking into shops and getting slowly more and more drunk. I thought thank Heavens for old Benckendorff, who had ordered a battalion of the Garde Equipage and various others to take up defensive positions around us. Decided to go myself to remind them quite particularly that the childrens' safety was in their hands, but as I was putting a coat on my Marie appeared at my side and said forcefully, 'I'm coming with you.'

We could hear shots now only five hundred or so yards away; I didn't want her out there, but she hung onto my hand and refused to budge, so I let her follow me, and Benckendorff came too, and we went from soldier to soldier telling them of our total trust in them. Many of them had their bayonets poised, fully expecting the rioters to rush into the courtyard at any moment, but our Mashka never once flinched. In the centre of them all was a huge field gun, and the sentries were stamping around it trying to keep warm. I had them brought indoors in little groups so they could be given tea and coffee to thaw them out. Anastasia wandered happily around the kitchens while they were there, chatting to old friends she remembered from their service on the yacht and feeling that everything was less strange and unnormal now the *Equipage* had come.

After that we had to sort out the sleeping arrangements for all the people stranded there with us. I put poor Maria Benckendorff on a sofa in the Pallisander room – I was quite worried, she isn't in the best of health, but dear Isa stayed with her and looked after matters. Benckendorff considered himself to be 'on duty' and he walked up and down the house and wouldn't sleep, dear old man. Brave Mashka followed me about, carrying blankets and fruit for everybody, and she volunteered to give up her bed to Lili – who wore Anastasia's dressing gown to sleep because she had nothing else, and we had a few moments' mirth at least seeing it strained round her great tall frame. I didn't go to sleep, although Marie eventually did, stretched out exhausted across my bed. Her sweet rosy face was so young and innocent and I felt so proud of the way she had been that night out in the courtyard, calm and steadfast although she knew well that the hordes of people lose in the town would be quite happy to kill us. Until then she'd never really had a chance to show the strength of character that lay beneath the jolly boisterous schoolgirl's exterior, but in the absence of Tatiana she suddenly came into her own.

The sick children upstairs could hear the firing from outside too; to them I said manoeuvres were going on in town. I was expecting an attack at any time, and I just remember pacing up and down the house, and chain-smoking like Victoria does and praying that Nicky's train would be on time. He was due at six in the morning, and I was firmly convinced that his presence would have a salutary effect on events: the ministers would brace themselves and deal with the situation. I'd have gone to them myself and shaken them and shown them my immortal trousers if I could have got out of the house!

Gradually towards morning the shots died down: for some reason the rioters had changed their minds and starting pulling back and dispersing – perhaps they were all drunk by then. There was a blizzard outside, and at first I thought this was why the train was late. I looked out of the window and saw that many of the soldiers had white handkerchiefs tied around their wrists. Benckendorff managed to find out what this meant: it was a symbol that the guards would not interfere with rioters in Tsarskoe so long as the rioters didn't come up to the house. This truce had been worked out by the Duma and I was angry:

suddenly the rotten Duma was turned noble protector against the storm it had itself whipped up.

Time passed and I began to feel edgy – several times Benckendorff or others rang the station to hear if there was any news. Finally at eight came a message: the Emperor's train has been diverted to Malaya Vishera. I immediately sent off a radiotelegram begging him for news. A little while later it came back to me – 'Address of person mentioned unknown' – and that was when the terror started creeping into my heart. All day I was trying to get hold of him, but each message was returned in exactly the same way. I went to the sick children and looked after them and chatted with them as if all was well, but there was a terrible cold knot of panic inside me. Never once in all our marriage had I not known where he was before, not been able to imagine his movements or count the time until I heard news from him. Every day at the same time his letters or telegrams had arrived and if they were even slightly late I worried, and now I had simply no idea at all where he was or what was happening to him. Clearly someone had detained him and was preventing news getting through to him – and as the hours wore on my fears got worse.

All that sleepless night I was talking to him inside my head – oh my love, what are they trying to make you do? Who has got you? – and with time I even stared praying that it was Duma members holding him, and trying to force him to sign for a responsible ministry – because the alternatives as to where he was were still more frightful – my own wee one, I'd know if you were dead, wouldn't I? – I'd feel it instinctively in my body and my soul and I couldn't go on, could I?

Benckendorff came very early in the morning and said to me simply that the guards had deserted – 'Kirill Vladimirovich has sent for them.' Thus Ducky's husband called his regiment away and left his cousin's children defenseless before a mob.

Thank God nothing at least happened.

That day - it was March 2 of course - the water and electricity went off - one had to cut the ice in the lake to supply the household. I was dizzy and exhausted by lack of sleep and running around the invalids, and now because the lift wouldn't work I had to drag myself up the stairs to the nurseries with a terrible pain in my chest - knew my heart was starting to act up again. I took vast quantities of veronal to keep myself going and I said to Lili that I'd be drug-addicted before this was over.

My little Anastasia was showing signs of measles too now, with a blinding headache and a temperature, and she cried and cried that she couldn't be a use to me helping with the others.

I wrote two long letters to Nicky and sent them off with a messenger, well-folded in case they were searched - but I didn't know if they could even find him. And then at last something came! - oh darling, just a little telegram to say you were at Pskov - but I breathed a bit easier.

During the night Botkin had a phone-call from the Duma, asking how Alexei was without saying why. Other household people started to arrive back to town as matters quietened there, and they brought all sorts of wild rumours - one of them that Nicky had abdicated and that leaflets to this effect were being distributed. I simply wouldn't believe it; I carried on as normal and tried to get news of other loved ones. N.P. was locked up by his own regiment for being our friend, Xenia and Misha were stuck in their houses in Petrograd, and poor Fredericks had his house burnt down. In the war I used sometime to look at old Benckendrff and Fred. and say that they were getting past it, and starting to be more an anxiety than a help in the household - especially when Fred would go with Nicky to the *Stavka* and start spitting blood and fainting so Nicky had to appeal to me in desperation 'order the Old Man to take some time off; he obviously only listens to you' - but when times were hard, these old soldiers rallied round and showed their mettle, truly, and the same could not be said of so many of the younger ones. Apart from the telegram there was no real news of Nicky all day and I started to feel nervous again.

At seven that evening Uncle Paul suddenly turned up and asked to see me, and in my mauve room he came straight out with it, 'Alix, I don't know what you have heard yet – but Nicky has abdicated with effect from yesterday.' I was simply knocked for six, I demanded details I am sure and I no doubt heard that vile Guchkov and Shulgin of the Duma had gone down to see him while he was trapped at Pskov and had talked and talked for several hours until he agreed to sign – and that General Ruszky and others of the general staff had been involved, otherwise how did the train come to be diverted in the first place? – And I felt such anguish for him – caught like a mouse in a trap and brow-beaten and bullied and humiliated until he did what they wanted him to do – tired and lonely as he was and with no-one at all there to support him. I remember saying to Paul, 'Oh God – what he's gone through!' – and then I had the presence of mind to ask how long he'd known the news himself and whether everyone else knew, and what happened now with Alexei to whom the throne now belonged and for whom I was immediately starting to worry. Paul said, 'The Duma members came to see Misha last night because it's on his behalf that Nicky abdicated. He has signed away Alexei's rights as well as his own, I can't explain his thinking – I can only presume he didn't want the boy to have such a worry at his age.' I said, 'So Misha has known all day.' Paul nodded and looked embarrassed, and I didn't have to say what I was thinking: 'So for twenty-four hours the Family knew and not one member of it had the human decency to come and tell me what had happened to my husband.'

I had to tell the Household. Many of them knew it already really, because of the leaflets, but I remember how Isa cried and clung to me when I confirmed it, and Benckendorff the rigid old soldier sat and held my hand with tears running down his face, assuring me again and again of his personal loyalty to our family. It was just awful, and I kept repeating, 'It must be for the best; it'll come right in whatever way God intends' and saying all the gentle stoic things Nicky would have said to them. I didn't tell the children yet, and I was still worried about Nicky himself because apart from the telegram there had been no news at all. I had no idea where they'd taken him now or if he was even still at liberty.

In the morning we got another message to say that Misha had declined the throne and everything was now in the hands of the Duma who were forming a Provisional Government. I was and am still just furious with Misha who deserted his post like all the rest of the cowards at the moment he was most needed. But in any case he would have been in the pocket of the Duma so the outcome would have been similar no doubt.

One letter came through to me from the Family: Xenia, sweetly writing to console us. Then during that day one of the footmen rushed in to say that my darling was on the phone, and I ran to it and seized it and he said immediately, 'You know?' - very softly and I answered, 'Yes' with a big lump in my throat to hear his dear voice again. - And we talked briefly about the practical details - that Guchkov and Shulgin and Ruszky had been there at the abdication, and that Nicky was now in the *Stavka* again to say farewell to the troops. He was writing them an address blessing them and urging them to fight on until victory, but I didn't want to talk too long about that for fear of upsetting him so I switched back to chatting about the children's health. We didn't once mention his motivation for abdicating - not on the phone, when people might be listening. He said his mother had telegraphed that she was coming from Kiev to visit him for a few days, and I was glad for him though I imagined that much of her conversation would consist of how it was all my fault. He hoped to be back after that: there had been no talk of detaining him or any such nonsense.

Marie was that day showing definite signs of measles and had to be put to bed, and Anastasia was at the worst stage, but the first three patients were on the mend, particularly Alexei who was out of bed and sitting in the playroom with Zhilik or Sig or me taking turns reading to him. There was nothing to stop Lili going home to Petrograd but she opted to remain, to help with the children and especially with Ania who continued rather poorly on the other side of the house. In the middle of it all she received a phone call that the little boy was ill, of course, and I could see her terrible dilemma, but she said with remarkable sacrifice - I wouldn't have been up to it - 'My first duty is with my sovereign's family when they need me.' The electricity and water were restored quite fast after the abdication became known, and the town was quiet, but suddenly on March 5th - day after Nicky rang, I suppose, though the time went like a snail through all these days - I got a message that Guchkov needed to see me. At once I sent for Paul, anxious about what was wanted because Guchkov was just my worst enemy in the whole of the Duma - this is the man who advertised our letters to Grigory around the capital - plus fakes - and who was just back from forcing my husband's hand! He came through our house followed by twenty members of the new Tsarskoe Revolutionary Council, and I could hear these men abusing members of the household as they passed - 'Bloodsuckers!' 'Lackeys!' It was eleven at night already. Paul and I waited in the formal rooms because for nothing was Guchkov and his suite going near my home. Of course they had a good contemptuous look round as though they thought we lived amid all this grandeur, but Guchkov was sickeningly polite. He was Minister of War now and all he wanted was to assure me that the government would protect us, and to ask whether I had everything I needed for the children. I told him I did, but I asked him to make sure that medicines were going through to the wounded in the hospitals too because of course I'd had no news at all from them since March 1st. He probably was enjoying being magnanimous to me now I'd got my come-uppance, but not for a moment was I going to let him see I felt patronised. After they'd gone Paul said to me - notwithstanding all that had passed between us concerning Dmitri - 'Dear Alix, that was done with such dignity. You look quite extraordinarily beautiful today.' - and he kissed me on the forehead. Good Uncle Paul, the mildest of his generation - I wonder where he is now?

CHAPTER SEVENTEEN

After that rumours started reaching us that the Duma was planning to put Nicky or me or both of us on trial for treason and spying for Germany. Newspapers and pamphlets that found their way in demanded to know why 'the ex-Emperor' was at Headquarters: was he rallying the troops against the revolution? There were demands that the house be searched for evidence of secret wireless communication with William. - The soldiers on duty outside began slouching at their posts and arguing with their officers; Benckendorff learned that from now on the officers would be elected by the men, order of the Petrograd Soviet. One afternoon a squadron of the Chevalier Grade turned up at the gates, and one went out to ask them why there were there. It was heartbreaking, simply - they had come from Novgorod to defend their Emperor, and on reaching Tsarskoe had been told that there was no longer an Emperor to defend. - But the picture it painted! - the country still loyal as one always knew it would be in spite of the hideous behaviour of the citizens of its capitals.

In the mauve room with Lili I started burning papers I didn't want seen by any possible trial - felt that more or less anything personal should go, so onto the fire went my letters from Granny, from Papa, from Ernie, Irène and Victoria, and my own letters to Granny which were sent back from Windsor after she died. In Ernie's case I was especially concerned that anything nationally indiscreet he had said should not survive in case one attempted to use it to compromise him with the German government - in any case God knows what sort off interpretation they were capable of putting on the most innocent of remarks.

I sat there and looked and looked at my letters from Nicky, the most precious and personal of all, and then I put them back in their box and locked it up because I just couldn't bear to destroy them. In any case if I had done immediate assumptions would have been made about what they might have contained. On March 8th General Kornilov of the Provisional Government came back to the house and told me that he had to put me under arrest for my own safety. Nicky would be arrested simultaneously at the *Stavka* and brought back to us tomorrow. In the meantime all our troops were to be replaced with men appointed by the Provisional Government. The household and our friends were free to leave today, but anyone who remained longer would be placed under arrest with us. He also said he was working with the British Government to get a cruiser to take us to England in a week or two.

After he left I finally had to tell my children the truth about the abdication. Zhilik went to Alexei to break the news to him and I dealt with the girls. Their reactions as I recall suited age and personality. The boy was sad that he wouldn't go to *Stavka* any more, and worried about who would govern Russia ('not a word,' Zhilik told me, 'about his own rights as Heir.'). Anastasia almost immediately started planning her new life in England and wondering if she could go to boarding school. Tatiana (who was at that point so deaf we had to write everything for her) said, 'If this government does a good job, then really we don't need to worry about anything. For you and Papa personally it's probably the best thing, now you can lead your own lives.'

Poor Marie was so sick that I don't think she took it in – she had pneumonia as well as measles and really we almost lost her once or twice over those dreadful days.

Olga was silent, and I knew that if the others had an appreciation of the potential spiritual and psychological impact of this event on their father than she alone would be disposed to express that knowledge.

We had another rotten night. The house was full of new soldiers, and we could hear them laughing and singing in the state rooms. Lili insisted on sleeping in the mauve room so I would not be alone on the ground floor, and I went to make her bed up on the sofa for her, astonished to find that she didn't know how to do it herself. Such were the Russian middle and upper classes, even an atypical specimen like dear Lili. All night there was a sentry pacing the corridor right outside the bedroom.

In the morning I went to wait with the children. Nicky's train was due at 11, but I was terrified it would be late or not come at all. Alexei too kept looking at his watch. And then eventually I heard the car draw up at the gate. Nothing happened; I went to the window and peered out anxiously and I could see a sentry looking into the car and asking something before going back into his gatehouse and using the telephone. Only then the gates opened, and I found out later from Benckendorff that this was because an officer had come onto the steps and bawled 'Who is there?' and the soldier had replied 'Nikolai Romanov!' so the officer gave the order he was to be allowed to pass, to come back into his own home. I ran down to the entrance to meet him, and I saw how none of those hanging about in the room returned the salute he automatically gave as he came through. For the moment I didn't care - I had my eyes on him and in a few seconds more we were behind the door to our own rooms and in each others' arms.

We had lunch with those of our dear children who were well enough to eat, and they bless them joked about their illnesses and asked after their grandmother and although we went over the events of the last few days they made light of the power cuts and the night of semi-siege. He sat then for a long time by the side of our darling Marie, stroking her hair and talking to her gently about nothing in particular while she hung on his hand and looked so happy to have him back and to herself for a while.

What followed was more painful. Nicky saw Lili and those members of the household who had actually remained, and I watched him mentally count all the absent faces – all those who had left when threatened with arrest. 'They had their families to think of, the others,' I reminded him, and he said, 'I know; Lili has given more than we had any right to ask' and he held out both his hands to her. I could see she was shocked at his appearance, and now I looked at him unblinded by the joy of the first moments of our reunion I was too. Pale and thin he'd been all winter, but now I found his face much more lined and his cheeks sunken, and his beard, once so sunny and blond, had grey hairs in it. 'I think I'll go for a walk,' he said, 'I need some fresh air.' – so then of course Lili and I had to watch from the window while little gangs of soldiers emerged from the park and blocked every path he tried to walk up, and they were saying things to him I couldn't hear – and in the end he turned and came back to the house with his head down – and the sight of him like that broke my heart. It was like – they couldn't have designed a scene more pathetic if they'd been writing a propaganda play on his behalf.

I kept him to myself that evening; I wouldn't let even the children near him. We had dinner in the mauve room, and I told him the full story of our experiences because he insisted on it, and he smiled at me and said, 'Sunny thrives on adversity – I must say you look marvelously well and beautiful – and look at the state of me!' He went to the window and looked out into the dark and said in quite a different tone of voice 'I feel so ashamed; I never did have any combative spirit, and now look where it's left us! Really – what you must be thinking in your heart of hearts, after all you've told me about sticking to my own opinions and standing up to people – and the first time I'm alone with a difficult decision on my hands look what I go and do! Since when does an emperor abdicate because of bread riots in the capital?!' I had expected this conversation, to be honest, and I flew across the room to him and took hold of his hands. 'Never never imagine I think badly of you for one moment! You know what you are to me and what your marvelous gentleness means to me and to our cherubs – and anyone would have abdicated when they were caught in a trap and the only other possibility was submitting to Guchkov and working with ministers appointed by the Duma. It was a brave strong act – you couldn't sign their constitution because it goes against what you swore at your coronation, I know that! – Not your fault that spineless Misha gave everything over to them anyway; you did what was best at the time to save Russia.'

'Is that what you think happened?' he asked me. 'That I gave up the throne so as not to break the coronation oath? –Oh Sunny – do you want to hear? – I telegraphed to the Duma just before I abdicated and I said to them that I would concede to their demands for a responsible ministry if it would stop the riots – and it's only because they told me it's too late that I decided to abdicate altogether and leave the throne to someone who could command the nation's confidence. Thus I broke the oath and I handed my country over to chaos because I didn't have the courage to face them down – and now I'm crying like I cried in terror when I knew I'd become Emperor, and in a minute you'll hear all the self-pitying little stories about people deserting me and how the troops took the oath to the Provisional Government loudly outside my train, and how the generals all bowed low to the Duma's carriage when it passed.' He was exhausted and devastated and just so torn apart – and there was nothing I could say or do to comfort him.

But in the days that followed he was a changed man; and, my darling, we have looked to you for your wonderful, Christian spirit of calm and acceptance of your own lot in all this. At least we were in our house. In due course the man Kerensky came to see us – he was Minister of Justice then, rough about the edges and very young, though his pock-marked face seemed older than his thirty-odd years. He separated Nicky and me while he interrogated us: about government, about Germany and our relationship with William. Had we sought a treasonous peace; was it true that we communicated with Berlin via telegraph from here in the house? I answered him as I could: that Nicky talked to me on government as he did on all things, and I had done no more than seek to help in whatever way I could during these hard war years. There had been no communication with William since 1914. I think he believed me, for he allowed us back together after that. He was rough with my friends as well though: poured scorn on Lili for leaving her own child in Petersburg to stay with mine; reduced poor Ania to hysterics by repeatedly entering and re-entering her sick room to check that she was not faking. And then they drove Ania away by car for questioning in Petersburg, her poor, dear round face the last thing visible at the back window as she went away. I have never seen my friend again, but I know she is alive and safe, for her letters make it through. I know she spent time in the Fortress, though, and they interrogated her. I wonder what the rest of her life will be?

And then we had the news that the British would not take us, and I remember a French newspaper printed a cartoon of Nicky sitting, groaning with his head in his hands, while the Allies bickered outside his window, ignoring him completely. 'Once,' the cartoon Nicky sighs, 'these scoundrels were my best friends.' Yes, it is a poor reward for years of faithful alliance, when one's friends turn one down in one's hour of need.

So they sent us here to Siberia instead, tracing the footsteps of so many political prisoners before us - but of many too who had found their lives here, in the wide-open spaces. Kerensky intended he said that we would spend the winter in Tobolsk before continuing on to Japan when spring came. Nicky was amused. 'So I am re-doing the journey I did in 1891 - but backwards,' he told the children as we waited for the last time in the Assembly Hall at home – July 31st it was, the day after Alexei's thirteenth birthday. 'I crossed from Japan and then went all through Siberia, and you know I was the first future Tsar that ever did so. My grandfather visited Siberia as a young man, but he did not cross the whole of it.' 'Siberia and the east is Russia's future – that I still believe,' he said to me. 'It is clearer than ever now that Europe has brought us nothing but harm.' I was thinking of another Russian family which went east many years ago: the Rosputin clan, who settled in Pokrovskoe in the seventeenth century and built their farm and made a better living there than they would have done in European Russia.

Finally, at five a.m., the cars came for us, and we left for the station in a terrible state: this was our home, our Alexander Palace, to which Nicky and I had come nearly twenty two years ago and decorated with such love and teasing over our different tastes; exclusive home to the girls and me these last three years when we had not taken a single holiday. Even the garden is full of vegetables we planted in that spring and summer of 1917, to feed our household, the dear children loving the physical hard work of digging over the earth and shifting it around. We saw it behind us for the last time, simple, long and low and clear yellow in the bright light of a summer morning so like the many mornings years ago when we had risen at this time or earlier to walk across the park in the luminous beauty of the northern sunrise.

The train I remember took us four days and we saw nothing but the familiar scenery of European Russia, because the blinds were drawn in stations so people could not see who was on board. Nevertheless, it was comfortable: we traveled in compartments belonging to the International Sleeping Car Company with the ladies and gentlemen from the suite and our servants too, and we had wines from the cellars and – packed away in the trunks – our favourite pictures and ornaments and carpets from home, which were to accompany us into exile abroad. At Tiumen we transferred to the steamer *Rus*, and that was how we saw Grigory's blessed home at last, as he'd often told us we would someday. Amid the one-storey wooden houses of Pokrovskoe we saw a taller, more affluent home with flowers around: this was the house that Ania had visited long ago and met Grigory's wife who lived there still. It was most strange and affecting to see it now, and mark the woods and fields where he'd played as a child and had his first religious experiences.

And then we came to Tobolsk, the ancient capital of Siberia, looking something of a backwater now. There we spent our winter, holed up in the big Governor's House while the suite took the house across the street, and we taught the children and went to church and strolled around the garden and waited for spring and our journey onwards. We, like those Siberian exiles of yore, found a paradoxical freedom in our imprisonment: freedom from the trappings of rank and wealth, from the cares of state. The children played cards in the guardroom and danced in the snow with the young men: after all, they have been around soldiers since birth and are used to military ways. They acted plays and wrote letters and complained sometimes about being bored and how they looked forward to Japan, of which their father had told them so much.

Meanwhile, we heard occasional news from outside. We heard that the Provisional Government had fallen, and that the Soviet town councils were now in charge – those who had been most radical and dangerous in the riots of 1905, and who harbored some real extremists in their midsts – the "Bolsheviks" of the Social Democrat party which was even illegal for many years. All of this is ultimately the fault of the Duma; neither of us has been shaken in that belief – look at what their loose tongues have unleashed! And Kerensky – he lost control of the Army, the fool, so after that he was doomed. Nicky said, 'You know, at least half these Bolshevik leaders are Jews, and they have lived in London and learned their craft there. My ally nurtured them while Russian soldiers died for our Alliance.' It made me uncomfortable; what he says of England is alas so true, and one hears this story about the Jews from so many friends now. I used to argue hard against this sort of belief once; I no longer know the truth of it all, but I remain firmly convinced that there are good and bad in all religions and all walks of life, and one day this country will be great again and will understand what wrong has been done it by its new leaders. All the pensions, all the wages - gone. What do people live on now? They even changed the calendar; they broke the link with the Church style at last and put Russia onto the western calendar, so all of a sudden in February 1918 thirteen days passed overnight.

And now here we are - Ekaterinburg. Late spring melts into stifling summer, and our house is surrounded by a huge palisade so no-one can see in. It is not a bad house, though far too hot as the windows are sealed shut; it has an over-decorated middle-class comfort. Nuns from a Convent nearby bring milk and bread for the children, so one feels signs of the old, good Russia all around. They have changed the guards again now: Avdeyev softened more and days as days went by, and he was so often drunk that the solders ran riot and stole little things from our luggage, and grew more friendly and familiar. No doubt the Ekaterinburg Soviet feared we might escape. We once in Tobolsk considered getting away, when letters came promising us that 'Good Russian men' were watching the house and would smuggle us out one night. But no-one came the first night that we waited up, and after that we urged them to leave us alone; it was all so dangerous, especially for Alexei - and we were in no real danger where we were, and had our doctors and tutors around us then. Here it is different; I would love to escape from this hot, closed world where we have just four people left: Trupp the footman, Kharitonov the cook, poor Nyuta, and dear Eugene Sergeevich, our own Doctor Botkin, who left his children to be with us, and who is sick himself and more in need of nursing than anyone. Lenka the kitchen boy, Alexei's playmate, has gone: they took him out of the house today, we don't know why. Alexei sits up in bed, playing with a toy ship like a much younger child, though he looks enormous now, perhaps older than his years, and thin with lack of real exercise. In less than a fortnight he will be fourteen. The girls take turns to stay with me, reading aloud, while Nicky and the other three pace about the little yard. My Olga wrote a poem for me, which she gave me when we left Tobolsk. Said how I was "filled with sorrow for the suffering of others" but harsh and merciless towards myself; that if I looked on myself gently from a distance I would weep. My darling girl, who feels everything so deeply with us! – but how to pity oneself adrift in this world where *everyone's* lives in all the world are strange and different now?

Boredom, and heat; boredom and heat; and endless circulating memories of the dear, lost past we pray someday to regain. One by one all earthly things slip away. But let them take away everything in life; nothing will take away the soul.

CAST OF CHARACTERS

CAST OF CHARACTERS

The narrator:

Alexandra Feodorovna, Empress of Russia, (1872-1918), formerly
  Princess Alix of Hesse; married:

Nicholas II, Emperor of Russia, (1868-1918) ("Nicky"), formerly Grand
  Duke Tsesarevich Nikolai Alexandrovich

Their children:

The Grand Duchesses:
  1. **Olga Nikolaevna** (1895-1918)
  2. **Tatiana Nikolaevna** (1897-1918)
  3. **Maria Nikolaevna** (1899-1918) ("Marie" or "Mashka")
  4. **Anastasia Nikolaevna** (1901-1918) ("Shvibzik")

The Heir Tsesarevich:
  Grand Duke Alexei Nikolaevich (1904-1918) ("Baby")

Alexandra's parents:
Princess Alice of Great Britain (1843-1878)
Grand Duke Ludwig IV of Hesse and by Rhine (1837-1892); (who
  married secondly Alexandrine de Kolemine, [1854-1941], marriage
  immediately annulled)

Her siblings:
  1. **Victoria** (1863-1950), married Prince Louis ("Ludwig") of
  Battenberg, later Marquess of Milford Haven (1854-1921)
  2. **Elisabeth** (1864-1918) ("Ella"), married Grand Duke Serge of
  Russia, (1857-1905)
  3. **Irène** (1866-1953), married Prince Henry of Prussia (1860-1927)
  4. **Ernst Ludwig** (1868-1937), ("Ernie"), married firstly Princess
  Victoria Melita of Coburg and Edinburgh (1876-1936), ("Ducky")
  [marriage dissolved]; secondly, Princess Eleonore of Solms (1871-1937)
  ("Onor")
  5. **Friedrich Wilhelm**, (1870-1873), ("Fritzie" or "Frittie")
  6. **Marie** (1874-1878), ("May")

Alexandra's nieces and nephews:

Children of Victoria:
    1. **Alice of Battenberg** (1885-1969), married Prince Andrew ("Andrea") of Greece (1882-1944)
        i. Margarita of Greece (1905-1981) [daughter of Alice]
        ii. Theodora of Greece (1906-1969) ("Dolla") [daughter of Alice]
    2. **Louise of Battenberg** (1889-1965), married Gustav VI Adolf of Sweden
    3. **George of Battenberg** (1892-1938), ("Georgie"), later Marquess of Milford Haven, married Nada de Torby
    4. **Louis of Battenberg** (1900-1979), ("Dickie"), later Earl Mountbatten of Burma

Children of Irène:
    1. **Waldemar of Prussia** (1889-1945), ("Toddy")
    2. **Sigismund of Prussia** (1896-1978) ("Bobby")
    3. **Henry of Prussia** (1900-1904)

Children of Ernst:
    1. **Elisabeth of Hesse** (1895-1903)
    2. **George Donatus of Hesse** (1906-1937) ("Don")
    3. **Louis of Hesse** (1908-1969) ("Lu")

Wards of Ella:
    1. **Grand Duchess Maria Pavlovna of Russia** (1890-1951)
    2. **Grand Duke Dmitri Pavlovich of Russia** (1891-1941)

Alexandra's grandparents:
    Queen Victoria of Great Britain (1819-1901) ("Granny")
    Albert, Prince Consort of Great Britain (1819-1861) [Albert of Coburg]
    Princess Elisabeth of Hesse (1815-1885) [née of Prussia]

Alexandra's (maternal line) aunts and uncles [offspring of Victoria and Albert]:
    1. **Victoria, Princess Royal** (1840-1901), ("Aunt Vicky"), married German Emperor Frederick III ("Uncle Fritz") (1831-1888)
    Children of Vicky and Fritz:
        i. German Emperor Wilhelm II (1859-1941), ("William"), married Auguste Viktoria (1858-1920) ("Dona")
        ii. Charlotte (1860-1919)
        iii. Henry (1860-1927), married Irène of Hesse, see above
        vii. Sophie (1870-1932)
        viii. Margarethe (1872-1954) ("Mossy")
        Three others unnamed in text

2. **Albert Edward, Prince of Wales; King Edward VII** (1841-1910), ("Uncle Bertie"), married Alexandra of Denmark, see below
[3. **Alice**, see above]
4. **Alfred, Duke of Coburg and Edinburgh** (1844-1899), married Grand Duchess Marie Alexandrovna of Russia, (1854-1920)
Children of Alfred and Marie:

> ii. Marie, (1875-1938), ("Missy"), married Ferdinand I of Roumania [Son of Marie and Ferdinand: Carol II of Roumania (1893-1953)]
> iii.Victoria Melita (1876-1936) ("Ducky"), married Ernst of Hesse; Grand Duke Kirill Vladimirovich, see above and below
> Three others unnamed in text

5. **Helena** (1846-1923), married Christian of Schleswig Holstein
Children of Helena and Christian:

> iii. Helena Victoria (1870-1948) ("Thora")
> iv. Marie Louise (1872-1956) ("Louie"), married Aribert of Anhalt
> Three others

7. **Arthur, Duke of Connaught** (1850-1942)
8. **Leopold, Duke of Albany** (1853-1884)
9. **Beatrice** (1857-1944), married Henry of Battenberg (1857-1896)
Children of Beatrice and Henry:

> ii.Victoria Eugenie Julie Ena (1887-1969) ("Ena"), married Alfonso XIII of Spain
> iv. Maurice (1891-1914)
> Two others unnamed in text.

Nicholas's grandfathers:
Tsar Alexander II (1818-1881)
King Christian IX of Denmark (1818-1906)

Nicholas's parents:
Tsar Alexander III (1845-1894) ("Uncle Sasha")
Empress Maria Feodorovna (1847-1928) ("Aunt Minnie"; "Motherdear"). [née Princess Dagmar of Denmark]

Nicholas's siblings:

> 1. **Grand Duke Alexander Alexandrovich of Russia** (1869-1870)
> 2. **Grand Duke Georgy Alexandrovich of Russia** (1871-1899)
> 3. **Grand Duchess Xenia Alexandrovna of Russia** (1875-1960), married G.D. Alexander Mikhailovich ("Sandro")
> 4. **Grand Duke Mikhail Alexandrovich** (1878-1918) ("Misha"), married Natalia Sheremetevskaia (1880-1952)
> 5. **Grand Duchess Olga Alexandrovna** (1882-1960), married Peter of Oldenburg ("Petia") (1868-1924) [marriage dissolved 1916]

315

Nicholas's niece and nephews:

Children of Xenia:

>   1. **Princess Irina Alexandrovna Romanova** (1895-1970), married
>   Prince Felix Felixovich Yusupov (1887-1967)
>
>   >   i. Princess Irina Felixovna Yusupova (1915-1983) [great niece;
>   >   daughter of Irina and Felix]
>
>   2. **Prince Andrew Alexandrovich Romanov** (1897-1987)
>   ("Andriusha")
>
>   3-7. Five more sons not named in the text

Nicholas's Romanov [paternal] aunt and uncles, offspring of Alexander II:

>   1. **Grand Duke Vladimir Alexandrovich** (1847-1909), married
>   Princess Marie of Mecklenburg (1854-1920) ("Miechen")
>   Their sons:
>
>   >   i. Grand Duke Kirill Vladimirovich, (1876-1938), married Victoria
>   >   Melita, former wife of Ernst of Hesse (see above)
>   >   ii. Grand Duke Boris Vladimirovich (1878-1943)
>   >   iii. Grand Duke Andrei Vladimirovich (1878-1956)
>
>   2. **Grand Duke Alexei Alexandrovich** (1850-1908)
>
>   3. **Grand Duchess Marie Alexandrovna** (1854-1920), married Alfred,
>   Duke of Edinburgh, see above
>
>   4. **Grand Duke Sergei Alexandrovich** ("Serge") (1857-1905), married
>   Elisabeth of Hesse (see above)
>
>   5. **Grand Duke Paul Alexandrovich**, (1860-1918), father of Ella's
>   wards Marie and Dmitri (see above)

Nicholas's aunt [maternal line], daughter of Christian IX:

>   **Princess Alexandra of Denmark** (1844-1925), married Albert Edward
>   Prince of Wales (see above)
>   Their children:
>
>   >   1. **Albert Victor, Duke of Clarence** (1864-1892), ("Eddy")
>   >   2. **George, Duke of York; Prince of Wales; King George V**
>   >   (1865-1936), married "May" of Teck; Queen Mary (1867-1953)
>   >
>   >   >   i. Edward VIII (1894-1972), ("David") [son of George
>   >   >   and Mary]
>   >
>   >   4. **Victoria** (1868-1935) ("Toria")
>   >   5. **Maud** (1869-1938), married Prince Charles of Denmark, later
>   >   King Haakon of Norway, (1872-1957)

Other relatives of Nicholas:

"The Michels" [cousins of Alexander III]

>   1. **Nikolai Mikhailovich** (1859-1918)
>   2. **Alexander Mikhailovich** (1866-1931) ("Sandro"; see above)
>   3. **Sergei Mikhailovich** (1869-1918)
>   Four others unnamed in text

Grand Duke Konstantin Konstantinovich [cousin of Alexander III]
(1855-1915) ("Kostia"), married Princess Elisabeth of Saxe-Altenburg
(1865-1927), ("Mavra")
Their children:
    3. Princess Tatiana Konstantinovna (1890-1970)
    5. Prince Oleg Konstantinovich (1892-1914)
    7. Prince Georgy Konstantinovich (1903-1938)
    9. Princess Vera Konstantinovna (1906-2001)
    Five others unnamed in text

"The Nikolaevichi" [cousins of Alexander III]
    1. **Grand Duke Nikolai Nikolaevich** (1856-1929) ("Nikolasha"),
    married Princess Anastasia of Montenegro (1868-1935), ("Stana")
    2. **Grand Duke Peter Nikolaevich** (1864-1931), married Princess
    Militsa of Montenegro (1866-1951)

Maternal cousins of Nicholas:
[nephews of Empress Maria and Queen Alexandra]
    1. **Prince George of Greece**, (1869-1957) ("Greek Georgie")
    2. **Prince Andrew of Greece**, (1882-1944) ("Andrea"), see above

Other royalty:
Franz Josef I, Emperor of Austria (1830-1916), married Elisabeth of
Bavaria (1837-1898)

Friends and members of their households:
Anna Stepanovna Demidova (1878-1918) ("Nyuta"): lady's maid to
the Empress; murdered with her employer in the Ipatiev House at
Ekaterinburg.
Doctor Evgenii (Eugene) Sergeevich Botkin (1865-1918): physician to the
Emperor and Empress, a member of a long-standing Russian medical
dynasty. Murdered with his patients in the Ipatiev House at Ekaterinburg
Prince Vassili Dolgoruky (1868-1918), "Valia," member of the imperial
suite, executed in prison at Ekaterinburg

Terenty Chemodurov (1849-1919), Nicholas's valet, released from the
Ipatiev House due to age and ill-health
Alexei Trupp (1858-1918): Nicholas's footman; killed with his employers in
Ekaterinburg
Ivan Sednev (1886-1918), Nicholas's valet; executed in prison in
Ekaterinburg
Leonid Sednev, (1904-1927) ("Lenka"), kitchen boy, nephew of Ivan
Sednev, playmate of Alexei in Ekaterinburg; released from the Ipatiev
House due to his age

Ivan Kharitonov, (1870-1918), chef; murdered with his employer in Ekaterinburg

Doctor Vladimir Derevenko (1879-1936): physician to the Tsesarevich Alexei; accompanied the family to Tobolsk and Ekaterinburg, but was not imprisoned with them

Nikolai Derevenko (1906-1999) ("Kolya"), son of Dr Derevenko, childhood playmate of Alexei; also accompanied his father to Tobolsk

Charles Sidney ("Sidney Ivanovich") Gibbes, (1876-1963), ("Sig"): English tutor to Alexandra's children; later an Orthodox archimandrite; accompanied the imperial family to Tobolsk and remained free due to his nationality

Pierre Gilliard (1879-1962), ("Zhilik"): Swiss-born French language tutor to Alexandra's children; later a lecturer at the University of Lausanne. Accompanied the imperial family to Tobolsk and remained free due to his nationality

Mrs Mary Anne Orchard (1830-1906) ("Orchie"), Alexandra's childhood nurse

Miss Margaret Hardcastle Jackson (1837-1918), ("Madgie"), Alexandra's tutor

Fraulein Anna Textor: Alexandra's tutor; later founded a school in Darmstadt

Antonia ("Toni") Becker: daughter of Princess Alice's secretary and librarian; closest friend of Alexandra in childhood

John Brown (1826-1883): Queen Victoria's notorious Highland ghillie and confidant

"Minnie" Cochrane: lady-in-waiting to Queen Victoria's court; friend of Alexandra in youth

Gretchen von Fabrice: Alexandra's girlhood lady-in-waiting

Konstantin P. Pobedonostsev (1827-1907): Russian conservative philosopher and statesman; tutored Nicholas as a boy. Later Procurator of the Holy Synod

Prince Max of Baden (1867-1929): German politician and last imperial Chancellor; early suitor of Alexandra

Ekaterina Schneider, (1856-1918) ("Trina"): Russian tutor to Ella and Alexandra. Murdered in prison in Perm by the Bolsheviks

Father John of Kronstadt (1829-1908): Russian mystic and demagogic priest; believer in the religious mission of the monarchy. Some connections to the court of Alexander III

Count Rostovtsev: Alexandra's personal Secretary

Marie Tutelberg ("Toodles"): Alexandra's lady's maid

Madeleine Zanotti: Alexandra's lady's maid

Margaretta Eagar (1863-1936): Governess to Alexandra's children, 1898-1904

Count Vladimir Fredericks (1838-1921), Minister of the Imperial Court [i.e. Head of the Household]

Princess Elisabeth Narishkina [Narishkin-Kurakin], ("Zizi"), lady-in-waiting to Alexandra

Alexander A. Mos[s]olov: Head of the imperial Court Chancellery; not an admirer of Alexandra, who in turn called him a "fogey"

Prince Vladimir Orlov ("Fat Orlov"): Chief of the imperial Secretariat; another household enemy of Alexandra's. His vocal criticism of her in 1915 led to Nicholas sending him away to join the household of Nikolasha instead.

Count Paul Benckendorff: Grand Marshall of the Imperial Court

Countess Maria Benckendorff: wife of the above

Princess Marie Bariatinsky: maid-of-honour, friend of Alexandra

General Alexander Alexandrovich Orlov: military governor, one of the few close friends Nicholas had. Alexandra's own resultant affection for him was the subject of St Petersburg gossip

Nikolai Pavlovich Sablin ("N.P."): naval officer from the yacht Standart; personal friend of Nicholas and Alexandra

Admiral Nilov: commander of the yacht Standart, and a personal friend of the imperial couple

Julia Dehn (1888-1963) ("Lili"): wife of a Standart officer, and a close friend of Alexandra.

Alexander Dehn (1908-1974) ("Titi"): son of the above; Alexandra's godson

Anna Alexandrovna Vyrubova, née Taneeva (1884-1964) ("Ania"). Maid-of-honour; usually, Alexandra's closest friend. Released from prison in St Petersburg, she emigrated to Finland and became an Orthodox nun

Alexander S. Taneev (1850-1918): composer; father of Anna Vyrubova

Maria Ivanovna Vishniakova ("Mary"): nursemaid to Alexandra's children

Klavdia Bitner (1878-1935): Russian schoolteacher from Tobolsk; briefly tutored Alexandra's children at the behest of the Provisional Government

Peter Vladimirovich Petrov ("P.V.P."): Russian mathematics tutor to the children of Nicholas and Alexandra

Andrei Derevenko: sailor; male nurse and supervisor to the Tsesarevich

Klementy Nagorny (1889-1918): sailor; male nurse and supervisor to the Tsesarevich; executed in prison in Ekaterinburg

Sophia Ivanovna Tiutcheva: governess to the daughters of Nicholas and Alexandra

Princess Sophia Orbeliani ("Sonia"): maid-of-honour, close friend of Alexandra

Countess Emma Fredericks: daughter of Vladimir Fredericks; friend of Alexandra

Alexander Vasiliev: the imperial family's priest and confessor

Archimandrate Feofan: confessor to the imperial family, inspector of St Petersburg Theological Academy; originally a friend, later a stern critic of Rasputin

Iliodor [Sergei Truvanov]: demagogue and unstable right-wing preacher. Once a friend of Rasputin; later a bitter enemy of his. Also an enemy of the Synod and established Church, who unfrocked him.

Philippe Nizier-Vachod (1850-1908) ("M. Philippe"): controversial French theosophist and lay preacher whom Nicholas and Alexandra befriended

Grigory Efimovich Rasputin (1869-1916): controversial Russian lay preacher whom Nicholas and Alexandra befriended; widely believed to exert huge influence over government. His widow, Praskovia, and younger daughter Varvara died of famine during the Civil War years

Matriona Rasputina (1898-1977) "Maria": daughter of Grigory; educated in St Petersburg, later a circus performer in the U.S.

Peter A. Badmaev ("Dr Badmaiev"): an alternative medical practitioner in St Petersburg: herbalist, Orthodox convert and friend of Rasputin

Sir Ian Malcolm (1868-1944): British M.P., traveled to Russia many times before 1918 on diplomatic business, including for the coronation, and was friendly with Alexandra. His wife, Jeanne-Marie, was the daughter of society beauty Lillie Langtry, and her father is thought to have been Alexandra's brother-in-law, "Ludwig" Battenberg, who acknowledged her as the offspring of a pre-marital affair. It is unclear whether Alexandra knew this.

Maurice Paléologue (1859-1944): French Ambassador in St Petersburg, 1914-1917, politician, novelist, and diarist. A member of high "society" circles in Petersburg

Sir George Buchanan (1854-1917): British Ambassador in St Petersburg, 1910-1917. A liberal who later developed ties to the Provisional government, he was distrusted by Nicholas and Alexandra. A previous appointment had been as British Minister in Darmstadt, and his family actually had close personal links to Alexandra's.

Politicians:

Benjamin Disraeli (1804-1881): British Conservative Prime Minister and novelist; a favourite of Queen Victoria and practiced royal sycophant.

Robert Cecil, Marquess of Salisbury (1830-1903): British Conservative Prime Minister

Félix Faure (1841-1899): French President and architect of the Franco-Russian Alliance. Now however best remembered for the Dreyfus Affair and for dying in his office in flagrante with his mistress, like a less-lucky former-day Bill Clinton

Raymond Poincaré (1860-1934): conservative President of France, 1913-1920

Vyacheslav Plehve (1846-1904): Russian politician of the hard right; Minister of the Interior whose assassination heralded the troubles of 1904-6

Sergei Iulevich Witte (1849-1915): Russian statesman, architect as Finance Minister of a radical industrial and agricultural policy. Later Chairman of the Council of Ministers and creator of the elected parliament. A talented man but with an arrogance and ego that fatally alienated many people including Nicholas II and Alexandra

Peter Sviatopolk-Mirsky (1857-1914): Russian liberal politician and Minister of the Interior, 1904-5; partially responsible for the government reforms of 1905

Ivan Goremykin (1839-1917) ("The Old Man" or "Dear old Man"): old-fashioned Russian monarchist politician; Prime Minister 1906 and 1914-1916. Killed by a mob during the revolution

Peter Stolypin (1862-1911): Russian politician of reformist conservative views. Prime Minister, 1906-1911. Assassinated in Kiev by a gunman

Alexander Guchkov (1862-1936): Duma deputy and sometime President, a constitutional monarchist and thus vocal opponent of Alexandra's role, perceived or real. Alexandra loathed him beyond all other politicians, and he was one of those who personally sought Nicholas's abdication

Vladimir N. Kokovstev (1853-1943): Russian politician and prime minister, 1911-1914. An economic liberal in the Witte mould, he alienated the Empress with continual scrutiny of her role in government, and the perceived role of Rasputin

Alexander Krivoshein (1857-1921): Russian politician; Minister of Agriculture 1908-1915. Trusted by the Tsar as well as by liberals he eventually declined to participate further in government, and this act may have been the death knell for competent leadership in wartime Russia

Sergei Sazonov (1860-1927): Russian Foreign Minister, 1910-1916. Alexandra disliked this man, whom she called "Long Nose," and who blamed her for his downfall, probably without direct reason. Her main issue with him concerned Polish autonomy, and the chief architect of his downfall may have been Maklakov.

Vladimir Sukhomlinov (1848-1926). War Minister scapegoated for military failures in 1915, beginning the popular witch-hunt for German agents.

Nikolai Maklakov (1871-1918): conservative Minister of the Interior, 1912-1915: an ardent Monarchist, he was dismissed to satisfy the demands of the Progressive bloc in the Duma. Shot by the Bolsheviks

Prince Nikolai Shcherbatov: Minister of the Interior, 1915. Appointed to satisfy the Progressive bloc in the Duma, Shcherbatov initially made a good impression on the Empress, but fell from grace due to his inability to control the press

Alexei N. Khvostov (1872-1918): Minister of the Interior, 1915-1916. A new-fangled (demagogue) monarchist and thoroughly sleazy character who impressed Alexandra with his ideas about managing elections. He first courted Rasputin and then turned on him and tried to have him murdered. Khvostov's actions did more than those of any single man to discredit Nicholas and Alexandra's personal government.

Boris Naumov: Russian minister of Agriculture, 1915-6. A vocal critic of Rasputin who the Empress nevertheless liked for his loyalty and ability

Boris Stürmer (1848-1917): Russian Minister of Foreign Affairs and later Minister of the Interior, 1915-16. Was tolerably well-thought-of before assuming office, but later gained a reputation for incompetence and was accused on the basis of his name only of being a German spy

Alexander Protopopov (1866-1918): Vice-President of the Duma, Minister of the Interior, 1916-17

Boris Shulgin: Duma deputy of constitutional monarchist leanings. One of those who went personally to seek Nicholas's abdication

Paul Miliukov (1859-1943): Duma member and liberal historian who in 1903 was imprisoned for a speech made at a private party. His release was a cause célèbre of 1905, seen by many as a test of the Tsar's intentions.

Vladimir Purishkevich (1870-1920): flamboyant and dishonest Duma deputy of the far Right, who murdered Rasputin believing he could save the monarchy by it.

Alexander Kerensky (1881-1970): left-wing Duma deputy and eventual leader of the Provisional Government that took power in 1917. Deposed by the Bolshevik coup and spent the rest of his life in exile, chiefly in America, writing volumes and volumes of memoirs

Soldiers, Bolsheviks and guards:

Vassili Yakovlev (1886-1938): extraordinary Commissioner who took Nicholas and Alexandra by a circuitous from Tobolsk to Ekaterinburg. Often thought to have been a double agent intending to help them escape during the journey, though nothing concrete came of this and the route may equally have been due to politicking between Moscow and Ekaterinburg

Alexander Avdeyev (1887-1947): first leader of the Ekaterinburg guard. A rough-spoken but not ill-intentioned man whose bark was worse than his bite.

Yakov Yurovsky (unnamed in the text) was the leader of the murder squad which killed Nicholas, Alexandra, their children and staff on July 16/17 1918.

Printed in the United Kingdom
by Lightning Source UK Ltd.
130337UK00001B/16-39/P